"Can you think of any reason your stepmother would be so upset about talking to me about the case?"

She shook her head, took a gulp and looked over at him. "You can't really think that she is somehow involved." When he didn't speak instantly, she snapped, "James, my stepmother wouldn't hit a child and keep going."

"I'm not saying she did. But she might know who did."

Lori shook her head, drained her paper cup and set it on the edge of his desk as she rose. "You really think she would keep a secret like that?"

"People keep secrets from those they love all the time," he said.

She glared at him. "What is that supposed to mean?"

"Just that she might be covering for someone."

Her eyes flared. "If you tell me that you think she's covering for me—"

He stood, raising both hands in surrender as he did. "I'm not accusing you. I'm just saying..." He met her gaze, surprised at how hard this was. He and Lori had gone through school together and had hardly said two words the entire time. It wasn't like that much had changed over the past few days, he told himself, even as he knew it had. He liked her. Always had.

B.J. Daniels is a *New York Times* and *USA TODAY* bestselling author. She wrote her first book after a career as an award-winning newspaper journalist and author of thirty-seven published short stories. She lives in Montana with her husband, Parker, and three springer spaniels. When not writing, she quilts, boats and plays tennis. Contact her at bjdaniels.com, on Facebook or on Twitter, @bjdanielsauthor.

Books by B.J. Daniels

Harlequin Intrigue

A Colt Brothers Investigation
Murder Gone Cold & Crossfire

Cardwell Ranch: Montana Legacy
Steel Resolve
Iron Will
Ambush before Sunrise
Double Action Deputy
Trouble in Big Timber
Cold Case at Cardwell Ranch

Visit the Author Profile page at Harlequin.com.

B.J.

NEW YORK TIMES AND USA TODAY BESTSELLING AUTHOR

DANIELS

MURDER GONE COLD & CROSSFIRE

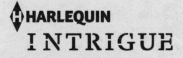

HARLEQUIN
INTRIGUE

HARLEQUIN®
INTRIGUE®

ISBN-13: 978-1-335-46290-9

Murder Gone Cold & Crossfire

Copyright © 2022 by Harlequin Enterprises ULC

Murder Gone Cold
Copyright © 2022 by Barbara Heinlein

Crossfire
First published in 2005. This edition published in 2022.
Copyright © 2005 by Harlequin Enterprises ULC

Harlequin Enterprises ULC
22 Adelaide St. West, 41st Floor
Toronto, Ontario M5H 4E3, Canada
www.Harlequin.com

Printed in U.S.A.

CONTENTS

MURDER GONE COLD

This new Intrigue series is dedicated to all my fans who have followed my books from Cardwell Ranch to Whitehorse and back again. I hope you like these wild Colt brothers and Lonesome, Montana.

Prologue

Billy Sherman lay in his bed trembling with fear as the thunderstorm raged outside. At a loud crack of thunder, he closed his eyes tight. His mother had warned him about the coming storm. She'd suggested he might want to stay in her room now that his father lived somewhere else.

"Mom, I'm seven," he'd told her. It was bad enough that he still slept with a night-light. "I'll be fine." But just in case, he'd pulled out his lucky pajamas even though they were getting too small.

Now he wished he could run down the hall to her room and crawl into her bed. But he couldn't. He wouldn't. He had to face his fears. That's what his dad said.

Lightning lit up the room for an instant. His eyes flew open to find complete blackness. His night-light had gone out. So had the little red light on his alarm clock. The storm must have knocked out the electricity.

He jumped out of bed to stand at his window. Even the streetlamps were out. He could barely see the house across the street through the pouring rain. He tried to swallow the lump in his throat. Maybe he should run down the hall and tell his mother about the power going off. He knew she would make him stay in her room if he did.

Billy hated being afraid. He dreamed of being strong and invincible. He dreamed of being a spy who traveled the world, solved mysteries and caught bad guys.

His battery-operated two-way radio squawked, making him jump. Todd, his best friend. "Are you asleep?" Todd's voice sounded funny. Billy had never confided even to his best friend about his fear of the dark and storms and whatever might be hiding in his closet. But maybe Todd was scared sometimes too.

He picked up the headset and stepped to the window to look out at the street. "I'm awake." A bolt of lightning blinded him for a moment and he almost shrieked as it illuminated a dark figure, walking head down on the edge of the road in the rain. Who was that and…? He felt his heart leap to his throat. What was it the person was carrying?

Suddenly, he knew what he had to do. He wasn't hiding in his room being scared. He would be strong and invincible. He had a mystery to solve. "I have to go," he said into the headset. "I saw someone. I'm going to follow whoever it is."

"No, it's storming. Don't go out. Billy, don't. Billy?"

He grabbed his extra coat his mother kept on the hook by his door and pulled on his snow-boots. At the window, he almost lost his nerve. He could barely see the figure. If he didn't go now he would never know. He would lose his nerve. He would always be afraid.

He picked up the headset again. "The person is headed down your street. Watch for me. I'll see you in a minute." Opening his window, he was driven back for a moment by the rain and darkness. Then he was through the window, dropping into the shrubbery outside as he'd done so many other times when he and Todd were playing their game. Only the other times, it hadn't been storming or dark.

He told himself that spies didn't worry about a thunderstorm. Spies were brave. But he couldn't wait until he reached Todd's house. Putting his head down he ran through the rain, slowing only when he spotted the figure just ahead.

He'd been breathing hard, his boots slapping the pavement, splashing through the puddles. But because of the storm the person hadn't heard him, wouldn't know anyone was following. That's what always made the game so much fun, spying on people and they didn't even know it.

Billy realized that he wasn't scared. His father had been right, though he didn't understand why his mother had gotten so angry with his dad for telling him to face his fears and quit being such a baby. Billy was facing down the storm, facing down the darkness, facing down all of his fears tonight. He couldn't wait to tell Todd.

He was smiling to himself, proud, when the figure ahead of him suddenly stopped and looked back. In a flash of lightning Billy saw the face under the hooded jacket—and what the person was carrying and screamed.

Nine years later

Chapter 1

Cora Brooks stopped washing the few dinner dishes she'd dirtied while making her meal, dried her hands and picked up her binoculars. Through her kitchen window, she'd caught movement across the ravine at the old Colt place. As she watched, a pickup pulled in through the pines and stopped next to the burned-out trailer. She hoped it wasn't "them druggies" who'd been renting the place from Jimmy D's girlfriend—before their homemade meth-making lab blew it up.

The pickup door swung open. All she saw at first was the driver's Stetson as he climbed out and limped over to the burned shell of the double-wide. It wasn't until he took off his hat to rake a hand through his too-long dark hair that she recognized him. One of the Colt brothers, the second oldest, she thought. James Dean Colt or Jimmy D as everyone called him.

She watched him through the binoculars as he hobbled around the trailer's remains, stooping at one point to pick up something before angrily hurling it back into the heap of charred debris.

"Must have gotten hurt with that rodeoin' of his agin," she said, pursing her lips in disapproval as she took in his limp. "Them boys." They'd been wild youngins who'd grown into wilder young men set on killing themselves by riding anything put in front of them. The things she'd seen over the years!

She watched him stand there for a moment as if not knowing what to do now, before he ambled back to his pickup and drove off. Putting down her binoculars, she chuckled to herself. "If he's upset about his trailer, wait until he catches up to his girlfriend."

Cora smiled and went back to washing her dishes. At her age, with all her aches and pains, the only pleasure she got anymore was from other people's misfortunes. She'd watched the Colt clan for years over there on their land. Hadn't she said no good would ever come of that family? So far her predictions had been exceeded.

Too bad about the trailer blowing up though. In recent years, the brothers had only used the double-wide as a place to drop their gear until the next rodeo. It wasn't like any of them stayed more than a few weeks before they were off again.

So where was James Dean Colt headed now? Probably into town to find his girlfriend since she'd been staying in his trailer when he'd left for the rodeo circuit. At least she had been—until she'd rented the place out, pocketed the cash and moved back in with her mother. More than likely he was headed to Melody's mother's right now.

What Cora wouldn't have given to see *that* reunion, she thought with a hearty cackle.

Just to see his face when Melody gave him the news after him being gone on the road all these months.

Welcome home, Jimmy D.

James hightailed it into the small Western town of Lonesome, Montana. When he'd seen the trailer in nothing but ashes, he'd had one terrifying thought. Had Melody been in it when the place went up in flames? He quickly assured himself that if that had happened, he would have heard about it.

So…why hadn't he heard about the fire? Why hadn't Melody let him know? They'd started dating only a week before he'd left. What they'd had was fun, but definitely not serious for either of them.

He swore under his breath, recalling the messages from her that he hadn't bothered with. All of them were along the line of, "We need to talk. Jimmy D, this is serious. Call me." No man jumped to answer a message like that.

Still, you would think that she could have simply texted him. "About your trailer?" Or "Almost died escaping your place."

At the edge of the small mountain town, he turned down a side street, driving back into the older part of town. Melody's mother owned the local beauty shop, Gladys's Beauty Emporium. Melody worked there doing nails. Gladys had been widowed as long as James could remember. It was one reason Melody always ended up back at her mother's between boyfriends.

He was relieved to see her old Pontiac parked out front of the two-story rambling farmhouse. A spindly stick of a woman with a wild head of bleached curly platinum hair, Gladys Simpson opened the door at his knock. She had a cigarette in one hand and a beer in the other. She took one look at him, turned and yelled, "Mel… Someone here to see you."

Someone? Lonesome was small enough that he could easily say that Gladys had known him his whole life. He waited on the porch since he hadn't been invited in, which was fine with him. He'd been toying with the idea that Melody was probably mad at him. He could think of any number of reasons.

But mad enough to burn down the double-wide out of spite? He'd known some women who could get that angry, but Melody wasn't one of them. He'd seen little passion in her before he'd left. He'd gotten the impression she wasn't that interested in him. If he'd had to guess, he'd say she'd been using him that week to make someone else jealous.

Which was another reason he'd known their so-called relationship wasn't going anywhere. In retrospect though, leaving her to take care of the place had been a mistake. It hadn't been his idea. She'd needed a place to stay. The double-wide was sitting out there empty so she'd suggested watching it for him while he was gone.

Even at the time, he'd worried that it would give her the wrong idea. The wrong idea being that their relationship was more serious than it was. He'd half hoped all the way home that she'd moved back in with her mom or a friend. That the trailer would be empty.

He just never imagined that there would be no place to come home to.

"Jimmy D?"

From the edge of the porch, he turned at the sound

of her voice. She stood behind the door, peering around it as if half-afraid of him. "Melody, I was just out at the place. I was worried that you might have gotten caught in the fire."

She shook her head. "I wasn't living there anymore when it happened."

"That's good." But even as he said it, he knew there was more story coming. She was still half hiding behind the door, as if needing a barrier between them. "I'm not angry with you, if that's what you're worried about. I'm just glad you're okay."

He watched her swallow before she said, "I'd rented your trailer to some guys." He took that news without reacting badly. He figured she must have needed the money and he *had* left her in charge of the place, kind of.

"Turned out they were cooking meth," she said. "I didn't know until they blew the place up."

James swallowed back the first few words that leaped to his tongue. When he did find his voice, he said, "You didn't know."

She shook her head. "I didn't." She sounded close to tears. "But that's not all I have to tell you."

He held his breath already fearing that the news wasn't going to get better. Before his grandmother died, she'd explained karma to him. He had a feeling karma was about to kick his butt.

Then Mel stepped around the edge of the door, leading with her belly, which protruded out a good seven months.

The air rushed out of him on a swear word. A million thoughts galloped through his mind at breakneck speed before she said, "It's not yours."

He felt equal parts relief and shock. It was that instant of denial followed by acceptance followed by regret that surprised him the most. For just a second he'd seen himself holding a two-year-old little girl with his dark hair and blue eyes. They'd been on the back of the horse he'd bought her.

When he blinked, the image was gone as quickly as it had come to him.

"Who?" The word came out strangled. He wasn't quite over the shock.

"Tyler Grange," she said, placing her palms on the stretchy top snug over her belly. "He and I broke up just before you and I..." She shrugged and he noticed the tiny diamond glinting on her ring finger.

"You're getting married. When?"

"Soon," she said. "It would be nice to get hitched before the baby comes."

He swallowed, still tangled up in that battle of emotions. Relief was winning by a horse length though. "Congratulations. Or is it best wishes? I never can remember."

"Thanks," she said shyly. "Sorry 'bout your trailer. I'd give you the money I got from the renters, but—"

"It's all right." He took a step toward the porch stairs. After all these years in the rodeo game, he'd learned to cut his losses. This one felt like a win. He swore on his lucky boots that he was going to change his wild ways.

From inside the house, he could hear Gladys laughing with someone. He caught the smell of permanent solution.

"Mama's doing the neighbor's hair," Melody said. He nodded and took a step off the porch. "Any idea where you're going to go?"

Until that moment, he hadn't really thought about it. It wasn't like he didn't have options. He had friends he could bunk with until he either bought another trailer to put on the property or built something more substantial. He and his brothers, also on the rodeo circuit, used the trailer only to stay in the few times they came home to crash for a while—usually to heal up.

Not that he was planning on staying that long. Once he was all healed up from his last rodeo ride, he'd be going back. He'd left his horse trailer, horse and gear at a friend's.

"I'm going to stay at the office," he said, nodding to himself. It seemed the perfect solution under the circumstances.

"Uptown?" she asked, sounding surprised. The word hardly described downtown Lonesome, Montana. But the office *was* at the heart of town—right on a corner of Main Street.

"Don't worry about me," he said. "You just take care of yourself and give my regards to Tyler." He tipped his hat and headed to his pickup.

As he drove away, he realized his heart was still pounding. He'd dodged a bullet. So why couldn't he get that image of him holding his baby daughter out of his head? Worse was how that image made him feel—happy.

The emotion surprised him. For just that split second, he'd had to deal with the thought of settling down, of having a family, of being a father. He'd felt it to his soul and now he missed it.

James shook his head, telling himself that he was just tired, injured and emotionally drained after his homecoming. All that together would make any man have strange thoughts.

Chapter 2

James reached high on the edge of the transom over the door for the key, half-surprised it was still there. He blew the dust off and, opening the door, hit the light switch and froze. The smell alone reminded him of his father and the hours he'd spent in this office as a child after his mother had died.

Later he'd hung around, earning money by helping any way he could at the office. He'd liked hanging out here with his old man. He chuckled, remembering how he'd thought he might grow up and he and Del would work together. Father and son detective agency. Unfortunately, his father's death had changed all that.

He hadn't been here since the funeral, he realized as he took in his father's large oak desk and high-backed leather office chair. More emotions assaulted him, ones he'd kept at bay for the past nine years.

This was a bad idea. He wasn't ready to face it. He might never be ready, he thought. He missed his father and nine years hadn't changed that. Everything about this room brought back the pain from the Native American rugs on the floor and the two leather club chairs that faced his dad's desk and seat.

He realized he wasn't strong enough for this—maybe especially after being hurt during his last ride and then coming home to find his home was gone. He took one final look and started to close the door. He'd get a motel room for the night rather than show up at a friend's house.

But before he could close the door, his gaze fell on an old Hollywood movie poster on the wall across the room. He felt himself smile, drawn into the office by the cowboy on the horse with a face so much like his own.

He hadn't known his great-grandfather Ransom Del Colt. But he'd grown up on the stories. Ransom had been a famous movie star back in the forties and early fifties when Westerns had been so popular. His grandfather RD Colt Jr. had followed in Ransom's footprints for a while before starting his own Wild West show. RD had traveled the world ropin' and ridin' until late in life.

He moved around the room, looking at all the photographs and posters as if seeing them for the first time. The Colts had a rich history, one to be proud of, his father said. Del Colt, James's father, had broken the mold after being a rodeo cowboy until he was injured so badly that he had to quit.

Del, who'd loved Westerns and mystery movies, had gotten his PI license and opened Colt Investigations. He'd taught his sons to ride before they could walk. He'd never stopped loving rodeo and he'd passed that love on to his sons as if it was embedded deep in their genes.

James limped around the room looking at all the other posters and framed photographs of his rodeo family. He felt a sense of pride in the men who'd gone before him. And a sense of failure on his own part. He was pushing thirty-six and he had little to show for it except for a lot of broken bones.

Right now, he hurt all over. The bronc he'd ridden two days ago had put him into the fence, reinjuring his leg and cracking some of his ribs. But he'd stayed on the eight seconds and taken home the purse.

Right now he wondered if it was worth it. Still, as he stood in this room, he rebelled at the thought of quitting. He'd made a living doing what he loved. He would heal and go back. Just as he'd always done.

In the meantime, he was dog tired. Too tired to go look for a motel room for the night. At the back of the office he found the bunk where his father would stay on those nights he worked late. There were clean sheets and quilts and a bathroom with a shower and towels. This would work at least for tonight. Tomorrow he'd look for something else.

Lorelei Wilkins pulled into her space in the alley behind her sandwich shop and stared at the pickup parked in the space next to it. It had been years since she'd seen anyone in the building adjoining hers. She'd almost forgotten why she'd driven down here tonight. Often, she came down and worked late to get things ready for the next day.

Tonight, she had brought down a basketful of freshly washed aprons. She could have waited until morning, but she'd been restless and it was a nice night. Who was she kidding? She never put things off for tomorrow.

Getting out, she started to unload the basket when she recognized the truck and felt a start. There were rodeo stickers plastered all over the back window of the cab, but the dead giveaway was the LETRBUCK personalized license plate.

Jimmy D was back in town? But why would he… She recalled hearing something about a fire out on his land. Surely, he wasn't planning to stay here in his father's old office. The narrow two-story building, almost identical to her own, had been empty since Del Colt's death nine years ago. Before that the structure had housed Colt Investigations on the top floor with the ground floor office rented to a party shop that went broke, the owners skipping town.

Lorelei had made an offer on the property, thinking she would try to get a small business in there or expand her sandwich shop. Anything was better than having an empty building next door. Worse, the owners of the party-planning store had left in a hurry, not even bothering to clean up the place, so it was an eyesore.

But the family lawyer had said no one in the family was interested in selling.

As she hauled out her basket of aprons, she could see a light in the second-story window and a shadow moving around up there. Whatever James was doing back in town, he wouldn't be staying long—he never did. Not that she ever saw him. She'd just heard the stories.

Shaking her head, she tucked the basket under one arm, unlocked the door and stepped in. It didn't take long to put the aprons away properly. Basket in hand, she locked up and headed for her SUV.

She couldn't help herself. She glanced up. Was she

hoping to see the infamous Jimmy D? Their paths hadn't crossed in years.

The upstairs light was out. She shook her head at her own foolishness.

"Some women always go for the bad boy," her step-mother had joked years ago when they'd been uptown shopping for her senior year of high school. They'd passed Jimmy D in the small mall at the edge of town. He'd winked at Lorelei, making her blush to the roots of her hair. She'd felt Karen's frowning gaze on her. "I just never took you for one of those."

Lorelei had still been protesting on the way home. "I can't stand the sight of Jimmy D," she'd said, only to have her stepmother laugh. "He's arrogant and thinks he's much cuter than he is."

"Don't feel bad. We've all fallen for the wrong man. And he *is* cute and he likes you."

Lorelei had choked on that. "He doesn't like me. He just enjoys making me uncomfortable. He's just plain awful."

"Then I guess it's a good thing you aren't going to the prom with him," Karen said. "Your friend Alfred is obviously the better choice."

Alfred was her geek friend who she competed with for grades.

"Jimmy D isn't going to the prom," she said. "He's too cool for proms. Not that I would go with him if he asked me."

Lorelei still cringed at the memory. Protest too much? Her stepmother had seen right through it. She told her-self that all that aside, this might be the perfect oppor-tunity to get him to sell the building to her. But it would mean approaching Jimmy D with an offer knowing he would probably turn her down flat. She groaned. From what she'd heard, he hadn't changed since high school. The only thing the man took seriously was rodeo. And chasing women.

Former sheriff Otis Osterman pulled his pickup to the side of the street to stare up at the building. Lorelei Wilkins wasn't the only one surprised to see a light on in the old Colt Investigations building.

For just a moment, he'd thought that Del was still alive, working late as he often did. While making his rounds, Otis had seen him moving around up there working on one of his cases.

The light in that office gave him an eerie feeling as if he'd been transported back in time. That he could rewrite history. But Otis knew that wasn't possible. One look in the rearview mirror at his white hair and wrinkled face and he could see that there was no going back, no changing anything. But it was only when he looked deep into his own eyes—eyes that had seen too much—that he felt the weight of those years and the questionable actions he'd taken.

But like Del Colt, they were buried. He just wanted them to stay that way. Blessedly, he hadn't been reminded of Del for some time now. He'd gone to the funeral nine years ago, stood in the hot sun and watched as the gravedigger covered the man's casket and laid sod on top. He told himself that had been the end of a rivalry he and Del had fought since middle school.

He watched the movement up there in Del's office. It had to be one of Del's sons back from the rodeo. Small towns, he thought. Everyone didn't just know each other. Half the damned town was related.

Otis drove down the block, turning into the alley and cruising slowly past the pickup parked behind Del's narrow two-story office building.

He recognized the truck and swore softly under his breath. Del Colt had left behind a passel of sons who all resembled him, but Jimmy D was the most like Del. Apparently, he was back for a while.

The former sheriff told himself that it didn't necessarily spell trouble as he shifted his truck into gear. As he drove home though, he couldn't shake the bad feeling that the past had been reawakened and it was coming for him.

Chapter 3

James woke to the sun. It streamed in the window of his father's office as he rose and headed for the shower. Being here reminded him of the mornings on his way to school that he would stop by. He often found his father at his desk, already up and working. Del Colt's cases weren't the kind that should have kept his father from sleep, he thought as he got dressed.

They were often small personal problems that people hoped he could help with. But his father treated each as if it was more important than world peace. James had once questioned him about it.

They may seem trivial to you, but believe me, they aren't to the people who are suffering and need answers, Del had said.

Now, showered and dressed, James stepped from the small room at the back and into his father's office. He hesitated for a moment before he pulled out his father's chair and sat down. Leaning back, he surveyed the room and the dusty window that overlooked Main Street.

He found himself smiling, recalling sitting in this chair and wanting to be just like his dad. He felt such a sense of pride for the man Del had been. His father had raised them all after their mother's death. James knew that a lot of people would have said that Del had let them run wild.

Laughing, he thought that had been somewhat true. His father gave them free rein to learn by their mistakes. So, they made a lot of them.

Everything was just as his father had left it, he realized as he looked around. A file from the case his father had been working on was still lying open on his desk. Next to it were his pen and a yellow lined notepad with Del's neat printing. A coffee cup, the inside stained dark brown, sat next to the notepad.

A name jumped out at him. Billy Sherman. That kid who'd been killed in a hit-and-run nine years ago. *That was the case his father had been working on.*

He felt a chill. The hit-and-run had never been solved.

A knock at the door startled him. He quickly closed the case file, feeling as if he'd been caught getting into things that were none of his business. Private things.

He quickly rose, sending the chair scooting backward. "Yes?"

"Jimmy D?" A woman's voice. Not one he recognized. He hadn't told anyone he was coming back to town. He'd returned unannounced and under the cover of darkness. But clearly someone knew he wasn't just back—but that he was here in Del's office.

He moved to the door and opened it, still feeling as

if he were trespassing. The light in the hallway was dim. He'd noticed last night that the bulb had burned out sometime during the past nine years. But enough sunlight streamed in through the dusty window at the end of the hall to cast a little light on the pretty young woman standing before him.

"I hope I didn't catch you at a bad time," she said, glancing past him before settling her gaze on him again. Her eyes were honey brown with dark lashes. Her long chestnut brown hair had been pulled up into a no-nonsense knot that went with the serious expression on her face. She wore slacks, a modest blouse and sensible shoes. She had a briefcase in one hand, her purse in the other. She looked like a woman on a mission and he feared he was the assignment.

Lorelei looked for recognition in the cowboy's eyes and seeing none quickly said, "I'm sorry, you probably don't remember me. I'm Lorelei Wilkins. I own the sandwich shop next door." When he still hadn't spoken, she added, "We went to school together?" She realized this was a mistake.

He was still staring at her unnervingly. When he finally spoke, the soft timber of his low voice surprised her. She remembered the unruly classmate who'd sat next to her in English, always cracking jokes and acting up when he wasn't winking at her in the hall between classes. She realized that she'd been expecting the teenaged boy—not the man standing before her.

"Oh, I remember you, Lori," he drawled. "Hall monitor, teacher's assistant, senior class president, valedictorian." He grinned. "Didn't you also read the lunch menu over the intercom?"

She felt her cheeks warm. Yes, she'd done all of that—not that she'd have thought he'd noticed. "It's *Lorelei*," she said, her voice coming out thin. She knew her reputation as the most uptight, serious, not-fun girl in the class.

"I remember that too," he said, his grin broadening.

She cleared her throat and quickly pressed on. "Look, Jimmy D. I saw your light on last night and I—"

"It's James."

"James...?" she repeated. She suddenly felt tongue-tied here facing this rodeo cowboy. Why had she thought talking directly to him was a good idea? She wished she'd tried his family lawyer again instead. Not that that approach had done her any good.

She took a breath and let it out, watching him wince as he shifted his weight onto his obviously injured leg. Seeing that he wasn't in any shape to be making real estate deals, she chickened out. "I just wanted to welcome you to the neighborhood."

"I'm not staying, in case that's what you're worrying about. I mean, not living here, exactly. It's just temporary."

She suspected that most everything about his life was temporary from what she'd heard. She was angry at herself for not saying what she'd really come to say. But from the look on his bruised face and the way he'd winced when he'd shifted weight on his left leg, she'd realized that this wasn't the right time to make an offer on the building. He looked as if he would say no to her without even giving it a second thought.

From her briefcase, she awkwardly withdrew a ten percent off coupon for her sandwich shop.

He took it without looking at it. Instead, his intense scrutiny was on her, making her squirm.

"It's a coupon for ten percent off a sandwich at my shop," she said.

He raised a brow. "Who makes the sandwiches?"

The question was so unexpected that it took her a moment to respond. "I do."

"Huh," he said and folded the coupon in half to stuff it into the pocket of his Western shirt.

What had made her think she could have a professional conversation with this…cowboy? She snapped her briefcase closed and turned to leave.

"Thanks," he called after her.

Just like in high school she could feel his gaze boring into her backside. She ground her teeth as her face flushed hot. Maybe she'd been wrong. Maybe some things never changed no matter how much time had gone by.

James smiled to himself as he watched Lorelei disappear down the hall. He hadn't seen her in years. As small as Lonesome was, he'd have thought that their paths would have crossed again before this. But she didn't hang out at Wade's Broken Spur bar or the engine repair shop or the truck stop cafe—all places on the edge of town that he frequented when home. Truth was, he never had reason to venture into downtown Lonesome because he usually stayed only a few days, a week at most.

Seeing Lorelei had made him feel seventeen again. The woman had always terrified him. She was damned intimidating and always had been. He'd liked that about her. She'd always been so smart, so capable, so impressive. In high school she hadn't seemed to realize just how sexy she was. She'd tried to hide it unlike a lot of the girls. But some things you can't cover up with clothing.

What surprised him as he closed the door behind her was that she still seemed to be unaware of what she did to a man. Especially this man.

He sighed, wondering what Lorelei had really stopped by for. Not to welcome him to the neighborhood or give him a sandwich coupon. It didn't matter. He knew that once he found a place to stay, he'd probably not see her again.

Something bright and shiny caught his eye lying on the floor next to his father's desk. He moved toward it as if under a spell. He felt a jolt as he recognized what it was. Picking up the silver dollar money clip, he stared down, heart pounding. Why hadn't his father had this on him when he was killed? He always carried it. *Always*.

James opened it and let the bills fall to the desktop. Two twenties, a five and three ones. As he started to pick them back up, he noticed that wasn't all that had fallen from the money clip.

He lifted the folded yellow lined notepad paper from the desk. Unfolding it he saw his father's neat printing and a list of names. As was his father's habit, he'd checked off those he had interviewed. But there were six others without checks.

James stared at the list, realizing they were from Del's last case, seven-year-old Billy Sherman's hit-and-run. His father had stuck the list in his money clip? Had his father been on his way to talk to someone on that list? Why had he left the clip behind? He'd always had so many questions about his father's death. Too many. Ultimately, after what the sheriff had told him, he'd been afraid of the answers.

Moving behind the desk, he sat down again and opened the case file. His father's notes were neatly stacked inside. He checked the notes against the list. Everyone Del had interviewed was there, each name checked off the list.

But the list had stopped with a name that made his jaw drop. Karen Wilkins? Lorelei's stepmother? Why had his father wanted to talk to her? She lived a half dozen blocks from where the hit-and-run had happened.

Chapter 4

James glanced at the time. Almost one in the afternoon. He'd lost track of time reading his father's file on the hit-and-run. Finding Karen Wilkins name on the list had scared him. He couldn't imagine why Del wanted to talk to her.

He'd gone through everything several times, including all of his father's neatly handwritten notes. Del didn't even use a typewriter—let alone a computer. He was old-school through and through.

James realized that after everything he'd gone through, he still had no idea why Karen's name was on the list or why it might be important.

His stomach growled. He thought of the coupon Lori had given him. Pulling it from his pocket, he reached for his Stetson. It was a short walk next door.

As James entered the sandwich shop, a bell jangled

over the front door. From the back, he saw Lori look up, her expression one of surprise, then something he couldn't quite read.

He walked up to the sign that said Order Here and scanned the chalkboard menu. His stomach rumbled again. He couldn't remember when he'd eaten—sometime yesterday at a fast-food place on the road. He'd been anxious to get home only to find he no longer had a home.

Lori appeared in front of him. "See anything you'd like?"

He glanced at her. "Definitely." Then he winked and looked up at the board again. He heard her make a low guttural sound under her breath. "I'll take the special."

She mugged a face. "It comes with jalapeño peppers and a chipotle mayonnaise that you might find too… spicy."

He smiled. "I'm tougher than I look."

She glanced at the leg he was babying and cocked a brow at that.

"It was a really big bronco that put me into the fence. For your information, it didn't knock me off. I held on for the eight seconds and came home with the money."

"Then it was obviously worth it," she said sarcastically. "Let me get you that sandwich. Is this to go?"

"No, I think I'll stay."

She nodded, though he thought reluctantly. When she'd given him the coupon, he could tell that she'd never expected he would actually use it. "If you'd like to have a seat. Want something to drink with that?"

"Sure, whatever's cold." He turned and did his best not to limp as he walked to a table and chair by the front window. This time of the day, the place was empty. He wondered how her business was doing. He wondered also if he'd made a mistake with what he'd ordered and if it would be too spicy to eat. He'd eat it. Even if it killed him.

What was it about her that he couldn't help flirting with her when he was around her? There'd always been something about her... He couldn't imagine how they could be more different. Maybe that's why she'd always made it clear that she wasn't in the least interested in him.

Fortunately, other girls and then women had been, he thought. But as he caught glimpses of her working back in the kitchen, he knew she'd always been an enigma, a puzzle that he couldn't figure out. Flirting with her sure hadn't worked. But, like his father, he'd always loved a good mystery and seldom backed down from a challenge.

Was that why he couldn't let this go? He needed to find out why her stepmother was on Del's list. Why the list was tucked in Del's money clip and why he hadn't had it on him that night. James knew he might never get those answers. Just as he might never know how his father ended up on the train tracks that night. So, what was the point in digging into Del's old unsolved case?

Wouldn't hurt to ask a few questions, he told himself. He wasn't going anywhere for a while until he healed. He had time on his hands with nothing to do—nothing but seeing about getting the wreckage from his burned trailer hauled away and replacing it with a place to live. He told himself he'd get on that tomorrow.

Lori brought out his sandwich and a tall glass of iced lemonade along with plastic cutlery and napkin roll. She placed the meal in front of him and started to step away. He grabbed her hand. She flinched.

"Sorry," he said quickly as he let go. "I was hoping since you aren't busy with customers that maybe you could sit down for a minute. Join me?"

"I guess I could spare a moment." She hesitated before reluctantly slipping into a chair across from him.

He smiled over at her. "I feel like you and I got off on the wrong foot somehow." He waited for her to say something and realized he could wait all day and that wasn't going to happen. She wasn't going to help him out. He took a sip of the lemonade. "Delicious. Let's start with the truth. What did you really come by for earlier? It wasn't to welcome me to the neighborhood."

She shook her head. "This isn't the time or the place." He raised a brow at that, making her groan. "You never change. Are you like this with every woman?" She raised a hand. "Don't answer that. I already know." She started to get up, but he stopped her.

"Seriously, you can tell me."

She studied him for a long moment before she asked, "Has your family lawyer mentioned that I've made several inquiries about buying your father's building?"

"Family lawyer?"

"Hank Richardson."

"Oh, him." James frowned. "He's our family lawyer? I guess I didn't realize that." She sighed deeply. "Why do you want to buy the building?"

"No one is using it. The place is an eyesore. I might want to expand into it at some point."

He nodded. "Huh. I'll have to give that some thought."

"You do that." She started to rise.

"Wait, I'm serious. I'll think about it. Now can I ask you something else?" She looked both wary and suspicious. "I was going through an old case file of my father's earlier. It was the one he was working on when he died. You might remember the case. Billy Sherman. Killed by a hit-and-run driver. So, I'm looking into it and—"

Her eyes widened. "What are you doing?"

He couldn't help but look confused. "Having lunch?"

"You're not a licensed private investigator."

"No, I'm not pretending to be. I just found the case interesting and since I have some time on my hands…"

She shook her head. "Just like that?" She sighed. "Are you living next door now?"

"For the moment. It's not that bad."

"Like your latest injury isn't that bad?" she asked, clearly upset with him.

"I'll heal, but if you must know my cracked ribs still hurt like hell." He took a tiny bite of his sandwich and felt the heat even though he'd mostly gotten bread. He knew instantly what she'd done. "This is good."

She was watching him as he took another bite. "I make my own bread."

"Really?" The heat of the peppers was so intense that they felt as if they would blow the top of his head off.

"You don't have to sound so surprised."

"Don't take this wrong, but back in high school, I never thought about you in the kitchen baking bread."

"Doubt you thought about me at all," she said and slipped out of her chair.

But as she started past, he said, "I thought about you all the time. But I was smart enough to know you were out of my league."

She'd stopped next to his table and now looked down at him. Her expression softened. "You don't have to eat that. I can make you something else."

He shook his head, picked up his sandwich and took

another big bite. He'd eat every ounce even if it killed him, which he thought it might. The intense heat made its way down his throat to his chest. It felt as if his entire body was on fire. He sucked in his breath. Somehow, he managed to get the words out. "This isn't too spicy."

She shook her head. At least she was smiling this time as she walked away.

Chapter 5

James had a lot of time to think since his spicy lunch had kept him up most of the night. It was a small price to pay, he told himself. He wasn't sure exactly what he'd done to Lori in high school or since that had her so upset with him. He'd been the high school jock and goof-off who'd gotten by on his charm. She'd been the studious, hardworking serious student who'd had to work for her grades. Why wouldn't she resent him?

But he suspected there was more to it than even his awkward attempts at flirting with her. He felt as if he'd done something that had made her dislike him. That could be any number of things. It wasn't like he went around worrying about who might have been hurt by his antics back then. Or even now, he admitted honestly.

He kept going over the conversation at lunch though. She'd tried to pass off her anger as something from high school. But he wasn't buying it. She hadn't been a fan of his for apparently some time, but when she'd gotten upset was when he'd said he was looking into his father's last case, Billy Sherman's hit-and-run.

Add to that, her stepmother's name was on his father's list. Del Colt had been meticulous in his investigations. He'd actually been really good at being a PI. Karen Wilkins wouldn't have been on that list unless his father thought she knew something about the case.

James was convinced by morning that he needed to talk to Karen. He knew Lori wasn't going to like it. Best that he hadn't brought it up at lunch.

But first, he wanted to talk to the person who'd hired his father to look into the hit-and-run after the police had given up.

Alice Sherman gasped, her hand over her heart, her eyes wide as she stared at James. It seemed to take her a moment to realize she wasn't looking at a ghost. "For a moment I thought… You look so much like your father."

James smiled, nodding. "It's a family curse."

She shook her head as she recovered. "Yes, being that handsome must be a terrible burden for you, especially with the ladies."

"I'm James Colt," he said, introducing himself and shaking her hand. "I don't think we've ever met." Alice worked at the local laundry. "I was hoping to ask you a few questions."

She narrowed her eyes at him. "About what?" She seemed really not to know.

"I hate to bring it back up and cause you more pain, but you hired my father to look into Billy's death. He died before he finished the investigation."

"You're mistaken," she said, fiddling with the collar of her blouse. "I didn't hire your father. My ex did."

That caught him flat-footed. He'd seen several checks from Alice Sherman in his father's file and Alice had been the first on Del's list of names. He said as much to her.

Her expression soured. "When my ex's checks bounced, I paid Del for his time. But what does that have to do with you?"

"I'm looking into the case."

Alice stared at him. "After all these years? Why would you do that? You…? You're a private investigator?"

"No. It was my father's last case. I'm just looking into it."

"Well, I'm not interested in paying any more money." She started to close the door.

"Please, Mrs. Sherman," he said quickly. "I don't mean to remind you of your loss. I just want to know more about your son."

She managed a sad smile. "Billy is *always* on my mind. The pain never goes away." She opened the door wider. "I suppose I have time for a few questions."

As James took the chair she offered him, she walked to the mantel over the fireplace and took down a framed photograph of her son.

"This is my favorite snapshot of him." She turned and handed it to him. It was of a freckle-faced boy with his two front teeth missing smiling broadly at the camera. "Billy was seven," she said as she took a seat on the edge of the couch facing him. "Just a boy. He was named after my father who died in the war."

"You've had a lot of loss," James said as she brushed a lock of her hair from her face. After the accident, it was as if she'd aged overnight. According to his father's file, Alice would now be forty-five. Her hair was almost entirely gray and there were deep lines around her eyes and mouth. "I'm so sorry. I don't want to make it worse."

"Have you found new information on the case?" she asked, her gaze intent on him. He realized that he might have given her the wrong impression.

"No, not yet. I'm not sure where my father had left the case. Had he talked to you about his investigation before his death?"

"He called me that afternoon, asked if I was going to be home. He thought he might be getting close to finding the hit-and-run driver," she said. "I waited for him but he never showed up. I found out the next day about his pickup being hit by the train."

"He said he thought he might be close to solving the case?" He felt hope at this news. Maybe he wasn't playing at this. Maybe there was something he could find after all. "Did he tell you anything else?"

She shook her head. "Unfortunately, that's all he said."

This news had his heart hammering. He'd always wondered if his father's so-called accident had anything to do with the case. If he was that close to finding the hit-and-run driver… Sheriff Otis Osterman's investigation had ruled Del's death an accident due to human error on his father's part. Either Del hadn't been paying attention and not seen the train coming at the uncontrolled railroad crossing or he'd tried to outrun the train.

Neither had sounded like his father.

The autopsy found alcohol in his father's system and there had been an empty bottle of whiskey found on the floor of his pickup.

James had never accepted that his father had been

drunk and hadn't seen the train coming. If he was close to solving the Billy Sherman case, there is no way he would have been drinking at all.

Alice had gotten up and now brought over more photographs of her son. He'd been small and thin. A shy boy, not an adventurous one. There'd been two theories of how Billy ended up outside on the street that night. The obvious one was that he'd sneaked out for some reason. The other was that he'd been abducted.

"Is there any reason Billy might have left the house that night after you put him to bed?" James asked cautiously.

"No, never. Billy would have never gotten up in the middle of the night and gone out for any reason. He was afraid of the dark. He hated admitting it, but he still slept with a night-light. He was also terrified of storms. There was a terrible storm that night. The wind was howling. Between it and the pouring rain you could hardly see across the street." She shook her head, her gaze unfocused for a moment as if she were reliving it. "He *wouldn't* have gone out on his own under *any* circumstances."

"So, you're still convinced that someone abducted him?"

"His bedroom window was wide open." Her voice broke. "The wind had blown the rain in. His floor and bedding were soaked when I went in the next morning to wake him up and found him gone." All of this he'd already read in his father's file. He could see it was a story she'd told over and over, to the sheriff, to Del, to herself. "I started to call the sheriff when Otis drove up and told me that Billy had been found a few blocks from here lying in the ditch dead." She made angry swipes at her tears. He could see that she was fighting hard not to cry.

"The sheriff said he didn't find any signs of a forced entry," James said. "According to my father's notes, you said you locked the window before tucking Billy in at nine. Maybe you forgot that night—"

"No, I remember locking it because I could see the storm coming. I even closed the blinds. It's no mystery. The only way Billy would leave the house was if his father came to his window that night. Sean Sherman. Not that he'll tell you the truth, but I know he took my boy. Have you talked to him?"

"Not yet." He was still working on the angle that Billy, like every red-blooded, American boy, had sneaked out a time or two. Having been a seven-year-old at one time, he asked, "Did Billy have his own cell phone?" She shook her head. "What about a walkie-talkie?"

"Yes, but—"

"Who had the other two-way radio handset?"

He watched her swallow before she said, "Todd. Todd Crane. But he swore he hadn't talked to Billy that night."

"I'm just covering my bets," James said quickly. He gathered that his father hadn't asked her this. "Did the sheriff talk to Todd?"

"I don't know. I think your father asked me about Billy's friends, but my son wouldn't have left the house that night even for his best friend, Todd."

James rose to lay a hand over hers as she gripped the stack of framed photos of her son. "Do you mind if I see his room?" Even before she led him down the hall, he knew Billy's room would be exactly like he'd left it even after nine years.

It was a classic boy's room painted a pale blue with

a Spiderman bedspread and action figures lined up on the bookshelf.

Moving to the window, James examined the lock. It was an old house, the lock on the window old as well. Maybe Billy *had* been abducted and the sheriff had missed something. But wouldn't there have been footprints in the wet earth outside Billy's window? Unless he'd been taken before the storm hit and the prints had been washed away.

James left, promising to let Alice Sherman know if he discovered anything helpful. The look in her eyes was a stark reminder of what he'd set in motion. He'd gotten her hopes up and the truth was, he had no idea what he was doing.

Karen Wilkins wasn't home. Her car wasn't parked in front of her freshly painted and landscaped split-level. Nor was it in the garage.

Todd Crane, who would now be around sixteen, hadn't been on his father's list. But Del had talked to Todd's stepmother, Shelby Crane.

Since it was a Saturday, James figured the boy wouldn't be in school. He swung by the house only a few blocks from Alice Sherman's. The woman who answered the door was considerably younger-looking than Alice. Shelby Crane was a slim blonde with hard brown eyes.

"Yes?" The way she was holding the door open only a crack told him that Alice might have already called her.

"I'm James Colt and—"

"I know who you are. What do you want?"

"I'm guessing that you spoke with Alice," he said. "I'd like to talk to your son."

"No." She started to close the door, but he stopped her with his palm.

"Your son might know why Billy Sherman was outside that night," he said, his voice growing harder with each word.

"Well, he doesn't."

"If that's true, then I can't see why he can't tell me that himself."

"He doesn't know. He didn't know nine years ago. He doesn't know now." Again, she started to close the door and again he put a hand on it to stop her.

"Did he and Billy talk on walkie-talkies back then?"

"My son had nothing to do with what happened to that boy. You need to go. Don't make me call the sheriff." She closed the door and this time he let her.

As he started to turn and leave, he saw a boy's face peering out one of the upstairs windows. Then the curtain fell back, and the boy was gone. He wondered why Shelby was so afraid of him talking to her son.

His phone rang as he was getting into his pickup. Melody? He picked up.

"I just got a call from the sheriff's department," she said without preamble. "Carl said you have to get a permit to remove the burned trailer from your land."

"Why would he call you?"

Silence, then a guilty, "I might have tried to hire someone to haul it away before you got back."

James shook his head. Did she not realize he would have noticed anyway? The missing double-wide and the burned area around it would have been a dead giveaway. "No problem. I'll swing by and pick up a permit. Thanks for letting me know."

He was still mentally shaking his head when he walked into the sheriff's department.

Sheriff Carl Osterman, younger brother of the former sheriff Otis Osterman, was standing outside his office with a large mug of coffee and the family sour expression on his face. A short stocky man in his late fifties, Carl believed in guilty until proven innocent. Word was that he'd arrest his own grandmother for jaywalking, which could explain why he was divorced and not speaking with his mother or grandmother, James had heard.

"Wondered when I'd be seeing you," the sheriff drawled. "Suppose you heard what happened out at your place."

"It was fairly noticeable."

Carl took a long moment to assess him over the rim of his mug as he slurped his coffee. "You know those meth dealers?"

"Nope. I was on the road. I didn't even know Melody had rented the place."

The sheriff nodded. "You need a permit to haul that mess off."

"That's why I'm here."

"What are you planning to do out there?" Carl asked.

James shook his head. "I don't have any plans at the moment."

"Heard you were staying in your father's old office."

News traveled fast in Lonesome. "My family still owns the building."

Carl nodded again, still eyeballing him with suspicion. "Margaret will give you a form to fill out. Could take a few days, maybe even a week."

"I'm in no hurry."

"That mean you're planning to stay for a while?"

James studied the man. "Why the interest in my itinerary, Carl?"

"There's a rumor circulating that you've reopened your father's office and that you're working one of his cases. Last I heard you weren't a licensed private investigator."

He hid his surprise, realizing that Shelby Crane had probably called. "No law against asking a few questions, but now that you mention it, I worked for my father during high school and when I was home from college and the rodeo so I have some experience."

"You need a year and a half's worth before you can apply for a license under state law."

He pretended he always knew that. "Yep, I know. Got it covered. Application is in the mail." It wasn't. But damn, he just might apply now.

The sheriff put down his coffee cup with a curse. "Why would you do that unless you planned to stay in town?"

James smiled. He *wasn't* planning to. "Just covering my options, sheriff."

"The state runs a criminal background check, you know."

He laughed. "Why would that concern me?"

"If you have a felony on your record—"

"I don't," he said with more force than he'd intended.

"Good thing they don't check finances or your mental health."

James laughed. "Not worried about either." With a shake of his head, he turned and walked over to Margaret's desk. Without a word, she handed him the permit application.

"You'll need to pay twenty-five dollars when you return that permit," Carl called after him.

Otis had just gotten through mowing the small lawn in front of his house. The summer air smelled of cut grass and sunshine. He turned on the sprinklers and, hot, sweaty and tired, went inside. He'd only just opened a can of beer and sat down when Carl called.

"You know what that damned Colt boy has gone and done now?" his brother demanded. James Colt was far from a boy, but Carl didn't give him a chance to reply. "He's been going all over town asking questions about his father's last case. He thinks he's a private eye."

He didn't have to ask what case. Otis was the first one on the scene after getting the call about the boy's body that was found in the ditch next to a house under construction in the new subdivision near where the Shermans lived. The memory still kept him awake some nights. He'd been a month away from retiring. Carl had been his undersheriff. The two of them had worked the case.

"Legally, James can't—"

"He's applied for a state license!" Carl was breathing hard, clearly worked up. "He says his experience working with his father should be enough. It probably is. It's so damned easy to get a PI license in this state, he'll get it and then—"

"And then *nothing*," Otis said. "He's a rodeo cowboy. I heard he's hurt. Once he feels better, he'll be back in the saddle, having put all of this behind him. Even if that isn't the case—which it is—he's inexperienced, the Sherman case is ice cold and we all know how hard those are to solve. And let's face it, he's not his father. I'll bet you five bucks that he quits before the week is out."

Carl sighed. Otis could imagine him pacing the floor of his office. "You think?"

"You know I don't throw money around."

His brother laughed. "No, not Otis Osterman." He sighed again. "I just thought this was behind us."

"It is," he said even though he knew it might never be true. Billy Sherman's death was unsolved, justice hadn't been meted out and what happened that night remained a mystery. There were always those who couldn't live with that.

Unfortunately, Del Colt had been one of them. Him and his damned digging. He'd gotten into things that had been better off left alone.

But Otis had five dollars that said James Colt was nothing like his father. For the young rodeo cowboy's sake, he certainly hoped not.

Chapter 6

After leaving the sheriff's office, James drove aimlessly around town for a while. He knew he should quit right now before he made things any worse. What had he hoped to accomplish with all this, anyway? Was he so arrogant that he thought he could pick up where his father had left off on the case and solve it just like that?

So far all he'd done was stir up a wasp's nest that was more than likely going to get him stung. If he hadn't left Melody in his trailer, if she hadn't rented it, if the renters hadn't blown it up, if he'd gone to a motel and never gone to his father's office…

He reminded himself that getting involved with Melody was all on him. He thought of one of his father's lectures he and his brothers had been forced to endure growing up.

Life is about consequences, Del would say. *Whatever*

you do, there will be a repercussion. It's the law of nature. Cause and effect.

What are you trying to say? one of his brothers would demand, usually himself most likely. *'Cause the effect I'm getting is a headache.*

His father would give him a reprimand before adding, *Don't blame someone else when things go wrong because of something stupid you did. Take responsibility and move on. It's called growing up.*

He and his brothers had made fun of that particular lecture, but it had never seemed more appropriate than right now.

His stomach growled. He looked at the time. Two in the afternoon. He hadn't had breakfast or lunch. He drove downtown. There was a spot in front of the sandwich shop. He took that as a sign.

"Tell me you aren't going to make a habit of this," Lori said when he walked in, but she smiled when she said it.

He smiled back at her. Distractedly he studied the chalkboard. The special today was a turkey club. He shifted his gaze to her. "I'll take the special and an iced tea."

"Do you want that on white, wheat or rye?"

"White." He hadn't been *that* distracted that he hadn't noticed her. Today she was dressed in a coral blouse and black slacks. The blouse was V-necked exposing some of the freckled skin of her throat and a small silver heart-shaped locket that played peekaboo when she moved. Her hair was pulled up again, making him wonder if it would fall past her shoulders if he let it down. "With mayo."

"It will be just a few minutes," she said, straightening her blouse collar self-consciously before hurrying into the back.

He took his usual seat. His leg was better today but his ribs still hurt. He kept thinking about his father's case, wishing he hadn't opened up this can of worms. Now that he had, what choice did he have?

Which meant he would have to talk to Karen Wilkins. Her stepdaughter wouldn't like it. Of that, he was certain. He just hoped that neither was involved. He liked Lorelei. He always had. Her stepmother owned a workout studio in town. Widowed, Karen was active in the community and had been as long as James could remember. He used to think "stepmother like stepdaughter." So why did Del have Karen on his list?

Deep in thought, he started when Lorelei set down the plate with his sandwich in front of him. She gently placed the glass of iced tea, giving him a worried look.

"You all right?" she asked. "You seem a little skittish."

He smiled at that. "I've been better."

"Is it true?"

"That's a wide-open question if I've ever heard one."

"Are you really applying for a private investigator's license?"

He chuckled. Thanks to the sheriff, he was. Probably also thanks to the sheriff everyone in town now knew. "Yep. How do you feel about that?"

She seemed surprised by the question. "It has nothing to do with me."

He nodded, hoping it was true. "Still, you seemed to have an opinion yesterday."

Lori looked away for a moment, licked her lips with the quick dart of her tongue, and said, "I was going to apologize for that."

"Really?" he said as he picked up his sandwich and took a bite. He chewed and swallowed before he said,

"And I thought you were going to apologize for trying to kill me with that sandwich you made me yesterday."

Her cheeks flushed. "You didn't have to eat it," she said defensively.

He held her gaze. "Yes, I did."

The bell over the front door jangled. She looked almost relieved as she went to help the couple that came in.

Chapter 7

After James finished his sandwich and iced tea, he wrote a note on the bill Lori had dropped by on her way past his table. The shop had gotten busy. He could see her through the small window into the kitchen. She was making sandwiches in her all-business way. It made him smile. Whatever she did, she did it with so much purpose.

He wondered what would happen if she ever let her guard down. He wished he could be there when she did.

As he left, he pulled out the list of names. It was time to talk to Karen Wilkins and relieve his mind. She couldn't be involved. He had to find out why she was on the list.

James was surprised how young Karen looked as she opened the door. A small woman with chin-length blond hair and large luminous brown eyes, the aerobics instructor was clearly in great shape. In her late forties, Karen and her stepdaughter could have almost passed for sisters rather than stepmother and stepdaughter.

From the expression on her face though, she wasn't glad to see him. He wondered if it had anything to do with him taking over his father's old case. Or if it was more about his reputation. Would he ever live down his misspent youth?

"I hope I haven't caught you at a bad time," he said. She was dressed in leggings, a T-shirt and sneakers as if on her way to her exercise studio. "Do you have a few minutes? I'd like to ask you a few questions."

The woman chuckled, reminding him of Lorelei for a moment. "Whatever you're selling Jimmy D—"

He raised his hands. "Not selling anything. I've taken over my father's old private investigative business temporarily. I'm looking into the last case he was working on before he died."

She raised an eyebrow and he saw her expression turn both serious—and wary.

"I'm here about Billy Sherman's hit-and-run."

Her eyes widened. "Wasn't that almost ten years ago?"

"It was. Please, I promise not to keep you long."

She didn't move. "Why would you think I would know anything about that?"

"Because you were on my father's list of people he wanted to interview."

Her face paled and he saw the fear. She quickly looked away. "I can't imagine how I could possibly help even if I didn't have a class in a few minutes." Her gaze shifted back to his but only for a second. "I was just leaving. I'm sorry. This really isn't a good time." With that, she closed the door.

He stood for a moment feeling shaken to his core.

He knew from experience what guilt looked like. Fear too. Turning, he walked out to his pickup and had just slipped behind the wheel when Karen Wilkins's garage door gaped open, and her car came flying out. She barely missed the front bumper of his pickup before she sped away.

She seemed to be in an awful hurry to get to her class, he thought as he gave it a moment before he followed her.

"What's wrong?" Lorelei felt panicked at the fear she heard in her stepmother's voice the moment she'd answered her phone.

"It's…nothing, I'm sorry."

"It's not nothing. I can hear it in your voice. Mom—" Lorelei's mother died when she was three. Both her parents had been young—her mother twenty-two when she died, her father twenty-four. She barely remembered her mother. After her mother died, her father went for ten years before even dating.

It had been a shock when he'd come home from an insurance conference with Karen who had looked like a teenager at twenty-five. Lorelei had been thirteen, Karen only twelve years older. People said they could be sisters. At the time, the comment had made her sick to her stomach. How could her father do this to her?

Lorelei hadn't accepted the woman into their lives for a long time, refusing to call her mom. But at some point, her stepmother had won her over and she'd begun calling her mom since she'd never really had a mother before Karen.

The only time she called her Karen had been when she was angry at her like for grounding her or mentioning that she had a boyfriend when her father had said she was too young to have one. Most of the time though, she and Karen had been as close as biological mother and daughter.

"I'm just being silly," Karen said now. "I had a little bit of a scare, for no good reason really. Let's forget it. Tell me how you are doing."

Lorelei looked to the ceiling of her shop kitchen. "I'm doing fine. Had a busy lunch crowd and now I'm prepping for tomorrow." Just like she did every day. "Mom, tell me what's wrong. You never call me at work."

"I shouldn't. I know how busy you are."

"I'm not busy right now. Talk to me."

Silence, then finally, "James Colt is back in town. Apparently, he's taking over his father's investigations business?"

"I don't know. Maybe. Mom, why—"

"That boy is trouble. He always has been. I just don't like the idea of him being in the same building as you."

"He's not in the same building," she said, unable to understand why her stepmother was so upset over this. "He's staying next door in his father's office."

"So, you've seen him?"

"He's stopped by for sandwiches a couple of times." She realized that her stepmother was calling from her car. "Are you in your car? Where are you going?"

"Nowhere. I mean…to the store. I'm out of milk."

Her stepmother didn't drink milk. Nor did she hardly eat anything but fruit and vegetables. Her stepdaughter owned a sandwich shop and her stepmother didn't eat even gluten-free bread. "Are you sure you're all right?"

"Sometimes I just need to hear my daughter's voice. I didn't mean to scare you."

Scare her? Lorelei realized that was exactly what

she'd done. Scare her. This wasn't like Karen. Whatever had upset her… She realized that it seemed to be James Colt and his plan to take over his father's PI business. It had upset her too, but Lorelei had her reasons going all the way back to middle school. She couldn't imagine first how her stepmother had heard and second why that would upset her unless…

"Mom," she said as a bad feeling settled in her stomach. "Did James come by to see you?"

"I'm at the store about to check out," her stepmother said. "I have to go. Talk to you later." She disconnected.

Lorelei held the phone feeling a wave of shock wash over her. Her stepmother had just lied to her. She wasn't in the store checkout. Karen had still been in her car driving. She'd heard the crunch of tires on gravel. Where had her stepmother gone? Not the store with its paved parking lot.

She quickly called her back. But got voice mail straight away. She didn't leave a message.

At first Karen Wilkins seemed to be driving aimlessly around town. James had finally pulled over on a side street with a view of Main Street near her exercise studio and waited. She pulled in front of the studio and he'd thought she was going to get out.

But a few minutes later, she took off again without getting out of the car. If she'd had a class, someone else was now teaching it apparently. This time, she headed out of town. James waited until another car got behind Karen Wilkins's car before he pulled out and followed.

A few miles out of town, he saw her brake lights come on ahead of him right before she turned down a gravel road and disappeared into the pines. He caught up, turned and followed the dust trail she'd made, wondering if she was finally going to park somewhere.

He didn't have to wonder long. Around a curve in the road, he saw her car stop in front of a large house set back in the pines. Pulling over, he watched her exit her car and hurry up the steps. As she rang the doorbell, she looked around nervously, before the door opened a few moments later.

The man in the doorway quickly pulled Karen Wilkins into his arms, holding her for a moment before he wiped her tears and then kissed her passionately. As he drew her inside, he glanced around—giving James a clear view of his face—before he quickly closed the door.

James felt as if he'd touched a live wire. He let out a low curse. He'd been hoping that he was wrong about Lorelei's stepmother. He'd hoped there was a simple explanation for her being on his father's list. James still didn't want to believe it, but there was no doubt that he'd upset Karen Wilkins on his visit to her house. Since then she'd been running scared.

And look where she'd run. Straight into the arms of Senator Fred Bayard.

Chapter 8

James drove back into town, stopping in at the local hardware store that his friend Ryan owned. He found him in the back office doing paperwork. "What is Senator Bayard doing in Lonesome?"

His friend looked up and laughed. "You don't get out much, do you? Fred had a summer home built here about ten years ago. He's one of my best customers, always building something out there on his property."

James didn't follow politics. The only reason he'd recognized the man was because his face had been in so many television ads before the last election. "Why here?"

Ryan leaned forward, his elbows on his desk. "His family's from here. It isn't that unusual. What has got you so worked up? I didn't know you were back in town, let alone that you cared about politics."

"Wait, the senator's from Lonesome?" That couldn't have been something he'd missed.

"His mother was Claudia Hanson, the postmistress. Fred grew up here. He was your father's age. Claudia moved them to Helena at some point when she married Charles Bayard, also a senator, and Bayard adopted Fred."

"I never knew that."

"His great-grandfather started the original sawmill here in Lonesome about the time the railroad was coming through. Heard he made a bundle making and selling railroad ties to the Great Northern. Did you pay any attention at all during Montana history class?"

"Apparently not." He vaguely remembered this, but it had been out of context back then. "You've met him then?"

"Fred? He's a good old boy. Like I said, he stops in when he's in town, which isn't often. Most of the time he's in DC. The rest of the time, he's building corrals or barns or adding onto the summer house, even though he spends so little time here during the year."

James sank into the chair across from Ryan's desk, thinking about what he'd just seen. Karen in the man's arms. "Doesn't he have a wife?"

"Mary? I don't think I've ever seen her. She doesn't spend much time here. They have a big place outside of Helena. I think she stays there most of the time doing her own thing. Why the interest?"

He shook his head. "Have you ever seen him with another woman?"

Ryan looked surprised. He leaned back in his chair. "I'm guessing you have. Someone I know?"

"I'm probably mistaken." He quickly changed the subject. "I'm back for a while. I supposed you heard about Melody and my trailer." His friend nodded. "I'm staying at my dad's old office for the time being." He chewed at his cheek for a moment. "I'm thinking about getting my PI license."

"Seriously?"

"I need to heal up before I go back on the rodeo circuit. I thought it would give me something to do."

Ryan narrowed his gaze. "If I didn't know you so well, I might believe that. What's really going on?"

He sighed. "I'm kind of working Del's last case, Billy Sherman's hit-and-run death. It's never been solved."

"Like a tribute to your old man?"

"Maybe."

"And you think Senator Bayard is involved?"

He shook his head. "I was following a lead that made me aware of Bayard. You said he had his summer home built about ten years ago? So, he might have been here at the time of Billy Sherman's accident."

Ryan gave him a wary look. "Where are you going with this?"

James pulled off his Stetson and raked a hand through his hair. "I have no idea. I'm probably just chasing my own tail."

His friend laughed. "I'd be careful if I were you. Bayard carries a lot of weight in this state. Talk is that he might run for governor."

"Don't worry. I'm just following a few leads. I hate that Del didn't get to finish the case." He thought about mentioning what Alice had told him. That Del said he was close to solving it—and was killed that very night.

But he knew what it would sound like and Ryan knew him too well. Conspiracy theory aside, he had his own reasons for fearing what he might find if he dug into his father's death. His father had been acting strangely in those weeks—or was it months—before his death. Something more than the case had been bothering him.

"How's things with you?"

Ryan motioned to the paperwork stacked up on the desk. "Busy as usual. More people are finding Lonesome. I bought the lumberyard a few years ago. Quite a few new houses coming up, so that's good. You thinking about building out there on your place?"

"I'll see what my brothers want to do when they get back after the rodeo season."

"You can't see yourself staying long-term?"

A fleeting image of Lorelei popped into his head, followed by the little girl on the horse. He shook his head. "Nope, can't see myself staying."

Lorelei closed the shop right after her last customer left. She usually stayed open until six, but tonight she was anxious to leave. She'd tried to call her stepmother numerous times, but each call had gone to voice mail. After how frantic Karen had sounded earlier...

She parked out front. No sign of her stepmother's car. As she started toward the front door, she checked the garage and felt a surge of relief. Her car was parked inside. At the front door she knocked. Normally she just walked right in. But nothing about earlier had felt normal.

"Lorelei?" Her stepmother seemed not just surprised to see her but startled. True, Lorelei hadn't stopped over to the house for a while. She'd been so busy with the sandwich shop. "Is something wrong?"

"How can you ask that?" Lorelei demanded. "You called me earlier clearly upset and when I tried to call you back, my call went straight to voice mail. I've been worried about you all afternoon."

"I'm so sorry. I guess I turned my phone off. Come in." She moved out of the doorway.

As she stepped in, she tried to breathe, admitting to herself just how scared she'd been and how relieved. Her stepmother seemed okay. But Karen wasn't easily rattled. Instead, she'd always taken things in her stride. In fact, she'd seemed really happy for a long while now. Except for the way she'd sounded on the phone earlier.

She turned to study her stepmother and saw something she hadn't before. How had she not noticed the change in her? Karen Wilkins was practically glowing. She was always slim and trim because she often led classes at her studio. But she appeared healthier and happier looking.

"You look so…good," she said, unable to put her finger on what exactly was different about her stepmother.

Karen laughed, brown eyes twinkling, clearly pleased. "Why, thank you."

"Has something changed?"

Her stepmother's smile quickly disappeared, replaced by a frown. "Why would you ask that?"

"I don't know. You just seem…different."

Brushing that off, Karen headed for the kitchen cupboard, saying over her shoulder, "I made some granola. I was going to call you and see if you—"

"Mom. Stop. Why were you so upset earlier when you called me?"

Her stepmother froze for a moment before turning to face her. "I feel so foolish. I got worked up over nothing." Lorelei put her hands on her hips, waiting.

Finally, Karen sighed and said, "James Colt paid me a visit."

Which explained her stepmother's reaction to him staying in the building next to the sandwich shop. "He came here? Why would he—"

"He's taking over one of his father's old cases apparently and was asking questions about something that happened years ago."

Lorelei noticed that her stepmother was twisting the life out of the plastic bag with the granola in it. "What case?"

"That hit-and-run… The boy, Billy Sherman."

"Why would he ask *you* about that?" But she was thinking, why would that upset her stepmother so much?

Her stepmother turned back to the cupboard. Lorelei watched her busy herself with fixing a bag to send home with her. "I have no idea. He's probably asking a lot of people in the neighborhood."

Lorelei frowned. The accident had happened probably a half mile from her stepmother's house. "I'm sure that's all it was," she said, even though her pulse was spiking. She knew her stepmother. Something was definitely wrong. "It still doesn't explain why you were so upset."

Karen sighed. "I was just sorry to find out that he's back in town and in the office next to you given the crush you had on him in high school."

"I didn't have a crush on him in high school!" she protested, no doubt too much.

"Lorelei, I was there. I saw your reaction to that boy. You're doing so well with your business. I'm just afraid you're going to get mixed up with him."

"I'm not getting mixed up with him. He's come over

to the shop a couple of times. I don't know where you got the idea I had a crush on him."

Her stepmother merely looked at her impatiently before she said, "Here, take this home." Karen thrust the bag of granola into her hands and looked at her watch. "I'm sorry I have a class I'm teaching this evening. I wish you could stay and we could watch an old movie." She was steering her toward the door. Giving her the bum's rush, as her father would have said.

She wanted to dig her heels in, demand to know why she was acting so strangely. Was it really because she was worried about Lorelei and James Colt, her new neighbor, the cowboy impersonating a PI?

That was ridiculous.

James had been at his father's desk, head in his hands, when the pounding at his door made him jump. What the— "Hold your horses!" he called as he rose to go to the door. "What's the big—" He stopped when he saw Lori standing there.

Her face was flushed, her brown eyes wide, her breathing rapid as if she'd run up the stairs. She was still wearing what she'd had on earlier.

"Is there a fire?" A shake of her head. "Are you being chased by zombies?" A dirty look. "Then I give up." He leaned against the doorjamb to survey her, giving her time to catch her breath. He had a pretty good idea what had her upset, but he wasn't going to bring it up unless she did.

"Why are you questioning my stepmother about the hit-and-run accident?" she demanded.

"Why don't you step in and we can discuss this like—"

"Do you have any idea how much you upset her?"

He nodded slowly. "Actually, I do. Which makes me wonder why, and now why you're even more upset."

Lori took a breath then another one. Her gaze swung away from him for a moment. He watched her regain control of her emotions. She swallowed before she looked at him again. "Why did you question her?" Her voice almost sounded in the normal range.

He moved aside and motioned her into the office. With obvious reluctance, she stepped in, stopping in the middle of the room.

"I love what you've done with the place," she said derisively.

James glanced around, seeing things through her eyes. "I've been meaning to buy a few things to make it more…homey. I've been busy."

"Yes," she said turning to glare at him. "Intimidating my stepmother."

"Is that what she told you?"

A muscle jumped in her jaw. "I will ask you again. Why my stepmother?"

"She was on my father's list."

Lorelei stared at him. "What list?"

He stepped around behind the desk, but didn't sit down. "My father had a method that worked for him. Did you know he solved all of his cases? He was methodical. I wish I was more like him." He could see her growing more impatient. "He would write down a list of names of people connected to the case that he wanted to talk to. He'd check off the ones as he went. Your stepmother was on the list. He hadn't gotten around to questioning her before he was killed. I decided to take up where he left off and ask her myself."

"And?"

"And nothing—she got upset, said she had a class and threw me out."

"Maybe she did have a class."

He gave her a you-really-believe-that look? He watched all the anger seep from her. She looked close to tears, her back no longer ramrod straight, her facial muscles no longer rigid.

"Why would she know anything about Billy Sherman?" she asked quietly.

He shrugged and stepped around the desk to dust off one of the leather club chairs. She moved to it as if sleepwalking and carefully lowered herself down. Behind the desk again, he opened the bottom drawer, took out the bottle of brandy his father kept there and two of the paper cups.

After pouring them each a couple of fingers' worth, he handed her a cup as he took the matching leather chair next to her. He noticed her hand trembled as she took the drink. She was scared. He was afraid she had good reason to be.

He waited until she'd taken a sip of the brandy before he asked, "Can you think of any reason your stepmother would be so upset about talking to me about the case?"

She shook her head, took a gulp and looked over at him. "You can't really think that she is somehow involved." When he didn't speak instantly, she snapped, "James, my stepmother wouldn't hit a child and keep going."

"I'm not saying she did. But she might know who did."

Lori shook her head, drained her paper cup and set it on the edge of his desk as she rose. "You really think she would keep a secret like that?"

"People keep secrets from those they love all the time," he said.

She glared at him. "What is that supposed to mean?"

"Just that she might be covering for someone."

Her eyes flared. "If you tell me that you think she's covering for me—"

He rose, raising both hands in surrender as he did. "I'm not accusing you. I'm just saying…" He met her gaze, surprised at how hard this was. He and Lori had gone through school together and hardly said two words the entire time. It wasn't like that much had changed over the past few days, he told himself even as he knew it had. He liked her. Always had.

"I think your stepmother knows something and that's why she got so upset." He said the words quickly.

Her reaction was just as quick. "My stepmother wouldn't cover for *anyone*. Not for such a horrible crime. You're wrong. She doesn't keep secrets." She started toward the door.

"You might not know your stepmother as well as you think you do." All his instincts told him she didn't.

She reached the door and spun around to face him, anger firing those brown eyes again. "What are you trying to say?"

"That your stepmother might have secrets. Maybe especially from you."

She scoffed at that, and hands on her hips demanded to know what he was talking about.

"After I questioned her about Billy Sherman's death, your stepmother headed for her studio, saying she had to teach a class. But instead of teaching, she drove out of town and into the arms of Senator Fred Bayard."

He saw the answer as the color drained from her face.

She hadn't known. "I'm sorry." He mentally kicked himself for the pain in her eyes before she threw open the door and stormed out.

He swore as he heard her leave. How did his father do this? He had no idea, but he suspected Del was a hell of a lot better at it than he'd been so far.

Chapter 9

For the next few days, James avoided the sandwich shop and Lori. He felt guilty for exposing her stepmother. But he'd hoped that Karen Wilkins might be honest with her stepdaughter. He needed to know what the woman was hiding—other than the senator.

He'd called out-of-town body shops and left messages for them to call if they had a front end–damaged car from hitting something like a deer after the date of Billy Sherman's death. He didn't have much hope, given how much time had passed. He also assumed his father had done the same thing nine years ago without much success.

While he waited to hear back, he mulled over the case as he cleaned up the office and back bedroom. He bought a few things to make the place more comfortable by adding a couch, a couple of end tables, a coffee table, a large rug and some bookshelves for more storage.

For the bedroom, he'd bought a new rug for the hardwood floor and all new towels, rug and shower curtain for the bathroom. He'd even replaced his father's old vacuum with a new one and dusted and washed the windows. By the time he was through with all the hauling and cleaning his leg hurt and his ribs ached worse.

But when he looked around the place, he felt better. He'd also sent in his application for his private investigator license and dropped off his permit at the sheriff's office to have the burned-out trailer removed from the property. Margaret had suggested a company that did that kind of work. After a call to them, he was told the work would be done this week.

James had to admit he was pretty impressed with what he'd accomplished. But he was no closer to finding Billy Sherman's killer. Also, he realized that he missed Lori's sandwiches and the time he spent with her. He'd been hitting the local In-N-Out, but had pretty much gone through the fried food menu over the past few days. He found himself craving the smell of fresh-baked bread— and the sweet scent of Lori.

He just wasn't sure what kind of reception he would get so he decided to do some real work first. After pulling out the list of names, he grabbed his Stetson and headed for the door.

Maybe he'd get a sandwich to go, he thought as he locked and closed the office door behind him. He'd worried about Lori since he'd dropped the bombshell. All she could do was throw him out if she really couldn't stand the sight of him, right?

Lorelei had driven straight to her stepmother's house the evening after James had told her about her stepmother's relationship. She'd seen a light on and movement behind the kitchen curtains. Her stepmother's car was in the driveway, which was odd. She'd slowed and was about to pull in when she saw a second shadow behind the kitchen curtains.

She'd quickly pulled away, feeling like a coward. Why hadn't she confronted her stepmother and whoever was in the house with her? She told herself she needed to be calm before she did. That it would be better if she spoke about this with her stepmother when she was alone.

When she'd run out of excuses, she'd driven home and looked up Senator Bayard online. There were publicity photos of him and his wife, Mary, and their three daughters—all adults, but all younger than Lorelei.

James had to be wrong. He'd misunderstood. Although she couldn't imagine what had made him think that her stepmother would have an affair with a married man—let alone keep it from her only stepdaughter.

She knew that was the part that hurt. She and Karen had been close, hadn't they? And yet, the other night when she'd driven by, her stepmother hadn't been alone. Could have been a neighbor over, but Lorelei knew it wasn't true. The shadows had been close, then moved together as if one before breaking apart and disappearing from view. Her stepmother did have secrets.

The bell over the front door of the sandwich shop jangled and she looked up to see James Colt come in. He was the last person she wanted to see right now. Or ever. Emotions came at her like a squad of fighter jets. Mad, angry, embarrassed, upset, worried, resigned and at the same time her heart beat a little faster at the sight of him.

"Any chance of getting a sandwich to go?" he asked almost sheepishly.

"I suppose," she said, still battling her conflicting emotions.

He glanced from her to the chalkboard. She studied him while he studied it. He was wearing a blue paisley-patterned Western shirt that matched his eyes. She wondered if he'd bought it or if it was purchased by a girlfriend. It was tucked into the waist of his perfectly fitting jeans. One of his prizewinning rodeo buckles rounded out his attire. He shifted on his feet, taking her gaze down his long legs to his boots. New boots? She'd heard him hauling stuff in and out the past few days and knew he'd been shopping.

"I'll take the special on a roll," he said.

After all that, he'd chosen the special? "Iced tea?"

"How about a cola?"

"Fine. Have a seat. I'll bring it to you."

He nodded and met her gaze. "Lori—"

Whatever he planned to say, she didn't want to hear it. Turning on her heel, she hurried into the kitchen to make his sandwich and try to calm her pounding heart. What was it about the man that had her hands shaking? He just made her so...so...so not her usual controlled self.

Lori. No one had ever called her anything but Lorelei. Leave it to James to give her a nickname. Leave it to James to say it in a way that made her feel all soft inside.

James couldn't get a handle on Lorelei's mood. He hated to think what she was putting in his sandwich. Maybe coming here hadn't been his best idea. But he was hungry, and at least for a few minutes he got to breathe in the smell of freshly baked bread and stretch out his legs.

He didn't have to wait long. When he saw her coming, he started to get up but she waved him back down.

"I thought you'd prefer I take it to go."

She shook her head. "Barbecued pork is hard to eat in your pickup, though I'm sure you've managed it before," she said as she sat down in a chair opposite him.

He wasn't sure the last was a compliment so he simply unwrapped his sandwich and carefully lifted the top piece of bun to see what was inside.

"It's just pulled pork, my fresh coleslaw and house special barbecue sauce," she said, sounding indignant.

"It's your special sauce that I'm worried about," he said.

"It's not too spicy. A tough cowboy like you should be able to handle it." Her gaze challenged him to argue.

He put the sandwich back together and took a bite. "Delicious." He took another bite. He really was starved.

"Do you have to keep sounding surprised that I can make a decent sandwich?" she demanded.

"Sorry, it's just that you're so…so…" He waved a hand in the air, wishing he hadn't opened his mouth.

"So? So what? Uptight? Too good to do simple things?"

He took a bite, chewed and swallowed, stalling. "You're so…sexy." He held up a hand as if expecting a blow. "I know it's a cliché that a sexy woman can't cook. Still…"

"Sexy?" She shook her head and let out an exasperated sigh, but she didn't leave his table. He continued eating. He could see her working through a few things. But when she finally spoke, her words took him by surprise. "I need to know why my stepmother is on your father's list."

He wiped his mouth with a napkin and took a drink of the cola. "I don't know. That's why I went to talk to her."

He could see she was struggling with the next question and decided to help her out. "After she got so upset I followed her. She drove all over town, at one point made a couple of phone calls and then drove out of town. I didn't even know the senator had a house here until he opened the front door."

"Just because she went to his house— Isn't it possible they're just good friends?"

He shook his head. "He took her in his arms and kissed her. It was passionate and she kissed him back. They both seemed nervous, worried that someone was watching and hurriedly closed the door."

"Someone *was* watching," she said under her breath. She looked sick to her stomach.

"I'm sorry to be the one to tell you. I was surprised to see her name on the list. I went there hoping she'd tell me why. It was a shot in the dark. But then when she got so upset before I even had a chance to ask her…"

She nodded. "Refill?" she asked, pointing at his cola.

He shook his head. "You haven't talked to her?"

"I haven't wanted to believe it. I was hoping you were wrong." Her gaze came up to meet his. "I suppose if anyone knows a passionate kiss when he sees one, it would be you though."

He laughed, leaning his elbows on the table to close the distance between them. "You give me a lot more credit than I'm due." She harrumphed at that. "Why do I get the feeling that I did something to you back in grade school or high school or this week and that's why you're so angry with me?"

"You didn't. It's just that I know what kind of man you are."

"Do you?" he asked seriously before shaking his head.

"I thought you were smarter than to believe everything you hear. Especially about me." He dropped his voice. "I've kissed a few women. But I'm still waiting to kiss the one who rattles me clear down to the toes of my boots."

She raised a brow. "You've been in town for a few days. I'm sure you have one in your sights already."

"Oh, I do," he said, realizing it was true. He just wondered if he'd ever get the chance to kiss her.

Lorelei called her stepmother after James left. "I was thinking we could have dinner together tonight if you don't have any plans. I could pick up—" She was going to suggest something vegan for her stepmother, when Karen interrupted her.

"You don't have to pick up anything. I can make us a nice salad for dinner."

She felt off balance. She'd been half expecting her stepmother to make an excuse because she was seeing her…lover again tonight? "Sure, that would be great."

"Good, then I'll see you about six thirty," Karen said.

"See you then."

She disconnected, telling herself that James was wrong. That what she'd seen last night might not even have been the senator. That her stepmother's name being on Del Colt's list meant nothing.

When she arrived at the house a little after six, her stepmother answered the door smiling and seeming excited to see her. She ushered her into the kitchen where she'd made a pitcher of lemonade. "I thought we could eat out on the patio. It's such a beautiful evening."

Lorelei had planned to question her after they ate, but she realized she couldn't sit through chitchat for an hour first. She watched her stepmother start to pour them each a glass of lemonade over ice.

"Are you having an affair with Senator Bayard?"

Her stepmother's arm jerked, lemonade spilling over the breakfast bar. Without looking at her, Karen slowly set down the pitcher, then reached for a dishcloth to clean up the mess. Without a word, she'd already admitted the truth.

"I can't believe this," Lorelei cried. "When did this happen? *How* did this happen? He's *married*!"

Her stepmother turned to her, her face set in stone. "He's getting a divorce and then we're going to get married."

"That's what they all say," she snapped. "Don't you watch daytime talk shows?"

"He's separated and has been for some time. He's been staying at the family's summer home here when he isn't in Washington." Karen looked down at the dishcloth in her hands. "We've been seeing each other for a while now." She looked up.

"Before he and his wife were supposedly separated." It wasn't a question.

"I'm not proud of it. It just happened."

Lorelei shook her head. *"It just happened?"*

"I love him and he loves me."

She bit her tongue, thinking how different this conversation would have been if she'd been the one having the affair. Her stepmother would be hitting the roof right now. Look how upset she'd supposedly gotten over James Colt being in the building next door to her stepdaughter. "You haven't said how you met him."

"Our paths crossed a few times while he was here

building his summer home," she said. "We found we had a lot in common."

Lorelei wanted to ask what, but she wasn't ready to hear this. "You're serious." Of course her stepmother was. That glow she'd noticed. Karen was in *love*. That her stepmother would even consider an affair with a married man told her how head over heels she was with this man.

"With him possibly running for governor, the timing isn't good, but we're going to get married once the fallout from his divorce settles."

She couldn't bring herself to say that she wasn't holding her breath and neither should her stepmother. But she was so disappointed and angry right now that she couldn't deal with this. Karen had cautioned her about men since she was thirteen.

"Let me get the salad and we can go out on the deck and—"

"I'm sorry," she said. "I've lost my appetite." With that she turned and started for the door.

"Lorelei, wait."

She stopped at the door, closing her eyes as she heard her stepmother come up behind her. She thought of all the tantrums she'd thrown as a teen, all the arguments she and Karen had had over the years. They'd always made up and gotten through it.

"I'm sorry I've disappointed you."

"I am too, Karen." She started to open the door, felt her stepmother tentatively touch her back and flinched.

Her stepmother quickly removed her hand. "Disappointed in me or not you have to understand, I'm an adult. I get to make my own decisions, right or wrong."

Her voice broke. "I'm still young. I've been lonely since your father died. Can't you try to be happy for me?"

Lorelei felt herself weaken, her love for her step-mother a constant in her life. Karen was right. She was still young and she'd been a widow for years now. Of course she was lonely; of course she wanted a man in her life.

"I'm trying," she said and turned to face her. "Tell me you aren't involved in what happened to the Sherman boy. Swear it on my life."

Her stepmother looked shocked. "Why would you ask—"

"Because I know you. For you to get so upset over James's questions about the case that you'd run to your lover and be seen, you must have something else to hide. Tell me the truth."

Her stepmother took a step back. "So, it was James who saw us and ran right to you to tell you. I should have known."

"He didn't run right to me. I cornered him, demand-ing to know why he would question you. But you still haven't answered my question," Lorelei said, that knot in her chest tightening. "Swear. On my life."

"Don't be ridiculous," Karen snapped and took an-other step back. "I would never swear to anything on your life. You're upset and don't know what you're say-ing. You should go before either of us says something we'll regret."

Lorelei felt tears burn her eyes. "You already have." With that, she opened the door and left.

Chapter 10

After leaving the sandwich shop, James had felt at loose ends. He drove out to his family's ranch. *Ranch* was a loosely used term since no one had raised much of anything on the land. It was close to a hundred acres covered with pines. Some of it was mountainous while a strip of it bordered the river.

He and his brothers had talked about selling some of it off since they didn't use it, but Willie, their eldest brother, talked them out of it.

"Land doesn't have to do anything and someday you're going to be glad that it's there and that it's ours," Willie had said.

The remains of the double-wide trailer had been removed leaving a scorched area of ground where it had been. But James could see where grass was already starting to grow. It wouldn't be long before nature healed the spot.

James stood looking at the rolling hillsides, towering pines and granite bluffs. He was glad Willie had talked them out of selling even a portion of it. This land was all that brought them back here. It was the one constant in their lives. The one tangible in their otherwise nomadic lives.

That and the office building. He thought about Lori wanting to buy it. He still thought of the place as Del's and felt himself balk at the idea of ever giving it up.

Back at the office, he found several notes tacked to his back door. Word had gotten out that he was in business. One was from an insurance company offering him surveillance work if he was interested. The other was from someone who wanted her boyfriend followed. He laughed, delighted that he had several new PI jobs if he wanted them.

But first he had to finish what he'd started. He drove out to Edgar Appleton's house some miles from town. Edgar owned a heavy equipment construction company. He and his crew had been working near where Billy Sherman's body had been found. One of his employees, Lyle Harris, had been operating a front loader that morning. He was about to dump a load of dirt into the ditch when a neighbor woman spotted the body and screamed—stopping him.

Edgar lived on a twenty-acre tract. His house sat off to one side, his equipment taking up the rest of the property. Several vehicles were parked in front of the house when James climbed the steps to knock. He could hear loud voices inside and knocked again.

A hush came from inside the house a moment before

the door opened. Edgar filled the doorway. He was a big man with a wild head of brown hair that stuck up every which way. He was wearing a sweatshirt with his business logo on it and a pair of canvas pants. It appeared he'd just gotten home from work.

"If this is a bad time…"

"James Colt," Edgar said in a loud boisterous voice. "Bad time? It's always a bad time at this house. Come in!" He stepped aside. "Irene, put another plate on the table."

She yelled something back that he didn't catch just a moment before she appeared behind her husband wiping her hands on her apron. "You'd think I'm only here to cook and clean for this man." She smiled, her whole face lighting up. "Get on in here. I have a beef roast and vegetables coming out of the oven. I hope your table manners are better than Ed's. I could use some stimulating conversation for once." Her laugh filled the large room as she headed back to the kitchen.

"The meanest woman who ever lived," Edgar said so she could hear it. Her response was swift, followed by the banging of pots and pans. "I don't know what I would do without her."

"That's for sure!" she called from the kitchen.

"I can't stay for dinner. I probably should have called first," James said.

"Sorry, but you have no choice now," Edgar said as he looped an arm around his shoulders and dragged him in. "She'll swear I ran you off and I'll have to hear about it the rest of the night."

He had to admit, Irene's dinner smelled wonderful. He heard his stomach growl. So did Edgar. The man laughed heartily as he swept him into the dining room off the kitchen.

"I didn't come for dinner, but it sure smells good," he told Irene as she brought out a pan of homemade rolls. "Let me help you with that." He grabbed the hot pads on the counter and helped her get the huge pot out of the oven. It was enough food to feed an army, he saw. "Are there other people coming?" he asked as she directed him to a trivet at the head of the large dining room table.

"At this house, you never know," Irene said. "I like to be prepared. As it is, Ed didn't bring home half the crew tonight so I'm glad you showed up."

"Me too," Ed said as he sat down at the head of the table and began to slice up the roast. Irene swatted him with the dishtowel she took from her shoulder before she sat to his right and motioned James into the chair across from her.

"James, I want to hear it all," she said smiling as she reached for his plate and Edgar began to load it up with thick slices of the beef. "You know what I'm talking about," she said, seeing his confusion. "Is it true? You've taken over your father's private investigative business? We'll get to Melody and what happened to your trailer later."

"Sorry, I should have warned you," Edgar said with a laugh. "The woman is relentless." As he said it, he reached over and squeezed her arm.

For the rest of the meal, they all talked and laughed. James couldn't recall a time he'd enjoyed more. Seeing how these two genuinely cared about each other was heartwarming and Irene's dinner was amazing.

"I know you didn't come by for dinner," Edgar said when they'd finished and Irene got up to clear the table.

James started to rise to help her but she waved him back down.

He explained that he was looking into his father's last case, the hit-and-run that killed Billy Sherman.

"We were working in that subdivision. You know Lyle, my front-end loader operator, was working that morning," Edgar said. "He was getting ready to fill in that ditch we'd dug when a neighbor lady came over with some turnovers she'd made for the crew. She saw Billy lying there and started screaming." He shook his head. "It wrecked us all." Irene came from the kitchen to place her hand on the big man's shoulder for a few moments before taking the rest of the dirty plates into the kitchen.

"That was a new neighborhood nine years ago, new pavement," James said. "Did you see skid marks, any indication that whoever hit him had tried to stop?"

Edgar wagged his big head. "The sheriff, that was Otis back then, said the driver must have thought he hit a deer and that was why he didn't stop. Plus it was raining hard that night. I reckon the car was going so fast when it hit the boy—he was pretty scrawny for his age—that the driver hadn't known what was hit."

"But the driver had to have known it wasn't a deer, even if he didn't stop," James said. "There would have been some damage to the car, a dent or a broken headlight." Edgar nodded. "I would think the car would have had to have been repaired."

"You're assuming the driver was local, but even if that was the case, he wouldn't have had it repaired in town."

James thought of the next name on his list that his father hadn't gotten to: Gus Hughes of Hughes Body Shop in town. But Edgar was right. If it had been a local, then the driver would have gotten the car repaired out of town.

Irene came in and changed the subject as she served coffee and raspberry pie with a scoop of ice cream.

"I can't tell you how much I've enjoyed this meal," James told her before Edgar walked him to the door.

"I hope you find out who killed that boy," the big man said, patting him on the shoulder. "It's time he was put to rest."

Lorelei woke feeling exhausted after a night of tossing and turning. She kept thinking about her stepmother and going from angry to sad to worried and regretful for the things she'd said. Her stepmother couldn't know anything about Billy Sherman's death. So why hadn't she sworn that? Why had she gotten even more upset and basically thrown Lorelei out of her house?

After a shower, she dressed for work. Owning her own business meant she went to work whether she felt like it or not. She had a couple of women she hired during the busiest seasons to help out, but she'd never considered turning the place over to one of them before this morning.

She reeled her thoughts back. What had she been doing nine years ago when Billy Sherman died? Working in a friend's sandwich shop in Billings, learning the business. Before that she'd had numerous jobs using her college business degree, but hadn't found anything that called to her. She'd always known that she wanted the independence of having her own business.

And what had her stepmother been doing nine years ago? Karen had her exercise studio and had been teaching a lot, as far as Lorelei could remember.

Frowning now, she tried to remember if it had been her stepmother who'd told her about Billy Sherman's hit-

and-run or if she'd heard it on the news. Didn't she remember a phone conversation about it? Her stepmother being understandably upset since it had happened not that far from her house in that new adjoining subdivision.

Lorelei felt sick to her stomach and more scared than she'd ever been. She had to know the truth. But if she couldn't get her stepmother to tell her...

It was still early. She called her friend Anita and asked her if she wanted to fill in today, apologizing for the short notice. Anita jumped at the opportunity, saying she had nothing planned and could use the money.

"I had already made a list of the specials," Lorelei told her. "Everything you need is in the cooler. You just have to get the bread going right away. I'll be in to help as soon as I can."

Anita said she was already on her way out the door headed for the shop, making Lorelei smile. Her business would be fine. Grabbing her purse, she headed for her car.

With the rising sun, James had awakened knowing he was going to have to talk to former sheriff Otis Osterman at some point. He had too many questions about how the sheriff had handled the investigation. According to his father's notes, Otis had refused to give him any information. James suspected it was one reason his father had taken a case that had still been active.

Del hadn't gotten along with the former sheriff and James had a history with Otis due to his wayward youth. So, he wasn't expecting the conversation was going to go well.

After getting ready for his day, he decided he would talk to Gus Hughes first, then swing by Otis's place out by the river. His father had already talked to Gus, but James thought it wouldn't hurt to talk to him again.

However, when he went downstairs to where his pickup was parked out back of the office building, he found Lorelei Wilkins leaning against his truck waiting for him.

He braced himself as he tried to read her mood. "Mornin'," he said, stopping a few safe feet from her.

She looked as if she didn't want to be there any more than he did. For a moment, he thought she would simply storm off without a word. "I want to hire you."

Of all the things that he'd thought might happen, this wasn't one of them. "I beg your pardon?"

"You heard me," she snapped, lifting her chin defiantly. "What do you charge?"

Good question. He had no idea. Legally, he wasn't a private investigator yet. The application and money had been sent in. He was waiting for his license. "If we're going to talk money, we should at least go somewhere besides an alley. Have you had breakfast?"

"I couldn't eat a thing right now."

"Could you watch me eat? Because I'm starved!" He gave her a sheepish grin. Even after that meal he'd had last night, he was hungry. He figured she might relax more in a public place. She also might not go off on him in a local cafe filled with people they both probably knew.

Because, he suspected before this was over, she would want to tell him what she thought of him.

Lorelei admitted this was a mistake as she watched James put away a plate of hotcakes.

"You sure you don't want a bite?" he asked between a forkful.

"I'm sure." The smell of bacon and pancakes had made her stomach growl, reminding her that she hadn't eaten dinner last night. But she still couldn't swallow a bite right now, she told herself. She just wanted to get this over with.

"So, are you going to do it or not?" she demanded.

He finished the hotcakes, put down his fork and pushed the plate aside. She watched him wipe his mouth and hands on his napkin before he said, "What exactly is it you want me to do?"

"I just told you," she said between gritted teeth. Leaning forward and dropping her voice even though there wasn't anyone sitting near them in the cafe, she said, "Find out the truth about my…" She mouthed, "Stepmother."

He seemed to give that some thought for a moment before he said, "Wouldn't the simplest, fastest approach be for you to ask her yourself?"

"I already tried that," she said and sighed.

"And she denied any knowledge?"

She looked away under the intenseness of those blue eyes of his. "Not exactly. She asked me to leave her house."

"Come on," James said, tossing money on the table before rising. "Let's go."

It wasn't until they were in his pickup that he said, "What is it you think I can do that you can't?"

"I thought you had some…talent for this."

"Like what? Throw my magic lariat around her so she tells the truth? Or use my brawn to beat the truth out of her?"

She mugged a face at him. "Of course not. I thought maybe you could break into her house and look for evidence."

Now they were finally getting somewhere, James thought. He disregarded the illegal breaking and entering part and asked, "What kind of evidence?"

She swallowed before she said, "A diary maybe. She used to keep one. Or…maybe a bill from like, say a… body shop for car repairs."

"What would make you think I'd find something like that even if nine years hadn't passed?"

"Because," she snapped, clearly losing patience with him. "If she was the one who hit Billy, then she would have had to have her car repaired, right? Has this thought really not crossed your mind?"

"My father already talked to Gus Hughes at his body shop."

She waved a hand through the air in obvious frustration. "Are you just pretending to be this dense? She wouldn't have taken it to the local body shop. She's smarter than that. She would have taken it out of town. It's not like she could keep it hidden in her garage for long."

"But she also couldn't simply drive it out of town either without someone noticing," he said.

"Maybe she did it at night."

He shook his head. "Still too risky. And how does she explain no car for as long as it was in the body shop?"

"It was summer. She always rides her bike to work in the summer. There must be some way she could get the car out of town to a body shop and get it brought back without anyone being the wiser."

"I have a couple of thoughts on the matter. In fact, I'm talking to someone on my list today about just that. I've already made inquiries of a half dozen body shops within a hundred-mile radius."

She sat back, looking surprised. "So, you *have* thought about all of this?" He didn't answer, simply looked at her. She let out a breath and seemed to relax a little. "You still haven't told me what you charge."

"Let's see what I turn up first, okay?"

Lorelei nodded and looked uncomfortable. "I'm starved. Would you mind stopping at a drive-thru on the way back to your office?"

He chuckled and started the engine. Out of the corner of his eye he watched her. She was scared, and maybe with good reason, that her stepmother was somehow involved.

He'd wanted to solve this case for his father. Also to prove something to himself. But right now he wanted to find evidence to clear Karen Wilkins more than anything else because of her stepdaughter. He wanted to put that beautiful smile back on Lori's face, even as he feared he was about to do just the opposite.

Chapter 11

After James dropped Lori off at her shop, telling her he'd think about what she'd asked him to do, he drove out to the river. It was one of those clear blue Montana summer days so he decided to quit putting it off and talk to former sheriff Otis Osterman. He'd save Gus Hughes for later, when he'd be glad to see a friendly face.

He put his window down and let the warm air rush in as he drove. He could smell the pines and the river and sweet scent of new grass. It reminded him of the days he and his brothers used to skip school in the spring and go fishing down by the river. One of his favorite memories was lying in the cool grass, listening to the murmur of the river while he watched clouds drift through the great expanse of sky overhead. His brothers always caught enough fish for dinner that he could just daydream.

The former sheriff lived alone in a cabin at the edge

of the water. Otis's wife had died of cancer a year before he retired. He'd sold their place in town and moved out here into this two-room log cabin. His pickup was parked in the drive as James knocked. He knocked louder, and getting no response walked around to the back where he found the man sitting on his deck overlooking the river.

"Hello!" he called as he approached the stairs to the deck. He didn't see a gun handy, but that didn't mean that there wasn't one.

Otis jumped, his boots coming down loudly on the deck flooring.

"Didn't mean to startle you," James said as he climbed the steps and pulled up a wooden stool to sit on since there was only one chair and Otis was in it.

"Too early for company," the former sheriff growled, clearly either not happy to be startled so early—or equally unhappy to see a member of the Colt family anytime of the day.

"I'm not company," he said. "I'm here to ask you about Billy Sherman's hit-and-run."

Otis gave him a withering glare. "Why would I tell you anything?" As if his brother Carl hadn't already told him.

"My father was working the case when he died. I've decided to finish it for him."

"Is that right? You know anything about investigating?"

"I worked with Del from the time I was little. I might have picked up a few things."

Otis shook his head. "You always were an arrogant little bastard."

"That aside, I'm sure you must have had a suspect or two that you questioned."

"Would have come out to your place and talked to you and your brothers but you felons were all too far away at some rodeo or other to have done it."

"Technically, none of us are felons," James said. "What about damage to the vehicle that hit him? You must have tried to find it."

"Of course we tried. Look, we did our best with what we had to work with. Your father thought he could do better. But he didn't find the person, did he?"

"He died before he could."

"To keep his record intact."

James shook his head. He'd known this would be ugly. "My father didn't kill himself."

"You really think his pickup stalled on the tracks with a train coming and he didn't have time to get out and run?" Otis shook his head. "Unless there was some reason he couldn't get out." He mimed lifting an invisible bottle to his lips.

Bristling, James warned himself to keep the temperature down. If things got out of control, Otis would have his brother lock him up behind bars before he could snap his fingers. "Del did have a shot of blackberry brandy on occasion, but according to the coroner's report, he wasn't drunk."

"But he could have been trying to get drunk after the argument he had with a mystery woman earlier that day in town," Otis said. "At least, that's the story I heard. The two were really going at it, your father clearly furious with her."

James pushed off the stool to loom over the man. "If anyone started that lie, it was you to discredit my father. The only reason he would have taken an open case like Billy Sherman's was if he thought you and your brother were covering something up. If he hadn't died, what are the chances that he would have exposed the corruption in your department?"

"I'd be careful making wild accusations," Otis warned.

"Why?" He leaned closer, seeing that he'd hit a nerve. "It's never stopped you."

Otis held up his hands. "You've got your grandfather Colt's temper, son. It could get you into a whole pack of trouble."

James breathed hard for a moment before he took a step back. That was one of the problems of living in small-town Montana. Everyone didn't just know your business, they knew your whole damned family history.

"I'm going to find out the truth about Billy Sherman's death. And while I'm at it, I'm going to look into my father's death as well. You make me wonder if they aren't connected—just not in the way you want me to believe."

"You're wasting your time barking up that particular tree, but it's not like you have anything pressing to do, is it? You should be looking for the mystery woman."

James smiled. Otis's forehead was covered with a sheen of sweat and his face was flushed. "You would love to send me on a wild goose chase. Are you that worried that I might uncover the truth about how you and your brother handled the Sherman case? You're wondering if I'm as smart as my father. I'm not. But maybe I'll get lucky."

"Get off my property before I have you arrested for trespassing."

"I'm leaving. But if I'm right, I'll be back, only next time it will be with the real law—not your baby brother."

* * *

Lorelei couldn't believe what she'd done. Now that she was away from James, she regretted hiring him and planned to fire him as soon as she saw him. The man didn't even have a private investigator's license. What had she been thinking? He was worse than an amateur. He thought he was more trained at this than he was because he'd run a few errands and done some filing for his father.

It had been a spur-of-the-moment stupid decision and not like her at all. She usually thought things through. She blamed James for coming back and turning her life and her upside down.

Worse, as the day stretched on, she'd also had no luck reaching her stepmother. By almost closing time, she'd already sent Anita home and was prepping for the next day, angry with herself. Not even rock and roll music blasting in her kitchen could improve her mood.

She felt so ineffectual. Had she really suggested to James that he break into her stepmother's house and search for incriminating evidence against her? She groaned at the thought that he might have already done it.

If she really believed he would find such evidence, then why didn't she simply look herself? She had an extra key to the house and she knew when her stepmother should be at the studio.

But she also knew the answer. She was afraid she *would* find something damning and do what? Destroy it?

The front doorbell jangled. She looked up to see the very pregnant Melody Simpson waddle in. "Hey," the young woman called. "Am I too late to get a sandwich?"

She hurriedly turned down the music as she realized

she'd forgotten to lock the front door. This was exactly the kind of behavior that was so unlike her.

"Not if you want it to go," Lorelei said, even though she was technically closed.

"Sure." Melody waddled up and studied the board. "White bread, American cheese, mustard and no lettuce."

Lorelei nodded. "Twelve inch?" A nod. "Anything to drink? I have canned soda to go."

The young woman shook her head and stepped to the closest table to sit down. "My feet are killing me."

Not knowing how to answer that, Lorelei hurried in the back to make her a cheese sandwich. It felt strange seeing James's pregnant former girlfriend. Not that they had dated long before he'd left town. Still...

"I heard about you and Jimmy D," Melody called back into the kitchen.

"Pardon?"

"Breakfast at the cafe this morning early, whispering with your heads together. The two of you were the talk of the town before noon."

Lorelei gasped as she realized the rumors that would be circulating. She groaned inwardly. Because it had been so early, people might think that she and James had spent the night together!

That thought rattled her more than she wanted to admit. She could just imagine Gladys's Beauty Emporium all atwitter. The place was rumor mill central. She started to tell Melody that it wasn't what it looked like, but the explanation of her early morning meeting with James was worse.

"I just wanted you to know that I'm not jealous," Melody added.

That stopped Lorelei for a moment. Melody wasn't jealous? Why would she be jealous? She finished wrapping up the sandwich, bagged it and went back out front to find the woman had kicked off her shoes and was rubbing her stocking-covered feet.

She put the bag on the counter along with the bill. After a minute, Melody worked her shoes back on and limped over to her. As she dug a wad of crumpled bills from her jacket pocket, Lorelei said, "Why would you be jealous? I heard you were marrying Tyler Grange and having…" Her gaze went to Melody's very distinct baby bump. "His baby."

Melody continued to smooth out singles on the countertop, her head bent over them with undue attention.

Lorelei felt a start. *It was Tyler's baby, right?* "Have your plans changed?" she asked, finding herself counting the months by the size of Melody's belly. What if it was James's? And why did that make her heart plummet?

"Naw, my plans haven't changed. Tyler's going to marry me," Melody finally said as she finished. Lorelei realized Melody had been counting the bills. She took the fistful of ones. "It's just that I really cared about James. I want him to be happy. I guess if you can make him happy…" She sounded doubtful about that.

"Sorry, but it isn't like that between me and James."

Melody picked up the sack with her sandwich inside. "If you say so. Just don't hurt him. He's real vulnerable right now." With that, she turned and left.

Lorelei followed her to the door and locked it behind her. James vulnerable? That was a laugh. But as she headed back to finish up in the kitchen, she wondered why Melody would even think that.

Shaking her head, she tried to clear James Colt out of

it. She hadn't seen him since this morning. She'd checked a few times to see if his pickup was parked out back. It hadn't been. She could have tried calling him—if she'd had his cell phone number.

She told herself she'd fire him when she saw him. She just hoped he hadn't done anything on her behalf and, at the same time wishing he had, but only if he hadn't found anything incriminating.

"Sounds like you had quite the day," Ryan said when James stopped by the hardware store. "I can't believe that you threatened Otis. Wish I'd seen that."

They were in the back office, Ryan's boots up on the desk as he sipped a can of beer from the six-pack James had brought. After his visit with Otis, James had driven around trying to calm down. He'd stopped at a convenience store, picked up the beer and headed for Ryan.

The two of them had roomed and rodeoed together in college. Ryan always knew he would come back and run his father's hardware store. James hadn't given a thought to what he would do after he quit rodeo.

"You'd better watch your back," Ryan was saying. "Otis hates you and his brother is even less fond of you."

"I'm not afraid of that old fart or his little brother." He took a drink of his beer. "I'd love to nail Otis's hide to the side of his cabin."

"I wouldn't even jaywalk if I were you until you leave town again. You know how tight he is with his younger brother. What all did Otis say that has you so worked up?" his friend asked.

James chewed at his cheek for a moment. "He insinuated Del killed himself possibly over a broken heart because of a mystery woman or because he couldn't solve the Billy Sherman case or because he was a drunk and couldn't get out of his pickup before the train hit him."

Ryan raised a brow. "What woman?"

"According to Otis, my father was seen arguing with a mystery woman earlier in the day before he was killed. Apparently not someone from around here since Otis didn't have a name."

"Seriously?"

"He was more than serious. He suggested I should find that woman. It was obvious that he's worried what I might find digging around in the Sherman case—and my father's death. I'm just wondering why he's so worried."

His friend took a long drink and was silent for a few minutes. "I've always wondered about your old man's accident."

"Me too. What was Del doing out on that railroad track in that part of the county at that time of the night? There are no warning arms that come down at that site. But the lights would have been flashing…" He shook his head. "I've always thought it was suspicious but even more so since I found out that Del told someone that he was close to solving Billy Sherman's case."

Ryan let out a low whistle. "Now you're a private investigator almost, investigate."

He smiled. "Just that simple?"

"Why not? Sounds like it's something you've thought about. Why not set your mind at ease one way or another?"

"Just between you and me? This is a lot harder than I thought. But you're right. I've already got half the town upset with me. Why not the other half?" He looked at his phone and, seeing the time, groaned. "I'd planned on stopping by Gus Hughes's garage. If I'm right, someone had to pay to get their car fixed out of town nine years ago."

"You're thinking it might have been Terry," his friend said. Terry Durham worked for Gus. "Now that you mention it, Terry bought that half acre outside of town a little over nine years ago and put a camper on it. Could be a coincidence. Not sure how much he would charge to cover up a hit-and-run murder vehicle. But since he's usually broke…"

James drained his beer, arced the can for a clean shot at the trash in the corner and rose to leave. "Thanks. I think I'll stop by his place and have a little talk with him."

"Thanks for the beer. Best take these with you." Ryan held up the other four cans still attached to the plastic collars.

James shook his head. "I figure you'll need them if the rumors are true. Are you really dating the notorious Shawna Collins?"

Ryan swore as he hurled his empty beer can at him.

James ducked, laughing. "And you're warning *me* to be careful." He stepped out in the hall before his friend found something more dangerous to throw at him.

Although Del Colt had talked to Terry Durham according to his list—and checked him off—James wanted to ask him where the money had come for his land and trailer.

Terry lived outside of town on a half-acre lot with a trailer on it. James pulled into the woods, his headlights catching the shine of a bumper. In the large yard light, he recognized Terry's easily recognizable car and parked behind it. The souped-up coupe had been stripped down to a primer coat for as long as James could remember seeing it around town.

Getting out of the pickup, he started toward the camper. But stopped at the sight of something parked deep in the pines. A lowboy trailer. The kind a person could haul a car on.

The lowboy trailer was exactly what he wanted to talk to the man about and he felt a jolt of excitement. Maybe he could solve this.

Whoever had hit Billy Sherman would have had some damage to their vehicle or at the very least would have wanted to get the car out of town and detailed to make sure there was no evidence on it. One way to get the car out of town was on the lowboy. Terry Durham always seemed to need money. Add to that his proven disregard for the law and the huge chip on his shoulder, and you had someone who would look the other way—if the price were right.

Moving toward the camper again, he saw that there appeared to be one small light behind the blinds at the back. He knocked on the door. No answer. No movement inside. Was it possible Terry had come home and left with someone else?

James was debating coming back early tomorrow when he started past Terry's car and caught a scent he recognized though the open driver's side window.

He stopped cold, his guts tightening inside him as he glanced over inside the car.

Terry was slumped down in his seat behind the wheel, his eyes open, his insides leaking out between his fingers.

Chapter 12

It was daylight by the time James had told the sheriff his story a dozen times before losing his temper. "I've told you repeatedly, I went out there to talk to Terry about a car he might have been paid to haul to another town."

"Whose car?" Sheriff Carl Osterman asked again.

James sighed. "Billy Sherman's killer whose name I don't know yet."

"You're back in town for a few days and now we have a murder. As I recall, you and Terry never got along. I recall a fistfight my brother had to break up out at the Broken Spur a couple years ago."

"That was between Terry and my brother Davey. I had nothing against Terry and I certainly had no reason to kill him. So, either believe me or arrest me because I'm going home!"

When the sheriff didn't move, James pushed out of

the chair he'd been sitting in for hours and headed for the door.

"Don't leave town!" Carl called after him.

He held his tongue as he strode out of the sheriff's department to take his first breath of fresh air. It was morning, the sun already cresting the mountains. He felt exhausted and still sick over what he'd seen earlier.

After he'd called 911 and the sheriff had arrived, he'd been ordered to wait in the back of Carl's patrol SUV while an ambulance was called along with crime techs. Eventually Terry Durham's body had been extricated from the car and hauled off in a body bag.

Even now, it took him a moment to get his legs under him. The last time he'd seen anything like that had been when a bull rider had been gored. He still felt sick to his stomach as he made his way to his pickup. He tried not to think about it. He'd wanted to ask Terry if someone paid him to take their damaged car out of town on that lowboy trailer of his nine years ago.

He'd been hoping the answer wasn't going to be Karen Wilkins. Terry wouldn't have done it for just anyone—unless the price was right.

Now he was dead. James feared it was because of the questions he'd been asking about Billy Sherman's death.

As he pulled up behind the office building, he saw that Lorelei's SUV was already parked behind her shop. He got out and was almost to his door, when she rushed out.

"I need to talk to you," she said. She smelled like yeast, her apron dusted with flour. There was a dusting of flour on her nose. He couldn't imagine her looking more beautiful.

But right now, he just needed some rest. He held up his hands. "Whatever it is, can we please discuss it later."

He opened his back door and started to step in when she grabbed his arm.

"Are you sick or drunk?" she demanded.

He turned to look at her. She sounded like the sheriff because he'd had beer on his breath earlier. "I'm not drunk, all right? Lorelei, it's just not a good time. Whatever it is, I'm sure it can wait until I get some sleep."

"Rough night?" she mocked.

"You could say that."

Her gaze suddenly widened. "Oh, no. You found something. You went to my stepmother's and—"

He sighed, realizing why she'd been waiting for him to return. "I didn't go to your stepmother's." She'd hear about this soon anyway. "I went out to Terry Durham's and found him…murdered. I've been at the cop shop ever since."

She let go of his arm. "I'm sorry."

He nodded. "Now I just need a shot of brandy and a little sleep. I've spent hours answering the sheriff's questions. I can't take any more right now." She nodded and stepped back. "Later. I promise. We'll talk then." He stepped through his door, letting it slam behind him as he slowly mounted the stairs.

It wasn't until he reached the office door that he saw the note nailed to it.

Tearing it off, he glanced at the scrawled writing.

Get out of town while you still can.

Inside the office, he unlocked his father's bottom drawer and pulled out the .45 he would be carrying from now on.

Lorelei started at the sound of her phone ringing. She pulled a tray of bread from the oven and dug her cell out of her apron pocket. "Hello?"

"I hope I didn't wake you." It was her stepmother.

"No. I'm at work. I've been here for hours."

"You must be expecting a big day." Her stepmother sounded almost cheerful.

Right, a big day, she thought remembering her encounter with James not long after sunrise. If that was any indication of how this day was going to go...

"I saw that you called yesterday," her stepmother said when Lorelei hadn't commented. "Sweetheart, I'm sorry about the way we left things. I had to get away for a while." With her lover? Lorelei didn't want to know. "I think we should get together this evening and talk. I'll make dinner. I thought you could come over after work." Her stepmother sounded tentative. "Please, Lorelei. You're my daughter. I love you."

She felt herself weaken. "Fine. But I need you to be honest with me."

"I am being honest with you. I don't know why seeing James upset me, but it had nothing to with Billy Sherman." A lie, she thought. "I was just worried that you were getting involved with him." Another lie? "He's all wrong for you." Yet another lie?

Lorelei closed her eyes to the sudden tears. "I'll see you this evening." She disconnected, hating this. They used to be so close. She feared everything had changed. Her stepmother had hidden a married lover. But that might not be the worst of it.

As she went back to work, she remembered what James had told her. Terry Durham had been murdered. She couldn't remember the last murder in Lonesome—then with a start, realized it would have been Billy Sherman's hit-and-run. James said he'd found Terry's body. He'd been so upset. Because he felt he might have caused it by asking questions around town from his father's list of people like her stepmother?

She felt a chill even in the warm kitchen. What if the two murders were connected? Hadn't she heard something about Terry getting beaten up after he tried to cheat during a poker game in Billings? But what if Terry was murdered because he worked at the local body shop and knew who killed Billy Sherman?

The thought shook her to her core. What if Billy Sherman's killer had felt forced to kill again? At the sound of a trash can lid banging in the alley, she quickly moved to the back door to look out in time to see James.

When she'd seen him coming in disheveled and exhausted she'd jumped to the conclusion that he'd been out on the town with a woman. It was reasonable given his reputation, but still she felt bad about how quickly she'd judged him. She'd been so ready to add this onto her list of reasons she couldn't trust the man. With a curse, she realized he'd probably thought she'd been jealous.

"Did you get some sleep?" she asked from the doorway.

"Some. Sorry I was short with you earlier."

She shook her head as if it had been nothing. As he joined her, she caught the scent of soap and noticed that his hair was still wet from his shower. He smelled good, something she wished she hadn't noticed. His wet dark hair was black as a raven's wing in the sunlight. It curled at the nape of his neck, inviting her fingers to bury themselves in it, something else she wished she hadn't noticed.

"You wanted to talk to me?"

"You look like you could use a cup of coffee," she said, stalling. "I have a pot on. Interested?"

He hesitated but only a moment. "Sure." He followed her into the kitchen at the back and leaned against the counter, watching her. She could feel the intensity of his gaze on her. She felt all thumbs.

Fire him. Just do it. Like ripping off a Band-Aid. Thank him and then that will be it. You can pretend that you were never so serious as to do something so stupid as hire him to investigate your own stepmother in the first place.

When she turned, he was grinning at her in that lazy way he had, amusement glinting in the vast blue of his gaze. His long legs were stretched out practically to the center of the kitchen as he nonchalantly leaned against her counter. "You want me to help you?"

She thought he meant the coffee and started to say that she had it covered.

"You aren't going to hurt my feelings," he said. "I figured you've changed your mind about hiring me. I don't blame you. Sometimes it's better not to know. And when it's your own stepmother—"

She bristled. "I didn't say I don't want to know if she's involved."

One dark eyebrow arched up. "So, what is it you're having such a hard time saying to me?" he asked as he pushed off the counter and reached her in two long-legged strides.

Lorelei swallowed the lump that had risen in her throat. The scent of soap and maleness seemed to overpower even the aroma of the coffee. Suddenly the kitchen felt too small and cramped. Too intimate.

She stepped around him to the cupboard where she kept the large mugs, opened the door and took down two. Her hands were shaking. "I didn't say I was going to fire you."

"No?" He was right behind her. She could practically feel his warm breath on the back of her neck.

She quickly moved past him with the mugs and went over by the coffee pot.

She heard him chuckle behind her.

"Do I make you nervous?" he asked as she filled both mugs shakily. When she turned around, he was back on the other side of the kitchen, leaning against the counter again, grinning. "I do make you nervous." He laughed. "What is it you're afraid I'm going to do? Or are you afraid I'm *not* going do it?"

"Sometimes you just talk gibberish," she snapped. His grin broadened. "I want to know when you're going to do what I'm paying you to do."

"Paying me?"

She stepped toward him, shoved one mug full of coffee at him and waited impatiently for him to take it. She wished she'd never suggested coffee. The less time she spent around this impossible man the better. Right now, she wanted him out of her kitchen.

Seeing that he had no intention of going anywhere, she said, "We can talk in the dining room." With that she turned and exited the kitchen, her head up, chin out and her heart pounding. She told herself with every step that she hated this arrogant man. Why hadn't she fired him?

She slipped into a chair, cupping the mug in her hands, her attention on the steam rising from the hot coffee.

He slid into a chair opposite her and turned serious. "Let's face it, Lori. You don't want to know about your stepmother. So let's just forget it and—"

She reached into her pocket, pulled out the key and

slapped it down on the Formica table. "That opens the back door to her house."

He stared at the key for a moment before he raised his gaze to her again. "You don't have to do this." She merely stared back, challenging him at the same time she feared she would change her mind. "Fine." He picked up the key and put it in his jeans pocket. Then he took a sip of his coffee.

"What does Terry Durham have to do with Billy's hit-and-run?" she asked.

He looked up in surprise. "I didn't say—"

"You didn't have to." She had a bad feeling that Terry's death had nothing to do with a poker game gone wrong.

"He works at the body shop. As you pointed out yourself, the vehicle that hit Billy would have some damage to it. How would you get it fixed without anyone being the wiser? Get it out of town quickly. Terry had a car-hauling trailer and now he's dead. Add to that, after the hit-and-run, Terry bought a piece of property and a small camper." James shrugged. "It's all conjecture at this point, but it stacks up. I start asking questions and now he's dead."

"What is it you'll look for at my stepmother's?"

"The person who owned the damaged car might have left a trail. Either a receipt from the body shop that fixed it. Or a lump sum withdrawal from a bank account to pay Terry off. But that's if they kept a record from nine years ago."

Her heart pounded. "Give me the key back."

He hesitated only a moment before he dug it out of his jeans and handed it over. "So, I'm fired."

Lorelei shook her head as she pocketed the key again.

"No, I'm going with you." He started to put up an argument, but she cut him off. "It will be faster if I go. I know where she keeps her receipts, and her bank account records. Karen keeps everything. Come on," she said, pushing away her unfinished coffee. "She'll be at her studio now."

"You sure about this?" he asked.

"Not at all, but I can't do this alone and I have to know."

He met her gaze. "If what we find incriminates her, I won't cover it up even to protect you."

"You come with integrity?"

"It costs extra," he said to lighten the mood for a moment. "But seriously, if you want to change your mind, now's the time, Lori."

She didn't correct him. In fact, she was getting to where she liked her nickname, especially on his lips. "I'm serious too." She knew she couldn't live with the suspicion. "I have to know the truth before tonight. I'm having dinner at her house."

"Great," he said under his breath as he downed his coffee and rose from the table as she called a friend to come watch the shop.

Chapter 13

James parked in the alley behind the house after circling the block. Karen Wilkins's car wasn't in the drive. Nor had there been any lights on in the house. He could feel Lorelei's anxiety.

He was about to suggest she stay in his pickup, when she opened her door and climbed out. Her expression was resigned. He could tell that she was doing this come hell or high water. She looked back at him, narrowing her eyes and he was smart enough not to argue.

Lori produced the key as they walked through the backyard. The sky overhead was robin egg blue and cloudless, the air already warming with the summer sun. A meadowlark sang a short refrain before they reached the back door.

He watched her take a breath as she unlocked the

back door and they stepped in. "Does she keep an of-fice here?"

With a nod, Lori led the way. The office was a spare bedroom with multipurpose use. There was a sewing machine and table and containers of fabric on one side. A bed in the middle and a small desk with a standing file cabinet next to it.

James headed for the filing cabinet only to find it locked. He looked at Lori who still hadn't spoken. He suspected she was having all kinds of misgivings about this but was too stubborn to stop it.

She opened the desk drawer and dug around for a few moments before she picked up a tiny wooden box that had been carved out of teak.

"My father gave her this." She opened the lid and with trembling fingers removed a tiny key and handed it to him.

He unlocked the top drawer and thumbed through the folders. Then he tried the second drawer. Karen's bank was still sending back the canceled checks nine years ago. He dug deeper and found small check boxes all labeled. She was certainly organized. He looked for personal checks from nine years ago, found the box, handed it to Lori. She sat down at the desk and began to go through them.

"You're looking for a check to Terry Durham or a tow-ing company after Billy Sherman's hit-and-run so after April 10th," James said. "Also, a check to a body shop in another town." She nodded and set to work.

He found Karen's monthly account statement in the third drawer and quickly began to sort through them looking for a large withdrawal after April 10 from nine years ago. He'd just found what he was looking for when he heard a car door slam.

They both froze. "I thought you said she was working," he whispered.

"She was supposed to be. Maybe it isn't her."

James heard a key in the front door lock. "It's her." He grabbed the months he needed of the checking account documents and carefully closed the file drawer. He saw Lorelei pocket a handful of checks and slip the box into the top drawer as he motioned toward the closet.

He opened the door as quietly as possible. It sounded as if Karen had gone to one of the bedrooms on the other side of the house. The closet was full of fabric and craft supplies. There was just enough room for the two of them if they squished together. He eased the closet door closed as the sound of footfalls headed in their direction.

A moment later Karen came into the room. He heard her stop as if she'd forgotten what she'd come in for. Or as if she sensed something amiss? He tried to remember if they had left anything out that could give them away. He didn't think so. But if she opened the desk drawer she would see the check box. As neat and organized as she was, she would know.

He held his breath. He could feel Lori, her body spooned into his, doing the same. Her hair smelled like a spring rain. He could feel the heat of her, the hard and soft places fitting into some of his. He tried to think about baseball.

With relief, he heard Karen leave the room. The front door slammed and he finally let out the breath he'd been holding. A few moments later, a car engine started up. James waited until the sound died away before he carefully opened the closet door.

Lori stepped out, straightening her clothing, looking flushed.

"Sorry about that," he said, his voice sounding hoarse. She pretended she didn't know what he was talking about, which was fine with him. "Let's finish and get out of here."

He went through the bank statements and then Karen's retirement papers. That's when he found it. A large withdrawal of ten thousand dollars.

"Lori?" He realized that she hadn't moved for a moment. She was staring down at a canceled check in her hand. All the color had drained from her face. "What is it?" Without a word, she handed him the check.

The check had been made out to the bank for ten thousand dollars. He flipped it over and saw that the money had been deposited into Lori's account. "I don't understand."

"Nine years ago I looked into getting a loan to open a sandwich shop," she said, her voice breaking. "The bank turned me down. My stepmother had offered to cosign on the loan but I didn't want her risking it if I failed. I had no experience."

"And then you did get the loan," he said.

She nodded. "The president of the bank called, said he noticed I had applied for the loan and that he knew me and was willing to take a chance on me. He lied. It was all my stepmother."

She looked as if she might burst into tears at any moment as she put the check back in the box and opened the file cabinet to put the box away. He watched her relock the file cabinet and put the key back where she'd found it and close the desk drawer.

"I can imagine what you're feeling right now," he finally said.

"Can you?" She turned to face him. "I didn't trust my stepmother. I hired you and then I sneaked in here with you looking for dirt on her. Did we find anything? No. Instead, I find out that she took money out of her retirement to help me open my sandwich shop, the woman I've been at odds with for days because of you."

He didn't feel that was fair, but was smart enough not to say so. "I'm sorry. But we didn't find anything." Instead, he'd found a large withdrawal from a retirement plan but not to cover a crime. "No checks to Terry Durham or a body shop." He held up his hands. "So good news."

She merely glared at him before she pushed past him and headed out the back door. He double-checked the room to make sure they hadn't left anything behind and followed. By the time he reached the pickup, she was nowhere to be seen.

He climbed behind the wheel and waited for a few minutes, but realized his first thought was probably the right one. She'd rather walk back than ride with him. He started the engine and drove out of the alley.

Another great day as a private investigator, he thought with disgust.

Cora swore she had a sixth sense these days. She'd been in the living room knitting while she watched her favorite television drama when she had an odd feeling. Putting aside her knitting and pausing her show, she went into the kitchen and picked up her binoculars.

These special night vision binoculars had paid for themselves the first night she got them. It truly was amazing what a person could see especially since she lived on a rise over the river.

First she scanned the river road. Only one car parked out there tonight and she recognized it. The same couple that often parked out there on a weekday night. She thought for a moment, wondering if there was any way she could benefit from this knowledge and deciding not, scanned farther downriver.

Tonight not even a bunch of teenagers were drunk around a beer keg. Slow night, she thought, wondering why she'd thought something was going on.

Out of habit, she turned the binoculars on the Colt place. At first she didn't see anything since she wasn't really expecting to—until she saw a pickup coming through the woods on the Colt property with no headlights on. Had she heard the driver pull in? Or did she really have a sixth sense for this sort of thing?

She wondered as she watched the pickup stop on the spot where the burned-out trailer had once stood. James Colt? She waited for the driver to exit the rig. Western hat and a definite swagger, she thought, but she couldn't see the face because he kept his head down.

Following him with the binoculars, she watched as he went around to the back of his pickup and took out a box. It must have been heavy because he seemed to strain under the weight. To her surprise, he carried the box over to where the debris from the burned-out double-wide had been. He hesitated, then put down the box before going back to the pickup. He returned with a small shovel.

She watched, transfixed as he began to dig a hole into which he dumped whatever was in the box. Then he shoveled the blackened earth over the hole.

Shoving back his hat to wipe a forearm across his

brow, Cora got her first good look at his face. She felt a start as she recognized him.

Her hand began to sweat because suddenly she was holding the binoculars so tightly, her heart racing in her chest. She watched former sheriff Otis Osterman carry his shovel and the empty box back to the pickup. A moment later he drove off.

Lorelei felt ashamed and guilty and not just because of her stepmother. She'd blamed James for all this when she'd been the one who'd hired him. How could she possibly think her stepmother was involved in Billy Sherman's death? Worse, that her stepmother would try to cover it up? She hated too that she'd felt a wave of relief when they hadn't found anything incriminating. Had she been that worried that they would? She was a horrible stepdaughter. She promised herself that she would make it up to Karen.

The walk back to the shop helped. Fortunately, the moment she entered her kitchen, she had work to do. Anita had a lot done, but there was still more bread to be made before she opened at 11:00 a.m. She thanked Anita, paid her and sent her on home, needing work more today than ever.

When she'd come in the back way, she'd been thankful that James's pickup wasn't anywhere around. She recalled the two of them in the closet, her body pressed into his, and felt her face flush hot as she remembered his obvious…desire. Fortunately, he hadn't been able to feel her reaction to it. At least she hoped not.

"Lorelei?"

She spun around in surprise to see Karen standing

in the kitchen doorway. She really needed to start locking the back door.

"Are you all right? You're flushed," her stepmother said as she quickly stepped to her, putting a hand on Lorelei's forehead.

"I'm baking bread and it's hot in here."

Her stepmother looked skeptical but let it go. "I hope you don't mind me stopping by."

She wiped her hands on her apron. "I'm glad you did."

"I know you're busy but I didn't want to do this over the phone. I'm afraid I have to cancel our plans for dinner tonight. I'm sorry. Something's come up."

Lorelei raised a brow, sick to the pit of her stomach at how quickly her suspicions had come racing back. "I hope it's nothing bad."

"No." Her stepmother looked away. "Just a prior engagement I completely forgot about." Lorelei nodded. "So, we'll reschedule in a few days." Karen let out a nervous laugh. "You and I are so busy."

"Aren't we though," she said, hoping the remark didn't come out as sarcastic as it felt. Her stepmother wasn't acting like herself. It wasn't Lorelei's imagination. She wanted to throw her arms around her and hug her although she couldn't thank her for the personal loan without telling her that she'd gone through her checks.

But at the same time, she wanted to demand her stepmother tell her the truth about what was going on. No matter what, she couldn't keep lying to herself. Something was definitely going on with her stepmother besides the affair.

"I'll call you." Her stepmother headed out of the kitchen.

"Mom!" Lorelei's voice broke. "Be careful."

Karen looked surprised for a moment. "You too, dear."

James felt as if he'd been spinning his wheels. He knew no more about Billy Sherman's death than he had when he started this. Now he'd alienated someone he had been growing quite fond of since his return to town.

As he was passing a house in the older section of town, he recognized the senior gentleman working in his yard. James pulled up in front of the neat two-story Craftsman with its wide white front porch. Getting out, he walked toward the man.

Dr. Milton Stanley looked up, a pair of hedge clippers in his hands. His thick white eyebrows raised slightly under small dark eyes. "You're a Colt."

He nodded. "James."

"You look like your father."

"My father's why I stopped when I saw you. Could we talk for a minute? I don't want to keep you from your work."

"I was ready for a break anyway." Milton laid down his clippers, took off his gardening gloves and motioned toward the house. "Take a seat on the porch. I'll get us something to drink."

James followed the man as far as the porch and waited. He could hear the doctor inside the house. Opening and closing the refrigerator. The clink of glass against glass. The sound of ice cubes rattling.

A few minutes later, the screen door swung open with a creak and Milton reappeared. He handed James a tall glass of iced lemonade and motioned to two of the white-painted wooden rockers. Each had a bright-colored cushion. James could imagine the doctor and his wife sitting out here often—before her death.

They sat. James sipped his lemonade, complimented it and asked, "You were coroner when my father was killed. I need to know if you ran tests to see if he was impaired."

The doctor drained half of his lemonade before setting down the glass on one of the coasters on the small round end table between them. James watched him wipe his damp hands on his khaki pants.

Milton frowned. "Why are you asking this?"

"Because of the case he was working on at the time of his death. It was ruled an accident by the sheriff, but I've since learned some things that make me think he might have been murdered."

"Murdered?"

"I'm not sure how, but I've only been working my father's old case a few days and already someone I wanted to talk to has been killed," James said. "I've always questioned my father's death but never more so than now. I've learned that he was close to solving Billy Sherman's hit-and-run."

The doctor frowned. "There was no alcohol or drugs in your father's system at the time of his death."

James blinked, swamped with a wave of relief. "None?"

"None."

The relief though only lasted a moment. "Then how did it happen?" Why didn't he get out of the pickup before the train hit him? Surely, he saw the flashing lights. Did he think he could beat the train? That wasn't like his father. Del was deliberate. He didn't take chances.

Milton shook his head. "Any number of things could

have led to it. He might have had something on his mind and didn't notice the flashing lights. The train hit him on the driver's side. He might not have had time to get out. The pickup engine could have stalled. He could have panicked. You can't see that train because of the curve until it's almost on top of you. Your father's accident wasn't the first one at that spot. The railroad really needs to put in crossing arms." He picked up his lemonade and drained the rest of it.

James drank his and placed the empty glass on a coaster on the table. He could tell the doctor was anxious to get back to his gardening. "Thank you for your help."

"I'm not sure I was much help," Milton said and followed him as far as the yard. The doctor picked up his clippers and went back to work.

Cora stewed. Her favorite television drama couldn't even take her mind off what she'd seen. She tried to work it out in her mind. That was the problem. She wasn't even sure what she'd seen—just that Otis Osterman hadn't wanted to be caught doing whatever it was. Of that she was sure.

Putting her knitting aside again, she picked up her cell phone and muted the television. She let the number ring until she got voice mail. Then she called back. It took four times, one right after the other, before the former sheriff finally picked up.

"What the hell do you want, Cora?" he demanded.

"I bought myself one of those video recorders."

"What?"

"I was trying to learn how to use it and I accidentally videoed the darnedest thing. *You.* You're right there on my video."

"What. Are. You. Talking. About?"

"I couldn't figure out why you would be on the Colt property, let alone why you would dump a box of something into the ashes where the Colt's burned-out trailer had been, let alone why you would then cover it up with that little shovel you keep in your pickup."

She listened to him breathing hard and knew that she'd struck pay dirt. "I'm thinking James Colt would be interested in seeing my little video. Heck, I suspect he'd pay good money given how he feels about you. Trespassing and so much more. So how much do you think my video is worth? Maybe I should just take it to the FBI."

Otis swore and Cora smiled. She could tell by the low growl on the other end of the line that she had him. She didn't care what he'd planted on Colt property. It was no skin off her nose. But she could certainly use a little supplemental income.

"You addled old woman. I don't know what you think you saw—"

"That's why I'm having this young person I met put the video up on the internet. Technology is really something these days. I bet someone has a theory about what you were doing, don't you? Even your brother the sheriff won't be able to sweep this under the rug—not after I make sure everyone knows the man in the video is a former sheriff. That should make it go viral, whatever that is. My new young friend assures me it's good though."

"Maybe I should come out to your place and we should discuss this," Otis said through what sounded like clenched teeth.

"I wouldn't suggest that. I get jumpy at night and you know I keep my shotgun handy. I'd feel terrible if I shot you."

"What do you want?" he demanded angrily.

"Five thousand dollars."

Otis let out a string of curses. "I don't have that kind of money."

"Well, not *on* you. You'll have to go to the bank and when you do, you tell them you borrowed money from me and want to pay it back. Just have them put it into my account. It's a small town. They'll do it. As soon as I get confirmation, I'll drop the video by your cabin. Maybe you'll have something cold for us to drink."

He growled again. "How do I know you won't make copies and demand more money?"

"Shame on you, Otis. They do say crooks are often the most suspicious people. I wouldn't have a clue how to make a copy."

"I want the camera too."

"Well, now that's just rude. I'm still learning how to use it. But I'll bring it when I bring the video. We can discuss it. With that night vision thing, the camera won't be cheap. Tomorrow then. Have the bank call me. Look forward to seeing you, Otis." She laughed. "In person. I've already seen enough of you in the movies." She laughed harder and disconnected.

Then she went to check her shotgun to make sure it was loaded, putting extra shells in her pocket, before she locked and bolted all the doors.

Chapter 14

When James returned to the office, he saw that it appeared someone was waiting for him. A bike leaned against his building in the alley with a young boy of about sixteen sitting on a milk crate next to it.

As he got out of his truck, the boy rose looking nervous. "Can I help you?" James asked.

"Are you the PI?"

He smiled. "I guess I am."

"I need to talk to you." He looked around to make sure there wasn't anyone else around. "It's about Billy."

In that instant, he realized who this boy must be. "Todd?" The boy nodded. "Does your mom know you're here?" The boy shook his head. "I'm not really supposed to talk to you without a parent present." Then again, he wasn't a licensed PI yet, was he?

"But I'll tell you what," he said quickly seeing the

boy's disappointment. The kid had been waiting patiently. He couldn't turn him away especially when Todd might have valuable information. He glanced at the time. "What if we have another adult present who can advise you?"

Todd looked worried. "Who?"

"Hungry?" He asked the boy, remembering himself at that age. His father used to ask if he had a hollow wooden leg. Where else was all that food going?

Todd nodded but then hesitated. "What about my bike?"

"It's safe there." James pushed open the back door into the sandwich shop. Once that smell of fresh bread hit the kid there was no more hesitation.

Lorelei saw James first and started to tell him he was the last person she wanted to see—when she spotted the boy with him. Her gaze went from the boy to James in question.

"This is Todd. He's hungry." James turned to the kid. "What kind of sandwich would you like?"

"I suppose you don't have a hot dog?" the boy asked her sheepishly.

"Let me see what I can do. Would you like some lemonade with that?" The boy nodded and actually smiled. Her gaze rose to James.

He shook his head since he didn't have a clue what was going on. "We'll just have a seat. We're hoping you can join us. Todd wants to have a talk with us."

"With *us*?"

"You're going to be the adult in the group," James said.

She smirked. "I always am."

He smiled. "I knew I'd picked the right woman for the job. Mind if I go ahead and lock the front door while we talk so we aren't interrupted?" He didn't wait but went to the door and put up the closed sign and locked the door.

She did mind, even though it was past closing time. What was this man getting her into? She made Todd a mild sausage sandwich with a side of ketchup and mustard and poured three lemonades before bringing them out on a tray to the table. She put Todd's in front of him.

"So, what's this about?" she asked as she slid into the booth next to the boy. Todd had already bitten into his sandwich. He gave her a thumbs-up as he chewed.

"Todd was waiting for me behind my office. He wanted to talk to the PI." She raised a brow. "I explained to him that we probably shouldn't talk without an adult present. It's kind of a gray area."

Lorelei shook her head. "I'm not sure I want to be part of this."

"I have to tell him about Billy," Todd said, putting down his half-eaten sandwich. He took a drink of lemonade. "I know what my mom told you when you came over to see her. She forgot that I did have Billy's other walkie-talkie headset that night and that after that, she threw it away."

"You and Billy talked on the two-way radios the night he died?"

Todd nodded, looking solemn.

"About what time was that?" James asked.

"He woke me up. The electricity had gone off but I looked at my Spiderman watch. It was almost ten thirty. I told him not to do it."

James shot her a look before shifting his gaze back to the boy. "Do what?"

"He said he had to go out. That he'd seen someone walk by his house in the rain and that he needed to follow whoever it was."

"His mom told me that Billy didn't like storms," James said. "Why would he go out and follow someone?"

He picked up his sandwich, took a large bite and chewed for a moment before swallowing. "Billy and I had this game we played. We pretended we were spies. We used to pick someone to follow. It was fun. They usually heard us behind them and chased us off. But sometimes we could follow them a really long way before they did."

"Who was he following that night?" James asked.

Todd shook his head. "He said he had to see what they were doing before he chickened out. I told him not to. He said the person was headed down the street in my direction and that I should watch for him and come out. I watched from the window, but I never saw him and then I fell asleep. I just figured he chickened out, like he said. Or his mom made him go to bed and quit using the walkie-talkies."

"How did you pick the people you followed?" James asked.

The boy shrugged. "Sometimes we would just see someone who looked dangerous."

"Dangerous?" Lorelei repeated.

"Sometimes we just wondered where they were going, so we followed them."

"So, Billy just saw someone out the window and decided to go out into the storm to follow them?" she asked, unable to hide her incredulity.

"I guess. It might have been someone he'd been following before that."

"Was it a man or a woman?" Lorelei asked.

"Billy said, 'I just saw someone outside my window. I have to follow and find out what they're doing.' He sounded…scared." The boy looked down at his almost empty plate. "When I heard you asking my mom about Billy, I knew I had to tell you." He bit into what was left of his sandwich and went to work on it.

"Does your mom know about the call from Billy?"

The boy shook his head adamantly. "Billy and I took a blood oath not to ever tell our parents about our spy operations. But I think she was worried that I told Billy to go out that night and that everyone would blame me. I didn't. I swear. I tried to stop him." Todd's eyes shone with tears. Lorelei watched him swallow before he said, "I think he would have wanted me to tell you."

"Thank you, Todd. I'm glad you did," James said.

Lorelei touched the boy's shoulder. "You did the right thing."

He nodded, swallowed a few times and ate the last bite of his sandwich.

She looked across the table at James. He held her gaze until she felt a shudder at what they'd just heard and had to look away.

Chapter 15

"Are you okay?" James asked Lori after Todd left. He'd helped her clear the table, then followed her back into the kitchen.

"Fine," she said, her back to him.

"I forgot about your dinner with your stepmother tonight. I'm sorry. I hope I'm not making you late."

She turned in his direction, avoiding eye contact. "She cancelled. Something came up." He said nothing. Finally, she looked at him. "She's scaring me."

He nodded. "But maybe it has nothing to do with Billy Sherman. At least now we know why Billy went out that night. We just don't know who he was following or why." He sighed. "I'm sorry. I feel like I never should have started this." She didn't exactly disagree with her silence.

"Hey," he said. "How do you feel about a big juicy rib eye out at the steak house? I'm buying."

She smiled and he could tell that she was about to decline when his cell rang. He held up a finger, drew out his phone and, seeing who was calling, said, "I need to take this. Hello?"

"Mr. Colt?"

He smiled to himself. No one called him Mr. Colt. "Yes?"

"My name is Connie Sue Matthews. I heard you have taken over your father's private investigations firm and that you've been asking questions about Billy Sherman's death."

"That's right."

"You probably know I was the one who found the body that morning. Could I stop by your office? I know it's after hours, but it's the only time I'm free this week. I might have some information for you." She lowered her voice. "I don't want to get into it on the phone."

He shot a look at Lori. He'd been looking forward to that steak but had really been looking forward to dinner with her. He hesitated only a moment, hoping Lori would understand. If this woman had any information for him… "You know where my office is?"

"Yes, I can be there in a few minutes."

"Use the back entrance. I'll see you then." He disconnected and looked across the room at Lori. Only moments before he was mentally kicking himself for digging into his father's unsolved case and here he was cancelling his dinner plans because of it. What was wrong with him? "I'm afraid I'm going to have to postpone that dinner invitation."

"Bad news?" she asked, looking genuinely concerned.

"No, maybe just the opposite." He could only hope.

Cora sat in the house, the shotgun lying across her lap. All the lights were out and there was no sound except when the refrigerator turned on in the kitchen occasionally. She'd always been a patient woman. She'd put up with her no-account husband for almost fifty years. She could sit here all night if she had to.

But she knew she wouldn't have to. She knew Otis Osterman. He was a hothead without a lot upstairs. He'd stop by tonight and she would be waiting.

The fool would be mad, filled with indignation that she'd called him out. He wouldn't be thinking clearly. She reminded herself to make sure he died in the house after he broke in. She didn't want any trouble with the law—especially Otis's baby brother, Carl. But an old woman like herself had every right to defend her life—and her property.

Otis should have taken her deal. He'd regret it. If he lived that long.

And to think back in grade school she'd had a crush on him. He'd been cute back then, blond with freckles and two missing front teeth. She shook her head at the memory. That was before high school when she found out firsthand about his mean streak. But she'd taken care of it—just as she'd taken care of everything else all these years. If he came around tonight, this time he would leave with more than a scar to remember her by. Or not leave alive at all.

Connie Matthews was a small immaculate-looking woman in her late fifties. She was clearly nervous as she stepped into his office. He'd had just enough time to pick up the room and close the door to the bedroom before she'd arrived.

She sat on the edge of one of the leather club chairs, her purse gripped in her lap as he sat behind his father's desk. Idly he wondered how long it would take for him to think of this office as his own.

"You said you might have information on Billy Sherman's death?"

Connie looked even more uncomfortable. "Those boys, Billy and that Crane boy. I found them hiding in my bushes one day. They were always sneaking around, getting into trouble, stomping down my poor flowers. One day I caught them going through my garbage! Can you imagine? Billy said they were looking for clues. *Clues.* Clues to what, I'd demanded. And the Crane boy said, 'We know what you've been doing.' Then they laughed and ran off."

It sounded like typical boy stuff to James. He hated to think of some of the shenanigans he and his brothers had pulled. "Did you tell my father about this when he interviewed you?" James knew it wasn't in his father's notes.

She shook her head. "It seemed silly at the time because that young boy had lost his life. But what was he doing out in that storm in the middle of the night in his pajamas?"

"Since your house is the closest to where he was found, did you notice anyone outside that night? Hear anything?" He already knew the answer. *That* was in his father's notes. But Todd said that his friend was following someone.

"No, but I went to bed early. I don't like storms. I

took some sleeping pills and didn't wake up until the next morning. By then the storm was over."

"What about your husband?"

"What about him?" Connie asked frowning.

"I wondered if he might have mentioned seeing anyone, hearing anything."

She shook her head. "George went to bed when I did so I'm sure he would have mentioned it, if he had seen someone or heard anything, don't you think? That's a busy road. Gotten even busier with all the houses that have come up. The mayor lives in the new section and I suppose you know that Senator Bayard lives just down the road from our place." She seemed to puff up a little.

That road was an old one used by a lot of residents who lived out that way. The subdivision had grown in the past nine years.

"Was there something more?" he asked. On the phone she'd sounded as if she might have new information. That didn't seem to be the case and yet she was still sitting across from him, still looking nervous and anxious. He waited, something he'd seen his father do during an interview.

"I hate to even bring this up, but I feel I was remiss by not doing it nine years ago," Connie finally said. "I think someone abducted that boy from his bed. Because what boy in his right mind would go out in a storm like that?" she demanded, clearly warming to the subject. "And I know who did it. It was the father." At his confused look, she said, "The *boy's* father, that ne'r-do-well, Sean Sherman. Weren't he and his wife arguing over the boy in the divorce? I think Sean snatched him out of his bed that night. That's why the mother didn't hear anything. The boy would have gone willingly with his own father otherwise he would have raised a ruckus, don't you think?"

"That is one theory. I wonder though how Billy ended up getting run over just blocks from his house?"

"Maybe the boy changed his mind, decided he didn't want to go with him and jumped out of the car. It would be just like his drugged-up father to run over the boy and then panic and take off."

James pretended to take notes, which seemed to please the woman. "I'll look into that," he told her, and she rose to leave, looking relieved.

"I wasn't sure if I should say anything or not," Connie said. "But you haven't been around much so you don't know a lot about this town and the people who live in it. I thought you should know." She let out a breath, nodded and headed for the door where she stopped to look back at him. "I'd be careful if I were you though. If Sean Sherman killed that boy, he thinks he's gotten away with it for nine years." She nodded again as if that said it all, but seemed compelled to add, "I hired Sean one time to do some landscaping. He made a mess of it. When I refused to pay him…" She shuddered. "The man has a terrible temper. He's dangerous."

"Thank you, Mrs. Matthews."

"I believe in doing my civic duty," she said primly and left.

Cora heard the sound of shattering glass in the basement of her small house and smiled. Otis was just too predictable. What was he thinking he was going to do anyway? Kill her? The thought made her laugh. He was a nasty little bugger, but she couldn't see him committing murder. No, he'd come out here to scare her.

She shifted the shotgun in her lap and waited. Her chair was in a corner where she would see him when he came upstairs. She could hear him moving around down there. After tonight, Otis was going to replace that window he'd broken and anything else she wanted done around here.

Over the years, she'd collected a few people who were indebted to her after she'd caught them in some nefarious act. Some paid her monthly, others paid in favors. She didn't like to think of it as blackmail. She preferred to call it penitence for misdeeds done. She never asked for more than a person could afford.

But she didn't like Otis. She would make him pay dearly—if she didn't shoot him on sight.

Her cell phone rang, startling her. She glanced at the time. Almost one in the morning. The phone rang again—and she realized no sound was now coming from the basement.

"Hello?" she whispered into the phone, planning to give whoever was calling a piece of her mind for interrupting her at this hour.

"I got your money," Otis said. "I'll put it in your account tomorrow. Why are you whispering?" He chuckled. "Oh, I hope I didn't wake you up."

She could hear what sounded like bar noise in the background. "Where are you?" she demanded.

"At Harry's as if that is any of your damned business," he snapped and disconnected.

She stared at the phone for a moment. Then she heard again a sound coming from the basement. Her blood ran cold. If Otis wasn't down there, then who was? Cora felt fear coil around her as she heard a sound she recognized.

A moment later, she smelled the smoke.

Chapter 16

James was awakened some time in the night by the sound of sirens. Sheriff's department patrol SUVs and several fire trucks sped down Main Street and kept going until the sirens died away. He'd rolled over and gone back to sleep until his cell phone rang just after 7:00 a.m.

"Did you hear about the fire?" his friend Ryan asked. "That old busybody crossed the wrong person this time. Cora says someone set her house on fire, but I heard the sheriff's trying to pin it on her. Arson."

"You've heard all this already this morning?"

"The men's coffee clutch down at the cafe. You should join us. It's a lot of the old gang along with some of the old men in town. Pretty interesting stuff most mornings."

James shook his head and told himself he wouldn't be staying in town that long. His leg was better, and his ribs didn't hurt with every breath. It was progress. "Thanks for the invite," he said. "I'll keep it in mind."

"How is the investigation going?"

He was saved from answering as he got another call. "Sorry, I'm getting another call. Talk to you later?" He didn't wait for an answer as he accepted the call. At first all he heard was coughing, an awful hack that he didn't recognize. "Hello?" he repeated.

"I want to hire you." The words came out strained between coughs. "Someone tried to burn me alive in my own house last night."

"Cora?" The last time she'd said more than a few words to him, she'd been chasing him and his brothers away from her apple trees with a shotgun.

In between coughs, she said, "You're a private detective, aren't you?"

"Isn't the sheriff investigating?" he asked, sitting up to rub a hand over his face. It was too early in the morning for this.

"Carl? That old reprobate!" He waited through a coughing fit. "He thinks I set the fire, that's how good an investigator he is. I put myself in the hospital and burned down my own house? Idiot." More coughing. "You owe me, James Colt, for all the times you and your brothers trespassed in my yard and stole my apples."

He wanted to point out that she'd had more apples than she could ever use and let them waste every year. But they *were* her apples.

"The least you can do is prove that I didn't start the fire. Otherwise, the sheriff is talking putting me behind bars."

"I'll look into it," he said, all the time mentally kicking himself.

"Good. Don't overcharge me."

James disconnected. He lay down again, but he knew there was no chance he could get back to sleep. After Connie Matthews had left last night, he'd hoped Lori was still around. She wasn't so he'd gone out and gotten himself some fast food and then driven to Billy Sherman's neighborhood.

From there, he'd walked toward the spot where the boy had died. He'd tried to imagine doing the same thing in a violent thunderstorm at the age of seven. Whoever Billy had seen couldn't have been some random person like anyone he and Todd normally followed. The boy must have recognized the person. But then why hadn't he mentioned a name to Todd? Or maybe there was something about the person that had lured him out into the storm. James couldn't imagine what it could have been.

An image from a movie during his own childhood popped into his head of a clown holding a string with a bright-colored balloon floating overhead. It had given him nightmares for weeks. A kid afraid of the dark and storms wouldn't go after a clown—especially one with a balloon.

Lorelei had driven past her stepmother's house last night only to see all the lights were out and her car wasn't in the garage. She'd been tempted to drive out to the senator's house to see if she was there. Earlier this evening on the news she'd heard that the senator and his wife were officially divorcing.

"They reported that they've been separated for some time now and believe it is best if they end the marriage," the newscaster had said. *"Senator Bayard said the di-*

vorce is amicable and that he wishes only the best for Mary."

It had sounded as if Mary was the one who'd wanted the separation and divorce. Maybe she had. Maybe Lorelei had been too hard on her stepmother.

The news had ended with a mention of Bayard being called back to Washington on some subcommittee work he was doing. She wondered how true that was. Maybe Fred and her stepmother had flown off somewhere together to celebrate the divorce.

What bothered Lorelei was that her stepmother felt the need to lie to her. Or at the very least not to be honest with her. Like providing the loan for the sandwich shop. Like falling in love without telling her. While Lorelei didn't approve of her stepmother's affair, she wanted her to be happy. She hated the strain in their relationship and promised herself that she would do what she could to fix it when she saw Karen again.

After a restless night, she'd gotten up and gone to work as usual. As she pulled in behind the shop to park, James was standing by the back door of his office grinning.

"My license came today. It's official—I'm a private investigator."

"Congratulations. You'll have to frame it and put it up on your wall."

"I know it seems silly being excited about it, but I am. It makes me feel legit. I also have a new client." She raised a brow. "I'll tell you all about it over dinner. I thought we'd go out and celebrate. I owe you a steak." She started to argue, but he stopped her with a warm hand on her bare arm. "Please? You wouldn't make me celebrate alone, would you?"

She knew he could make a call to any number of women who would jump at a steak dinner date with him. When she'd awakened this morning, she'd promised herself that she would see her stepmother tonight—if her stepmother was in town.

James waved the license in the air and grinned. "How can a Montana girl like you say no to a slab of grain-fed beef grilled over a hot fire?"

Lorelei laughed in spite of her sometime resolve to keep James Colt at arm's length. "Fine. What time?"

James couldn't help smiling as he drove out to Cora's. Lori had agreed to have dinner with him. He hadn't been this excited about a date in… Heck, he wasn't sure he ever had been. That should have worried him, he realized.

Cora's house had sat on a hill. Smoke was still rising up through the pine trees and into the blue summer sky as he pulled in.

After parking, he got out of his truck and walked over to the firefighters still putting out the last of the embers. One of the fears of living in the pine trees was always fire. But the firefighters had been able to contain the blaze from spreading into the pines. The small old house though seemed to be a total loss.

"I'm looking for the arson investigator," James said and was pointed to a man wearing a mask and gloves and a Montana State University Bobcats baseball cap digging around in the ashes.

"I'm Private Detective James Colt," he said introducing himself.

The man gave him a glance and continued digging. "Colt? That your property next door?"

"Yep."

"A lot of recent fires out here." He rose to his feet and extended a gloved hand before drawing it back to wipe soot onto his pants. "Sorry about that. Gil Sanders."

James couldn't help his surprise. "Gilbert Sanders?" he asked, remembering seeing the name on his father's list. But why would his father be interested in talking to an arson investigator as part of Billy Sherman's hit-and-run?

"Have we met before?" Gil asked, studying him. "You look familiar."

"My father, PI Del Colt, might have contacted you about another investigation."

The man frowned. "Sorry. Can you be more specific?"

"He was investigating the hit-and-run death of a local boy about nine years ago."

Gil shook his head. "You're sure it was me he spoke with?"

"Maybe not." Now that James thought about it, there hadn't been any notes from the interview in his father's file. "I'm here about another matter. Cora Brooks called me this morning. Anything new on the fire?"

"It was definitely arson. The blaze was started in the basement. The accelerant was gasoline. It burned hot and fast. She was lucky to get out alive."

James nodded. "The sheriff seemed to think Cora started the fire herself."

The investigator shook his head. "I've already reviewed the statements from the first responders. The property owner was in a robe and slippers carrying a shotgun and a pair of binoculars. That's all she apparently managed to save. She couldn't have outrun that fire if she started it. Not in those slippers. I'm told she is in her right mind."

"Sharp and lethal as a new filet knife."

Gil chuckled. "She told first responders that she'd heard someone breaking into her basement. That's why she had her shotgun. Not sure why the binoculars were so important to her, but I don't see any way a woman her age could have started the fire in the basement and high-tailed it upstairs to an outside deck. Not with as much gas as was used downstairs. I'm not even sure she can lift the size gas can that was found."

Cora was apparently in the clear. "Thank you. If I figure out why I saw your name in my father's case file…"

"Just give me a call. But unless it pertains to a fire, I can't imagine why he had wanted to talk to me."

James shook the man's hand and nodded at Gil's cap. "Go Bobcats," he said and headed back to his pickup. Too bad all his PI cases weren't this easy, he thought. He headed for the hospital to give Cora the good news. This one was on him, no charge. He knew she'd like the sound of that.

Otis stumbled to his cabin door hungover, half-asleep and ticked off. Whoever was pounding on his door was going to regret it.

"What the hell did you do?" his brother Carl demanded, pushing past him and into the cabin. The sheriff turned to look at him and swore. "On second thought, I don't want to know."

"If this is about that fire out at Cora's—"

"What else? I saw you yesterday. You were going on about the woman and last night her house burns down."

Carl raised a hand. "There's an arson investigator out there. I told him that I think Cora did it for the insurance money, but he sure as the devil isn't going to take my word for it."

"I didn't do it." Otis stepped past him to open the refrigerator. He needed the hair of the dog that bit him last night. Pulling out a can of beer he popped the top, took a long drink and looked at his brother.

"How deep are you in all this?" Carl demanded.

"I did something stupid."

His brother groaned. "I wouldn't be here if I didn't suspect that was the case."

"I took something out to the Colt place. I was going to make an anonymous call and let you find it. I know you'd like to get that arrogant little turd behind bars as much as I would."

The sheriff swore. "Tell me it isn't anything explosive. You get anyone killed—"

"No, just some illegal stuff. Doesn't matter now. I'll get it hauled away. It was stupid. Then Cora saw me, said she made a video of me dumping it…" He hung his head again.

"Otis, swear to me you didn't burn down Cora's house."

The former sheriff looked up, his expression one of disbelief and hurt. "I was at the bar. You can check. I was there until closing. Even better about the time it was catching fire, I called Cora from the bar. See I have an alibi so I'm gold."

His brother swore.

"What's wrong? There will be a record of the call— just before I heard the sirens. So it couldn't have been me."

Carl told himself that his brother had been at the bar

to establish that alibi, which meant Otis had hired someone to set fire to the place. He wished he didn't know his brother so well. "If it wasn't you, any idea who might have wanted Cora dead?"

Otis chuckled. "Anyone who's ever crossed her path."

"Let's just hope Gil Sanders doesn't find any evidence out there that would make him think you had anything to do with this."

Cora took the news as would be expected. She nodded, told James he'd better not send her a bill and ordered him out of her room.

A near-death experience didn't change everyone apparently, he thought as he left chuckling.

He was still wondering if the Gilbert Sanders on his father's list was the arson investigator and if so what Del thought the man could offer on the hit-and-run case.

Meanwhile, he tracked down Sean Sherman. His call went straight to voice mail. He left a message asking Sean to call him and hung up. Sherman lived in a town not far from Lonesome. If he had to, James would drive over and pay the man a visit.

With that done, he considered his father's list again. Connie Matthews had said something in her original interview with his father that kept bothering him. Lyle Harris had been operating the front-end loader the morning Connie had seen the body and stopped him from covering it up.

James knew it was a long shot. His father had already talked to the man and there wasn't anything in his notes that sent up a red flag. But he was running out of people to interview and getting worried that he'd missed something important.

At forty-five, Lyle Harris had quit his job with the local contractor after a work comp accident that had put him in a wheelchair. As James pulled up out front of his place deep in the woods, he noticed the ramp from the house through the carport to the garage. He recalled Ryan telling him that he'd donated the lumber and the men Lyle used to work with had donated their time to make the house more wheelchair accessible.

After parking, he got out and walked toward the house, changing directions as he heard the whine of an electric saw coming from the garage.

"Lyle!" he called. "Lyle, it's James Colt!" The sound of the saw stopped abruptly. He heard what sounded like a cry of pain and quickly stepped through the door into the large garage.

The first thing he saw was the wheelchair lying on its side. Past it, he caught movement as someone ran out the back door and into the pines. He charged into the garage thinking it had been Lyle who'd run out.

But he hadn't gone far when he saw that Lyle had left a bloody trail on the concrete floor where he'd crawled away from the wheelchair, away from the electric saw lying on the floor next to it, the blade dripping blood.

"What the hell?" he said, rushing to the man on the floor. He was already digging out his phone to call 911.

"No, don't. Please. Don't call. I'm okay," Lyle cried as he pressed a rag against the wound that had torn through his jeans to the flesh of his lower leg. "It's not fatal."

James stared at the man, then slowly disconnected before the 911 operator answered. "I just saw someone running out of here. What's going on?"

Lyle shook his head. "Could you get my chair?"

He walked over, picked it up and rolled the wheelchair over to the man, holding it steady as Lyle lifted himself into it.

"It looks worse than it is," Lyle said as he rolled over to a low workbench. He grabbed a first aid kit. "But thanks for showing up when you did."

"That blade could have taken off your leg," James said.

"Naw, it wouldn't have gone that far."

Lyle winced as he poured rubbing alcohol on the wound then began to bandage it with shaking fingers. From what James could tell, the man was right. The wound wasn't deep. "You want help with that?"

"No. I'm fine," he said, turning his back to him.

"You're in trouble." Lyle said nothing. "And whatever it is, it's serious." James took a guess on how many times he'd seen Lyle's rig parked in front of the casino since he'd been back in town. "Gambling?"

Lyle finished and spun the wheelchair around to face him. "I appreciate you stopping by when you did. Now what can I do for you?"

He sighed. His father used to say that you couldn't help people who didn't want to be helped. He knew that to be true. He chewed at his cheek for a moment, thinking. "Were you gambling nine years ago when Billy Sherman died?"

The question took the man by surprise.

James saw the answer in Lyle's face and swore. "Connie Matthews said that if she hadn't seen Billy Sherman's body lying in that ditch when she did, you would have dumped dirt on him with your front-end loader and he would never have been found. She also told my father that she'd been surprised that you were already working that morning since you usually didn't start that early. In fact, she'd been afraid you were going to get fired since she'd heard Edgar Appleton, your boss, warning you before that day about coming to work late so often. She thought that's why you were there so early that morning and that still half-asleep, you didn't see the boy and would have buried him in that ditch. You would have known that the concrete had been ordered for the driveway. It was going to be delivered that day. Had you covered Billy's body with dirt, it would have never been found."

Lyle stared him down for a full minute. "Like I said, thanks for stopping by."

"I don't believe you ran that boy down, but I do wonder if you weren't hired to get rid of his body. Maybe hired is the wrong word. Coerced into making Billy Sherman disappear?"

"You can see your way out," Lyle said, wheeling around and heading toward his house.

Chapter 17

Lorelei couldn't believe that she'd agreed to have dinner with James. He'd caught her at a weak moment. The small table at the back of the steak house was dimly lit. A single candle flickered from a ceramic cowboy boot at the center. The candlelight made his blue eyes sparkle more than usual and brought out the shine of his thick dark hair.

If she had been on a real date, it would have been romantic. But this was James. A woman would be a fool to take him seriously.

James lifted his wineglass in a toast, those blue eyes taking her captive. "Thank you for indulging me tonight."

"My pleasure," she said automatically and realized she meant it as she lifted her own wineglass and tapped it gently against his. She couldn't remember the last dinner date she'd been on with a man. She took a sip of the wine. It was really good. "I'm surprised you know your wines."

He grinned. "You're impressed, aren't you?" He shook his head. "I called earlier and talked to the sommelier. I didn't want to look like a dumb cowboy."

"You could never be a dumb cowboy," she said, feeling the alcohol loosen her tongue. She'd have to be careful tonight. The candlelight, the soft music, the wine, the company, it made her want to let her hair down—so to speak. She'd pulled her hair up as per usual, but in a softer twist. She'd worn a favorite dress that she'd been told looked good on her and she'd spritzed on a little perfume behind each ear.

She felt James's intent gaze on her a moment before he said, "You look beautiful." His tone sent a tremor through her that jump-started her heart.

Lorelei sipped her wine, fighting for a control she didn't feel. "Thank you. I could say the same about you." He'd worn all black from his button-up shirt to his jeans to his new boots. The outfit accented his long muscular legs and cupped a behind that could have sold a million pairs of jeans. The black Western shirt was opened just enough to expose the warm glow of his throat and make her yearn to see more.

There'd been a time when she'd dreamed of being with James Colt. When she'd fantasized what it would be like if he ever asked her out. But he never had. Until now. She had to remind herself that this wasn't a real date and yet it certainly felt real the way he was looking at her.

She was surprised to see that she'd finished her wine. James started to refill her glass—and not for the first time. She shook her head. Given the trail her thoughts had taken, the last thing she needed was more wine.

James suddenly got to his feet and reached for her hand. "Dance with me."

She took his hand before the words registered. Dance? She glanced at the intimate dance floor as he drew her to her feet. No one was dancing. But he was already leading her to it. He turned her to the middle of the dance floor and pulled her directly into his arms.

He drew her close and she let him. She pressed her cheek against his shoulder knowing she couldn't blame the wine. Their bodies moved in time to the music as if they were one of those older couples who'd danced together for decades.

Lorelei drew back a little to look into his eyes and wanted to pinch herself. Not even in her fantasies had she dreamed of James Colt holding her in his arms and looking at her like this. She'd been only a girl and, like her Barbie dolls, she'd long ago stored all that away. And yet here they were.

She pressed her cheek against his warm shoulder again, closed her eyes and let herself enjoy this moment. Because that's all it was. A moment. Just like in the closet with him. The memory made her smile. He'd actually been embarrassed by his reaction to her.

The song ended. There was that awkward moment when they stood looking into each other's eyes. She was certain that he wanted to kiss her, but the waiter came by with their salads. The moment gone.

Her heart was still triple-timing as James walked her back to the table, holding her hand, squeezing it before letting it go.

"You dance well," she said.

He grinned. "My brother Willie taught me."

She laughed and felt herself relax a little. He had been

about to kiss her, hadn't he? Another awkward moment before they dug into their salads, both seemingly lost in their private thoughts.

By the time their meals came they were talking like friends who owned businesses next door to each other. They'd both grown up in Lonesome so it made it easy to talk about the past and stay away from the future. That moment on the dance floor had passed as if it had never happened. She suspected they both were glad of that. Otherwise, it could have made being business neighbors awkward. Neither of them wanted that.

Asking Lori to dance had been a mistake. Not that James hadn't enjoyed having her in his arms. He'd loved the sweet scent of her, nuzzling his way into her hair to get at its source behind her ears. She'd smelled heavenly. She'd felt heavenly.

He'd lost himself in the feel of her, wishing the song would never end. It was as if they'd called a truce, shared no uncomfortable past, had only this amazing few minutes moving together as one, in perfect sync.

And then the song ended and he'd looked at her and all he'd wanted to do was kiss her. She'd parted those lips as if expecting the kiss. He'd seen something in her eyes, a fire burning like the one burning inside him. And then the waiter had been forced to go around them to put their salads on their table and he was reminded of all the reasons he shouldn't get involved with this woman. He wasn't staying. Getting the PI license was a hoot, but he was a rodeo cowboy. If he solved this case, then it would make all of this worthwhile. But once he was healed, he would be leaving again. Long-distance relationships didn't work. Just ask Melody.

But all that aside, he'd mentally kicked himself for not kissing her when he had the chance. Maybe he'd known deep inside that once he kissed her there was no going back with this one. Lori wasn't like anyone he'd dated—if you could even call it dating. The others had known what they were getting into and had ridden in eyes wide open.

Lori was different. She expected more. Would want more from him. More than he had to give at this point in his life. One of these days he'd think about settling down, but he hoped those days were still a long way off.

Even as he thought it, he couldn't help looking over at Lori as he walked her to her door later that night. He felt the pull of something stronger than the road, maybe even stronger than the rodeo, stronger than even his resolve.

"Thank you for a lovely evening and congratulations again," she said as she pulled out her keys and turned to unlock her door.

He didn't feel like himself as he touched her arm and gently turned her back toward him. "Lori." It didn't feel like his arms that drew her to him. Or his lips that dropped hungrily to her mouth. Or his fingers that released her hair and let it fall in waves of chestnut down her slim back.

Her perfume filled his senses as her arms looped around his neck and he pushed his body into hers until the only way they could have been closer was naked in the throws of passionate lovemaking.

The kiss and that thought sent a bolt of desire rocketing through him. He had never wanted a woman like he did this one. He felt humbled with desire. He wanted to be a better man. He wanted to be her man. He wanted her. For keeps.

He felt her palms on his chest, felt her gentle push as she drew her mouth from his and leaned back to look into his eyes. He saw naked desire as well as the battle going on there. She was as scared as he was.

She shook her head slowly. Regretfully? And pulled free of his arms. He watched her straighten, brushing her long hair back as she lifted the keys in her hand and turned toward the door again.

He let her fumble with the key to the lock for a moment before he took the keys from her and opened her door. Then desire still raging through him, he handed her the keys and took a step back. He feared that if he took her in his arms again there really would be no turning back. He looked at her and knew he couldn't do it. He wouldn't let himself hurt this woman.

"Thanks again for tonight," he said, his voice rough with emotion. "I'll see you tomorrow." He turned and hurried down the steps to his pickup. He hadn't noticed the car that had gone by. Hadn't heard it. Only the taillights turning in the distance made him even aware that anyone had driven past. Nor did he give it more than a distracted notice as he climbed behind the wheel and, thinking of Lori, allowed himself to glance back at the house.

She was no longer standing there, thank goodness. The door was closed and a light glowed deep in the house. He sat for a moment, still shaken before he started the engine and headed toward home, knowing he wouldn't be able to sleep a wink.

But to his surprise, he fell asleep the moment his head hit the pillow only to be assaulted by dreams that wove themselves together in a jumbled pattern that felt too real and too frightening. In the dream, he'd known that it wasn't just him who was in danger. Lori was there and he was having trouble getting to her when the little blond-haired girl appeared on her horse. She was laughing and smiling as she cantered toward him. "Watch this, Daddy!"

He half woke in a sweat. The nightmare clung to him, holding him under even as he tried to surface. He was in uncharted waters on a leaky boat and it was impossible to swim with the concrete blocks that were tied to his ankles.

Chapter 18

Lorelei woke and panicked for a moment, thinking she was late for work. She hadn't gotten to sleep until very late last night. It had taken her a while to process everything. James had kissed her. He'd called her Lori in a way that made her heart race. No one had ever given her a nickname. She hadn't been that kind of girl. Until James.

And that was the problem. He'd upset her orderly world. He'd made her burn inside with a need she knew only he could fulfill. He'd made her want to throw caution to the wind.

And then he'd been a perfect gentleman, unlocking her front door, handing her the keys and leaving.

She'd been shocked. But mostly…disappointed. She hadn't planned to invite him in. But he hadn't even tried. A man with his reputation? Surely, he had to know the power he had over women. He would know she was vulnerable after a kiss like that. So why hadn't he asked to spend the night?

Lorelei knew it was ridiculous that she was angry with him for not hitting on her. Everything the man seemed to do made her angry with him, even when he was well-behaved. Maybe it wasn't him. Maybe it was her who was the problem. Maybe he didn't find her attractive.

Those thoughts had her tossing and turning and losing sleep because of him. That too annoyed her with him.

She told herself that her life had been just fine before he'd showed up next door. Her stepmother was right. Having James Colt living next to her shop was a bad idea. The man was too...distracting.

As daylight crept into the room, she lay in bed staring up at the ceiling reliving the kiss, reliving the way he'd cupped the back of her neck, the way he'd buried his face in her hair, the way he said Lori.

"Oh, for crying out loud!" she snapped and swung her legs over the side of the bed. She was acting like a teenager.

The thought actually made her smile. She'd been so driven from middle school on that all she'd thought about was excelling in her school work so she could get into a good college. Then at college she'd worked hard to get top grades so she could get a good job. She hadn't let herself be a teenager and do what a lot of other teenagers did—like James Colt.

She'd missed so much. No wonder she'd never felt like this, she realized. Until now. Now she wanted it all. And she wanted it with James.

He had wanted her, hadn't he? That kiss... She'd seen the desire in his blue eyes. So why had he just walked away last night?

Because for the first time maybe in his entire life he was being sensible, something she'd been her whole life? Oh, that was so like him, she thought angrily as she stepped into the shower. *Now* he decided to be responsible.

James threw himself into work the next morning. His thoughts and emotions had been all over the place from the moment he'd opened his eyes. The cold shower he'd taken hadn't helped so he'd left the office early to avoid seeing Lori.

He knew it was cowardice, but after that kiss last night he didn't trust himself around her. That had been a first for him. Normally after a kiss like that, he would only avoid a woman if he didn't want to see her again. But Lori wasn't just some woman and that was the problem.

Because it was Montana, the drive to the next town gave him plenty of time to think—more than an hour and a half. In this part of the state, the towns were few and far between.

Alice Sherman's ex worked as a maintenance man at the local hospital. As it turned out, today was Sean's day off. A helpful employee told him that the man lived only a block away in a large apartment house.

James walked, needing to clear his head. On the drive over, he'd had plenty of time to think. Too much. He'd finally turned on a country station on the radio. Not that even music could get his mind off Lori Wilkins.

He went from wishing he hadn't come back to town to being grateful that he had because of her. He went from wishing he could get right back on the rodeo circuit to being too involved in not just this case to want to leave now. He knew the best thing he could do was give Lori a wide berth, but at the same time, he couldn't wait to see her again.

Now as he shoved open the front door of the large apartment house, he tried to focus on work. According to the mailboxes by the door, Sherman was in 322. He turned toward the large old elevator and decided to take the stairs.

The man who answered the door at 322 was tall and slim and nice-looking. He was nothing like James had been expecting. Nor was the man's apartment. It was neat and clean, much like the man himself. "May I help you?"

"I'm James Colt. I'm a private investigator in Lonesome."

"Did Alice hire you?"

"No. I believe my father, Del Colt, was hired by you to look into the death of your son. As you know, he died before he finished the case. I've taken it over. I'd like to ask you a few questions."

Sean Sherman seemed to be making up his mind. After a moment, he stepped back. "Come on in. I'm not sure how I can help," he said after they were seated in the living room. "Alice and I were separated at the time and in the middle of a divorce. I was fighting for joint custody, but I would imagine she already told you that." She hadn't, but James had read as much in his father's notes.

"Were you in Lonesome that night?"

The man hesitated a little too long so James was surprised when he finally answered. "Yes." That definitely wasn't what Sean had told Del.

"You were?"

Sean sighed before he said, "I lied to your father about that. I had my reasons at the time."

"Then why tell me the truth now?"

"Because if it will help you find out who killed my son, then nothing else matters."

"But that wasn't the case nine years ago?" James asked.

"Other people were involved. It was a very traumatic time in my life. The divorce, arguing over Billy. I don't know if Alice told you this or not." He met James's gaze and held it. "I was having an affair. Alice found out and our marriage was over. The affair was a mistake, one I will always regret. I didn't want all of that made public and having it thrown in Alice's face. We'd lost our son. We were both devastated. The rest of it wasn't important."

"I understand drugs were involved?"

"I'll be honest with you. I couldn't take the pain of what I'd done, blamed myself for not being in the house with my family that night and I turned to drugs. It's taken me a long time to climb back out of that. Being honest is part of my recovery."

"If you were in Lonesome that night, but not at your house, where were you?" James asked.

Sean looked away for a moment before he said, "I was at Karen Wilkins's house."

He couldn't help his surprise. "She was the woman you were having the affair with?"

The man nodded. "I was in the middle of breaking it off with her."

"Were you there all night?" James asked.

"I think so. Things got very emotional. Karen left. She ran out into the storm. I started to go after her but turned back."

"She left on foot?"

He nodded. "But not long after that I heard her take her car and leave."

"What time was that?"

"I think it was about ten."

"You didn't go after her in your car?" Sean shook his head. "When did she come back?"

"I don't know exactly. I got into her booze, got disgustingly drunk and passed out; and when I woke up, she was standing over me distraught, screaming, crying and telling me to get out. It was daylight by then. I left and the only time I went back to Lonesome was for my son's funeral. I tried to mend things with Alice but..." He shook his head. "That's it."

James thought about it for a moment. "When you woke to find Karen home again what kind of shape was she in? I know she was upset. There was a thunderstorm that night. Was she still wet from being out in it?"

The man frowned. "No. Her clothes must have dried because they weren't wet. Stranger was the fact that she'd fixed her hair. She had to have been home for a while, I guess." He shook his head. "You can tell how out of it I was."

"She was wearing the same clothing though?"

"She was. She had to have been home for a while before she woke me up. I could tell that she'd had a shower." He shrugged. "I liked the smell of her shower gel."

James shook his head. If he knew anything about women who felt scorned, it was that they didn't calmly come home shower, fix their hair, put on the same clothing and then decide to wake you up to throw you out. So where had Karen been that she'd spent the night, taken a shower and gotten her clothes dried? He supposed it was possible that she'd gone to her exercise studio. They probably had showers there. Karen could even have a washer and dryer down there for all he knew. Still, it seemed odd.

"Did you hear any more from her?" he asked.

Sean shook his head. "That night pretty well ended everything in Lonesome for me."

"She's never tried to contact you?"

"Never. Nor did I ever contact her. It was over almost before it started. We both regretted it. I'm sure I could have handled it better than I did."

James thanked the man and showed himself out. He couldn't help being surprised about Karen. But at least now he knew why she was on his father's list. She'd been upset and out driving that night in the storm. Had she done something? Had she seen something?

He felt a start. But how had Del found out about her possible involvement in Billy's death? Sean hadn't told him and Karen certainly hadn't shared the information when James had tried to question her.

Had someone seen her that night?

Lorelei did what she always did on Sunday morning. She went to church; only today she was asked to help with the toddlers in child care during the service and jumped at it. She loved the job, especially toddler age. They were so much fun as they raced around, laughing and screaming and keeping her on her toes. Seriously, she later thought. What had she been thinking volunteering for this since she had thirteen toddlers between her and another volunteer? It was wonderful madness.

For several hours she forgot about everything, especially James.

Then it ended, parents picked up their children and

she was facing what she did at home each Sunday after church: cleaning house. Today, the place got an extra good scrubbing even though it didn't need it. Her house was small—just the way she liked it since she spent so little time there.

She'd just finished when her doorbell rang. Her first thought was that it was probably her stepmother. They often did something together on a Sunday every month or so. But when she opened the door, it was James standing there. She blinked in surprise and then horror as she realized what she was wearing. Leggings and an oversized sweatshirt that hung off one shoulder. Her hair was pulled up in a high ponytail. She never wore much makeup, but now she wore none. And she smelled like cleaning solution.

"We need to talk," he said without preamble as he stepped in, seemingly not even noticing her appearance.

"Iced tea or beer?" she asked as she followed him into the kitchen.

"Beer." He looked around. "Nice house."

"Thanks." She took two beers from the refrigerator and handed him one as she led the way into the small living room and curled up on one end of the couch. He took the chair next to it, looking uncomfortable.

"If this is about last night—"

"No," he said too quickly. "I mean." He met her gaze. "No. It's about your stepmother." Lorelei groaned inwardly and thought, *Now what?* "I drove over to Big Timber and talked to Sean Sherman this morning."

She frowned. "Billy's dad?"

He nodded. "He told me something. Are you aware that your stepmother was seeing him nine years ago?"

James could have told her almost anything about her

stepmother and she wouldn't have batted an eye. Karen had proven to her how little she knew about the woman who'd raised her.

"What do you mean 'seeing' him?" When James merely looked at her, she let out a cry and shot to her feet. "If you're trying to tell me that my stepmother is a serial philanderer with married men…"

"It might be worse than that," he said. "Sean told me he broke up with her that night. Upset, Karen left the house in the storm, at first on foot, but later came back for her car."

Lorelei had moved to the fireplace but now put her free hand over her mouth, her eyes filling with tears as her heart dropped like a stone, bottoming out.

"We don't know that she was the one who hit Billy—" he choked out. "But she went somewhere. When she returned to her house, she'd either gone straight to the shower, fixed her hair and dried her clothing and put on the same outfit before confronting Sean who'd passed out after being into her booze, or…"

She rolled her eyes. "Or what?"

"She'd been somewhere and showered and fixed her hair before returning to the house to make it look as if she'd been home longer than she had."

Lorelei removed her hand from her mouth and took a drink of her beer without tasting it. She thought she might throw up. "All you have is Sean's word for this, right?" she asked, already looking, hoping, for a way that none of this could be true.

"He's on the wagon, in a program that requires him to be honest, he said, which is why he was willing to talk now. I called Alice on my way back. It's true."

"What am I supposed to say?" she asked, her voice breaking.

"I'm worried about your stepmother. Do you have any idea where she is?" She shook her head. "I've been trying to reach her. From what I can tell she hasn't been home. Neither has the senator."

"Maybe they ran away together to celebrate his divorce," she said. "She thinks he's going to marry her."

"I hope she is with him. I would hate to think that she's alone. It might be my fault that she's left town. I need her side of the story."

Lorelei couldn't believe this and yet she could. It explained why her stepmother had gotten so upset that James was digging into the old hit-and-run case. Because she had a whole lot to hide. But Lorelei couldn't let herself think that her stepmother had killed that boy. She wouldn't.

"I'm sorry to be the one to tell you," he said, sounding as miserable as he looked. "I wish…" He shook his head. He didn't need to say it. She had her wishes too.

She put down her half-full beer. "I'll let you know when I hear from her."

James finished his beer, set the empty bottle on the small table by the chair and rose. He had taken off his Stetson when he'd come in. It now dangled in his fingers by the brim. She couldn't help but think about those fingers on her face, in her hair, last night as he'd kissed her. He'd been so gentle, his caress soft, his callused fingertips sending shivers through her.

He took a step toward her. She couldn't move, couldn't breathe, couldn't think. She felt her eyes widen as he leaned toward her and brushed his lips over hers. "About last night," he said, his voice low. "It was the best date I've ever had." He drew back, his gaze locking with hers before he turned and left.

Chapter 19

James felt as if he'd been kicked in the gut by a bronc. But he'd come this far. He couldn't stop now. He had to finish his father's case. That meant finding Billy Sherman's killer—no matter where the path led him.

When his phone rang, he hoped it would be Lorelei. If not her, then her stepmother. But it was Lyle Harris.

"I've been thinking. I want to talk," Lyle said. "Can you come here?"

"I'm on my way." He turned and went back the way he'd come, turning and going east on a dirt road until he came to the small homemade sign that marked the way into Harris's place hidden in the pines.

James tried not to be anxious, but he'd known that there was more to Lyle's story. He'd just never thought he was going to hear it. Because Lyle was afraid of the person who'd hired him to cover up the body? Or out of loyalty to that person? Either way, James thought, he needed a break in this case. And this just might be it.

He parked, got out and checked the garage shop first before going up to the side door of the house. At his knock, Lyle called, "Come in."

Shoving open the door, he stepped first into a mud room, then a hallway with a lot of doors. "Lyle?" No answer. He felt his skin prickle as he realized belatedly that he might be walking into a trap. The garage had been large, easy to see if someone had been hiding to jump him.

You're getting awfully paranoid.

"In the kitchen," came Lyle's voice.

He headed slowly down the hall, pushing aside half-open doors on his way. True to his word, Lyle was in the kitchen, which had been remodeled to accommodate a man in a wheelchair.

"I was just making chili," Lyle said, his back to him. "My stepmother said no one eats chili in the summer." He turned then to look at James. "I do." Wheeling back to the pot on the stove, he stirred, turned down the heat, and putting down the spoon spun around. He looked nervous, which made James nervous too. "I called you at a weak moment. I'd just talked to my mom on the phone."

"Does that mean that you've changed your mind about telling me the truth?" James said, hoping that's all there was to this.

"Look, I know you're going to keep digging. I've heard around town. A lot of people are getting upset."

"They shouldn't be unless they have something to hide."

Lyle laughed. "Hey, in case you haven't noticed, Lonesome is a small town. It's tight, man. I don't think

you realize the position you're in. This is dangerous because you've stirred things up after nine long years when
everyone thought it was over."

"Why would they think that? Billy Sherman's killer
was never found. Why would people not want the boy's
killer to be found?"

"I'm going to level with you," Lyle said. "I think
you're an okay dude. Well-meaning enough but treading where you shouldn't be treading unless you have a
death wish. So, you're right. I *was* told to cover up the
body in the ditch before anyone saw it—especially the
neighbors' kids. But I was told it was a coyote."

"A coyote?"

"I saw the blood on the road where it had been hit
that morning when I came to work. I had no reason to
think otherwise. It was god-awful early in the morning.
I was half asleep, half loaded too. I climbed up on my
front loader—"

"You didn't go look at the coyote?"

"Why would I? I just loaded up the bucket and was
about to dump it when that woman came out and started
screaming. That's the truth."

James realized that he believed him. "There's just
one thing you left out. Who told you it was a coyote?"

Lyle looked down at his feet for a long moment. "You
see all these ramps out here? You see this kitchen? You
think the state picked up the bill?" He shook his head.
"My friends and the people I worked with did all this."

James felt an icy chill begin to work its way up his
spine. "You ever think that the person who told you to
bury the...coyote...was lying to you?"

Lyle met his gaze with an angry one. "No, I did not.
Because I admire the hell out of the man who told me

to do it. It's the kind of thing he would think to do if he saw a dead coyote in the road in a nice neighborhood where he thought it might upset the kids. You think he would have done that if it had been a little boy lying in that road?"

"I don't know. I guess it depends on who we're talking about." He watched Lyle's temper rise and fall before the man turned back to his chili. James thought he knew where this was headed. He didn't want it to be the man and his wife that he'd had dinner with a few nights ago. He didn't want to believe it and yet he knew that Lyle couldn't be talking about anyone else.

"Edgar told you about the coyote, didn't he? He's the one who told you to come in early and cover it up. You didn't question it because you'd been coming in late and he'd been threatening to fire you. And like you said, you would do anything he asked you—even before your accident."

"It *was* a coyote," Lyle said as if trying to convince himself. "You say otherwise and you're going to destroy a good man. You don't want to do that in this town unless you're planning to leave and never come back. It might already be too late anyway."

James left the man to his chili, hearing the warning, knowing well enough how small towns worked. He suspected his father had made an enemy while working the case and it had gotten him killed.

He felt sick at the thought of Edgar Appleton being involved. He was thinking of the dinner that night, the love he saw between husband and wife, as he climbed into his pickup and started the engine. He didn't want to believe it. Worse, he didn't want to confront the man. Edgar and Irene were good people. But his father always said that even good people made bad decisions and ended up doing bad things sometimes.

Still… He'd turned around and driven through the dense pines toward the main road when he heard it. A rustling sound followed by the distinct rattle. His blood froze as his gaze shot to the passenger side floorboards of his pickup.

He hadn't noticed the paper sack when he'd gotten in. His mind had been on what Lyle had told him. Now though, it drew his attention like a laser as the head of the rattlesnake slithered out, its body coiling, the head rising as the rattles reached a deafening sound.

James slammed on the brakes, throwing the pickup into Park as he flung open the door and bailed out. Even as he did he felt the snake strike his lower calf, sinking its fangs into the top of his cowboy boot.

Chapter 20

As Edgar Appleton opened the door, James grabbed his hand and dropped eleven rattles into his palm. He saw the man's startled expression. "What the—"

"Someone put a rattlesnake in my pickup," James said and reached down to draw up his jeans pant leg to show where the snake had almost bitten through the top of his boot before he'd dragged it out and killed it, cutting off the rattles. "Want to guess why?"

The older man frowned. "If you're suggesting—"

"I was at Lyle Harris's house when the snake was put in my pickup. Nine years ago, you told Lyle Harris to bury the body."

Edgar blinked. "You should come in. Irene is out working in the garden. I can see that we need to talk." He turned and walked into the dining room.

Through the window, James could see Irene bent over

weeding in the huge garden. He turned to Edgar, wishing this hadn't brought him to this house of all places. He waited, sick at heart.

The older man sighed and dropped into a chair, motioning for James to take one as well. But he was too anxious to sit. He stood near the window and kept waiting.

"Irene and I had been to a movie and stopped for milkshakes at the In-N-Out. We were headed back. It was pouring rain. Irene was driving. There was a car pulled off to the side of the road. Irene went around it and hadn't gone far when she hit something. She stopped, terrified of what she might have run over. We'd both been distracted by the car beside the road. Because of the storm, I had wanted to stop and see if the person needed help, but Irene was anxious to get home. She was worried that she'd left the oven on." He rubbed a hand over his face.

"You didn't check to see what she'd hit?"

"Of course I did," Edgar snapped. "I got out and ran back through the rain. I knew it hadn't been a person. It had been too small." He looked up at James, holding his gaze with a steady one of his own. "It was a coyote. I shoved it off the road. On the way home, I got to thinking about all those kids in that neighborhood seeing it on their way to school. Coyotes remind me of the dogs I've had over my life. So I called Lyle and told him to come in early and make sure it was buried before anyone got up."

"How did the coyote turn into a little boy's broken body?"

"I don't know." He lowered his voice, looked toward the garden. Irene still had her back to them. "I'm telling you the truth."

James didn't know what to believe. "What time was this?"

"A little after ten, I think."

"Did you see anyone else out that night? Did you see Billy?"

"No one other than the car pulled off the road."

"You didn't notice who was in the car or the make or model?"

"It was an SUV, like half the town drives. On top of that the night was pitch-black and with it raining hard... It was tough enough to see anything that night." Edgar swore. "Don't look at me like that. I can tell the difference between a coyote and a kid." His voice broke. "When I heard the news about Billy Sherman..." He looked out the window to the garden. "Irene was beside herself. My wife didn't even believe me. She really thought that I would cover up that child's death to protect her."

"I think you would too," James said. "But if you had, I think it would have eaten you up inside after all these years. I also don't think Irene would have let you."

The older man nodded, smiling sadly. "You're right about that. I'd hoped your father would find out who did it." He met James's gaze. "Find out who killed that boy. Do it for all our sakes."

He saw Irene headed back in. "About the snake—"

"I'll talk to my guys, if that helps, but Lyle has some of his own friends who I have no control over."

"Thanks. Give Irene my regards," he said and left.

Lorelei had already made up her mind that if she didn't hear from her stepmother today she was going to track her down. The day seemed to drag even though she was busy most of it. She was still reeling from what she'd learned from James about Karen and Sean Sherman. How could you think you knew someone so well, only to realize it was a lie?

All day long she'd thought James might stop in for a sandwich. He didn't. She wondered if he was avoiding her. Or just busy with his case. He'd already dug up so much about her stepmother, she feared it would get worse. So maybe not seeing him was good news.

That evening as she locked up, she noted that James's pickup wasn't parked out back. She felt a strange tremor of worry that something might have happened to him. Since he started asking questions about Billy Sherman's death, at least one person had been murdered.

She was almost to her stepmother's house when she saw her pull in. The garage door went up and her stepmother's car disappeared inside. Lorelei pulled in as the garage door closed. She didn't know what she was going to say now that she was here. Accuse Karen of yet another affair? Or of murder and covering it up?

Maybe all her stepmother had been hiding was her relationship with Billy Sherman's father and the divorce that followed. But was there more? Lorelei feared there was.

She climbed out of her SUV and walked to the front door. She didn't have to knock. The door opened and her stepmother was standing there with such a resigned look on her face that Lorelei wanted to cry.

Without a word, Karen stepped back to let her in. She followed her into the kitchen where her stepmother opened the refrigerator and pulled out a bottle of wine. Opening it, she poured herself a glass and, without asking, poured another. She set Lorelei's in front of her at the breakfast bar, then walked into the living room to sit down.

For a moment, Lorelei stared at the wine. Then impulsively, she picked it up and downed it before turning her phone to Record and walking into the living room. Even as she did it, she felt as if she was about to betray the woman who'd been her mother. But if Karen had killed that boy...

"I'm at a loss as to what to say to you," Lorelei said as she watched her stepmother sip her wine.

"And yet here you are." There was defiance in her words, in her look.

"You had an affair with Sean Sherman. You destroyed his marriage. Did you also kill his son?" She'd thought her words would get a quick and violent reaction.

Instead, her stepmother took another sip of her wine and set the glass down on the end table next to her before she spoke. "I hate small towns. I told your father that when we moved here. It's like living in a fishbowl." She met Lorelei's gaze. "You were the best part of that marriage. I'd always wanted a child and couldn't have one of my own. I felt like you were my flesh and blood daughter, but I wasn't happy. I loved your father, but he definitely wasn't the love of my life. He couldn't...satisfy me."

"Could anyone?" She regretted the retort at once, sighed and sat down as a long silence fell between them.

"When Fred and I get married, I'm going to put this house up for sale," Karen said, looking around. "I'll sell the studio as well since we're going to get an apartment in Washington. We'll come here in the summer so it's not like I'm leaving forever, and you can always come visit us in Washington if you want to."

"What about Billy Sherman? You were upset and out driving that night."

Karen got a faraway look in her eye for a moment. "I loved Sean and he loved me. But he was determined to go back to his wife even knowing it would have never worked." She made eye contact again. "Remember when I told you that some women always go for the bad boys?" She chuckled. "That was me. And maybe you since I've seen the look in your eye whenever James Colt's name is mentioned."

"I'm nothing like you," Lorelei said, shaking her head.

Her stepmother chuckled again. "Sean had a wild side."

"What about Fred? Does he have a wild side?"

Karen looked away.

"It's all going to come out," Lorelei said. "Everything. James isn't going to quit, and neither am I."

Her stepmother looked at her again and she saw resignation in Karen's eyes. She felt her heart drop as her stepmother said, "That was one of the worst nights of my life."

When Lorelei spoke, it came out in a whisper. "What did you do?"

Karen took another drink of her wine. "I drove around. I was upset. I wasn't thinking clearly. I was crying and it was raining. I couldn't see anything so I pulled over beside the road. I knew I shouldn't be driving in the condition I was in and yet I couldn't stay in the house with Sean, knowing he was leaving me. My chance of happiness had been snatched away and right or wrong, I blamed Alice."

Lorelei lifted a brow. "After you stole her husband,

you blamed her because her husband was going back to her?"

"You can't steal anyone's husband," she snapped with obvious disgust. "That's just what wives say so they don't have to take responsibility for their husbands being unhappy with them."

"I'm sorry, but that sounds like an excuse for what you did," Lorelei said and then quickly waved it away. "I don't care. Are we finally getting to what you did that night?"

"I was sitting in my car crying when this car went by. I heard this *thump-thump* and the brake lights came on and a man jumped out and ran back through the rain. The driver had run over something. I could see a small form lying in the road. The man kicked it off to the edge of the ditch with his boot, ran back and jumped into the car and they drove away."

Lorelei's heart had lodged in her throat. "You saw who killed Billy Sherman?"

"It wasn't Billy. I got out and went over to see. At first I thought it was a dog, then I realized it was a coyote. It was a young one. I picked the poor thing up. It was dead. I don't know where I planned to take it. As I said, I wasn't in my right mind. It doesn't make any sense now, but right then I felt this connection to that dead animal. I started walking down the road holding this dead animal in my arms and crying. I didn't know where I was going or what I was going to do with it."

Lorelei saw the pain in her mother's face, then the anger.

"I decided to leave it on Alice's front doorstep. She was killing me. I wanted her to suffer."

"As if she wasn't suffering enough?"

Karen looked away. "If you'd ever been in love—"

She thought of James and how he'd turned her life upside down. "So you left this dead coyote on her doorstep?"

"That was what I'd planned to do. But as I started by the house I saw her. She was out on her porch having a cigarette. She stubbed it out and went inside, slamming the door. I realized how small and cruel and juvenile my plan was so I turned around and headed back. I can't tell you how badly I felt about all of it, the affair, the people I'd hurt, but most of all the pain in my heart. I wanted so desperately to be loved like I felt I deserved." She glanced at Lorelei. "No offense to your father. He did the best he could, but he—"

"Back to Billy," she said, cutting her off.

Karen nodded. "I hadn't gone very far when I realized there was someone behind me. I turned and…" She swallowed, tears filling her eyes. "It was Billy. He'd been following me."

Chapter 21

James was headed back into town from the Appleton house when he got the call from Lori. He heard it at once in her voice. "What's wrong?"

"I need to see you." The quaver in her voice sent his pulse rocketing.

"Are you all right?" She had him scared.

"Just meet me at your office, okay?" Her voice broke. "It's important."

"I'm headed there right now," he said and sped up. "Just be careful." But she'd already disconnected.

As he pulled into the alley behind their buildings, she climbed out of her SUV and started toward him. The look on her face made him rush to her and pull her into his arms. She leaned into him for a moment, resting her head on his shoulder, before she pulled back.

He saw the plea in her eyes. Whatever was wrong,

she needed to get it out. "Let's go upstairs," he said as he opened the door. He felt a draft, accompanied by a bad feeling. Slowly he began to climb upward, hesitating just before the top to peer down the hallway. Empty. But he could see the door to his office standing open.

Moving closer, he could see that the wood was chewed from where the lock had been jimmied. He wanted to send Lori back to her car. Or into her shop, but he also didn't want to let her out of his sight.

"Stay behind me," he whispered as he pulled his weapon. A cone of light from inside the office shone golden on the hallway floor. He watched it as they moved quietly toward it. But no shadow appeared in the light. No sound of movement came from within the office.

At the door, he motioned Lorelei back for a moment before he burst into the office, his weapon raised and ready to fire. He saw no one and quickly checked the bedroom and bath. Empty.

Turning, he saw Lori framed in the ransacked office doorway. "Who do you think did this?"

"Someone worried about what I've discovered in the case," he said without hesitation as he holstered his gun and, ushering her in, locked the office door and bolted it. Turning to her, he said, "Tell me what's happened. I can see how upset you are."

She reached into her pocket and pulled out her phone. A moment later, he heard Karen Wilkins's voice—and her stepdaughter's.

When the recording ended, Lorelei turned off her phone. At some point, she'd taken the chair James had offered her along with the paper cup of blackberry brandy.

"So, when Billy came face-to-face with your stepmother he screamed and ran into the storm. She didn't go after him. She didn't see him again."

She nodded. "You heard her. She swears it's true. She took the dead coyote into the trees and then she walked back to her car and drove home."

"Billy was killed in the same block from where your stepmother said she'd pulled off the road. I have a witness who saw her car there. Unfortunately, there were no video cameras in that area because of the empty lots and construction going on at the time. The witness killed the coyote just after ten that night. I need to know what time she saw Billy. And what time it was when she returned to her car and where she went after that. She didn't go home until daylight. Sean was at her house waiting for her. He said that she'd fixed her hair and wasn't wet from the storm. So where had she been?"

Lorelei shook her head, drained her blackberry brandy and rose. "I need to go home and try to get some rest. I have to work early tomorrow."

"I'm sorry you got dragged into this," James said as he got to his feet as well. "You look exhausted."

"I am. I knew she was hiding something." She met his gaze. "I honestly don't know what to believe. I thought she and my father had a good marriage. I was wrong about that. I was wrong about so many things. I thought I knew her. Now... I'm not even sure she's telling me the truth. What will you do now?"

"I'll talk to her. I'll tell her what you told me. I won't tell her about the recording. If I can establish a time sequence..."

"You think she did it, don't you?"

"I think she might have blotted it out of her memory. As she said, she wasn't in her right mind. Picking up a dead young coyote and carrying it down the street to play a mean joke? Clearly she wasn't herself."

"But upset enough to run over a little boy on her way home and not remember?" Lorelei shook her head. "We've already established that she's dishonest about at least her love life. We both know there is a part of her story that she's leaving out."

He stepped to her and took her shoulders in his big hands. His touch felt warm and comforting. She wanted to curl up in his arms. "I'm going to find out who killed Billy. Please, I need you to be careful. Someone doesn't want me to know the truth. I doubt they found what they were looking for in my office. I'm afraid of how far they might go to cover up their crime. I don't want you involved."

She smiled sadly. "Too late for that."

"But promise me you won't do any more investigating on your own."

She was too tired and drained and discouraged to argue.

"I'll see you tomorrow?" he said, meeting her gaze.

She nodded numbly and he let her go but insisted on walking her down to her car. He'd wanted to follow her home, except she wasn't having it. It was flattering that James cared, but she wasn't some helpless woman who relied on a man. She wasn't her stepmother. Lorelei wanted a man in her life, but she didn't need one.

"I'm fine," she assured him. "I'm more worried about you."

"Indulge me. Please. Call me when you get home, so I know you made it okay. Promise me?"

James didn't care what Lori said. He was going to follow her home to make sure she was safe. He felt as if he'd dragged her into this. Just being associated with him could be bad enough. Add in her stepmother...

As she drove away, he reached for his keys and swore. He'd left them upstairs in his shock at finding his office broken into and ransacked, not to mention the information Lori had gotten on her stepmother.

He turned and rushed upstairs in time to hear his phone ringing. The phone and his keys were on his desk. He scooped up the phone, thinking it might be Lori. It was Gilbert Sanders, the arsonist investigator. He glanced at the time and had a feeling the man wouldn't be calling now unless it was important.

He picked up the call on his way out the door.

"I was thinking about what you said about your father wanting to talk to me about a hit-and-run case he was working on," Gilbert said after a few pleasantries were exchanged. "I couldn't imagine why he'd want to talk to me about anything but a fire. But then I remembered. I *did* talk to him. He told me he was working on a case about a young boy who'd been killed, right?"

"Right. Billy Sherman."

"But that wasn't why your father called me. He wanted to know about a house fire. One fatality. The wife."

James frowned. "Whose fire?"

"His own. Del Colt wanted to know about the fire that killed his wife."

"I don't understand," James said as he reached his pickup and stopped. "My mother died of cancer."

"It was his first wife."

James couldn't speak for a moment. "His *first* wife."

"I'm sorry, you didn't know that your father had been married before?"

"No. What did you tell him about the fire?"

"Just that it had been ruled an accident, a faulty lamp cord. But I wasn't the one who handled that investigation. It was my uncle, the man I was named for, Gilbert T. Sanders, who did the investigation. Your father asked me to look into it for him. Something must have come up in his investigation of the hit-and-run that made him believe the fire that killed his first wife had been arson and was somehow connected to his case."

This made no sense. "Did you look into the fire?" James asked as he climbed into his pickup. Lori would probably be home by now and probably trying to call him.

"I did. I think your father might have been right."

"Wait, right about what?"

"The fire that killed his first wife," Gilbert said. "My uncle suspected it was arson, but there were extenuating circumstances. An eyewitness swore he saw the lamp ignite the living room."

"Who was the eyewitness?"

"Sheriff Otis Osterman. He was the first person on the scene. But I saw in my uncle's notes on the case that there was a string of small fires that summer around Lonesome. There was a suspect at the time."

James felt all the air rush from his lungs as Gilbert said, "Freddie Bayard, now Senator Fred Bayard. Freddie had apparently been a firebug since he was little. But there was no proof and his father, also a senator, made Freddie untouchable. The boy was sent away to a private school where his father promised he would get him the help he needed. In the report, there was also mention of Del and Fred being at odds, some rivalry that went back years."

"How is that possible?" James asked. "I didn't think Fred moved here until about ten years ago."

"His grandparents lived here and he stayed with them more than he stayed with his parents. His father was in DC a lot of the time and he and his mother weren't close. I'm not sure how any of this will help with your investigation."

"Me either, but thank you for letting me know." James pulled in front of Lori's house. No lights on. No Lori. She hadn't come straight home or she would be here by now. Fred Bayard was involved with Karen Wilkins and Lori was involved because of it.

He felt a tremor of fear. Why hadn't Lori gone straight home like she'd planned? Had her stepmother called? Had something happened?

He started to call Lori's cell when he knew where she'd gone. Making a sharp U-turn in the middle of the street, he headed toward her stepmother's house.

As he drove, he couldn't get what Gilbert Sanders had told him out of his mind. He called his brother Davey only to get voice mail. He tried his brother Tommy. Same thing. He was about to give up when he realized the brother he needed to ask was his eldest brother, Willie.

"What's up?"

"Did you know Dad was married before?" he demanded.

Willie hesitated before saying, "Who told you that?"

"You just did! And you never said anything?" James couldn't believe this.

"Why would I? It had nothing to do with our family," Willie said. "Also, it was too painful for Dad. I wanted to protect him. They were married less than a month when she was killed. Luckily, he met our mom."

"Protect him from what?" James demanded.

"Heartbreak. He blamed himself for her death. Like us, he was on the rodeo circuit all the time. He'd left her alone in a house that had bad wiring. He didn't need to be reminded of the past. That's why I didn't tell you or the others."

"How did you find out?" he asked as he pulled up in front of Lorelei's stepmother's house.

"Otis Osterman told me. He was the cop who investigated the fire. He threw the fact that Dad left his wife in a house with faulty wiring in my face the first time he hauled me in on some trumped-up charge. I told him that if he ever said anything like that to me or my family again, I'd kill him. Apparently, he believed me."

"I'm getting another call," James said, hoping it would be Lori. "We'll talk about this soon." He disconnected from Willie and said, "Lori?"

Silence. He realized that the other call had gone to voice mail. He listened, still hoping it had been Lori. It was one of the out-of-town body shops he'd called inquiring about a vehicle being brought in from Lonesome nine years ago after Billy Sherman's death. He didn't bother to listen to the message. Right now he only cared about Lori. He couldn't shake a bad feeling that she was in trouble.

Lorelei had grudgingly promised to go straight home and call James when she arrived. Her intentions had been good when she'd left him. Until her stepmother called crying and hysterical.

"What's wrong?" Karen didn't answer, just kept crying. "Mom."

Calling her mom seemed to do the trick. "We broke up."

It took Lorelei a minute to realize that she must be talking about the senator.

"Why?"

More awful sobbing, before her stepmother said, "It was all based on a lie. How could I have ever trusted that he was really in love with me? Or that he wasn't just marrying me so I couldn't testify against him?"

At those words, Lorelei felt shaken to her soul. Marry her so she couldn't testify against him? "What are you talking about?"

"That night on the road. Billy." She was sobbing again. "I left out that part. When I was walking back to my car, Fred picked me up. On the way to my car…" More sobbing. "He ran over something in the road. It didn't seem like it was anything. I told him about the coyote… He didn't stop to check but he did look back in his side mirror. I saw his expression. I knew it wasn't a coyote."

Lorelei felt her blood run cold. Her stepmother was sobbing.

"I was so upset and freezing and there didn't seem to be any damage to his vehicle."

"He took you to his house," Lorelei said, seeing now how it had happened with her mother and the senator.

"He was so kind, so caring. I wanted to believe in him." More uncontrollable bawling.

She didn't need her stepmother to tell her what had happened after that night. Fred had been afraid that Karen could come forward with what she knew. He must have seen how much she'd needed a man in her life. He became that man to protect himself. Until Karen finally admitted the truth—and not just about the night Billy Sherman had died.

Lorelei had known women her own age who went from one man to the next, desperate to have someone in their lives. She'd felt sorry for them. She felt sorry for her stepmother. Karen would have been flattered at the senator's attention. She'd been lonely, had needed a man so desperately, that she would rather live a lie than admit the truth about her relationship with Fred Bayard.

Until now.

"You told him what you told me," Lorelei said.

"I knew you were right," her stepmother wailed. "James was going to find out. Fred became so angry. It's over." She began to cry harder.

Why hadn't she noticed how unhappy Karen had been? Why hadn't she known what her stepmother had been going through? Because Karen had seemed happy. And because Lorelei had been busy living her own life, seeing what she wanted to see.

"Mom, I'm almost to your house." But she didn't think Karen heard her. "Mom?" She kept hearing her stepmother's words. *I knew it wasn't a coyote.*

She could hardly make out her stepmother's next words, "Someone's at the back door. It can't be Fred. He's promised to go to the sheriff..." Then Karen's voice changed, and Lorelei knew her stepmother was no longer talking to her. "What are you doing here? I thought—"

Lorelei heard what sounded like the phone being knocked out of Karen's hand. It made a whishing sound as it skittered across the hardwood floor.

She couldn't make out the words, but it sounded like Karen and a man arguing. Then to Lorelei's horror, she heard her stepmother scream followed by a painful cry an instant before she heard the sound of what could be a body hitting the floor.

"Mom?" she cried into the phone. Silence. Then foot-falls. The line went dead.

Her hands were shaking so hard on the wheel that she had to grip it tightly. She was calling 911 as her step-mother's house came into view and she saw the smoke.

Chapter 22

The smoke seemed to be coming from the back of the house. The man had come in the back door. Lorelei knew who the man was, knew what he'd done and why. But as she made a quick turn and swung down the alley, she was surprised to see him jump into his large dark-colored SUV. She sped toward him as he ducked behind the wheel and took off in a hail of gravel. But not before she'd seen his license plate number. The senator had vanity plates.

She hit her brakes behind the house and bailed out of her vehicle. She could see smoke rolling out of the open back door. She was running toward the house when James came running around the side of the house toward her.

"My stepmother's inside," she screamed over the crackle of the blaze. "The senator was here. I heard him attack her, then set the house on fire." She could see flames rising at the kitchen windows.

"Stay here," James ordered as he pulled off his jean jacket, and putting it over his head ran into the open back door and into the smoke and flames.

Lorelei stood there, feeling helpless. She could hear sirens growing closer. The fire trucks would be here soon. But soon enough? She wanted to race into the house through the smoke and flames and find James, find Karen. She felt her panic building. James was here because of her. He couldn't die because of her.

She began to cry tears of relief as she saw him come out of the smoke carrying Karen. She ran to him as the first of the fire trucks pulled up out front along with an ambulance and the sheriff.

"She's unconscious," James said, coughing. "But since she was on the floor, I don't think she breathed in much smoke."

Lorelei wiped at her tears as she ran to keep up with him as he carried Karen toward the waiting ambulance. James had risked his life to save her stepmother. She loved this man. The thought whizzed through her mind as they reached the sidewalk and were immediately surrounded by frantic activity as James handed over Karen and the EMTs went to work on her.

"Want to tell me what's going on here?" the sheriff asked as he sauntered up to Lorelei.

"My stepmother was attacked and left in a burning house to die," she snapped. "That's what happened. I saw the man who assaulted her and started the fire. I was on the phone with her when he attacked her. I was only a block away so I saw him running away as I drove up. I took down his license number. But I also saw his face. It was Senator Fred Bayard."

Carl started to argue that she had to be mistaken. "Fred is a godsend to this community. Without him and the donations he'd made—"

Karen, now conscious, pulled off her oxygen mask. She narrowed her gaze on the sheriff, stopping the EMTs from loading her gurney into the back of the ambulance.

"Senator Fred Bayard tried to kill me and then he set my house on fire," her stepmother said through coughing fits. "He also killed Billy Sherman. I know because I was in the car with him. He didn't stop to see what he'd run over. He just kept going. He would have killed me too."

The EMTs got the oxygen back on Karen as she gasped for breath.

"If you don't arrest the senator," Lorelei said, turning to the sheriff, "I will call the FBI and tell them that you refused to pick up the man who assaulted my stepmother, started the fire and left her to die. I don't think you want them looking into the other things you and your brother have done over the years to cover up crimes in Lonesome."

The EMTs loaded Karen into the ambulance. "I have to get to the hospital," she said and pushed past the sheriff.

"I'll take you," James said, suddenly at her side. He put his arm around her as they hurried to his pickup. She leaned into him, for once happy to have someone to lean on.

As she climbed in and he slid behind the wheel, she told him what her stepmother had told her on the phone before she'd heard Karen being attacked.

"When I drove up, I saw him running from the back

of the house," she said. "He tried to kill my stepmother to cover up his crime." She fought tears, fearing that Fred would get away with it. The sheriff certainly didn't have the guts to arrest him.

Sheriff Carl Osterman swore as he watched the ambulance leave, siren blaring and lights flashing. James Colt and Lorelei Wilkins took off behind it. When had those two become so tight, he wondered. He'd thought Lorelei had more sense. Shaking his head, he watched the firefighters trying to put out the blaze and then sighing, climbed into his patrol SUV and headed out to the senator's place.

He knew how this was going to go down so he was in no hurry. It would come down to the senator's word against the woman he'd just broken up with and Lorelei, a younger woman protecting her stepmother. Not the best witnesses especially if all this had been caused by a domestic disagreement between the senator and Karen Wilkins. He certainly didn't want to take the word of a hysterical woman.

As he pulled up in the yard in front of the large summer house, he slowly got out. He wasn't surprised when Fred came out carrying a small suitcase and walked toward his helipad next to the house in a clearing in the pines.

Carl followed him. "If you have a minute, Fred?"

"Sheriff, good to see you. Actually, I don't. Something's come up. My chopper should be here any minute. I need to get to the airport. Government business."

The senator smelled as if he'd taken a quick shower, so quick that there was still that faint hint of smoke on him. "We have a problem," Carl said.

Fred smiled. "I'm sure it's nothing that you can't handle, Sheriff. It's one of the reasons I backed your campaign. Please don't tell me I supported the wrong man."

He could hear the sound of the helicopter in the distance. "You did back the right man," Carl said, bristling. "But money can only buy so much. This time I'm going to have to take you in for questioning, Fred. Lorelei Wilkins saw you leaving her stepmother's house. You stepped over a line. What you did can't be undone."

The senator shook his head. "I was at her house. I'm not sure what happened after I left, but I had just broken up with her stepmother. Karen was overwrought, threatening to kill herself. Of course Lorelei is going to blame me if the woman did something…stupid."

"It's more serious than that, I'm afraid, Fred. Karen regained consciousness. She says you assaulted her and set her house on fire. Lorelei was on a phone call with her stepmother and heard it all. Karen also says that you killed Billy Sherman—that she was in the car that night and will testify in court that you didn't even stop."

"She's lying. I told you. I broke it off. She'd say anything to get back at me." The helicopter came into view.

Carl pulled out his handcuffs. A part of him had known that this day was coming and had been for years. Fred had gotten away with numerous crimes over the years since he was a boy. Back then he'd been a juvenile, his father a respected senator, his grandparents churchgoing people. But now that the man's house of cards had started to tumble, the sheriff suspected a lot more was about to come out.

Worse, Carl knew that he and Otis would be caught in the dirt once it started flying. He laid his hand on his weapon and slowly unsnapped the holster. Fred saw the movement, his eyes widening. The senator had to know that there was an easy way out of this for Carl, for his brother. If Fred were dead there would never be a trial, a lot of old cases wouldn't come to light.

"I hope you'll come peacefully, senator," Carl said. "But either way, you're going to have to come down to the station for questioning." He met the man's gaze and held it for a long moment.

Fred swore. "All the things I've done for your two-bit town." He angrily pulled out his phone and called his attorney.

"I'll tell the helicopter pilot that you won't be going anywhere for a while," Carl said, then turned back to the senator. "By the way, I heard from Gilbert Sanders, the state arson investigator, earlier today. He told me that he's reopening the Del Colt fire case. He thinks he has some new evidence." He watched Fred's spray-on-tanned face pale. "He was especially interested in talking to you."

"The statute of limitations on arson is five years."

"I guess you forgot. Del's first wife died in that fire. There is no statute of limitations on murder."

Chapter 23

Lorelei found her stepmother to be in good spirits when she stopped by the hospital the next morning. Karen had a concussion from the blow the senator had dealt her and a mild cough from the smoke, but she was going to be fine.

"The prosecutor said he didn't think I would be arrested for withholding evidence," Karen said. "I'm just glad to be alive. But I can't stay in Lonesome. I should have left a long time ago."

She took her stepmother's hand. "You stayed because of me."

Karen smiled. "You always did give me the benefit of the doubt. I will miss you, but you need to get on with your life. You need not worry about me anymore."

She wasn't sure about that. "You put up the money for my shop from your retirement account."

"It was the right thing to do. I inherited the house and your father's money. It's what your father would have wanted me to do."

"I'm sorry things didn't work out for you," Lorelei said.

"I chose the wrong men for the wrong reasons." She shook her head. "I've learned my lesson. Don't look at me like that. Even old dogs can learn new tricks."

Lorelei laughed. "You're still young. There's someone out there for you."

"I hope so." She took a ragged breath. "What's going on with you and James Colt?"

She shrugged. "We had a moment, but now he's done what he set out to do. Solve his father's case. I'm sure he'll be going back on the rodeo circuit."

"I'm sorry."

"I'm sure it's for the best," Lorelei said. "I heard you're getting out of here today."

"I'm thinking of going to Chicago. I'll be back for the trial, if Fred's case goes to trial. But first I have to tie up some loose ends with the insurance company and the house. I've had an offer for the exercise studio and I've decided to take it. I'm looking forward to a fresh start in the big city."

She squeezed her stepmother's hand. "Please keep in touch."

"You know I will. You're my daughter." They hugged and Lorelei left before she cried. She would miss Karen. Her stepmother had been the last link she had with her father and the last reminder of her childhood. With Karen gone, she had no family left here.

The thought made her sad as she drove to her shop. Anita had volunteered to come in and work, which Lorelei had happily accepted. Given everything that had happened, she needed a little time off. Karen thought she was like her because of James Colt. Was he her bad boy? He had played that part in high school and for some time after, but she no longer thought of him that way. He was her hero. But he was also a rodeo cowboy at heart. The circuit would be calling him now.

As she got out of her SUV, James drove up. Just seeing him made her heart soar. Yesterday evening he'd gone to the hospital with her, but she'd sent him home after the doctors checked him over. He had smoke inhalation and she could tell he needed rest. He'd called to make sure she and Karen were both all right late last night. She hadn't had a chance to talk to him since.

He got out of his pickup and sauntered toward her. Had she really not noticed how good-looking he was that first day when she'd seen him again after all the years? She could laugh about it now. She'd thought his hair was too long, that he dressed like a saddle tramp, that he was too arrogant for a man who obviously lacked ambition. So why did he seem perfect now? He hadn't changed, but the way she saw him definitely had, she realized. She'd gotten to know the man inside him and fallen in love with him.

The thought struck her at heart level like a blow. She'd had the thought yesterday after he'd gone into a house on fire to save her stepmother. This time the thought carried no raw emotion. It just happened to be the truth.

And now he would be leaving Lonesome, leaving her.

"I'm starved," he said, grinning as he joined her.

"You're always starved," she said with a laugh.

He put his arm around her as they headed into the

back of her sandwich shop. He did it casually and yet it sent a jolt through her. "What's the special today?"

"Pulled pork. Your favorite."

He looked over at her and smiled. "You know me so well. Anita must be working. Thank goodness since I don't want you going anywhere near my sandwich."

She thought of that day when she'd added hot sauce and sliced jalapeños to his sandwich—and he'd eaten every bite of it. "I'm still sorry about that."

"Sure you are," he said with a laugh as he headed for his usual table. "Have an early lunch with me?"

Lorelei nodded, fighting tears. She didn't want to think about the days he would no longer stop by. When his pickup wouldn't be parked in the alley next door. When she wouldn't see him. "Let me place our orders. I'll be right back. Iced tea or lemonade?"

"Both." He looked so happy. He'd solved his father's last case. Why wouldn't he be happy? But she feared it was more about going back on the rodeo circuit.

James took his usual seat at the booth and looked out on the town. Funny how his attitude toward Lonesome had changed. It had been nothing more than a stopover on his way somewhere else for so many years. He realized that he hadn't appreciated it.

Now he felt more a part of the place. It was a good feeling, one he would miss if…when he went back on the rodeo circuit. He'd done what he'd set out to do. Solve his father's last case. Still, it felt unfinished. There was the question of his father's death. He thought the truth about it still might come out—if as he suspected Otis had something to do with Del Colt's death.

The senator's arrest had a domino effect. The feds

had stepped in and taken over the case. Gilbert Sanders turned over new evidence to the prosecutor regarding the Del Colt case along with other fires that were quickly attributed to Fred. He was being held without bail.

A small-time criminal Otis Osterman had arrested back when he was sheriff was picked up and charged for drug possession. He copped a plea, giving up Otis as the one who'd hired him to burn down Cora Brooks's house. The prosecution, closely watched by the feds, began looking into how other investigations had been handled by both Carl Osterman and his brother Otis. Under pressure, Carl had resigned, and the reign of the Osterman's was over. More of their misdeeds would be coming out, James knew.

He dragged himself out of his thoughts as Lori appeared with a tray full of food and drinks. "I'm sorry. I could have helped you with that."

She gave him a dismissive look. "I do this for a living. I can handle it."

He watched her slide into the chair across from him and take everything off the tray. He'd never imagined he would have these kinds of feelings for Lorelei Wilkins and yet he did. Once, it had been flirting. Now… Now it was so much more. She had a pull on him stronger than gravity.

"What will happen now with the case?" she asked after they'd tucked into their sandwiches in companionable silence.

"Probably the most Fred will go down for will be assault, arson and manslaughter even if the prosecution can prove he set the fire that killed my father's first wife. He might get some time in prison, but probably not much. But his career is over. He'll be a felon. He won't even be allowed to vote, own a gun or hold office in most states and there are countries that won't allow him in."

She put down her sandwich. "It's not enough. What about Billy?"

James shook his head. "I doubt a jury will convict him on that because of lack of evidence. Karen says he ran over something. All Fred has to do is lie and say he didn't. It's her word against his. There apparently wasn't any damage to his large SUV."

"He's in a position where he can lie and there will be people who will believe him over my stepmother."

James couldn't argue that. "Taking away his career and ruining his reputation will hurt the most. He'll lie, say he was railroaded by a scorned woman. That he was innocent of all of it. But he ran from your stepmother's house after assaulting her and setting her house on fire. Add to that the other fires... His reputation is toast."

He watched her pick at her sandwich as if she'd lost her appetite. "Do you think he would have married Karen?"

She shook her head. "I think she realized there was no happy ending with the lie between them. She would have always questioned his love for her."

James reached across the table to cover her hand with his own. "People disappoint us but ultimately we're all human. That's what my dad used to say. We do what we have to do to survive. For some, that's lying, cheating, stealing and even killing. For others it's small lies and secrets. My dad was good at uncovering them and finding a little justice or at least peace for those in pain. I understand now why he loved doing this."

"So you're hooked on the PI business?" She'd said it jokingly, but he knew at the heart of her question what she was asking. This year's rodeo season was in full swing. He was healed. There was nothing to keep him from getting back to his life. He'd accomplished what he'd set out to do. Solve his father's last case—with Lori's help. If he didn't go soon...

Lori. He looked into her face, saw her compassion, her spirit, her desire that mirrored his own. How could he leave her for months to go back on the rodeo circuit? But then how could he not? He wasn't getting any younger. He didn't have that much time left in the saddle and there were a lot of broncos he'd yet to ride.

Lorelei stood in the kitchen of her shop after James left. He'd said there were some things he had to take care of and that he would see her later. She and her friend Anita were prepping for the next day and getting ready for the lunch crowd. It was Saturday and a beautiful summer day. There would be a lot of picnickers coming for her special weekend basket.

"I keep thinking about everything that happened," she said, voicing her doubts out loud. "It doesn't feel over."

"I'm sure it's going to take a while to process everything." She and Anita had been good friends in high school. While Lorelei had gone to college, Anita had married her childhood sweetheart, had babies and settled in Lonesome. Lorelei looked up to her since Anita had definitely had more life experience because of it.

"I keep thinking about something Karen said. She heard a car go by moving fast when she was in the trees getting rid of the coyote. She hid, so she didn't see the car or the driver. She said that's when she realized that she couldn't do what she'd been doing anymore. That she needed to find a man who appreciated her and wanted to marry her and that things were really over between her and Sean."

Anita stopped to plant one hand on her hip. "Where are you going with this?"

"I'm not sure. Right after that, she stepped back on the highway in the pouring rain and was picked up by the senator," Lorelei said. "Of course, Karen thought it was fate."

"Until the senator hit Billy."

"That's just it. Karen said he ran over *something* in the road. Not that he *hit* something."

"I'm not sure I see the difference."

"That car that sped by too fast while Karen was hiding in the trees, what if that's the driver who actually hit and killed Billy Sherman?"

"But you don't know who it was."

"No. Minutes later the senator would pick up Karen and run over something in the road and not bother to stop." She grimaced. "He must have seen the boy lying on the road in his rearview mirror."

"Well, you know what kind of man he is already," Anita said.

"But what if Billy was already dead? What if the senator panicked, thinking he had killed the boy and believing Karen would know he'd done it? When he looked back in his side mirror, he would have seen the boy's clothing. From that moment on, he had to keep my stepmother from ever telling so he seduced her that night."

Anita shuddered. "And when he realized he could no longer trust her, he tried to kill her and burn down her house."

"Maybe that's what he planned all along. I really doubt he would have married her and yet he couldn't break up with her for fear of what she might do. He must have felt trapped. How ironic would it be if he was innocent?"

"Innocent is not a word I would use with him, but I see what you mean," Anita agreed. "But how can you prove that Billy was already dead, hit by the car before the senator's vehicle drove over the remains?"

"I have no idea," Lorelei said. "But I'm going by Alice Sherman's today. My stepmother was going to stop by her house, but I talked her out of it. Karen wanted to send her a card to tell her how sorry she was about everything. She's now decided that to change she needs to apologize to those she hurt."

"Not a bad idea."

"No, but I think Karen showing up there might not be a great idea. So I said I'd drop off the card she wrote instead. I wanted to see if Alice might remember a car flying past that night. My stepmother said Alice had been outside smoking a cigarette when she'd seen her but had gone back inside. I would imagine she'd been at the window making sure Karen kept going past."

Anita looked skeptical. "Are you sure she'll want to talk to you? I mean, you are Karen's daughter. But what's the worst that can happen? She'll throw you out."

"That's a pleasant thought," she said as she tossed her apron in the bin and headed for her SUV parked outside. But she had to try.

She noticed that James's pickup was still parked in the alley. She considered sharing her theory with him but decided otherwise. There was a good chance that the senator had been the one to hit Billy in that big SUV of his with the huge metal guard on the front. Questioning Alice Sherman probably wouldn't go anywhere anyway.

On top of that, she could see a shadow moving around in the upstairs apartment. Was James packing? Would he tell her goodbye?

James had looked around the office, his gaze lighting on his private investigator's license. He'd taken Lori's advice. He'd framed it and put it on the wall next to his father's. It had felt presumptuous. But he liked the look of it there.

He knew he should start packing. He needed to pick up his horse and trailer. He turned and saw the Colt Investigations sign in the front second-story window. He should take that down. He'd already had several calls from people wanting to hire him as the news had swept through Lonesome.

The crazy part was that he would never have solved it without Lori's help. He still didn't know what he was doing. He was playacting at being a PI. But it had given him some experience. Maybe with more…

The worst part was that something was still nagging at him about the case. He told himself that the FBI would get to the bottom of any questions he might have. Everything was in good hands.

He turned to look at his framed PI license hanging on the wall over the desk next to his father's again. He felt torn about leaving. When he thought about Lori he wasn't sure he could leave. But would he regret it later if he didn't go at least one more year on the circuit? It would probably be his last.

His cell phone rang. "Congrats," Willie said. "You're all over the news. Dad would be proud."

"Thanks."

"I suppose I know what you're doing. Packing. Did I hear you might catch up to us in Texas?"

"Thinking about it."

"What? You aren't already packed? What's going on?"

James knew he had to make a decision. He still didn't know how or why his father had died that night on the railroad tracks. He feared that he never would.

He'd been offered more cases since the senator's arrest. Maybe he could make a living at this PI thing. He and Lori had found Billy Sherman's killer. They'd made a good team.

"I'm packing," he told his brother. "I'll let you know, but probably Texas." He disconnected. But something was still nagging him. About the case? About leaving?

He stepped over to the desk and sat down. Earlier, he'd filed the case away. Now he pulled it out. There were his own notes in with his father's. Would his father be proud?

What was bothering him? He flipped through the file, stopping on the coroner's report. He'd read it over when he'd first started the case. Billy's injuries had been consistent with being hit by a vehicle. Numerous bones had been broken but it was a massive head injury that was listed as cause of death.

Numerous bones had been broken, he read again and looked through the list. Billy's right arm had been shattered and was believed to have been run over by the vehicle's tire after initial impact.

He picked up his phone and called Dr. Milton Stanley. He figured the man would be out working in his yard and was surprised when he picked up. "This is a bit unusual, but I was looking at the coroner's report on

Billy Sherman. I need to know if this is consistent with a small boy of seven being struck by a large vehicle."

"It would depend on the size of the car. If it was a large SUV or pickup or a small car, the injuries would be different. The state medical examiner did this autopsy. Send me the report and I'd be happy to give you my opinion."

James glanced around the office and spotted his father's old fax machine. "I can fax it to you. I don't have a copy machine."

The doctor laughed. "How about a computer? No? If you're going to stay in business, son, you need to get into at least the twentieth century. Just take a photo of it with your phone and send it to me."

He'd just hung up, wondering what it was he was looking for when his cell phone rang. When he saw it was one of the out-of-town body shops he'd called, he remembered that one of them had called him back but he'd never listened to the message or returned the call. He'd forgotten about it with everything else that had been going on.

"You still looking for a vehicle that might have been involved in a hit-and-run?" a man asked.

He wasn't and yet he heard himself say, "What do you have?"

"I saw the message you left about looking for a damaged vehicle after April 10th nine years ago. I killed the message before my boss saw it," the man said. "Otherwise, no one would be calling you right now."

Did the man want money? Was that what this was about? "So why are you calling me?"

"After that date you mentioned, we had a car come in. It was late at night on a lowboy trailer. My boss had it dumped off. He pushed it into one of the bays. He didn't know I was still in the garage. I was curious so after he left I took a look at it. It wasn't the first car that rolled in that was…questionable. This one bothered me because there was blood on it and…hair."

Even as James told himself that this wasn't Billy's hit-and-run, he felt his heart plummet. This vehicle had been involved in a hit-and-run somewhere. Unless this guy was just leading him on. "Why didn't you report it?"

"My boss was an ass but I needed the job. My old lady was pregnant."

"You don't work there anymore?" He waited for the man to ask for money.

"I won't after this. I was suspicious so I bagged the hair and a scrap of clothing that was stuck in the bumper. Now I find out that the clothing matched the description of what that boy was wearing. I also took a piece of clean cloth and I wiped up some of the blood and put it into the bag for insurance. Look, I could get in trouble for this in so many ways. But now I've got a kid and when I heard about the trial of that senator for running over that boy… I want to see him hang."

So did James. "The FBI is going to want that bag with the evidence in it and your statement. Will you do it?"

Silence, then finally, "What the hell. My old lady says it's bad karma if I don't. It's been bothering me for the past nine years."

"They'll also want the make and model of the car."

"No problem. I even took down the license plate number." He rattled it off and James wrote it down. He was frowning down at what he'd written, when the man said, "It was a mid-sized sedan. I took a photo. Hold on, I'll send it to you."

A few moments later, the photo appeared on James's phone. By then he knew deep down what he'd been fearing. The car wasn't Senator Fred Bayard's large black SUV. The license plate number had been wrong as well.

Heart in his throat, he stared at the car in the photo and remembered where he'd seen it. Parked in front of Alice Sherman's house.

Chapter 24

Lorelei was about to give up. After ringing the doorbell several times and finally knocking at Alice Sherman's door, she still hadn't been able to raise anyone. She'd seen the car in the garage so she suspected the woman was home. There had been a news van parked outside when Lorelei had driven up, but it left after she hadn't gotten an answer at the door.

She was about to leave the card from her stepmother when the door opened a crack.

"What do you want?" Alice wore a bathrobe and slippers. Her hair looked as if it hadn't been washed in days. The woman stared at her, clearly not having a clue who she was.

"Mrs. Sherman, I'm—"

"It's not 'Mrs.' You're a local. I've seen you before. You one of those reporters?"

"No," she quickly assured her before the woman could close the door. "I'm Lorelei Wilkins. I own the sandwich shop in town. I just stopped by to—"

"Wilkins?" She grabbed hold of the door as if she needed it for support. "You're related to Karen?"

"She's my stepmother. She's in the hospital—"

"Like I care." Tears welled in Alice's eyes. "I hate her. I hope she dies."

"I'm sorry." Lorelei was still holding the card in her hand.

"What's that?"

"It's a note from my...from Karen."

Alice's eyes widened. "She sent you with a card for me? How thoughtful after what she did to my life," she said, her voice filled with rancor. Suddenly the woman opened the door wider. "You should come in."

That had been her hope originally, using the card as an excuse. But now she wasn't so sure. "I don't want to disturb you—"

"Too late for that. Come in."

Lorelei hesitated for a moment before stepping in. As she did, Alice Sherman snatched the card from her hand.

"Sit." She tore into the envelope. "Did she tell you what she did to me?" Alice didn't wait for an answer. "She destroyed my life and now everyone is going to know and she and her boyfriend are going to pay. It's just too bad my ex-husband isn't going to prison too."

"The senator's not her boyfriend anymore," Lorelei said as Alice motioned her into a chair. This was clearly not the best time to be asking questions about Billy's death, she thought. But then again she couldn't imagine a time that would be. The senator's arrest and Karen's part in it had obviously opened the old wounds—wounds Lorelei suspected hadn't ever started to heal.

"But he *was* her boyfriend," Alice said, showing that she had been listening. "Karen lied to protect him and herself after they killed my boy."

Lorelei took a seat. She watched her read the card not once, but twice before she ripped it up and threw it into the fireplace.

Alice reached into a container on the hearth, drew out a match, struck it and tossed it into the shredded paper. Flames licked through the card in a matter of seconds before dying out.

"What did you really come over here for?" Alice asked, turning to face her. "It wasn't to bring me a card from your mother."

She didn't correct her. She thought of Karen as her mother. "You're right. I had wanted to ask you about the night Billy died."

Alice looked surprised. "Why? The cops have Billy's killers."

"I was hoping you could help me with something. Karen was in the pines not too far from here when she heard a car go racing past."

The woman's eyes narrowed. "The senator."

Lorelei shook her head. "He didn't drive by until minutes later when Karen was walking back up the road toward her car. I was wondering if you saw the vehicle go by? If you might have recognized it."

"I had other things on my mind besides looking out the window."

She couldn't help her surprise or hide it. Alice was looking at her expectantly, waiting as if almost daring

Lorelei to call her a liar. "It's just that you saw my step-mother."

"I don't know what you're talking about." Alice rubbed the back of her neck as she turned to look at the ashes in the fireplace, her back to Lorelei.

"My mother had been headed for your house but when she saw you and when you saw her, she changed her mind."

Alice picked up the poker and began jabbing at the charred remains of the card lying in the bottom of the fireplace. "I just told you I didn't look out the window."

Lorelei felt a chill move slowly up her spine. One of them was lying and this time, she believed it wasn't Karen. A thought struck her as she watched the woman's agitation increasing with each jab of the poker. "She said you quickly disappeared from the window. Not long after that, she heard the car go racing by." The chill moved through her, sending a wave of goose bumps over her flesh.

In that instant, she knew. Worse, Alice knew that she'd put it together. Lorelei shot to her feet, but not quickly enough. Alice spun around, the poker in her hand, getting between Lorelei and the door.

Brandishing the poker, the woman began to make a wailing sound. Lorelei took a step back and then another as she shoved her hand into her pocket for her phone and looked for a way out.

The wailing stopped as abruptly as it had started. Alice got a distant look in her eyes that was more frightening than the wailing. "I saw her out there through the rain. She'd taken my husband, destroyed my family. I knew Sean had broken it off with her. I knew that was why she was out there in the rain. I hated her. I just wanted her dead. Then I saw her turn and head back up the road toward her house."

Lorelei felt her phone in her pocket, but she didn't dare draw it out as Alice advanced on her, brandishing the poker.

"I went into the garage and got into my car. I opened the garage door, hoping it wouldn't wake Billy. I planned to be gone for only a few minutes. I knew exactly what I had to do. She'd asked for it and now she was going to get what she had coming to her."

Lorelei bumped into the kitchen table. She glanced toward the back door, but knew she'd never reach it in time. Alice stopped a few feet away. Her eyes looked glazed over as if lost in the past, but Lorelei didn't dare move as she took in her surroundings—looking for something she could use for a weapon.

When Alice spoke, her voice had taken on a sleep-walking kind of sound effect. "It was raining so hard, the night was so dark. I saw the figure running down the road. I hit the gas going faster and faster. The rain was coming down so hard, the wipers were beating frantically and…" Alice stopped talking, her eyes wide with horror. She began to cry. "I didn't know. How could I know? It was so dark, the rain… I didn't know." The poker wavered in her hands. "What was he doing out there in the storm? I thought he was in bed. I thought…" She looked at Lorelei, her gaze focusing and then hardening as her survival instincts took over. "I thought I killed Karen. She took my husband and then my son.

"And now I'm going to take her daughter."

Lorelei's cell began to ring, startling them both.

James tried Lorelei's cell on his way over to Alice's. At lunch, he remembered their discussion. Something had been nagging at Lori too, he realized. The same thing that had been bothering him.

Karen had said that the senator ran over something. Not hit something. That had been the clue the whole time. When the call to Lori went to voice mail, he called Karen. She said she'd just gotten home from the hospital after being released.

"Have you see Lorelei?" he asked, trying not to sound as worried as he was.

"She was going over to Alice Sherman's house. I had a card I wanted her to deliver."

James swore. "Call 911 and tell them to get over there. I'm on my way. Lorelei could be in trouble."

He sped toward Alice Sherman's house. He remembered Karen saying that she'd heard a car go racing past while she was in the pines getting rid of the coyote. That was after seeing Alice—and after Alice saw her walking down the road in the rainstorm. He desperately wanted to be wrong.

Just the thought of what Alice might have done, what she'd been living with... If he was right, she'd killed her own son and then covered it up. What would she do if forced to face what she'd done? That was what terrified him. If Lorelei asked too many questions...

He was almost to Alice's house. He could see Lori's car parked in the driveway. He just prayed he was wrong, but all his instincts told him that she was in trouble. He just prayed he could reach her in time.

Chapter 25

Alice ran at her, swinging the poker, aiming for her head. Lorelei had only a second to react. She grabbed the back of the wooden chair next to her at the table and heaved it at the woman. The chair legs struck the poker, knocking it out of Alice's hands and forcing her back. The poker clattered to the kitchen floor and then skittered toward the refrigerator away from both of them.

Shoving the fallen chair aside, Alice came at her like something feral. "You and your boyfriend just couldn't leave it alone. Billy is buried. Why can't you let him rest in peace?"

"Alice, you don't want to do this," Lorelei cried as she managed to get on the other side of the kitchen table. "It was an accident. You didn't know it was Billy."

But the woman was shaking her head as she suddenly veered to the right. She thought Alice was going for the poker on the floor in front of the refrigerator deeper in the kitchen. She decided to make a run for it. She had just come around the end of the table and was headed for the living room and the front door beyond it at a run when she heard the gunshot. Sheetrock dust and particles fell over her, startling her as much as the loud report of the gun.

"Take another step and the next bullet will be for you," Alice cried.

Lorelei turned slowly to look back. The woman held the gun in both hands, her stance a warning that she was no novice at this.

"We're going to go for a ride," Alice said and motioned with the gun toward the door to the garage.

Lorelei had seen enough movies and read enough thrillers to know that you never wanted to be taken to a second location. That was where someone would eventually stumble over your shallow grave. Or their dog would dig up your remains. It was how you made the headlines.

But she also thought that as desperate as Alice appeared, maybe she should take her chances. From the look in the woman's eyes, she would shoot her here and now—just as she'd warned. Maybe during the drive Lorelei might see an opportunity to get the upper hand.

Out in the garage, Alice ordered her behind the wheel. As she climbed in, Alice got in the other side and ordered, "Start the car. I will shoot you if you do anything but what I tell you."

The key was in the ignition. As Alice hit the garage door opener, Lorelei snapped on her seatbelt, started the car and drove out of the garage.

"Go left."

She turned onto the street, her brain whirling. So far

Alice hadn't buckled up. Lorelei was debating what to do when she saw James's pickup racing up the other side of the street. She swerved in front of him hoping to get his attention.

"What do you think you're doing?" Alice demanded, shoving the gun into her face as they sped past James. Had he seen her? Had he seen Alice and the gun pointed at her head?

"You called him!" Alice screamed. "I told you not to do anything stupid, but you did." She had turned in the seat and was looking back.

In her rearview mirror, Lorelei saw James make a U-turn and come after them. He had seen her, but Lorelei realized it had been a mistake to draw his attention. James couldn't save her. Alice would kill her before that.

Worse, Alice had put down her window and was now shooting at James. In the rearview mirror, she saw the pickup's windshield shatter.

Lorelei swerved back and forth as she tried to keep the woman from getting a clean shot at James. He'd knocked out the rest of the windshield and was still coming up fast behind them. She swerved again and Alice banged her head on the window frame.

"You silly fool," the woman screeched, turning the gun on her. "I told you. Didn't I tell you? You've left me no choice."

Lorelei hit the gas again. She knew she had to act fast. Alice was too close to the edge. It would be just like her to pull the trigger and then turn the gun on herself. She slammed her foot down hard on the gas. The car jumped forward, the speed climbing quickly.

"What are you doing?" Alice cried. They were on the straightaway almost to the spot where Billy had died.

Alice was screaming as if she'd realized where they were. "No! No!" She took aim and Lorelei knew what she had to do.

Keeping the gas pedal to the floor, she suddenly swerved to the right. The car bounced down into the shallow ditch. Alice, still not belted in, was slammed against the door, throwing her off balance in the seat as she tried to aim the gun at her.

But Lorelei didn't let up on the gas as she pointed the vehicle toward the stand of pines in the empty lot across from where Billy died.

"I should have killed you at the house!" Alice screamed as she took aim at Lorelei's head.

The car bucking and bouncing across the field, she let go of the steering wheel with one hand to try to grab for the gun. The shot was deafening, but nothing like the sound when the car hit the trees.

James couldn't believe what he was seeing. He'd never felt more helpless as he watched Alice's car leave the road. It roared down into the ditch then headed for the pines. He hit his brakes, barely getting his pickup stopped before the car crashed into the pines.

He leaped out and ran toward the wrecked car. Steam rose from the engine. He could see that the front end of the car was badly damaged—mostly on the passenger side. Lori had been behind the wheel. As he raced to that side, Connie Matthews came out of her house.

"Call 911. Hurry!" he yelled at her as he reached the driver's side door and saw that the window had been shot out. He felt his heart drop. Had Alice shot her? Is that why the car had left the road, why it had crashed into the pines?

Inside he could see Lori. Her airbag had gone off and was now deflated over the steering wheel with Lori draped over it. There was blood dripping onto the deflated airbag.

He noticed it all in a split second as he tried unsuccessfully to open her door. Past her, he could see Alice. She'd gone through the windshield and now lay partly sprawled across the hood. She hadn't been wearing her seatbelt. Nor had her airbag activated.

James could hear sirens headed their way. He put all his weight into opening the door, surprised when he looked down and noticed his own blood. He'd taken a bullet in his arm but hadn't even realized it.

The door groaned and finally gave. In an instant he was at Lori's side. He felt for a pulse, terrified he wouldn't find one. There it was. Strong, just like her. He felt tears burn his eyes as relief rushed over him.

"Lori?" he said as he knelt beside the car. "It's going to be all right, baby. It's all going to be all right now. You're a fighter. Don't leave me. Please, don't leave me."

Soon he heard the EMTs coming, telling him to step aside. He rose and moved away, running a hand over his face as he watched them go to work. One of the EMTs noticed he was bleeding and pulled him aside.

More sirens and more rigs pulled up. Workers rushed past with a gurney for Lori. He turned away as he saw them checking Alice. It had been clear right away that she was gone.

He didn't remember going back to his pickup and following the ambulance to the hospital. Just as he didn't remember calling his brothers. Just as he didn't remember the doctors taking care of his gunshot wound or giving his statement to a law enforcement officer. All he'd thought about was Lori.

Hours later, he was walking the floor in the waiting room, when Willie arrived, followed soon after by Davey and Tommy. The surgeon had come in shortly after that to tell him that Lori had survived and was in stable condition.

"You should go on home and get some rest," the doctor told him. "You won't be able to see her until later today anyway."

He hadn't wanted to leave, but his brothers had taken him under their capable wings. When he'd awakened hours later in his bed, he'd gotten up to find them sitting in their dad's office. His arm ached. He'd looked down at the bandage, the horror of what had happened coming back to him.

"I just called the hospital," Willie said as James walked into the room. "I talked to a nurse I know. Lorelei's good. If she keeps improving as she has, you can see her later today."

James's knees felt weak with relief as he dropped into his father's office chair his brother Tommy had vacated for him.

"Now tell us what the hell has been going on here," Willie said. "Tommy went out to get us something to eat and came back with newspapers. You're a famous detective?"

"Not quite or Lori wouldn't be in the hospital right now," he said.

"Lori, is it?" Willie asked, grinning. "We saved you something to eat and made coffee. You fixed up the place pretty nice. But I think you'd better tell us what's been going on."

When he finished telling them between bites of breakfast washed down by coffee and a pain pill, his brothers were staring at him.

"You're good at this?" Davey said and laughed.

"Not quite," he said. "I almost got myself and Lori killed."

"You solved the case," Willie said.

James shook his head. "I almost got Lori killed."

"It's pretty clear to me what's going on here," Davey said. "James is in love."

His three brothers looked at him as if waiting for him to deny it. But he couldn't. It was true. He loved Lori. He repeated it out loud. "I love Lori."

His brothers all laughed, stealing glances at each other as if they couldn't believe it. James was the last one they'd have expected to get serious about anyone.

"Wait, what are you saying? You're giving up rodeo?" Tommy said.

Lori opened her eyes and blinked. She thought she was seeing double. No, not double, quadruple. Four men dressed in Western attire standing at the end of her bed. All tall, dark and handsome as sin. One in particular caught her eye. She smiled at James and closed her eyes again.

When she woke up again, James was sitting by her bed. "I dreamed that there were four of you," she said, her hoarse voice sounding strange to her. "Four handsome cowboys."

He rose quickly to take her hand. "My brothers."

"I haven't seen them in years. They're…gorgeous."

James grinned down at her. "You're still drugged up, aren't you."

She nodded, smiling. "I can't feel anything but this one spot on my head." She reached up to touch her bandage. "Alice shot me."

"Fortunately, the bullet only creased your scalp, but it did give you a concussion and bled a lot. The doctors had to stitch you back up, but you're going to be fine." He squeezed her hand. "You scared the hell out of me, Lori. I thought for sure..." She saw him swallow. "I wish you would have told me you were going to see Alice."

"You were busy packing."

It was true. He'd planned to leave. He'd put the case behind him even though something had been nagging at him. "You hadn't been gone long when I got a call from one of the auto body shops that had fixed her damaged car after the hit-and-run. When I saw the photo of the car..."

"The senator didn't kill Billy," she said.

"No, he did apparently run over part of his body though and he didn't stop. Not to mention what he did to your mother. So he's still toast."

She nodded and felt her eyelids grow heavy. "I thought you might have already left."

He shook his head. "I'm not going anywhere. You rest. I'll be here."

Lorelei closed her eyes, hoping the next time she woke he wouldn't be gone and that this would have been nothing more than a sweet dream.

Willie Colt stood in the small second-floor office about to propose a toast. James had dug out a new bottle of blackberry brandy and paper cups.

"To my brother James," Willie said. "The first of the brothers to take his last ride."

There was laughter followed by rude remarks, but as James looked around the room at his brothers he'd never been happier. It had been so long since they'd all gotten together. "I've missed you guys." He still couldn't believe that they'd dropped everything and come running when he'd needed them.

The four of them had always been close, but definitely lived their own lives. They'd see each other at a rodeo here and there, but often went months without talking to each other. But when the chips were down, they always came through. They would squabble among themselves as boys, but if anyone else got involved, they stood together.

"You're really doing this?" Davey said, throwing an arm around his brother. "You're going to marry this woman?"

James nodded, grinning. "I really am. Well, I'm going to ask her to marry me. She hasn't said yes yet. I thought I should wait until she's not doped up on the drugs they're giving her for the pain."

He'd been to the hospital every day. Lori was getting better. She was strong, just as he knew. She had bounced back fast and would be released from the hospital today.

"When are you going to ask her?" Davey wanted to know.

"I'm not sure. Soon, but I want to do it right, you know." He looked over at Tommy who'd wandered behind their father's desk and was now inspecting both James's and their father's private investigator licenses.

"You'll miss the rodeo," Davey predicted.

He couldn't deny it. "Not as much as I would miss Lori. I don't expect you to understand. I wouldn't have understood myself—until I fell in love."

Davey laughed. "I've been in love. It comes and goes. Mostly goes."

"I'm talking about a different kind of love other than buckle bunnies on the circuit," he said. "I can't even explain it. But you'll know it when it happens to you."

"So you're sticking with this PI gig?" Willie asked. "It sounds even more dangerous than bronc riding."

James chuckled. "Sometimes it definitely is. But I like it. I see why Dad liked it. Lori has her sandwich shop. Not sure what we'll do when we have kids."

"Wait a minute. *Kids?*" Davey said before the others could speak.

"She's not pregnant."

Willie chuckled. "You haven't even…"

"Nope. We literally haven't gotten that far." He grinned. "But I know she'll want kids. I'm just hoping she'll want to start trying right after the wedding."

Willie was shaking his head. "Boy, when you fall, you fall hard. You sure about this?"

"I've never been more sure of anything," he said. He couldn't describe what it had felt like when he'd leaped out of his pickup and run toward Alice Sherman's car. The driver's side window had been blown out. There was blood everywhere. His knees had threatened to buckle under him when he'd realized that Lori had been shot.

"I'm thinking about building out on the ranch," he said. "There's plenty of room for all of us. As long as there are no objections." There were none. He knew that right now his brothers couldn't see themselves settling down. Eventually they would and the land would be there for them all.

"You going to keep the name, Colt Investigations?"

Tommy asked. It was the first time he'd spoken since they'd come back from the hospital.

James studied him. "I guess, why?"

"Any chance you might want a partner?" his brother asked. Everyone turned to look at Tommy.

"Are you serious?" Davey sounded the most surprised. "You just turned thirty. You have a lot of rodeo ahead of you."

Tommy shook his head. "I've been thinking about quitting for some time now. I guess I was waiting for someone to go first." He smiled at James.

"You have even less experience at being a private investigator than James," Willie pointed out. "No offense."

"It can't be that hard," Davey joked. "If James can do it."

"Right, nothing to it. James and Lorelei both almost got killed," Willie said, sounding genuinely worried.

But Tommy didn't seem to be listening. "Look at this office. I could start by getting it up to speed technologically." He continued, clearly warming to the subject. "We could invest in computers, an office landline, equipment and even filing cabinets."

James realized that his brother was serious. "You've given this some thought."

Tommy nodded. "I didn't work with Dad as much as you did, but I could learn on the job while I helped do whatever you needed done. Didn't you say a lot of the jobs you've been offered were small things like Dad used to do, finding lost pets, tracking cheating husbands and wives, filming people with work comp injuries Jet Skiing, that sort of thing. What do you say?"

"I actually think he's serious," Davey said with a shake of his head.

Willie had been watching them. "It sounds like a pretty good deal. We all know we can't rodeo forever."

"I say great," James said, surprised and yet delighted. He stepped to his brother and started to shake his hand, but instead pulled him into a bear hug. "Let's do this."

Willie was smiling broadly. "You could change the name to Colt Brothers Investigations."

"I like that," James said and looked to his brother. Tommy smiled and nodded. He looked at Willie and Davey. "That way if the two of you ever—" Before he could get the words out, Davey stopped him.

"Not happening," Davey said. "I have big plans. None of them include getting myself shot at unless it's by an irate boyfriend as I'm going out a bedroom window."

They all laughed. Willie had been quiet. As James looked at him, his older brother winked at him. "Let's just see how it goes, but I know one thing. Dad would have loved this," he said, his voice breaking. He lifted his paper cup. "To Dad." They all drank and James refilled their cups.

"There is one more thing," James said. "One of the investigations I'll be working on involves Dad. I don't think his death was an accident." As he looked around the room at each of his brothers he saw that they'd all had their suspicions. "Maybe we can find out the truth."

"I'll drink to that," Davey said, and the rest raised their paper cups.

Chapter 26

Lori looked forward to James's visits each day at the hospital. And each day she'd waited for him to tell her he was leaving. She knew she was keeping him in town and hated that he felt he had to stay because of her.

I'm fine, she'd told him yesterday when he'd come by. *I know you're anxious to get back on the rodeo circuit. Please don't stay on my account.*

I'm not going anywhere, he'd said. *I just spoke to the doctor. Told me that you're going to be released tomorrow. Which is good because I have a surprise for you.*

A surprise?

Yes, a surprise and no I'm not giving you any clues.

She'd been allowed to dress but had to wait for a wheelchair to take her down. She'd begun to worry that James wouldn't show up. Maybe that was the surprise, she'd been thinking when he walked in. She felt a wave of relief wash over her and felt herself smiling at just the sight of him.

He grinned. "Ready to blow this place?"

She nodded, a lump in her throat. He'd stayed for her. He had a surprise for her. She tried not to, but her heart filled like a helium balloon even as she warned herself that this was temporary. James never stayed anywhere long, and he'd been here way past time. Those boots of his would be itching to make tracks.

He wheeled her down to his pickup and helped her into the passenger seat. "I want to show you something," he said as he started the engine. "You feel okay, comfortable, need anything?"

She laughed. "I'm fine," she said as she buckled up her seat belt and settled in, wondering where he was taking her. "Still no clue as to this surprise of yours?"

James shook his head, still grinning. The radio was on to a Western station. Lorelei felt herself relax. She breathed in the warm summer air coming in through the open window. She was alive. Suddenly the world seemed bigger and brighter, more beautiful than she remembered—even the small town of Lonesome.

When she voiced her euphoric feeling out loud, James laughed and reached over to take her hand.

He gave it a squeeze, his gaze softening. "It sure seems brighter to me too, being here with you."

Lorelei felt her heart fill even more and float up. She felt giddy and as hard as she tried to contain her excitement, she couldn't as he headed out of town. She glanced over at him, again wondering where he was taking her.

He turned off onto a dirt road back into the pines and kept driving until the road ended on the side of a mountain overlooking the river. He stopped, cut the engine and turned toward her.

She wasn't sure what surprised her more, that he'd brought her here or that he seemed nervous.

"Do you like it?" he asked, his voice tight with emotion. She must have looked perplexed because he quickly added, "The view. I'm thinking about building a house on this spot. What do you think?"

She looked out at the amazing view. "It's beautiful." He was thinking about building a house here? This was the surprise? "How long have you been thinking about building here?"

"For a while now," he said. "Do you feel up to getting out? There is a spot close by I wanted to show you."

James had never been so nervous in his entire life. He'd climbed on the back of rank horses without breaking a sweat. He'd even ridden a few bulls he shouldn't have in his younger days. He'd been stomped and almost gored and still, he'd never hesitated to get back on.

But right now, as they walked through the wildflowers and tall summer grass toward his favorite spot, he felt as if he couldn't breathe.

He couldn't help being nervous. He'd planned out his life and Lori's and he wasn't even sure she wanted to marry him. They'd been through a lot in a short time. They'd gotten close. But they'd had only one date. One kiss.

It had been one humdinger of a kiss though, he thought with a grin.

As he walked, he reached into his pocket and felt the small velvet box. The engagement ring was an emerald,

Lori's birthstone. The moment he'd seen it, he'd known it was perfect for her. He just hoped she liked it.

He took his hand out of his pocket, leaving the ring in its box. He had to do this right, he thought as he glanced over at her. Her bandages had been removed all except for one. The headaches were only occasional and minor. The doctor had said that she was good to go.

"This isn't too much for you, is it?" James asked, his voice sounding tight.

Lori laughed. "I'm fine, James. Are you sure you're all right though?"

His laugh sounded even more nervous than he felt. He was glad when they reached the outcropping of rock. "This is my favorite spot."

"I can see why," she said, smiling up at him. "It's beautiful."

He reached down and picked a couple of wildflowers, held them in his fingers for a moment before he offered them to her. As she took them, he watched her expression soften. Her brown eyes seemed to turn golden in the summer sun. She was so beautiful that she took his breath away.

"Lori." He swallowed.

"James?" she asked, suspicion and concern in her voice.

"I'm in love with you." He spit out the words so quickly that he had to repeat them. "I'm madly in love with you." He waited for her reaction.

Lorelei couldn't help being shocked. He was looking at her as if he couldn't believe she really hadn't seen this coming.

"I brought you here because this is where I want to build our house. I know this is fast," he added quickly.

"And maybe out of the blue," she said, unable not to smile. "We've never even been on a real date."

"You didn't think dinner at the steak house was a real date? How about when we danced?"

She nodded and felt her cheeks warm. "That did feel like a date."

He grinned as if not as nervous as he'd been before. "How about when we kissed?"

She nodded as she felt color rising to her cheeks.

He cocked his head as he looked at her. "We packed a lot into a few weeks time, you and me. We solved a mystery together and almost got killed."

Chuckling, she said, "I suppose you could say we got to know each other."

His grin broadened. "I remember being in the closet with you."

She flushed and had to look away. "If that's your idea of courtship—"

"My idea of courtship is to spend every day loving you for the rest of my life."

"James, I know you feel responsible for what happened to the two of us and that's why you're saying this. But what about the rodeo?" she asked.

"I'm not asking you out of guilt, although I do feel responsible. I jumped into my father's case not realizing how many lives I was risking—especially yours. But over this time, you've changed me."

She couldn't help her skeptical look.

He laughed. "Changed me for the better. You've made me see what it is I want out of life. I want to be with you. When I almost lost you—"

"You didn't lose me. Once you realize that I'm fine, you can go back to the rodeo—"

"I'm not leaving. I figured I had maybe another year or two max. It was time, Lori. I love rodeoing, but I love you more."

Lorelei watched him drop to one knee. Reaching into his pocket, he came out with a small velvet box. "James?" She felt goose bumps ripple across her skin.

"Lorelei Wilkins? Will you marry me and make me the proudest man in the county?" he asked, his voice breaking.

"James."

"I want to go on dates with you, dance, kiss and make love. But I want to do it right. I want to do all of it with my wife. Say yes. You know you love me."

She laughed. "I do love you, Jimmy D."

He opened the small velvet box. "I saw this ring and it reminded me of you. One of a kind."

"My birthstone," she said. "Oh, James, it's beautiful." She met his gaze as tears filled her eyes. "Yes. Yes, I want to do all those things with you. As your wife."

He slipped the ring on her finger and rose to take her in his arms. The kiss held the promise of many days living on this mountainside overlooking the river. She could hear the laughter of their children, smell the sweet scents of more summers to come and feel James's arms around her always, sheltering her, loving her.

Chapter 27

Lorelei wanted to pinch herself as she stared into the full-length mirror at the woman standing there.

"You look beautiful," her stepmother said as she came up beside her. They smiled at each other in the mirror. "Such a beautiful bride."

"I'm doing the right thing," she said. "Aren't I? I know it's sudden. James and I hardly know each other."

"Hush," Karen said as she turned to her. "I've never seen anyone more in love than the two of you. You know James. And he knows you. I could see this coming for years. He was always trying to get your attention back in high school. You used to blush at just the sight of him."

"I still do," Lorelei confessed with a laugh. "It's the way he looks at me."

Her stepmother laughed. "I've seen it. It's the way

every woman wants to be looked at. The way every woman wants to feel. You're very lucky."

"He makes me happy."

"I can see that." Karen looked at the time. "Ready?"

Lorelei took one last look at the woman in the mirror. She was glowing, radiating happiness and excitement. Life with James would never be dull. Anita had offered to buy the sandwich shop. At first Lorelei had been surprised that her friend would think she wanted to sell it.

I just assumed you'd be working with James in the PI business until the babies start coming, Anita had said with a wink.

She'd laughed at the thought, but only for a moment. *James mentioned the same thing. He says he can't do it without me.*

When she'd mentioned selling the sandwich shop to James, he'd been excited to hear that she was going to do it. *We'll change the name of the business to Colt Investigations.*

No, Lorelei had said. *I think it should be Colt Brothers Investigations. I won't be working there. I'll be too busy. We have a wedding to plan, a house to build and decorate to get ready for the babies we're going to make.*

I do like the sound of that last part, he'd said with a laugh. *Let's get on that right after the wedding.* And he'd kissed her.

"Shall we do this?" her stepmother asked, bringing Lorelei out of her reverie.

Lorelei nodded. She couldn't wait.

The church was full to overflowing. Her three bridesmaids were ready. So were the three Colt brothers, but all she saw was James standing at the end of the aisle, waiting for her. The look in his eyes sent heat rocketing through her. Last night he'd told her about this vision he'd had of a little girl of about two on a horse.

I know she's ours, he'd said. *Our little girl.*

She'd had the same dream. *I've seen her. She has your blue eyes.*

Lorelei took a step toward James and their future. She wanted to run to him, to throw her arms around him, to tell him again and again how much she loved him, how much she wanted him.

But instead, she took another slow step and then another. There was no reason to run. They had the rest of their lives together.

* * * * *

CROSSFIRE

Many thanks to Twyla Geraci,
who trained to be a SWAT paramedic.
Also, Sergeant Jason Becker with the local SWAT team.
This book is dedicated to you
and the other men and women who risk their lives
every day to keep us safe.

Chapter 1

Lee Harper was no longer sure he could trust himself. Sometimes he would be in the living room and call to Francine to come see a show on TV. When she didn't respond, he would go looking for her.

And only then would he remember that his wife was dead.

She'd been killed seven weeks ago at the convenience store where she worked part-time. An aftershock from the earthquake had caused the store to collapse. Help hadn't arrived until it was too late to save her.

Knowing all of that, Lee Harper still found himself turning to speak to her and was always shocked and a little disoriented to find her gone. Not that unusual after forty-six years of marriage. No children. Francine had conceived four times, all miscarriages, all heartbreaking. They had stopped trying, stopped talking about children. It was better that way.

He'd been an English professor until last year, when he retired. He could recite complete Shakespeare plays from memory, knew hundreds of poems, and in all those years had never forgotten even one of his students' names.

Until lately.

"It's just grief," friends and colleagues had said. They'd been supportive at first. But as the weeks went by, they suggested he see a doctor.

No one understood that his mind had started to go when Francine was killed.

Now sometimes he left the stove on. Sometimes he didn't know where he was or how he'd gotten there. His grief felt like a tumor inside him, eating him alive, destroying a mind that had once been "sharp as a tack."

For a while the question—when he was thinking straight—had just been what to do. How could he right the terrible wrong of Francine's death? That question had kept him awake for days and left him feeling impotent. There was no way to fix things. No way.

Then he'd met Kenny Reese. And for the first time in weeks, he'd no longer felt confused. Kenny had a plan.

Lee Harper stared down at the crude drawing he'd made of city hall. It was a historic building, U-shaped, one wide marble stairway up the middle, one elevator at the back. For the past week he had staked out the place and knew exactly when everyone arrived each morning and who stopped for lattes and doughnuts, as well as the security system and the exits.

But as he took off his watch and set it next to the blasting cap and explosives, he felt a tremor of doubt. Was this what Francine would have wanted? He no longer knew.

It was the *only* thing he could think to do, and he had to do something. He couldn't explain this urgency in him, a feeling that if he didn't act now, he might not be able to later.

Anyway, the plan was already in place. In a matter of hours it wouldn't be just one old man who mourned Francine Harper's death. When Lee finished, the entire city of Courage Bay, California, would finally feel her loss.

9:50 p.m.

Anna Carson lifted the last item from the suitcase. A worn extra-large white T-shirt, the lettering faded almost beyond recognition: Property of Courage Bay Police Department.

Instinctively she brought the soft cloth to her face and sniffed, as if Flint's scent would still be there after five years. Funny, but for a moment, she thought it was. A masculine, clean scent that had always made her heart pound.

She couldn't believe she'd been dragging his old T-shirt around with her all these years. At first, after the breakup, she'd slept in the shirt. It was huge on her, falling past her knees, wide enough for two of her. Just the size of it reminded her of how she'd felt in Flint's arms. Totally wrapped up.

Wishful thinking. And that wasn't like her.

Well, she didn't need the shirt anymore, or the memories, she thought as she glanced out the open patio doors of her new apartment, breathing in the sight and smell of the Pacific. The sea was glassy, golden in the last of the day's light. From the third-story deck, she could hear the waves breaking on the sandy beach. It was one of the reasons she'd taken this apartment. Here she had the view, the sounds and smells of the only place that had ever felt like home.

Too bad everyone in her family had moved away after her parents divorced. Her dad at least was only upstate, a few hours away by plane, in Sacramento. Her mother was in Alabama with her family. Her sister Emily and husband Lance were in Seattle.

It was as though everyone had scattered after Anna left. As if the family had blown apart. Not that it hadn't been ready to blow before Anna had announced that her engagement to Flint was off.

"You didn't really throw the ring at him!" Her sister Emily had given her the eye roll that meant she thought Anna had done something irrational. Her younger sister had been giving her the eye roll for as long as Anna could remember.

"The ring is yours to keep," her mother had said, always the mercenary.

Anna had looked at the two of them as if they'd lost their minds. "I never want to see that ring again. Ever."

Her mother and Emily had exchanged a she-is-never-going-to-get-it look. To them, there was no higher calling than a wedding ring on a woman's finger.

Anna had figured the timing was as good as any to tell them the rest of her news. "I'm going to Washington, D.C., to become a SWAT team paramedic." She was rewarded with gasps from both mother and sister. She'd looked to her dad, expecting his support.

Anna frowned now at the memory. She'd thought he would be excited about her decision.

Instead he'd looked worried and upset. "If you're certain that's what you want to do," he'd said. "But make sure you're doing this for the right reasons, Anna." Not exactly what she'd been expecting.

"Isn't it…dangerous?" Emily had asked.

"That's what she likes about it," her mother had said. "She wants to turn my hair completely gray." Everything was always about their mother.

Anna shrugged off the past and the memories that had tried to weigh her down the last five years. She wasn't responsible for her parents' divorce—no matter what her sister said.

"You becoming a SWAT whatever was the straw that broke the camel's back," Emily had accused her at the time.

"Thank you, Emily, I really needed that," Anna had replied. "I'm sure it was me and not the fact that our parents have never gotten along, were never compatible in any way, and now, finally free of children, can happily go their separate ways."

"They used to be in love," Emily had said indignantly. "Before…before everything that happened."

Anna turned now to survey her apartment, not surprised that coming back to Courage Bay would stir up the ghosts of her past. The apartment, though, was perfect—small, but the view of the ocean made up for space. She took another deep breath of the night air and let it out slowly. It did feel good to be back.

A tremor of excitement rippled through her. She hugged herself, wrapping her arms around Flint's T-shirt, still in her hands. The excitement was quickly replaced with anxiety. Flint. Eventually she would run into him. He must be a detective by now and on the fast track for the chief of police job. Hadn't that always been his dream?

She wondered how he'd take the news that she was back in town. Unfortunately she didn't have to guess how he would react to her new job. Not that it mattered to her one way or the other. Not anymore.

It probably wouldn't matter to him, either, she realized. Not after five years. Flint was a formidable ghost, one she'd spent years trying to exorcize from her thoughts. She doubted it had taken that long for him to forget her.

Walking to the open deck door, she breathed in the sea air, trying to clear her thoughts. There was nothing more to do tonight. She was moved in and would start work in the morning. She had a 7:30 a.m. meeting with Chief of Police Max Zirinsky.

She doubted she'd be able to sleep a wink, she was so excited. She had the job she'd set out to get. A great apartment. And she was back in Courage Bay. Nothing could spoil it. Not even the thought of Flint Mauro.

She glanced back over her shoulder at the phone book, which she'd left open on the bed. Okay, she hadn't been able to help herself. She'd looked up his number. Just to see if he was even still in town. He was, although he had a different number from the one they'd had when they'd lived together. It seemed he'd moved to the harbor area. She didn't recognize the address, but then, Courage Bay had grown since she'd left.

Anna had made a point of not keeping up with local news during those years she'd been gone. Since her family had moved away, there had been no reason to come back to Courage Bay until this job offer.

For a while after she'd left, she'd stayed in touch with friends in town, but quickly realized she didn't want to know what Flint was doing, didn't want to hear about his latest girlfriend or any stories about his latest case.

For all she knew, Flint could be married by now with a couple of kids.

The pang of regret surprised her. She thought she'd long ago forgotten those silly talks they used to have lying in bed, debating what their babies would look like. They had both wanted a large family. They'd even come up with some names. What was the one that had made them both laugh so hard?

She shook herself out of that thought pattern and closed the deck doors. She had put Flint and Courage Bay behind her. Until Max had called with the job offer and she'd realized there was nothing she wanted more than to come back home. Courage Bay had been her home all but five of her twenty-nine years.

Now she wondered why she hadn't asked Max about Flint when he'd offered her the job. Max had known them both well. He'd known how devastated she'd been when she'd had to break off the engagement and leave.

She guessed the reason she hadn't asked Max was that she didn't want him thinking she was still hung up on Flint Mauro. Because she wasn't. Flint had nothing to do with her life anymore. Nor she with his.

As she turned, she realized she still had his T-shirt in her hands. She walked over to her new wastebasket and dropped the shirt into it. Tomorrow she started her new life in Courage Bay. No regrets. No looking back. She wasn't the same young woman who'd left here, and she was bound and determined to prove it.

10:15 p.m.

Flint Mauro stood on the stern of the boat he called home and stared out at the Pacific. A cool breeze stirred his thick black hair, lifting it gently from his forehead. He frowned as he took in the familiar horizon.

Do Whatever It Takes. That was his motto, wasn't it? Do Whatever It Takes. And that's what he did every day. Focusing on his job, his boat, his workouts. Not thinking about the past. The past was too painful. And yet it was there. A splinter just under his skin. On nights like tonight he could feel it pricking him, making him itch for something he'd once had—and had lost.

The flag on the bow flapped restlessly in the breeze coming off the sea. He closed his eyes, concentrating on the familiar scents of the ocean and the night. He'd bought the boat and moved aboard five years ago, the only place that he found any peace.

And yet sometimes he thought he smelled her perfume on the sea breeze. On those nights, he would swear that he heard her soft chuckle next to his ear, felt her pass by so close that her skin brushed against his, making him ache with a need that only she could fill. Unfortunately tonight was one of those nights.

Why was he thinking about Anna now? After all this time? He'd jumped right back into dating after she'd broken off their engagement.

"Get back on the horse before you forget how to ride," his friends had advised.

So he'd dated. A lot. But none of the women, no matter how pretty or sweet or capable, was Anna Carson.

"You can't replace cream with water," his boss, Police Chief Max Zirinsky, had said.

"If you're suggesting I was the one who threw out the cream, the cream being Anna, you're wrong. She's the one who broke up with me," Flint had told him. "And don't give me that look. It wasn't my fault."

Max had just shaken his head. "Someday you'll figure it out. I hope."

Max. Flint had a meeting with him first thing in the morning. He knew he wouldn't be able to sleep—not knowing what was waiting for him tomorrow morning at the office. There'd been a rumor going around at work that the chief was going to be making some changes. And just before Flint had left work today, Max had called him into his office.

He and Max had always been close. Not that they didn't disagree at times. Nor did Flint ever forget who was boss.

But when he'd followed Max into his office, Flint had been surprised that the chief had gone behind his desk and immediately begun to busy himself with some papers.

Max didn't look up. Nor did his voice convey any warmth, as if he'd been expecting an argument out of Flint.

"I'd like you at a meeting tomorrow morning. Seven a.m." Max continued sorting the paperwork on his desk.

"Seven a.m.?" Flint asked in surprise.

"Is that a problem?" Max finally looked up.

"No," Flint said quickly, wondering what he'd done that had put Max on edge. "Can't you tell me what this is about?"

"Seven a.m.," Max repeated. "We'll discuss it then."

Flint had wisely left without another word. He knew

Max well enough not to argue. At least not all the time. Flint had learned to pick his battles.

Was he looking at a battle in the morning? He had a bad feeling he was. He stared out at the sea, surprised again that his thoughts drifted back to Anna. What was it about tonight? Whatever it was, he'd play hell getting a decent sleep this night.

10:30 p.m.

Lorna Sinke opened a can of cat food and set it on the counter. As soon as she did, the cat jumped up and began eating with enthusiasm. A cat eating on the kitchen counter. Her mother must be rolling over in her grave, Lorna thought with a smile. There'd never been pets in this house. Not while Lorna's parents had been alive, and they'd both lived to their eighties.

"Pets are filthy and messy," her mother used to say. "Who needs them?"

Lorna needed them. She'd spent her whole life in this house with its spotless, lifeless furnishings. It had taken some time after her parents had died, but she'd finally gotten rid of the smell of pine cleaner.

She looked around the kitchen, pleased. The first thing she'd done was strip the curtains from all the windows and discard them. Then she'd painted over the flowered wallpaper. The furniture had had to go, as well. Her father's recliner. Her mother's rocker. She hadn't been able to bear looking at them, thinking she could see her parents' impressions in them, if not their ghosts come back to haunt her.

Lorna opened several more cans of cat food for the

other cats and set them on the floor. How odd that her
neighbors and some old family friends would think she
was lonely in this big old house without her parents.

All those years spent taking care of the two of them.
When other women were getting married, having children, making homes for themselves, Lorna Sinke had
been nursing her aging parents. The *good* daughter.

And to think that her sister was shocked that their parents had left Lorna the house. Hadn't she earned it? Her
younger sister had gotten out as quickly as she could,
purposely getting pregnant to escape, Lorna had always
suspected.

Well, it was her house now, she thought as she made
herself some toast, standing at the kitchen window to
butter it and smear a thick layer of jam on it. Her mother
would have thought so much jam wasteful. Lorna could
feel her mother's disapproval as she ate the toast and
stared out into the darkness. She realized that she'd been
waiting all those years for her life to begin. Too bad it
had taken the deaths of her parents. Not that Lorna hadn't
felt a huge weight lifted from her shoulders when they
were finally gone.

She shuddered, remembering finding the two of them
at the foot of the basement stairs. Her mother must have
gone down to the basement for something, fallen and
cried out. It would be just like her father to go down
there instead of calling 911.

Two nasty falls. Both fatal. It hadn't surprised Lorna,
given her father's condition. Couldn't remember anything, even what had happened just moments before.
And her mother, always nagging him to do one thing
or another.

Lorna had warned them both about those basement steps, but neither of them had ever listened to anything *she* had had to say.

She tried not to think about it. Her parents were both in a better place. She liked to imagine her father floating on a cloud, at peace at last. Her mother was no doubt making hell more hellish.

Getting out her mother's cookbook, Lorna went to work making her famous sugar cookies. Her mother and father had loved them. She'd made the cookies the night before their fatal falls, putting in her secret ingredient, just like she did tonight.

When the cookies were finished baking, she put them in an airtight container and set them by the front door so she wouldn't forget to take them to work, then she checked her watch.

Time to get to bed. As aide to the city council for years, she had the run of city hall and she loved it. Hers was the real power in Courage Bay. Without her, the city would come to a screeching halt.

She turned out the kitchen light. Tomorrow she could wear her new blue dress, the one the saleslady said brought out the blue in her eyes. She wondered if her favorite councilman would notice.

There was just one fly in the ointment, as her mother used to say. Councilwoman Gwendolyn Clark.

Lorna glanced at the container of cookies by the door. But she planned to take care of that problem tomorrow. Her life was finally going the way it always should have gone, and she wasn't about to let anything—or anybody—mess it up.

10:37 p.m.

Kenny couldn't sit still. He paced the trailer feeling as if his skin itched from the inside out. There was only one way to scratch it, but the pills were all gone.

He tried to concentrate on tomorrow. Lottery day, and he was going to be the big winner. All he had to do was to hold it together until then. He knew he'd never be able to sleep tonight. He was too excited at the prospect of being rich.

He picked up the photograph of his sister as he passed the corner table, looking into her face. "It's all going to work out, Patty. Thanks to you."

It was pretty amusing when he thought about it. Even from her grave, his big sis was looking out for him. And to think just days ago he didn't know what he was going to do. He didn't have money to pay his rent, the creditors had been calling every day—that was, until the phone company had disconnected the phone—and there was no one to turn to for help with Patty gone. It had looked as if he'd be out in the street.

And then his luck had changed when he met Lee Harper at that bar near city hall. What a wack job that guy was. Talk about hanging from a slim thread, and to think the guy used to be some well-known professor. Kenny had listened to the guy go on and on about the meeting he'd been to at city hall and how he blamed the city for his wife's death, until finally Kenny had said, "Why don't you do something about it besides cry in your club soda?"

"Like what?"

"Like make the bastards pay for what they did." Pay

had been the word that had echoed in his own head. Yeah, *pay*.

"How?"

Kenny gave it a little thought. Hell, people did it all the time on TV. "You could take over city hall, make them sit up and take notice."

Lee perked right up after that.

"But they won't unless you're serious," Kenny pointed out.

"Serious how?"

"Have a weapon or two to hold off the cops until your demands are met," Kenny said, the idea growing on him. Demands. How much money would the city come up with if a wacko had city hall? Better yet, if the wacko had a hostage? A hundred thousand bucks? More?

Lee was crying in his club soda again. "Forcibly take city hall for what purpose besides getting arrested? Anyway, nothing can bring Francine back."

Kenny thought fast. "You said you wanted to make a difference? So you're just going to give up?"

"What choice do I have? I've been to the city council meetings. I'm just one small voice in a city that has too many other problems to care about mine."

"Exactly," Kenny said. "You need to make yourself heard. If you took city hall hostage, you could demand that something be done. Hell, you would be on television. Everyone would know what happened to your wife. The city would have to do something."

"A bit drastic—"

"Seems to me drastic measures are needed," Kenny said, trying to come up with something to appease the old fart. "How else can you be sure that the city won't let something like this happen again? You want your wife's life to count for something, right? Think of the lives you might save."

Lee was looking at him through his wire-rimmed glasses, as if actually considering what Kenny was saying. The guy tended to zone in and out, but Kenny thought he finally had the old fool's attention.

"We both lost someone we loved because of this city, man," Kenny said, realizing when it came down to it, he'd been wronged, too. "We can't just sit back and do nothing." This might actually work. "You want to get the city to listen to you? Stick with me. We'll get their attention all right, man."

"You would support my efforts?" Lee sounded so surprised and touched that Kenny almost laughed.

"Damn straight. You and I are going to teach this city a lesson that won't soon be forgotten." He patted the old man's shoulder. "So do you think you can get yourself some firepower?"

Lee looked vague again, then nodded. "I suppose there is no other way?"

Kenny had shaken his head. "Sometimes you got to take a stand," he'd said, already seeing how this was going to play out. The city would pay to keep the hostages alive. He'd demand five hundred thousand, a passport and a plane out of the country to some place where he couldn't be extradited, just like the guys did on TV.

But it would only be a ticket for one. The old man wouldn't be coming along. Kenny would make sure of that.

Chapter 2

"Is the chief in yet?" Flint Mauro asked as he walked through the employee entrance to the police station.

The desk sergeant looked up and nodded. "Said to tell you to come straight to his office. He's waiting for you."

Flint didn't like the sound of that as he started down the hallway toward the watch commander's office. He was early, but Max was already waiting for him? What the hell was that about? What the hell was any of this about?

Max's door was closed. He tapped lightly.

"Come in," said a gruff, impatient voice.

Flint stepped in, ready to take a good chewing out. He just wished he knew what for. "Chief," he said.

Max motioned him into a chair without even looking up. Flint sat down uneasily and watched as his commander raked a hand through a head of thick, dark hair, then finally leaned back in his chair and looked at him, as if bracing himself for the worst.

At forty-five, the six-foot-two chief of police was as solid as a brick outhouse. He could be tough as nails, and yet normally, humor and compassion shone in his green eyes. Not this morning though.

Flint felt the full weight of his gaze. He waited, growing more worried by the moment. Something had happened, that much was clear. And it wasn't something Flint was going to like.

"Flint, you and I have discussed at length my idea to put a paramedic on the SWAT team," Max said after a moment.

Flint looked at him in surprise. This was what Max wanted to talk about? He relaxed a little. "And you know how I feel about it."

Max sighed. "As you know, we had a court reporter, Lorraine Nelson, who suffered a heart attack during that shooting incident back in September. She lived, but suffered extensive damage to her heart and was forced to retire because of it. If the fire department's paramedics could have gotten to her quicker, maybe she would have had a full recovery. George Yube died after the sniper shot him. Same story there. Had he gotten help faster, he might be alive today." Max took a breath and let it out with a sigh. "The way it is now, we can't get the victims any help until the area is secured. That's not acceptable."

"It's not acceptable to send a paramedic into a dangerous situation until it is secured," Flint said. "Otherwise you're risking the paramedic's life or simply offering the criminals another hostage. The bottom line is, we end up having another person to try to protect, as well as the victims, when our main priority is to stop the bad guy before he hurts anyone else."

"I've taken all that into consideration," Max said.

"Have you forgotten that the last time we let a paramedic in with the team, the paramedic almost got killed?"

"That paramedic wasn't SWAT trained."

Flint shook his head in frustration and shifted in his chair. "Why are we discussing this again? You already know my feelings on this subject and I know yours. How long are we going to debate this?"

Max tented his fingers under his chin, his gaze suddenly steely. "I didn't ask you here to try to convince you. Or to ask for your approval."

Flint felt his heart drop. "I see. Well, if your mind is made up, then why get me in here so damned early?" He swore under his breath as he rose to his feet. "You're obviously moving ahead with this no matter how I feel."

"Sit down, Flint."

Flint dropped back into the chair with a sigh.

"I agree with all your arguments," Max said quietly. "It is a risk, but one that I feel has to be taken for the victim's sake."

There was no talking Max out of this. Flint could see that now. "We have a couple of SWAT members with paramedic training who might be interested in the position, I suppose."

Max shook his head. "I've found a paramedic with SWAT training and experience in situations we've been forced to deal with and some we haven't yet."

"Really?" Flint couldn't hide his surprise. "So when

does he start?" He knew his men weren't going to like this any more than he did. This guy better be flat amazing.

There was a knock at the door. Max glanced at his watch. "The new SWAT team paramedic is here now, early, just like you were," Max said with a wry smile as he got to his feet to answer the knock personally.

Flint turned in his chair as Max opened the door. He felt as if a Magnum .45 had been emptied into his chest when he saw the tall, slim figure framed in the doorway. He staggered to his feet, his brain telling him it was a mistake. Dear God, this couldn't be the SWAT team paramedic.

7:15 a.m.

Lorna Sinke loved to get to city hall before anyone else. She lived in the older section of town, close enough to city hall that she walked to work. She liked the fresh air, the exercise and the quiet. There were few people on the streets and traffic was light this time of the morning.

She was a creature of habit, leaving her house every weekday morning at the same time. This morning was no different. Only today, she carried more than her usual lunch and thermos of coffee. Today, she had the cookies in the airtight container in her bag. They made a thumping sound as she walked, reminding her of what she planned to do before the day was over.

City hall came into view, the white-stone, three-story building shimmering in the bright blue morning. Lorna always experienced a sense of pride when she saw it. She loved the inside even more, with its ornate moldings and high ceilings.

Some people thought the old city hall building was

cold and a waste of space, too much like a tomb, but Lorna loved it. A few years ago there was talk of tearing city hall down and building something modern. Over her dead body, Lorna had declared. After all the years she'd worked here, she felt as if it were her building. Fortunately the historical society had saved it. Lorna had led the charge—and made a few enemies along the way, including Councilwoman Gwendolyn Clark.

But that was just the tip of the iceberg when it came to her problems with the councilwoman. Gwendolyn Clark was on a mission to get Lorna fired, saying it was time that Lorna retired and the council got some "new blood" in the position. Over Lorna's dead body.

Crossing Washington Avenue, she walked down Robbin Street around to the employee entrance at the rear of city hall. Kitty-corner across the intersection of Bright and 12th streets, she caught a glimpse of the police department. She'd been taken there for questioning after her parents' deaths. The building was new and impersonal, nothing like city hall. She was glad the city had put up a tall oleander hedge along the back of city hall that hid the newer buildings. Especially the police station. The sight of it only brought back bad memories and Lorna Sinke wasn't one to dwell in the past.

As she walked through a narrow entrance in the oleander hedge, she stopped to pick up a candy wrapper someone had irresponsibly dropped. Muttering to herself, she stuffed the candy wrapper into her bag and pulled out the key she kept on her kitten key ring.

Her mind was on the day ahead and the outcome. She felt a ripple of excitement. If this day ended the way she'd planned it, she would be free of Gwendolyn Clark.

As Lorna inserted the key into the lock, she sensed

someone approaching from behind but didn't bother to turn around. Blast the woman to hell. Gwendolyn Clark had taken it upon herself to come in at the same time as Lorna every morning for the past two weeks. The councilwoman was spying on her. Gwendolyn said she was working on a special project. Lorna knew she *was* that special project. The woman was trying to dig up some dirt, something she could use to get rid of Lorna.

It was all she could do not to turn around and hit the woman with the heavy bag. Of course she wouldn't do that. She did her best not to let Gwendolyn see how she felt about her. That alone had become a full-time job and one of the reasons Lorna had decided today she'd do something about the councilwoman.

Lorna turned the key in the lock, planning to say hello to Gwendolyn, pretending, as she had been for weeks, that she didn't suspect what the woman was up to. Today she would be especially nice to her. It would make it easier later this afternoon when Lorna offered her one of her special cookies. If there was one thing Gwendolyn Clark couldn't pass up, it was sweets.

As the door swung open, Lorna plastered a smile on her face and turned, expecting to see Gwendolyn Clark's round, pinched face and disapproving gaze.

To Lorna's surprise, it wasn't Gwendolyn behind her but an elderly police officer, gray-haired, slim, wearing wire-rimmed glasses. He looked familiar. He was hunched over, as if in pain.

"Can you help me?" he said, his voice barely audible.

"Are you sick? Injured?" She fished for her cell phone and had just found it when a thirty-something man appeared from the edge of the oleander hedge along the street. Like the first, he, too, was dressed in a police uniform. But his hair was long and stringy, he'd done a poor job of shaving that morning, and part of his uniform shirt wasn't tucked in. Her gaze caught on his shoes. He wore a pair of worn-out sneakers.

Lorna felt her first real sense of fear. This man, she thought as he ran toward her, was not a policeman. Before she could react, the first man straightened a little, reached out and grabbed her wrist.

She swung her bag with her lunch, the pint-size thermos and the container of cookies in it, catching the older of the two on the side of his head. He yelped and stumbled back, bumping into the disheveled-looking man. Lorna had stepped backward into the building with the swing of her bag. Now she fought to close the door, but the younger man was faster and stronger.

He drove the door back. She turned and ran deeper into the building, her cell phone still in her hand, her fingers punching out 91—

The younger man was on her before she could get out the last number.

7:18 a.m.

Anna felt all the breath knocked out of her as she looked past Max and saw Flint. She was shocked at how little he had changed. For a moment it was as if the last five years hadn't happened and at any moment he would smile and she would step into his strong arms.

But then she saw his expression, a mixture of anger, bitterness and hurt, assuring her the years had been real, just like her reason for leaving.

His gaze turned colder than even she had expected. But it was her own reaction that surprised her. She had wondered what it would be like to see him again. She'd told herself she was over Flint Mauro. That there were no feelings left. For the past five years, she'd worked hard to forget him and get on with her life. She thought she'd done just that.

But she'd never expected it would hurt this much just seeing him.

"Anna," Max said warmly. "Flint, Anna is our new SWAT team paramedic. Anna, Flint is our SWAT team commander."

Anna could only stare in disbelief. Flint had always said he was going to be a detective and work his way to chief of police. He wanted to be one of those cops who used his brain instead of brawn, who didn't have a job where he was always in the line of fire.

"I want to be able to come home to my wife and kids at night," he had said. "I don't want to be out there risking my life any more than I have to."

Now he wore SWAT fatigues and a T-shirt with Do Whatever It Takes printed across the chest. What had happened in the last five years to change his mind?

"Please come in and sit down," Max said to her, cutting through her painful memories.

Behind him, Flint was shaking his head. "What the hell? Max, you can't be serious. This isn't going to work."

Max acted as if he hadn't heard him. "Anna, are you all settled in?"

She nodded, afraid she couldn't find her voice to speak.

Flint had turned away, anger in every line of his body. "I can't believe you kept this from me."

"Both of you—sit down," Max ordered.

"Max, I had no idea that Flint was the SWAT commander," Anna finally managed to say.

"Sit."

They sat in the two chairs in front of his desk, neither looking at the other. But Anna couldn't have been more aware of Flint. This close she could smell the light scent of his aftershave, the same kind he'd used when they'd been together. He exuded an energy that seemed to hum in the air around him, that buzzed through her, reminding her of what it was like being in that force field, the excitement, the dynamism.

"One of the reasons I had the two of you come in early is so that we could get this over with," Max said. "Bitch and moan and then get past it. Flint, that's why I didn't tell you until now that I'd hired Anna. I didn't want you stewing for weeks over this. The two of you will be working together. You have the jobs you do because you're the best at what you do."

"Why *Anna?*" Flint demanded as if she wasn't in the room. "Anyone but Anna."

"Excuse me?" she said, turning in her chair to look at him. "Is it possible I qualify for the job?"

Flint shot her a withering look. "I'm sure there are dozens, if not hundreds, of other paramedics who also qualify for the job."

"For the past three years," Max said, an edge to his voice, "Anna has excelled at this position in Washington, D.C., where she was in tougher situations than we've had in Courage Bay. She knows what she's doing and she's damned good at it."

Flint was shaking his head. "Does it matter how I feel about this?"

"No," Max said. "Anna's good and she knows how

our SWAT team operates because of her earlier experience as a paramedic with the Courage Bay fire department. She's the perfect person for the job. That's what's important here. Not any petty differences the two of you might have."

"Petty differences?" Flint snapped. "You might remember, Max, we were engaged to be married. Hell, you were going to be my best man. *This* is what tore us apart. Her insisting on endangering herself by training to go in with the SWAT team."

"You endanger yourself with your job every day," Anna pointed out. "I don't see the difference."

"You know damned well what the difference is." Flint swung his gaze from her to Max. "She's a *woman*. She needs to be there for our children."

"You have children?" Max asked.

Flint shook his head in obvious frustration. "You know what I'm saying."

Anna stared at Flint. When she'd first seen him after five years, all those old loving feelings had washed over her like a rogue wave, drowning her in wonderful memories of the two of them together, making her question how she'd ever been able to leave him.

But now as she looked at his obstinate expression, listened to him go on about a woman's place, she knew she'd made the right decision five years ago. The man was from the Stone Age.

"Anna was the best candidate for this job. She can handle it. So don't fight me on this, Flint."

Max turned his attention to her. "Flint has excelled with the SWAT team. He's shown himself a leader. That's how he got the job of commander. There is only one question I want answered here this morning. Can you work together, or are you going to let your differences make it impossible? I have to know right now. Is your past relationship going to interfere with your performance?"

"As you pointed out, we have no relationship anymore," Flint said. "Anna made that quite clear five years ago."

Max shot him a warning look.

"It's not going to be a problem for me," Anna said, sounding more convinced than she was. She'd never dreamed she'd be working so closely with Flint. Was that why Max hadn't told her? "Were you afraid I wouldn't take the job? Is that why you didn't warn me about Flint?"

"Would you have taken the job if I *had* told you?" Max asked her.

Her quick response surprised her. "Yes. This job is what I've wanted from the beginning. I'm not going to let anyone take that from me." She glanced over at Flint. His jaw was set, rock-hard in anger. She knew that look too well. "I have no problem working with Flint. It's been five years. I've moved past all that."

Flint turned his head slowly to look at her and his wounded gaze pierced her heart.

"What about you, Flint?" Max asked.

Flint's dark-eyed gaze was still on her. "Like she said, it's water under the bridge."

Anna heard the bitterness and anger. He hadn't forgiven her for breaking off their engagement. No, she thought, what he hadn't forgiven her for was not being the woman he wanted her to be. And to think she'd almost married the turkey.

"I need a united front here, Flint," Max said.

Flint nodded. "I will treat her like my other SWAT team members. No problem."

Anna recognized that sarcastic tone. Flint would make her life miserable on the team. But she wasn't about to let him run her off. She wanted this job, she'd worked for it, she deserved it.

"I don't want any special treatment," she said, meeting Flint's gaze. "I'm just one of the team."

"You've got it," he said.

Max sighed and got to his feet. "I'm going to leave the two of you alone to talk. Work it out between you. I'm meeting with the rest of the SWAT team in a few minutes. I'll expect the two of you in the briefing room in ten minutes." His gaze fell on Flint. "You're both professionals. Act like it."

Flint grunted.

"That's the attitude," Max said, but he smiled as he came around the desk and put his hand on Flint's shoulder. "It's great to have you on board, Anna. Five years was too long to be away. I'm glad you're home."

7:30 a.m.

The room seemed to shrink the moment Max left it. Flint got to his feet, needing to put distance between himself and Anna. He could smell her shampoo. The same kind she'd used when they'd been together. And her hair was the same: long, shiny, golden brown. Just as it had been the first time he'd seen her.

He'd thought about that day more times than he'd wanted to admit over the years. She'd been walking along the sidewalk by the ball field during one of the police department games. Something about the way she moved had caught his eye. There had been energy in her step. This was a woman who knew who she was and where she was going.

He hadn't been able to take his eyes off her, hoping she would look up. When she did, it had knocked the breath out of him. Her face was striking—the wide, brown eyes, the straight, almost aristocratic nose, the full, sensuous mouth. Her gaze radiated intelligence. Then she'd smiled; a bewildered smile, but still dazzling, blinding, enchanting.

It was as if Cupid had sunk an arrow into his heart. Not that he had ever told his buddies that. They'd have thought him crazy. What? Love at first sight? Get out of here.

He'd been so transfixed he hadn't heard the crack of the bat, hadn't seen the fly ball headed to left field, hadn't seen anything but the woman of his dreams.

He still didn't remember the ball hitting him in the head. He wasn't sure how long he'd been out. But when he opened his eyes, there she was, leaning over him.

"I'm a paramedic," she'd said. "Lie still." She'd gazed into his eyes, so close he could smell her sweet, slightly sweaty scent.

And he'd known this was the woman he was going to marry.

How wrong he'd been, he thought now as he looked over at Anna. The department's new SWAT team paramedic. Great. He'd spent five years trying like hell to forget her. It could have been fifty years and it wouldn't have made a difference, but now he would be working with her. The woman who'd walked out of his life after throwing his engagement ring at him. And after he'd spent days looking for the perfect ring for the perfect woman. What a fool he'd been.

And nothing had changed. Not his feelings of pain and regret. Not her lack of feelings for him, that was for sure. Except she was back, and now the SWAT team paramedic—the job he'd never wanted her to have.

He looked into her face, searching for some imperfection that would release her hold on him. She wasn't beautiful. Not in the classic sense. She was striking, the kind of woman who made you do a double take when you saw her. A face you never forgot. Imperfect and yet perfect for him in a way that made him ache inside.

The more he'd been around her, the more deeply he'd fallen in love with her. He'd gotten caught up in her enthusiasm for life, her generosity, her sense of humor, her do-or-die attitude. He'd once told her that if he could bottle whatever it was that made her so special, he'd be a millionaire.

"Flint?"

He blinked, so deep in his thoughts he hadn't realized she'd been talking to him.

"I was hoping we could do this in a civilized manner," she said in a calm voice that irritated him more than if she'd sworn at him.

He stared at her. She didn't even seem ruffled. Hell, maybe she was telling the truth. Maybe she had gotten over him while he'd been wallowing in regret all these years. Maybe he was the biggest fool on the planet. Maybe there was no maybe about it.

"I see no reason why we can't work together, two professionals, just doing our jobs," she said.

He snorted. "You have to be kidding." He was furious

at her for walking out on him, for coming back for an even more dangerous job. Didn't she know how impossible this situation was for him? Did she care?

"Why are you doing this?" he demanded. "You know how I felt about you working with the SWAT team. Are you just trying to rub it in my face?"

"That's ridiculous. This has nothing to do with you."

He glared at her. "My mistake."

"You know what I mean."

"No, I don't think I do."

She lifted her chin, stubborn determination in her brown eyes and a coolness that had always brought out heat in him. He'd seen that look way too many times. Unfortunately he could also remember desire in those eyes.

"If you're doing this just to get back at me—"

She laughed and shook her head, eyeing him as if she couldn't believe him. "You haven't changed a bit. You still think everything is about *you*."

"Damn it, Anna, you're wrong. I'm concerned as hell for you. You have no idea what you're up against. I can just imagine what my men are going to think of a paramedic on the team—let alone a woman—let alone you, my ex-fiancée." He tried to imagine this being any worse and couldn't.

"You are underestimating your men," Anna said coolly. "In my experience, the men follow the lead of their commander."

He laughed. She'd just put it all on him. Anna had always been good at turning the tables on him. He glared at her, wanting desperately to take her in his arms and to kiss some sense into her. If only his love for her was enough that he could talk her out of this.

But it hadn't been enough five years ago and it sure as hell meant nothing to her now.

"So, is there a man in your life?" he heard himself ask, and mentally kicked himself.

"I think we should keep our personal lives out of the office," she said.

He wanted to laugh again. "Is that a yes or a no?"

"I've been busy the last five years. I really haven't had time to—" She seemed to catch herself. "What about you?"

He raised an eyebrow. Did she really care one way or the other? "I guess we've both been too busy." He looked into her eyes, searching for just a little of what they'd once had together.

She was the first to drag her gaze away. She brushed a hand through her hair. He couldn't help but remember how her hair had felt in his fingers. He wondered if it would feel the same.

He turned away, unable to look at her as he found himself drowning in memories of the two of them together, laughing late at night, walking the beach as the sun rose over the city, talking for hours on the phone, making love—oh, lordie, yes, making wonderful, passionate love.

"Flint, this has been my life's dream," she said behind him. "This job. I've trained for years for it. Isn't it possible that I just want to help people, that I want to make a difference?"

He felt anger bubble up inside of him as he turned to look at her again. "Being the mother to our children wouldn't have made a difference in the world? No, sorry, that job wasn't exciting enough for you."

"That's a cheap shot even for you," she said. "I was twenty-four years old. I had worked hard to become a paramedic. I wasn't ready to quit a rewarding, exciting job to become a mother yet. But after a while I would have loved to have been the mother of our children. You were the one who said I had to choose. Either I stayed home and started a family right after we were married, or I could pursue a career—without you."

He shook his head. He hadn't meant to take that position. He'd regretted it for years. "We could have worked it out if you'd given us a chance. Instead you threw the engagement ring at me and walked out, left town and obviously never looked back."

"You mean, the way we're working it out now?" she asked with an exasperated sigh.

"Damn it Anna, I know what it was like to grow up without a mother, remember? I didn't want that for my kids. Is that so hard for you to understand?"

"No, but it was all right for their father to be a cop?" She narrowed her gaze at him. "I thought you were going to be a cop who used his brain and wasn't risking his life all the time. What changed?"

He shook his head. "It doesn't matter now, does it. We have no kids to worry about, and it seems we both think we can take care of ourselves just fine." She was right. They never could have worked it out. He didn't want his wife risking her life at her job. He wanted her at home with their kids.

"Flint, I had hoped you might understand."

He shook his head. "This has to be the worst decision you've ever made, but then, I thought leaving me was the worst, and obviously you've proven me wrong. You seem perfectly happy with your decision."

She raised her chin, that defiant, obstinate look in her eyes. "I am."

"Then we have no problem," he said, and opened the door. "Let's get this over with."

Chapter 3

Lee Harper had been feeling odd all morning. Now as he glanced around the main floor of city hall, everything had a surreal feel to it. He and Kenny were on the ground floor at the back of city hall and they had their hostage. Kenny's plan had worked.

"Could you help me over here?" Kenny snapped.

He turned to see Kenny wrestling with the woman. Lorna Sinke. That was her name. She was a tiny little thing, thin with brown hair and a small face that made her dark eyes seem larger. He'd seen her when he'd come to the city council meetings. She reminded him of Francine.

"Lee? Could you get your ass over here?"

He shook himself. "Sure." He moved, feeling bulky in the large, cumbersome police jacket.

Kenny had her down on the floor but she was fighting him, kicking, scratching, biting him.

"Get my gun," Kenny ordered. "Shoot the bitch."

"You said no one would get hurt."

"Shoot her, damn it! Or I'll shoot you!"

Lee picked up the assault rifle, which Kenny had dropped, and walked over to where the two were struggling on the floor. The woman's eyes were on him. She looked more angry than scared.

"Who are you fools?" she cried. "What do you think you're doing? This is a city building on the historic registrar."

"Shut the hell up," Kenny said. "Shoot her, damn it!"

Lee just tapped her with the butt of the rifle, a light tap that connected with her skull. Her eyes rolled back in her head and she quit fighting. "Did I kill her?" he asked, feeling sick and confused. "I didn't mean to kill her." He was having trouble remembering what he was doing here.

Kenny snatched the rifle from him. "I told you to shoot her."

"I don't want anyone to get hurt," Lee said.

"Yeah. Sure. You got the cuffs on you?"

Lee frowned, then felt in the pocket of his large jacket, producing one of a half dozen pairs. He remembered Kenny saying there could be cleaning people or repairmen in the building. Better to be prepared than not. Or maybe he'd said that. Not that it mattered. He handed a set of handcuffs to Kenny.

Kenny was looking oddly at Lee's big police coat. He shook his head and slapped one end of the handcuff on

Lorna's wrist. She was coming around, only dazed, not dead. Lee felt a surge of relief. Francine wouldn't like it if anyone got hurt.

Yes, he recalled now. The handcuffs had been his idea. "Easy and faster than rope," he'd told Kenny, who hadn't been that impressed. Kenny had liked it, though, when Lee had told him about the Internet supply shop he'd found where they could get real police handcuffs. "They even have police uniforms and badges."

Kenny had gotten excited then. "Lee, you're a genius. We'll dress as cops. It will make it that much easier to get the old broad to let us in."

"The old broad," as Kenny called her, was wide awake again. Lee could feel her gaze on him as he glanced up. He thought he heard a sound from one of the floors above them. The building should have been empty this time of the morning on a Friday. But he would have sworn he heard a door open upstairs.

7:37 a.m.

Lorna memorized the men's faces. If she were called in for a lineup, she wanted to identify these two without the slightest hesitation. The younger of the men grabbed her shoulder and tried to flip her over onto her stomach, no doubt so he could cuff her wrists behind her. He appeared to be in his thirties; his face was thin, hair dishwater-blond, and he looked slovenly even in the police uniform. Especially in the scruffy sneakers. He held some sort of assault rifle in his free hand, his fingernails grimy.

"Help me roll this bitch over," he ordered the older one, his breath smelling of garlic and alcohol.

With the handcuff dangling from her wrist, Lorna gripped the canvas bag with her purse, lunch and the cookies inside. Her cell phone was palmed in her other hand where he couldn't see it. She lay perfectly still, hardly breathing as he turned to the other man, the soft-spoken elderly man who'd first approached her.

"Lee? Are you going to help me over here or not?"

Lee was in his late sixties, early seventies, neat as a pin. Even his black lace-up leather dress shoes were shined, creases ironed into his uniform pants. He wore a large, bulky-looking uniform jacket, which, now that she thought about it, was far too heavy for Southern California. He was still kind of slumped over a little, looking uncomfortable, still giving her the impression that he was in pain.

But she thought she remembered where she'd seen him. Wasn't he the man who had come to the council meeting the last two months? Something about his wife.

"Wait a minute," the young one said, straightening as he stared back at the man. "Where the hell is your gun, Lee?"

"You said to bring firepower, Kenny."

"Yeah, so where is your firepower?"

Lee carefully unzipped his coat.

"Holy Mother of— What the hell is that? A bomb, Lee? You got a friggin' bomb taped to your chest?"

"An explosive device, yes," Lee said.

"Why the hell did you do that? Jeez. What if it goes off before you want it to?"

"Little chance of that," the older man said.

"Unless you get shot or fall down?"

"I have to discharge it with this switch," Lee told him,

calmly pointing to a hole in the green-colored plastic explosives.

The hole was just large enough for his finger and a small red toggle switch. Lorna knew the switch was attached to a series of colored wires that ran to a digital watch and a blasting cap. She had recently watched a show on TV about bombs, curious how they worked. But she'd decided bombs were messy and too obvious. She preferred a more subtle approach.

Kenny was shaking his head and running his free hand through his hair. "Oh, man, you're crazy, you know that? Beyond postal."

From what Lorna had seen, they both fit in that category.

Kenny was so upset he wasn't paying any attention to her. His kind took one look at her and saw a forty-something old maid, a woman afraid of her shadow, no threat at all.

His kind deserved everything they got.

"Never mind," Kenny said. "I can do this by myself. I don't want you blowing me up because you accidentally flip that damned switch while you're helping me." He put down the rifle, though not within her reach, and turned back around to her on the floor.

As he straddled her and started to reach down to try to roll her over again, she kicked him in the groin.

His knees buckled and she had just enough time to pull her legs to her chest and roll away. Scrambling to her feet, with her bag and the cell phone, the handcuffs still dangling from one wrist, she ran toward the front of the building and the staircase.

Kenny let out a howl that echoed through the rotunda. She raced up the wide central staircase, looking down

through the railing only once, with satisfaction, to see
that her kick still had Kenny on his knees.

"Get her, damn it!" Kenny wheezed. "Don't just stand
there, Lee! Get her!"

Lee was handicapped by the bomb on his chest and
his age. Lorna, on the other hand, took all three flights
of stairs every day, many times. She hated elevators and
closed-in spaces.

She bounded up the stairs. She could hear Lee labor-
ing up the steps behind her. He was breathing heavily
and falling behind.

On the second floor she looked up and was shocked to
see a group of people coming out of the meeting room,
obviously to see what the racket was about. What were
they doing here? Lorna thought as she recognized three
of the city council members: Gwendolyn Clark, Fred
Glazeman and James Baker, along with District Attorney Henry Lalane and City Attorney Rob Dayton. A
secret meeting?

They all seemed surprised to see her running up the
stairs with a handcuff dangling from one wrist.

"What is going on?" Gwendolyn demanded. She was
a frumpy matronly type, with a round face and a large
mouth that dominated her face. It didn't help that her
mouth was usually open.

Lorna could have asked her the same thing, but it
seemed pretty obvious. The city councillors were having a "secret" meeting, and there was only one topic
Lorna could imagine they would be talking about: her.

"Why is that policeman chasing you, Lorna?"

For just an instant Lorna was too stunned to answer.
Gwendolyn had called a special "secret" meeting with
these council members to try to get her fired? Lorna

should have known the woman would pull something like this.

Lee's labored steps behind her brought her back to the present problem. "That's not a cop chasing me. He has a bomb taped to his chest. There's another one down below with an assault rifle. They're taking city hall hostage. Get back into the meeting room. Now!"

Lorna herded everyone back down the hall to the meeting room, Gwendolyn arguing all the way. Lorna shoved her into the room after the others, closed the door and locked it. Lee had been only a few yards away. She leaned against the door and looked at the others.

She'd worked hard for these councillors, and here they were, meeting in secret to get rid of her. The traitors. She almost wished she'd left them all outside the door for whatever those two men had planned for them.

Except for Fred, she thought, letting her gaze fall on her favorite councilman. He wasn't like the others. He was kind and intelligent. A nice man. But Lorna knew that Gwendolyn had been trying to turn him against her.

"Barricade the door," Lorna ordered. She'd have to deal with that problem later. Right now, there was something more pressing to take care of. "Barricade the door!"

For a moment no one moved. They all just stared at her as if *she* was the crazy one. D.A. Lalane started to call someone on his cell phone. "Don't touch that cell phone. It might set off the bomb. Barricade the door, then get back from it. The man on the other side of this door has enough explosives taped to him to take out this entire room."

She could hear Lee outside the door, trying the knob, kicking the door, then turning and retreating back down the hall.

Gwendolyn let out a shriek. "Oh, God, we're all going to die." She began to cry loudly. But it got the rest of them moving. D.A. Lalane pocketed his cell phone and ordered the others to help him with the large conference desk. Fred, of course, joined in to help Councilman James Baker and City Attorney Rob Dayton. Gwendolyn stood in the center of the room, wringing her hands and crying.

Lorna's fingers were trembling, but more out of anger than fear as she carefully turned off her own cell phone. Two crazy men had barged their way into her city hall while upstairs a secret meeting had been in session to get rid of her. She didn't know which made her angrier.

The law required all city council meetings to be public—unless the meeting was about personnel. If it had been about city personnel, the city manager would have been here. And since Lorna was the council's only aide and Gwendolyn was dead-set on getting her fired, that definitely narrowed down the agenda of this meeting.

Tossing down her purse and the bag with her lunch and the cookies, Lorna picked up the meeting room phone, hoping the land line wouldn't set off the bomb as she tapped out 911.

7:48 a.m.

Kenny cursed the woman who'd kicked him and mentally listed all the things he was going to do to her when he caught her. And he *would* catch her. She couldn't get out of the building and there wasn't anyone around to help her. All he had to do was trap her on one of the upper floors.

He was so sure they were alone in the building that

he was startled by the sound of raised voices overhead. A woman let out a shriek. Not the woman who'd kicked him. Then he thought he heard several men's voices. What the hell?

He listened to the sound of voices, then footfalls upstairs, a door slamming, locking. He swore under his breath. Where the hell was Lee? Why hadn't he stopped the woman?

This should have been a piece of cake. They were supposed to overpower the Lorna Sinke woman. Hell, as small and frail-looking as she was, it should have been a cinch.

Once he had a hostage and city hall, Kenny thought he'd be calling the shots. He could hear Lee's arduous footsteps coming back down the stairs. He'd never expected the damned fool to show up wearing a bomb.

As Kenny got to his feet, he told himself that this wasn't going as he'd planned, and it was all that damned Sinke woman's fault. He swore he could hear her upstairs giving orders. The bitch.

He looked up at the sound of Lee's shuffling feet.

"They all went into a room and locked the door," Lee said.

"*They* all?" Kenny demanded.

"I recognized most of them. Three city council members, the district attorney and city attorney." Lee nodded. "I think that was all. I only got a glimpse of them before they closed the door. Ms. Sinke was with them."

Ms. Sinke? Lee was calling the bitch *Ms. Sinke?* Kenny swore. He was going to kill Ms. Sinke. The only good thing was that it sounded like he had some more hostages he could use as leverage. He didn't need Sinke anymore.

As he turned toward the front of city hall and the wide staircase, he heard a sound that made him freeze and the hair stood up on the back of his neck. It was the click of a door opening.

Spinning around, Kenny brought his rifle up, shocked to see that Lee hadn't locked and barricaded the door as Kenny had told him to.

A man in his middle forties, dressed like an undertaker in a dark suit, came walking in with an air about him as if he owned the place. Who in the hell was this? He looked vaguely familiar in a way that made Kenny nervous.

What were all these people doing here?

The man was so preoccupied he didn't see them at first. He stopped when he did, not showing any concern at first to see two policemen in city hall before it opened for the day.

But then his gaze took in the assault rifle in Kenny's hands. Kenny pointed the barrel at the man's chest.

"Well, if it isn't Judge Lawrence Craven," Kenny said, and laughed, finally recognizing him. He looked different without his robe on and that bench in front of him.

Craven studied him for a moment. "Four years for burglary."

Kenny smiled. "You remembered. I'm touched. What the hell are you doing here before city hall opens, anyway?"

Craven glanced toward the stairs but didn't answer.

Obviously he'd come by to see someone, but he didn't want to say who. Now why was that?

Not that it mattered. This was a stroke of luck. "Lee, we just got a real break. This hostage is better than your Ms. Sinke or all the councilmen and lawyers in the world. Make sure no one else can come through that damned door and let's go see what other hostages we have."

7:54 a.m.

As Anna walked with Flint down the hallway to the briefing room, she couldn't have been more aware of him. After all these years, they were here together. Only not together. Not even close.

When she thought back to when they'd first met... She shook her head. What happened to those two people who were so head-over-heels in love?

She smiled to herself at the memory of the first time he'd asked her for a date. She could practically smell the salt, hear the Pacific breaking on the sandy beach, feel the sun on her back. She'd been coming out of the water, her surfboard tucked under her arm, happy in her element, when she'd seen someone waiting for her.

She'd squinted into the sun, seeing first the dark silhouette of a man, then the uniform. A cop. Her heart sank. Bad news. Something to do with her family?

"Hi," he said. "You probably don't remember me." He seemed so different in the uniform, sand sticking to his freshly polished black cop shoes, and looked as out of place and uncomfortable as anyone she'd ever seen.

"You're a cop," she said, relieved and yet feeling foolish. Of course he was a cop. She knew that. She'd just forgotten that part and hadn't recognized him in uniform for a moment. He hadn't been in Southern California long; his skin was not yet tanned. His hair was straight black. One errant lock hung down over one dark eye.

How could she have forgotten that deep, wonderful voice? Or that boyish face? Or that bump on his forehead?

She reached out to gently touch the knot on his head. "I see some of the swelling has gone down."

He grinned. "You remember me, I guess."

"How could I forget?" she joked, remembering the huge bump he'd gotten on his head from being hit by a fly ball during a cop tournament baseball game, then the crazy ambulance ride to the hospital, where the doctor had assured them both that it was only a slight concussion. And all the time, the guy'd been trying to get her home phone number.

He'd insisted she not leave his side, even with the entire police department baseball team packed into the hospital emergency room, all laughing as Flint pleaded his case for her phone number, saying it was her fault he got hit by that fly ball. If he hadn't been admiring her....

She'd finally given him the number. But he'd never called.

Instead he'd shown up at the beach, and he was so shy, so sincere, so nervous he seemed like a different guy.

"You saved my life," he said.

Right. "It wasn't quite that dramatic."

"You're wrong." He settled those dark eyes on her. "It was for me. It was the luckiest day of my life."

That day at the ballpark he'd been wearing the T-shirt she'd carried around with her for the last five years. His lucky shirt, he used to call it. Lucky because he'd been wearing it the day he met her.

She normally didn't date his type. Jocks. Stars of one sport or another. The kind of guys her sister Emily always dated. And ended up marrying.

Anna had only given him her number that day at the

hospital to shut him up. She'd never expected him to call. If he had called, she would have turned him down. And saved them both a lot of grief. Instead he'd shown up at the beach, looking sweet and shy and anxious as he asked her to dinner.

And fool that she'd been, she'd said yes. Look where that had gotten them, she thought now, dragging herself out of the memory as Flint halted at the door to the briefing room.

He opened the door and stood back to let her enter.

"After you," she said. "Just one of the team."

He made a face. "Right." He turned and entered the room ahead of her.

She braced herself. There were always a few men on a SWAT team who had trouble accepting a woman among them. Fortunately most of the men were younger, more in tune with the times. Flint, she hoped, would prove to be the exception rather than the rule, since the Courage Bay SWAT team was all men.

As she stepped into the briefing room, she heard a male voice ask, "You are aware that the last time a paramedic went in with us, she was injured?"

There was some grumbling agreement.

"That's why I've gone with a paramedic with SWAT training *and* experience," Max answered. "Anna can handle herself under pressure. She knows the danger. She's going to surprise you all."

Anna flushed. "Thank you, Chief Zirinsky," she said, moving out from behind Flint to meet a lot of very male faces.

To her surprise, Flint stepped to her side. "Gentlemen, this is Anna Carson, our new SWAT team paramedic. Anna, if you will," he said, giving her the floor.

She looked at the men, then laid it out for them in a flat, no-nonsense account. "I am SWAT trained, second in my class. I spent three years on a Washington, D.C., SWAT team. I received several medals for bravery and dedication to duty. I have been involved in tactical situations from bank robberies and terrorist attacks to domestic disputes and hostage-suicides." She stopped before adding, "I'm honored to be part of your SWAT team, and I look forward to working with all of you."

Silence. Then, "This isn't Washington, D.C. We don't have the same kind of manpower." It was one of the older men. His name tag read T.C. Waters. "I, for one, don't like the idea of a woman on the team. Call me old-fashioned—"

"Old-fashioned and a true chauvinist," Flint said, and laughed. "Welcome to the twenty-first century, T.C. They're even letting women vote nowadays."

"Aw, T.C. even gripes about women reporters on the field during a football game," a younger SWAT member called from the back.

"Yeah, he says he doesn't like the sound of their voices," said another one. More laughter.

"The bottom line here is that Anna's on the team," Flint said, looking over at her. "We treat her like we would any other team member. Forget she's a woman."

There were some chuckles. "Yeah, right," one of the guys retorted. "At least you could have hired an ugly one, Chief."

Even Max laughed this time. The desk sergeant stuck his head in the doorway. "Chief."

Max went to the door and immediately called Flint over.

Anna didn't have to hear what they were saying. She

saw Flint's face, saw the color drain from it and the look he gave her.

His gaze met hers, then moved past to his men. "City hall. Possible hostage situation. Suit up."

Chapter 4

8:02 a.m.

Flint knew the drill by heart: contain and control. The command center was quickly set up in the briefing room with a view of city hall out the window.

"Lock down that building," he ordered into the high-tech headset that let him communicate with the tactical force.

Behind him, Max was barking out orders, as well. "Get me blueprints. I need an exact location of the meeting rooms on the second floor, all air-conditioning vents and the phone panel."

Techies raced into the room with TV monitors, both visual and audio devices and phone systems. Outside, barricades had gone up and the streets were swarming with firefighters and policemen. An ambulance pulled through the barricade. Just a precaution, he told himself. Just like Anna being here.

He couldn't believe Anna had chosen this day to begin work. All his fears seemed to be coming true. He had to diffuse this situation stat before someone got hurt and Max wanted to send Anna in.

Max pulled him aside, moving the two of them to the northwest corner of the room to look kitty-corner across the street at city hall. Normally they would have set up the command center across the street from the incident. But with the police station so close, it made sense to set it up here.

From the window Flint had a good view of the right wing and part of the back of the building. The large, old, white-stone building, U-shaped and three stories high, glistened in the sun, the windows like mirrors. Even at this angle, the back employee entrance was partially hidden from view by the oleander hedge. Nothing looked amiss. Nothing gave them any indication that a siege was going on inside.

"I've ordered an evac of the area and the perimeter cleared for four blocks," Max said.

Flint looked at the chief in surprise. "Four blocks?"

"We have the aide to the city council, Lorna Sinke, patched through dispatch. She says one of the subjects has an assault rifle." He met Flint's gaze. "The other has a homemade bomb duct-taped to his chest. I've put the bomb squad on notice. Unknown type."

Flint felt his heart drop. Oh, yeah, Anna had picked one *hell* of a day to start her new job. It would be a miracle if he and his team could defuse this crisis without anyone getting hurt and needing a paramedic.

"Do we have any idea who these guys are or what they want?" Flint asked.

"So far all we know is their names. Kenny and Lee. But Sinke says she thinks Lee's name is Harper. She thinks he's been at the city council meetings the last couple of months talking about the loss of his wife... blames the city. She said she got the impression he wasn't well. We're trying to find out just who all is in the building. Thank God this is happening so early in the morning, but once the media gets wind of it.... I'm going to put Sinke on the speaker phone as soon as the techies get everything hooked up." They would be able to hear her, but Max would talk to her on a private line. "Bradley is out with the flu, the other negotiators are on vacation, so I'm taking this one myself."

Flint glanced over at him, but Max gave no indication he was doing it for any other reason. Like the fact that it was Anna's first day and he wasn't taking any chances because of it.

Sirens blared outside as police and fire departments responded to the call. Fire Chief Dan Egan reported in that he had the four-block area secured.

Overhead came the whoop-whoop of a helicopter taking off from the pad on the roof.

"Building perimeter secure," came the report from one of the tactical teams. "Marksmen observers in place. Tactical team in position. Waiting for orders to breach building."

Flint looked over at Max. Every incident was situational. No one thing was ever the same. That meant each incident was handled differently. Facts were gathered as quickly as possible, then a rational decision was

made based on what approach would cost the least number of lives.

There was always a risk. Flint had been in explosive
domestic situations that turned violent. He'd confronted
armed subjects holed up in alleys, barricaded suicidal
subjects and hostage situations involving drunks, crazies,
suicidal maniacs with sawed-off shotguns and crying
little kids being held by doped-up, drugged-out parents.

Every situation had the potential to blow up in your
face at any moment. This one wouldn't have been any
different from all the others—if it hadn't been for Anna
being here.

Flint looked up, as if sensing her presence. Anna entered the room and came toward them. Five years hadn't
dulled his awareness of her any more than it had his
feelings.

Their eyes met for a moment, then Anna pulled away.
Flint swore under his breath and Max looked up. "Anna,
good. I want you in on all of this so we know what we're
up against if you have to go in."

Unlike the other SWAT team members now securing
the perimeter of city hall, she was dressed in fire department paramedic gear except for the Kevlar vest over her
short-sleeved shirt. She carried a jump kit with the basic
paramedic supplies and stood, waiting for orders. The
hostage takers would think she was just another paramedic. Flint swore under his breath as he realized how
vulnerable she would be. This was exactly what he'd
feared five years ago.

Max listened to dispatch on his headset, nodding. A
frown furrowed his brows increasing Flint's concern.

"Sinke isn't the only civilian in the building," Max
said when he got off. "The mayor's out of town, but one

of the councilmen home sick with the flu that's going around said there was an early morning meeting to discuss an employee problem. The district attorney was in attendance, as well as the city attorney and three council persons."

"Employee problem?" Flint repeated. "But the council only has one employee directly under them."

Max nodded. "Lorna Sinke."

Flint lifted a brow. A closed meeting to discuss personnel problems, and yet the district attorney was there? What exactly did they have against Sinke, or were they just being cautious?

Max turned to Anna. "So far it sounds as if there is Sinke, two councilmen and a councilwoman, the city attorney and the district attorney in the building. Sinke's got them all in the second-floor meeting room with the door locked and barricaded." He showed both Flint and Anna the position of the meeting room on the map.

The room was at the end of the U-shaped wing with three large old windows along the outer wall. The windows opened, but they were now closed and the blinds drawn. According to Sinke, Councilwoman Gwendolyn Clark said the light bothered her eyes.

"Get Sinke to open the blinds and the windows," Flint said. Max nodded and passed on the message.

Flint's radio beeped in his ear. He listened for a moment, then turned his attention back to Max. "My men are in position. We're ready to lock down the building. Marksmen are positioned in buildings on all sides of city hall. They're just waiting for the word. No sign of the subjects, though."

Flint knew that old building. It was solid, but if the hostage takers wanted into the meeting room badly enough, they would find a way in, one way or another. He wanted to take city hall before the situation escalated. Before anyone got hurt.

He met Anna's gaze again. Hers was cool, calm and collected. He wondered what she was feeling inside. Hell, he had wondered that for five years, but even looking into her eyes now, he couldn't tell.

"We've got your hookup," one of the techies announced, and pressed the speaker phone button.

Flint heard a female voice. She was talking to someone else in the room. He could hear crying in the background, and male voices trying to soothe the distraught woman.

"Ms. Sinke, this is Chief Zirinsky," Max said on his extension. "Are there any other people in the building that you know of, other than the ones in the meeting room with you now and the two subjects dressed as police officers?"

"Not that I know," she said after conferring with the others. It sounded as if D.A. Lalane tried to take the phone from her, but Lorna was making it clear she was running this show.

"What can you tell us about the two men now in the building?"

She didn't hesitate. "They are both armed. One with what looks like an assault rifle. The other with a homemade bomb. He has it duct-taped to his chest. There is a timer and a switch. He keeps his finger on the switch most of the time."

"What about the men themselves?" Max didn't need to explain to her what he meant.

"They don't know each other very well."

"What makes you say that?"

"The way they act," she said flatly. She described the

two men, making Flint shake his head at the extensive descriptions she'd been able to get while facing a man with an assault rifle and another with a homemade bomb duct-taped to his chest.

"Lee's the smart one," she continued. "I remember him from the city council meetings. Lee Harper, that's his name. I remember him now. He's educated, moderate to high income, a retired professor. College English, I think he said at the first meeting he showed up at. That would have been about two months ago. Kenny is a bum, probably has a criminal record. I've never seen him before."

"Think they're related?"

"I don't think so. They don't like each other much, either." A noise. "They're on our floor."

Max looked at Flint, his expression grim. "What was this Lee Harper doing at the city council meeting?" he asked Sinke.

"His wife was killed in the earthquake's aftershock. He wanted the city to make sure their medical response time could be improved."

Max shut off his extension so Sinke couldn't hear. "A bad situation all around, but if we can keep them from getting into that meeting room…. Let's see if we can get to the two of them before they can take the hostages. It's risky, especially with a bomb, but it could get a whole lot riskier once they have hostages."

Flint gave the order. "Breach the building."

"Ms. Sinke? This is Chief Zirinsky again. We're sending you some help. Please move away from the door, get under desks, anything you can, and wait until you hear our men outside. But stay on the line, if that's possible."

Lorna began giving orders. Flint could hear desks being

moved, someone screaming and crying harder, Lorna telling her to shut up, then several male voices arguing.

"Kenny and Lee are outside our door," Lorna said into the phone.

"The SWAT team is coming into the building," Max said, and hung up his phone as he turned to Anna and Flint. "There is something about Sinke you should both know. She would have been prosecuted for killing her elderly parents a while back, but evidence found in her car was ruled inadmissible because the warrant was improperly executed."

Flint couldn't hide his surprise. "What kind of evidence?"

"A drug that was also found in both parents' systems following the autopsies," Max told him.

"And now she's locked in a meeting room with the council members who were in the process of possibly firing her," Anna observed.

"She's had some run-ins with Councilwoman Gwendolyn Clark," Max said. "I guess there is no love lost between them. Gwendolyn has been trying to find some grounds to can her for months, at least that's what the councilman said."

"You think there's some connection between the two armed men who've taken city hall and the special meeting this morning about Sinke?" Flint asked.

"I don't think so, but you never know," he said, and stepped over to talk to one of the techies, leaving Flint alone with Anna.

Flint couldn't bring himself to look at her. He still couldn't believe she was back in Courage Bay. Or why. Sure as hell not for any reason he'd imagined. Or hoped for. Not even close.

* * *

Anna watched Flint, his eyes hooded, his body tense, facial features a set mask of determination. She braced herself, praying he didn't try to fight her on this, because he would be fighting Max. She didn't want Flint jeopardizing his job because of her, and as stubborn as he was....

But he didn't say a word. He just looked at her, his look saying, "You asked for this."

She raised her chin. Not only had she asked for it, she had trained for it. And she was ready. She had her supplies together and was dressed. The Kevlar vest was cumbersome but essential. At her feet was a jump kit with basic supplies. Now it was just a matter of waiting for instructions, should someone be injured in the breach.

"We were able to reach the mayor," Max said, joining them again. "He confirmed Lee Harper's been coming to the city council meetings. He's the husband of the woman who was killed in that convenience store collapse during the aftershock almost two months ago. His name is Lee Harper, just as Sinke said. He's been demanding that the city do something about its medical response time."

Flint swore. "What's his connection to the other man?"

"We don't know yet."

"They have to have something in common to take over city hall together," Flint said.

Max nodded and turned to Anna. "You ready?"

"Yes, sir."

"Nothing like being thrown right into the fire on your first day." Max studied her for a moment, then handed her a headset. "I knew I hired the right person for the job."

Anna was calm. She'd seen enough of these types of situations to know they often escalated quickly. She didn't think about the danger or what she'd find if she were called inside. All she would concern herself with was the injured and keeping the situation from escalating.

Flint was communicating with the team again. She put on the headset and listened to him work, grudgingly impressed. But then she would have expected nothing less from him.

"No civilians found," came the report. "Floors one and three secured. Something happening on level two."

"Take level two," Flint ordered, and looked up at her.

He would do his job. No matter what. That was Flint. He was tough and determined, seemingly even more tough and determined than he'd been five years ago. But wasn't that strength of mind what she had loved about him? Yes, she thought, but he'd also had another side, a gentle, loving side that had stolen her heart.

"Breaching second floor, all teams on count of three," came a voice over the headset. "One, two, three!"

Anna waited, her heart in her throat. Where were the two armed men? Were they waiting to ambush the team?

Through the speaker phone came Lorna Sinke's voice over the sound of people shouting and a woman crying. "They have Judge Craven."

Judge Craven? There was screaming coming over the phone line from the meeting room.

"Shut her up so I can hear," Lorna ordered.

Max turned to Anna and said, "Judge Craven is Councilwoman Gwendolyn Clark's uncle. What the hell is *he* doing there?"

"Subjects holding gun to civilian's head," came T.C. Waters's voice from the SWAT team. "Please advise."

"Can you get a shot?" Flint asked.

"Negative."

Flint took a breath and looked at Max, who shook his head. "Stand down."

There was shouting in the background, louder crying, then Sinke was back on the phone, her voice tight. "Chief Zirinsky?"

It surprised Anna how little fear she heard in the woman's voice.

"They demand that you call back your men and we open the door or they will kill the judge."

"Don't open the door," Max ordered. There was louder crying in the background, voices arguing, then the sound of something scraping across the floor. "Do not open that door. I repeat. Do not open that door."

"They're breaking down the door!" someone cried above the screams of Gwendolyn Clark.

Lorna wished she had a gun so she could shut Gwendolyn Clark up. The councilwoman wouldn't quit screaming and crying. Even when the men had tried to console her. Even when Lorna had threatened to send her out with the crazies.

Now Gwendolyn was hysterical because her uncle, the honorable Judge Lawrence Craven, was going to die if they didn't open the door.

"You hear me in there?" It was Kenny, the craziest of the two crazies. "I'm going to count to three."

After that, things happened so fast, Lorna remembered little of it. Councilman James Baker had his arm around Gwendolyn as she screamed for them to open the door, her makeup running down her chubby cheeks. She looked like hell. Lorna thought about giving her a cookie just to shut her up.

D.A. Henry Lalane, City Attorney Rob Dayton and Councilman Fred Glazeman had all been huddled in the corner, discussing what to do. Lorna had known Fred would be strong in a crisis. He was short with brown hair and eyes, not the kind of man the opposite sex would even notice, much like herself, but there was a kindness in his eyes, a gentleness that made her ache with the desire to put her arms around him.

She'd wondered if he'd even had a chance to notice her new blue dress. Probably not. D.A. Lalane had been talking, but quit in midsentence as she joined them, setting her teeth on edge.

"The chief of police said not to open the door," Lorna told them.

Earlier, the D.A. had tried to take over talking to the chief. Lorna had refused to give him the phone, and Fred had supported her, saying, "She's doing fine, don't you think, Henry?"

Fred smiled reassuringly at her now, making her feel soft inside.

"We can't keep them out of this room if they decide to come in," Lalane said. "There are only two of them. We might be able to disarm them and put an end to this right now."

Lorna had never liked the D.A. She knew he would have loved to see her behind bars. She knew that he and Gwendolyn were friends. Both of which made him her enemy.

"One of the men is a walking time bomb," Lorna reminded the D.A. "The other has a bomb taped to his chest."

Lalane glared at her as if she hadn't been invited to this discussion. "You know anything about bombs, Lorna? It might not even be a working bomb. He could be bluffing."

"Or it could go off and blow off this part of the building, us with it," she said over the pounding on the door. "The chief of police said not to open the door. He probably knows more about this than you do, Mr. D.A."

Kenny was yelling for them to open the damned door. A second later something large and heavy hit the door. Gwendolyn screamed. The rest of them stepped back, Fred shielding Lorna as he said, "I believe it's about to become a moot point."

The door splintered, the lock broke. The three burst into the room in a blur of confusion, panic and gunfire.

8:32 a.m.

"Shots fired!" T.C. Waters reported from tactical force. "We have shots fired!"

Flint listened to the pandemonium over the speaker phone. Voices arguing, someone screaming, then the loud thunder of what sounded like a battering ram, wood splintering and shots fired. More shots fired to the sound of screaming.

"Shots fired!" T.C. repeated. "Shots have been fired."

"Tell your men to hold their positions," Max ordered Flint.

"Hold your positions!" Flint said into the headset.

"Lorna? Lorna, are you still there?" Max was calling into the phone.

It wasn't Lorna's voice Flint heard next but a man's he didn't recognize. "She's been shot! We need help! Lorna's been shot and they're—"

A scuffle, a male voice yelling for everyone to get down, more shots. The receiver hit the floor.

In the horrible quiet that followed, Flint glanced up at Anna. He had feared this from the beginning when he'd heard city hall had been taken. Oh, God.

"Who is this?" demanded a rough male voice as the phone was picked up. "Who the hell is this?"

"Chief of Police Max Zirinsky. Who is this?"

"You can call me Kenny," the man said, a cockiness in his tone. "I have your city hall and some of your fine, up-standing citizens, including the infamous Judge Craven."

"I understand Lorna Sinke has been shot," Max said. "How badly is she hurt?"

"I'd say she was toast," Kenny said.

In the background came an older man's voice. "I didn't mean to shoot her. I didn't mean to shoot her."

"Where was she shot?" Max asked.

"In the chest. Now listen to me. If you want to see any of the others alive again, I want five hundred thousand dollars in unmarked bills, a passport and a private jet out of the country."

Max was looking at Anna now, a silent understanding passing between them. A chest wound. Flint swore. She would be going in.

"We need to talk about the injured woman," Max said.

But Kenny was gone, the line suddenly dead.

"I need a clear phone line into that room," Max barked. "Now!"

Chapter 5

8:47 a.m.

"What are you doing?" Lee asked Kenny. When Kenny kept talking on the phone, Lee jerked the phone out of Kenny's hand and turned it off, dropping it on the floor.

"What the hell?" Kenny demanded. "I was talking on that."

Lee looked down at the gun still in his hand. Kenny had shoved it at him right before they'd broken down the door to the room. He didn't remember firing it, didn't remember a lot of things about the morning.

He couldn't be sure what had happened except that there'd been a boom and he'd felt the pistol buck. He'd thought the bullet went wild, hitting high in the wall next to the windows. But it couldn't have, because as the boom echoed through the room, Lorna Sinke clutched her chest and dropped to the floor.

Sinke was on the floor. Lee was still shocked that he'd shot her. He hadn't meant to. The bullet must have ricocheted. He would never have shot her. She reminded him of Francine.

"Is she what this is about?" Kenny grabbed the pistol from him with a look of disgust. Not because Lee had shot the woman, but because he didn't know anything about guns. "If you hadn't shot her, I would have."

Lee stared at Kenny, confused. Had he really just asked for five hundred thousand dollars and a plane? That wasn't the plan. That wasn't the plan at all.

"Why did you change the plan?" Lee asked as Kenny picked up the phone from the floor.

"It was my plan. I can change it anytime I want."

Lee reached up and put his finger against the bomb switch. "We agreed on the plan."

Kenny froze. "Hey, what's the problem here? Let's talk about it, all right? But first, Lee, you need to get everyone handcuffed to the radiators beneath the windows, right?"

Lee glanced at the hostages lined up against the wall by the windows, where Kenny had ordered them. The D.A., the city attorney, one of the councilmen, the judge, the councilwoman. She was bawling and carrying on. The judge was trying to calm her down without calling too much attention to himself.

Lorna Sinke, the council aide, was sprawled on her back on the opposite side of the room. Fred Glazeman, the councilman whose name Lee remembered, knelt at her side, pressing his suit jacket against her chest. The jacket was soaked in blood.

"No one was supposed to get hurt," Lee said, turning back to Kenny.

"Lee, I just knocked down a door. You're the one who pulled the friggin' trigger. How was I supposed to know you didn't know squat about guns, huh? It was an accident. Are you going to cuff the hostages, Lee, or am I going to have to do it?"

Lee looked at the hostages sitting under the windows, but didn't move. "Those weren't the demands we agreed on. You are changing the plan."

"You didn't give me a chance to tell them all of our demands," Kenny said.

Lee was shaking his head.

"Hell, Lee, this isn't rocket science. I'm sorry the woman got hurt, but it was her own fault. Had she opened the door like we said…." Kenny shrugged. "You asked me not to shoot the judge and I didn't—even when you let him get away and run into the room."

Everything had happened so quickly, Lee couldn't be sure how Lorna had been hit. The judge had broken away from him and rushed into the room. There was so much confusion. Lee had watched in horror as the pistol in his hand went off. That's when he'd looked up to see that Lorna had been hit, blood blossoming across her chest as she fell.

He felt sick. This wasn't what he wanted at all. And he didn't want money or a plane or passport. "I have the demands we agreed on in my pocket. I wrote them down so I could read them on television." He reached into his coat pocket. He'd spent most of last night getting the wording right. He looked up, the folded paper in his hand, realizing that Kenny wanted something entirely different and probably had from the beginning.

No wonder Kenny had agreed to help him. Kenny was planning to help himself.

Lee felt his finger twitch on the bomb switch, but his gaze strayed from Kenny to the hostages. They shouldn't have to pay because he'd been stupid and let Kenny talk him into this. His head ached and he suddenly felt very tired.

"I decided to ask for retribution and a new life in another country," Kenny was saying. "That's only a slight change in the plan."

"Money won't bring back Francine." Lee wasn't sure why he bothered to argue the point. Clearly, Kenny had made up his mind a long time ago.

Nervously, Kenny began to swing the assault rifle in his hands. "That's true, Lee. But neither will blowing up this building. You want to have the last word? Then have it on some tropical island drinking fancy cocktails with umbrellas in them. You ever have one of those, Lee?"

"I don't drink alcohol."

"Now, how did I know that? Look, Lee, we need to get these guys handcuffed before anyone else gets hurt, and then we can talk about this. Okay?"

Lee saw the judge look up. He thought he saw something pass between the judge and the district attorney. He knew Kenny was right. If one of the hostages did something stupid like try to rush Kenny, more people could get hurt. "I want to make my own demands."

"You got it," Kenny said affably, his gaze going to the bomb switch and Lee's finger. "So, handcuff these guys and then we'll make our demands, okay?"

Lee saw that the assault rifle was now pointed at him. "Are you going to shoot me, Kenny?"

"Nah, Lee, why would I do that?"

"If you did, the bomb would explode," Lee said quietly. "It would kill a lot of innocent people."

Kenny looked at him as if innocent people were the least of his worries. "I'm not going to shoot you, Lee." He lowered the barrel of the rifle. "But I need you to go along with this. I'm not ready to die. I want Patty's life not to have been wasted. Me dying would just be a waste of two lives, you know what I'm saying?"

Lee just stared at him. He knew exactly what Kenny was saying. His mind was as clear as it had been in weeks.

"Francine doesn't want to see your body blown to bits, either," Kenny said. "Let's ask for money and a passport for you. There's nothing keeping you here. You might as well come with me." Kenny was shifting from one foot to another.

The movement was starting to make Lee sick. He wanted to scream for Kenny to stop. He wanted it all to stop. He hadn't wanted this. No, not like this.

He could feel the switch against the pad of his finger. All he had to do was to move his finger the slightest bit and he would be with Francine. He closed his eyes.

"He's right, Lee."

He opened his eyes to see who had spoken. It was the woman who reminded him of Francine. She was lying on the floor, shot, bleeding. Probably dying. "This isn't what your wife would have wanted. Not the deaths of innocent people."

He liked her voice. It was soft. Like Francine's. Not like that other woman, Gwendolyn. She was crying on the floor by the radiator and the judge. Her voice was like a fingernail scraping down a blackboard.

Lee looked at Kenny. "You can have your money and your plane. I just want my statement read on the television news like we discussed. Once you are gone, I will release the hostages." As his gaze shifted to Lorna Sinke, he looked into her eyes. One person at least knew he wasn't leaving this building alive.

"Hey, that's cool, man," Kenny said, excited now. "So handcuff everyone and let's make that call."

Was Kenny just trying to get him to let go of the switch? "Here," Lee said, reaching into his pocket with his free hand to give Kenny the ball of metal cuffs. "You cuff them. I'll make sure no one does anything. After all, I have the real firepower, right?"

Kenny tried to hide his anger without much luck. He glared at Lee for a long moment, then slowly he took the handcuffs and walked over to the line of hostages. He carried the assault rifle, all the time keeping an eye on Lee. He was finally forced to put the rifle on the window ledge above the hostages's heads and untangled the handcuffs.

He started with Gwendolyn Clark, snapping a cuff on one wrist, then jerking her back to loop the cuff through the radiator pipe and snap the bracelet on the other wrist.

"No, leave me alone," the councilwoman was crying. "Don't touch me! Someone do something!"

Lee watched Kenny start to cuff the judge and was startled when the desk phone rang. It rang again.

"Answer it," Lorna said impatiently. "I'm sure it's for you."

Lee started to answer the phone, but Kenny pushed him out of the way and picked it up. "Yeah?"

9:11 a.m.

"Kenny?" Max said. Someone was crying in the background. "What's going on?"

"I'm busy," Kenny said.

Something jingled like a chain. "How is Lorna Sinke?"

"How should I know? She's still alive. I don't want to talk about the bitch. How are you coming on my demands?"

Max heard someone protesting in the background.

"Let me handle this," Kenny snapped. "Cuff the rest of them." A louder jingle.

"Maybe we can make a deal," Max said. "I'll do something for you and you release Lorne Sinke so we can get her medical attention."

"Yeah, right. You just hold your breath on that one," Kenny said. "Here's the deal. Either you give me what I want or I kill them all. That's the—"

The sound of a gunshot echoed over the speaker phone, followed by a blood-curdling scream.

"Kenny, did you do that?" Max demanded. A commotion in the background. "Who's been shot?"

"Get me a doctor," Kenny cried, coming back on the line. "You hear me? If you want to see any of these people alive again, get me a friggin' doctor. Now!"

9:23 a.m.

Anna felt the adrenaline shoot up, then the calm that always followed. She could hear the confusion in the meeting room at city hall. She desperately needed to get in there. One of the hostages had been shot in the chest and needed medical attention stat.

"Chief, you have to get me in there," Anna said, ignoring the look Flint was giving her.

Max shook his head. "I'm not sending another person in there. If there is any more shooting, I'm calling for a full breach."

"A lot of people could get killed if you do that," she suggested.

"Even more could get killed if I don't," Max said. "This is about preserving life at all costs, Anna, you know that. My SWAT team's lives, as well. The situation is too volatile."

"That's why you need to send me in," she said quietly. "You need someone who can contain that situation."

"And you think you're that person?" Flint asked, shaking his head.

"Yes," she said simply. She had seen his expression when the first shots were fired, when someone had come on the cell phone to say that Lorna Sinke had been shot. A chest wound. "We need to find out what is happening in there before this situation literally blows sky high. He's demanding a doctor. He will let me in. But we have to act quickly."

"We don't even know who shot Kenny," Flint pointed out. "Who else has a gun in there besides Kenny and Lee?"

"One of the councilmen?" Max suggested, then swore under his breath. "It's turning into a free-for-all." He glanced at Anna, then picked up the phone again. "What is the extent of your injuries?" Max asked Kenny.

"My arm. God, it hurts like hell. Get me a doctor, damn it. Now! Or I'm going to start killing everyone in this room, you hear me? Just the doctor. No one else comes in. You hear?"

"I'm getting you someone, but I need you to assure me that she will be safe," Max said.

"*She?* You can't find a *male* doctor?" Kenny cried.

"Not on short notice."

Kenny was swearing profusely. "Send the bitch in."

Flint raked a hand through his hair and shook his head at Anna.

The more they learned about Kenny, the more dangerous this situation became. Anna could understand Flint's concern.

"How is Lorne Sinke doing?" Max asked Kenny.

"How the hell should I know?" came the reply.

Max hung up the phone and looked at Anna. "I can't send you in there. It's just too dangerous. I'm not giving this guy another hostage."

"What about the wounded hostage, Max?"

He shook his head as one of the techs motioned that he had an outside call. He went to take it.

Flint looked relieved but equally worried about the hostages. This situation could blow at any time.

Max returned a few moments later. "That was the police commissioner and the governor on a conference call. Judge Craven is involved in some sensitive cases that the state doesn't want to lose. The police commissioner and governor want us to handle this as quickly and discreetly as possible. They don't want anything to happen to Judge Craven."

Flint shook his head. "Politics! What about the other hostages?"

Max shot him a look. "Don't preach to the choir, Flint."

"Well, Anna isn't going in there alone," Flint said, a finality in his voice that made even Max raise a brow. "I don't want her to go in at all, but I know there is no stopping her."

"Kenny is allowing only one person in and only because he's injured," Max explained quietly, calmly. "Anna might be just the person we need in there. She might be able to defuse the situation."

"Or get herself killed," Flint said. "I'll go. Tell Kenny you found a male doctor."

"It's a chest wound," Anna said. "You don't have the training. I do. Stop arguing and tell me how I can help once I'm inside."

"You don't even know if he will let you work on Lorna Sinke when you get in there," Flint told her. "He's been shot. But once you fix him up, you'll just be another hostage. He won't let you leave."

No one argued that point. They couldn't depend on Kenny to keep any of his promises. Quite the opposite.

"All your experience aside," Flint said. "You have no idea what you're walking into this time."

"We seldom do," she said.

"This is what she's been trained for," Max said. "Once she's inside and has stabilized the victim, she can use her SWAT training to help contain and control the situation."

Max turned to Anna. "We have marksmen observers on the roof across the street in the law offices." He rolled out the map of the second floor of city hall.

"The problem is the guy with the bomb," Flint said. "We can't take a shot if there is any chance Lee Harper really did build a working bomb."

Max nodded. "That's why I need someone to get a

good look at the bomb." He glanced at Flint. "I need that audio and visual to that meeting room."

"My men tried to get it in," Flint told him. "But the building is old and every sound echoes. They can't do it without being detected unless there is enough noise in the meeting room to cover the sounds."

"Like during the commotion when everyone is watching the door as they're letting me into the room," Anna said, looking at Flint, knowing that was what he was getting at. It surprised her. There had to be more to his plan, since he'd already said he wasn't letting her go in there alone.

"We can't risk having one of the marksmen take out either of the subjects until we can verify the status on that bomb," Max said, looking over at Anna. "I'm going to need you to get a good look at the device. You'll have to pass a signal. One hand, five fingers splayed and held up, is a yes, it's a bomb. Ten fingers, both hands, fingers splayed, is a no, period. If we can't get the visual in through the vents, you'll have to go to the window. Can you do that?"

She nodded.

Flint was shaking his head.

"I'll see what I can do," she said. "The way Lorna described the man with the bomb, I think I might be able to talk him down. Get me everything you have on his wife and the accident."

Max met her gaze with approval. "You got it." He turned to one of his men and gave the order.

"She can't send a detailed diagram of a bomb with a yes or no," Flint said when Max was finished. "Even if you get visual through the vents, it won't be clear enough for us to know how to disarm that bomb."

"Flint—"

"I'm not saying that Anna can't pull this off. I don't doubt she can do anything she sets her mind to." He glanced at her, a half smile curling his lips. "I've seen her determination." He swung his gaze back to Max. "But I might be able to *disarm* that bomb. If I can't, I can make sure that bomb doesn't go off in that room with all those hostages. Anna can't do that. You need me in there and you have just the opportunity to get me inside. Tell him you've found a male doctor."

Anna started to remind him again that he didn't have the medical experience.

"Your other option is to take the chance with Anna and all those hostages," Flint said. "What if it really is a bomb and Anna can't talk him down?" Flint shook his head. "Tell him you found a male doctor—and a nurse." He looked over at Anna. "Anna and I will both go in."

Anna saw where he was headed with this. "The doctor needs a nurse to help him. Kenny is obviously a bigger chauvinist than Flint. He'll expect a nurse to do the dirty work while the doctor saves his life."

Flint actually smiled. "I love it when we're on the same wavelength." His smile faded as he obviously realized what he'd said. "Max, you have to talk Kenny into letting us both come in. Look how quickly things have escalated in that room. You know it will only get worse if you don't send in a doctor. If you breach now, he'll try to kill as many people as he can."

Max sighed as the phone began to ring. Kenny calling back. He picked up after four rings.

"You'd better be getting me a doctor in here and now," Kenny cried. "I'm going to finish off the one bitch, then kill the other one unless there is a doctor here in fifteen minutes. You got fifteen minutes, you hear me?" The connection was broken with the sound of Kenny slamming down the phone.

"I'm not sure we shouldn't go full breach and take our chances," Max said.

Flint frowned. "You could lose everything, including the judge and part of the building. You aren't going to do that."

"I don't want to lose you and Anna, either," Max snapped. "You are no doctor, Flint. If Kenny figures that out, he'll kill both of you."

"Don't you think I know that?" Flint looked over at Anna. "Anna's going to make me look good. She can tell me everything I need to do, and if I fumble, I can call her over to help me. If the guy is just shot in the arm…"

"He's right, Max. I can talk him through it. I'll get him to stall as much as he can to give me time to work on Lorna Sinke…if she's still alive by the time we get in there."

"Send us in. Anna and I are the best bet you have to end this without a lot of bloodshed. If you go full breach," Flint added, "you know he'll kill as many people as he can before you can get into that room, even if the other guy doesn't blow everyone to kingdom come."

Max looked from Flint to Anna, then nodded. "I'll try to talk Kenny into it. But if I can't, we're going full breach. Anna isn't going in there alone."

"That is something we can agree on," Flint said.

Anna watched Max pick up the phone, knowing that if something happened to Judge Craven, it would mean the end of Max's career. And probably Flint's, as well. She turned away, settling her gaze on Flint. "Tell me you aren't doing this to try to protect me."

He gave her a look. "You're just one of the SWAT team, sweetheart. I wouldn't let any of my men go in there alone."

"I hope you mean that. You know how I feel about this," she said.

His jaw muscle tightened, his eyes dark. "You've been abundantly clear about everything, especially how you feel."

What a lie that was, she thought. Even *she* didn't know how she felt about this man right at this moment. Seeing Flint again had made her feel things she'd thought long dead and buried. He made her think about the past, about the two of them and their dreams and plans. True, their reasons for breaking up five years ago hadn't changed. But the feelings were still there, feelings she had denied until today.

Of course, she wasn't about to tell Flint that. This situation was bad enough as it was. If she wanted to be treated like one of the SWAT team, then telling him she still felt something for him was definitely out.

Anyway, by the time this was over, all of Flint's male chauvinistic bias would have come out again and she probably wouldn't be able to stand the sight of him.

He was nice to look at right now, though. Dark in a very intense sort of way that made any woman still breathing notice him. Anna was no exception. She wondered if Flint had been honest about being too busy the past five years to get serious about anyone.

She told herself she was only thinking about this to keep her mind off what was really going on in city hall. She'd always prided herself on her cool, calm and collected demeanor while under the gun. Today was no different from any other on the job, she told herself. She couldn't let even the thought of Flint change that.

"I've found you a male doctor," Max was saying on the phone with Kenny. "But he won't come in without his nurse."

"What?" Kenny bellowed. "His nurse? I don't give a damn if he brings his wife, as long as he gets in here."

Max looked at Flint and nodded. "But I will need the release of one hostage for the doctor."

"Listen, you—"

"It's the way it's done," Max said. "I know you've seen enough of these kinds of shows on television and you're a smart man. I'm trying to work with you, but I'm not the last word here."

Kenny was grumbling but obviously coming around. "One hostage. I have just the one in mind. The sniveling, crying one." Gwendolyn Clark.

"I was thinking the injured one," Max said. "We need to get her to a hospital."

"No way, that bitch isn't going anywhere," Kenny snapped.

Max continued to negotiate, but one thing was definite: Flint and Anna were going into what they would call an explosive situation—if they were alive later to joke about the danger.

"You'll need to change into Courage Bay Fire Department paramedic clothing," Anna said to Flint. "With you going in, too, we can take more oxygen for the chest wound victim and extra bandages."

Flint looked at her, realizing what he'd done. He was going into that situation with her, and even if he admitted she was right and the only reason he'd done it was to try to protect her, he was smart enough to know how impossible that was going to be. They were walking into a potentially lethal situation unarmed.

This was Anna's dream job? And at one time he'd wanted to have babies with this obviously demented woman.

He watched her make a call for the supplies they would need.

"Flint?" she said as she hung up. "I have a paramedic uniform coming for you. I think that will be better than street clothes. Definitely better than your SWAT gear. And extra oxygen is coming in by helicopter."

He nodded. All he could be thankful for right now was that he was going in with her. Just the thought of her going into that room alone... And while Max had said he wouldn't send Anna in, Flint knew she would have eventually worn him down and gone in alone if he hadn't come up with a plan. He knew Anna. Oh, God, how he knew her. "Anna, please reconsider—"

"Don't try to stop me," she said. "Just let me do my job."

He heard the plea in her tone. He nodded. "Just tell me what you suggest I do once we're inside."

She nodded. "Just remember you're a doctor. Look... smart." She actually smiled at that. "If you get in trouble, ask for my help. But try to give me time to stabilize Lorna." She didn't say, "If Lorna is still alive" again, but the words hung in the air between them. They might be going in too late for the council's aide.

"Just follow my lead," Anna continued. "You check his wound, frown a lot, convince him he needs to be at the hospital if possible. If it's just a flesh wound, cut away any cloth, stop the bleeding with four-by-four trauma dressing and then take your time bandaging him up."

Flint nodded. "I need to get a good look at that bomb."

"I'll do what I can to help you," she said.

He smiled then, remembering how good they used to be together. He'd missed her, missed those late-night meals they used to whip up in his kitchen, missed after dinner, lying on the couch in each other's arms. Yeah, they used to work together well.

"We always did make a hell of a team," he said, and smiled at her, knowing there was no changing this woman's mind. "We used to say it was magic, whatever it was between us."

Her gaze seemed to soften. "We can do this, if anyone can."

He nodded. That was just it. He wasn't sure anyone could stop the two hostage takers from what they planned to do. He looked away, not wanting her to see how worried he was. It made him sick at just the thought of the danger she would be in. Didn't she realize this was killing him?

He fought the urge to reach out and brush his fingers across her cheek. He wanted to touch her, to assure himself that she was real. He didn't want to consider that if he did touch her, it might be the last time.

They were going to need all the magic they could make together today.

Max joined them again, his gaze taking in the two of them. He frowned. "Everything all right between the two of you?"

"Fine," Flint said. "We're ready."

Max looked at Anna. She nodded.

"He's agreed to let the male doctor and his nurse

in. He sounds like he's in pain, but not critical." Max glanced at Flint. "He's right on the edge, Flint."

Flint heard the hesitancy in the chief's voice and knew what was coming, but not how to stop it.

"You're all wrong for the role of the doctor, Flint," Max said. "I'm afraid you'll only make things escalate in there once they see you. Someone other than you needs to go in."

Flint started to argue but Anna cut him off.

"You're right, Max. Flint looks too much like a cop, but I have an idea." Anna could see that Flint was treading on thin ice with his job because of her. She hadn't wanted this, but she understood Max's reservations. Flint was a large man and in obvious good shape. He didn't look like a doctor. Nor would he be able to perform like one once they were inside.

But there was no one she trusted more to go in there with her. He was right, the two of them had made one hell of a team. She trusted him with her life. And even more important, he could trust her with his.

"The problem, Flint, is that you look too tough," she said to him. "Max, we need a metal leg brace." She met Flint's gaze. "You have a bum leg, a *bad* limp—something that weakens you in their eyes."

Max nodded, smiling as he turned to one of his men. "Find us a leg brace that will fit Flint. Hurry. Good thinking, Anna."

Flint gave her a nod. "Nice work."

She wasn't sure he was sincere but it didn't matter. She just might have saved his job. She prayed it wouldn't come down to her having to save his life.

"Can we get any kind of weapon into the brace?" Flint asked.

Max was shaking his head. "Too risky. I'd like to send in a radio, but if they search your bag, which I'm sure they will, we don't want them to know everything we're doing by stumbling onto our channel. But I do have something for Anna." He motioned to a techie, who handed him a device that looked like a hearing aid. "Here, put this in your ear behind your long hair. You won't be able to communicate with us, but we can at least talk to you."

She nodded and inserted the device in her ear, then covered it with her hair.

"You realize if they find it on her they'll be able to hear, as well," Flint said.

"That's why I need that audio and visual in the room," Max said.

Flint nodded. "We'll make as much noise as possible when we go in. Have the team try to put in the audio and visual receivers then. If they succeed, watch me for the same signals you gave Anna, five fingers being yes, ten, no. If we need you to go full breach, I'll give you a count of five, one finger to start the five-minute count."

"If things get out of control, I'll warn Anna before we go full breach. You know what to do with the guy wearing the bomb if that happens. No heroics. Sometimes you have to sacrifice a life for the good of the rest."

Flint nodded solemnly. He knew what to do. Take out Lee Harper. He was not to attempt to disarm the bomb if it would jeopardize himself or Anna or the hostages or even the other hostage taker. The area beneath the second-story windows had been cleared. If things went badly, Flint was to send Lee and the bomb out the window.

"I hope to hell it doesn't come to that," Max said.

"Me, too." Flint looked at Anna. "Me, too."

Chapter 6

Lee listened to Kenny yelling, "Someone shot me! Who the hell shot me?" Kenny had slid down onto the floor by the phone, holding his arm, cursing and glaring at the hostages as if thinking of turning the assault rifle on the whole bunch.

Lee knew he couldn't let Kenny do that. But stopping Kenny was proving to be a problem. Lee was too old and no physical match for Kenny. His only weapon was the bomb, literally, and while it made a good threat, the reality was flipping the switch and killing everyone. He'd already shot poor Lorna Sinke. He didn't want any more bloodshed. If he could prevent it.

Lee swung his gaze over the hostages, trying to understand where the shot had come from. The blinds were down, but he could see the windows were all intact, so it hadn't been a sharpshooter from one of the other buildings or one of the helicopters that had been circling outside.

He looked up. No holes in the ceiling. The shot had to have come from inside this room. And yet none of the hostages appeared to have a gun.

Lee stared at Lorna Sinke lying in a pool of her own blood. Councilman Fred Glazeman was bending over her, pressing his good suit jacket to the wound. Neither seemed interested in what was happening on Kenny's side of the room.

"Damn it, *now* will you get the rest of them handcuffed to the radiator pipes?" Kenny was yelling at Lee. Councilwoman Gwendolyn Clark was crying hysterically. "One of those sons of bitches shot me. Find the gun."

Lee moved across the room to where Kenny had dropped the last two pairs of cuffs when he'd gone to answer the phone. Lee picked up the handcuffs with his free hand, keeping his gaze on the hostages, his finger on the bomb toggle switch.

One of them had to have shot Kenny. He cuffed the district attorney, then the judge, and searched them all. "I didn't find a gun."

"What about them?" Kenny cried, indicating Lorna Sinke and Fred Glazeman.

Lee shuffled over to them. He felt exhausted, his head was hurting. He hated getting old. He used to have so much energy. Now any little thing wore him out. And he hadn't slept very well last night. Plus, he couldn't remember spending this much time on his feet lately.

Being careful not to disturb the suit jacket soaked with

the woman's blood, he searched the two of them with his free hand. The other hand stayed on the bomb switch. Then he turned to shake his head at Kenny.

"Maybe he shot himself," Lorna suggested in a whisper.

More and more the woman reminded him of Francine, Lee thought as he looked down at her and saw the slight smile on her lips. A strong woman, he thought. Wounded, probably dying, and still she had a sense of humor. Francine had been like that.

"Damn it, Lee, what are you doing?" Kenny demanded.

Lee turned to look at him. Kenny was sprawled on the floor, his back to the wall, the assault rifle in his lap, blood seeping out from between his fingers as he squeezed his upper arm in obvious pain.

The thought surprised Lee, but he wished he had the handgun Kenny had given him earlier. Even after accidentally shooting Lorna Sinke, Lee wouldn't have minded having the gun in his hand again. Only this time, he would have used it on Kenny. He would have walked right over to him and shot him between the eyes and ended this the way it was supposed to have ended.

Kenny was trying to turn what was to have been a statement into something else, something crass and crude. Francine definitely wouldn't have liked it.

"Shut up!" Kenny yelled at the hysterical councilwoman. "Shut her up or I swear…"

The judge was trying to reason with Gwendolyn.

Lee looked down at the bomb, at the tiny red switch. He could end this in an instant. End it all. And take Kenny with him.

But then he looked at the woman on the floor again, the woman who reminded him of Francine.

"No one was supposed to get hurt," Lee said, more to himself than her. She didn't say anything. But Kenny overheard.

"*I* got hurt," Kenny bellowed. "If you had gotten them handcuffed like I told you… Find that damned gun. Find the bastard who shot me. I'll kill them all if you don't."

Lee couldn't let Kenny do that. Maybe once Kenny got the money and the plane… But Lee knew the city wasn't going to give Kenny Reese anything except a pauper's burial when this was all over. If there was enough of Kenny left to bury.

As Lee looked again at the hostages, he noticed something he hadn't seen before the shot was fired. Behind the blinds, one of the large old windows was open a crack— wide enough to get rid of a handgun.

He studied the faces of the hostages, knowing that they would never tell who'd fired the shot even if one of them had seen it. The shooter must have gotten rid of the gun during the confusion after Kenny was shot.

"If you can't get them all handcuffed," Kenny said, "I can just shoot them."

Lee felt light-headed. Clearly, Kenny wanted to kill someone. He didn't care whom. "I'm sorry, but you'll have to go over with the others," Lee said to Councilman Glazeman, who was still beside the council's aide. Fred continued to hold the woman's hand and press his jacket to her wound. There was an awful lot of blood.

"She needs medical attention," Fred whispered so Kenny wouldn't hear.

Lee remembered that Fred had been genuinely compassionate when Lee had told him at the council meet-

ings about Francine and how he felt the city needed to do
something about what had happened. The other councillors had treated him like an addled old man.

"Someone has to keep this pressed to her chest," Fred
said.

"If you can't get him handcuffed to a radiator soon,
Lee, I'm going to shoot him," Kenny hollered.

Lee looked at Fred. "Please," he whispered. "I don't
want you to get hurt."

"It's all right," Lorna said. "I can hold the jacket on
the wound." She placed her hand over Fred's and slowly
he pulled his bloody hand free and moved to the radiator against the wall. Lee took the cuff off Lorna's wrist,
the last handcuff he had, and walked over to the outside
wall to attach one end to Fred's wrist, the other to the
pipe. He didn't think Kenny would notice that he hadn't
cuffed both of the man's hands around the pipe the way
he had with the others. It was the one kindness he could
show the man who had been kind to him.

"What about her?" Kenny demanded, motioning toward Lorna.

"I don't have another pair of cuffs," Lee said. "It isn't
as though she's going anywhere."

"Maybe next time she'll shoot *you*," Kenny said, looking at her as if he wouldn't be surprised if she was the
one who'd shot him.

"She doesn't have a gun." Lee glanced down at Lorna.
She had closed her eyes. He just hoped she wasn't dead.
He also hoped she wouldn't turn out to be the one who'd
shot Kenny. Lee knew he wouldn't be able to save her
if Kenny found out.

"I'm really sorry I shot you," he whispered to Lorna.
She didn't open her eyes.

When he turned, he saw that Kenny had forgotten about Lorna and the gun. He was grimacing in pain and staring at his bleeding arm. "Where the hell is that doctor?"

10:37 a.m.

Flint led the way to the ambulance parked behind the police station. He and Anna had gone out the back and would backtrack a few blocks before turning on the siren and racing toward city hall—just in case the hostage takers were watching from the window.

Flint could see how anxious Anna was to get there. He just hoped the injured woman hung on long enough for them to get inside the building—and to get her and Anna out again.

That would be the first step, to get the injured woman and Anna out and size up the situation. First, he would determine whether or not they were dealing with a live bomb. Then he would see how many other weapons were involved, make an evaluation of the two men and decide his next course of action.

He took a seat in the back of the ambulance across from Anna, the medical bags between them. He would have to take his lead from Anna when it came to the medical part of the mission. He'd had a little paramedic training, but Anna would be calling the shots. Nothing new there, he thought. She'd been calling the shots for years.

"Once we get inside, stop the bleeding first," Anna repeated. "Take your time. He won't notice that I'm working on the woman as long as you're busy with him."

Flint nodded. She didn't seem nervous, just anxious

to get to work. He would have gladly given his life twice over to keep her out of that building. But the best he could do was to try to protect her once they were inside.

Without thinking, he reached over to tuck a lock of her hair behind her ear. Her hair felt exactly as he remembered it, and he knew if he took her in his arms and kissed her, it would be like the first time—the night of their first date.

He'd taken her to his favorite restaurant, a small seafood place on the beach. They'd sat at a table looking out over the water, the warm sea breeze stirring her hair, the sound of the sea beneath them. He remembered the way the candlelight flickered in the breeze, the light played on her face. God, she was beautiful that night.

He had stared at her, watching her talk, watching the way her lips moved, thinking how badly he wanted to kiss her. He'd known she hadn't been so sure about going out with him. He'd feared it was because he was a cop.

"I had an uncle who was a cop," she'd said, and he'd sensed there was something there, something painful.

He hadn't pried, sensing that she didn't want to tell him. He later learned that her uncle had been killed in the line of duty. He'd changed the subject, asking her about Courage Bay. He'd been on the city's police force for only a few weeks, the same amount of time he'd been in Southern California, but he liked it here more and more, he'd thought, looking at her.

She was smart and funny and he'd known he had to see her again. But he'd also sensed he needed to take it slow—the very last thing he'd wanted to do.

When they'd finished dinner, they'd gone for a walk on the beach. She'd insisted he take off his shoes and roll up his pant legs. "You have to feel the sand between your toes," she'd said, laughing at how white his feet were.

She had pulled off her shoes, then taken off down the beach, splashing in the shallow water as she ran, the moonlight turning her hair to gold, the sound of the surf mixing with her laughter, her footprints washing away behind her.

He'd run after her, catching her, turning her in his arms, kissing her. He would always think of that first kiss, the warm lushness of her mouth, the taste of her on his tongue, her scent mingling with that of the Pacific breeze. "My surfer girl," he'd called her. He'd sworn that night that he was going to marry this woman or die trying.

10:46 a.m.

"What?" Anna whispered as the ambulance turned a corner. Flint's expression had softened, his gaze almost dreamy, a slight smile on his lips. "Flint?"

He blinked, some of the softness going out of his face, his eyes. She regretted saying anything. For a few moments he'd been the Flint she'd fallen in love with.

"I was just thinking about the first time we kissed," he said quietly.

He couldn't have surprised her more. She shook her head, dragging her gaze away, not wanting him to see the impact his words had had on her. How many times over the past five years had she relived that first date on the beach, her body achingly recalling the feel of being in his arms, the sensation of his lips on hers, the effect just one kiss had had on her?

But it was the last thing she wanted to think about now.

After that kiss, all her reservations about dating him had seemed to have gone out with the tide. When they'd walked back up the beach, holding hands, the surf ebbing around their bare feet, she'd known she would see him again if he asked.

He'd asked.

And she'd said yes, the taste of him still on her lips, the feel of him still humming through her veins. It was that kiss, their first kiss, that had convinced her. Flint Mauro had made one thing perfectly clear with all his actions—especially the kiss. He wanted her. She'd never been able to resist a man who knew what he wanted and went after it. She'd thought they'd had that in common.

"That night I thought nothing could keep us apart," he said now.

"So did I," she told him as the siren came on and the ambulance sped toward city hall. She could smell his light aftershave in the small enclosed space. It brought back the feel of his rough jaw, the whisper of his lips at her temple, then on her mouth. How could she have left this man?

"Anna." He leaned closer, his lips just inches from her own, his fingers brushing her cheek, warm, a feather of a touch that sent a shock wave through her.

The ambulance braked to a stop in front of city hall. "Anna, let me go in alone," Flint said. "It's not too late to stop this."

She pulled back from him, remembering now why she'd been forced to leave him. But for just an instant there, she'd almost kissed him, almost thought things could change between them, thought there was hope for them.

Shaking her head at her own foolishness, she popped

open the back door and jumped down to the ground, turning to look back inside at him. "Just do your job, Flint."

His gaze turned hard again and she realized that was what she needed. She needed him to be the man who did whatever it took, just like his T-shirt had said. She didn't want to think of him as flesh and blood. She didn't want to remember their past.

She reached for one of the medical bags. "Once we're inside, remember, you're the doctor and I'm the nurse," she said. "Don't try to protect me."

Flint nodded abruptly, the moment lost. Just for an instant there, he'd thought he had seen that old devil desire in her eyes, he'd thought there was still a connection between them, he'd thought he could change her mind about this suicidal mission into hell. It was one thing for him to go in there. Another for her.

He climbed out. The brace hurt his leg. Limping wasn't a problem. He grabbed the oxygen tank and the other bag of medical supplies. They didn't look at each other as they started up the sidewalk.

He could feel eyes on them from inside the building but didn't look up. He stopped just in front of the door to put down the oxygen tanks and equipment as if they were too heavy for him.

Anna turned at the sound of his grunt. "Aren't you taking this a little too far?"

"I don't think so. I'm trying to act weak and helpless. How am I doing?"

She met his gaze and quickly looked away. "Good." Moving to the door, she waited until he joined her, then knocked. Her back was ramrod-straight, her expression unreadable. She could have been waiting for a bus.

This woman knew no fear, he told himself. That's why she was so calm. Fear, he'd always thought, was a good thing. It had saved his life more times than he wanted to count.

He looked over at Anna again, wondering if he'd ever really known her, as he waited for the SWAT team inside the building to open the door, waited to enter what might be the last door they ever walked through. Worst of all, he was walking through it with the only woman he'd ever loved.

The panic came out of nowhere and with such acuteness that it took Anna's breath away. She'd done this hundreds of time, gone into situations that she'd known could get her killed, and yet she'd always been calm, trusting in her training. She'd thrived on this, pitting herself against whatever was behind the door she was just about to enter. She'd loved the challenge, loved the exhilaration, loved that her training could save lives, her own included.

But as she stood at the back door to city hall with Flint beside her, the panic took hold of her and she realized this time was different. This time she would be going in with a man she had loved, had planned to marry, a man who could have been the father to her children. This time the stakes were higher. This time she wasn't sure she could do this.

She felt herself begin to shake all over. This had never happened before. The SWAT team in Washington, D.C., used to make fun of her because she was so serene in some pretty hairy situations. Where was that unshakable cool now?

She glanced over at Flint. This was all his fault. He'd had to remind her of their first date, their first kiss. He'd had to remind her of what they'd shared all those years ago and thus remind her of all they had lost. Worse, he'd reminded her how much it had meant to her. Flint had been her first love. Her only love.

She hadn't let any man close since her breakup with Flint. Instead she'd gone back to being afraid of making the wrong decision when it came to men. With Flint, she had been so sure. And if he wasn't the right one, would she pick a man who was even more wrong for her next time? At the back of her mind was always the nagging fear that she would make the same mistake her older sister had made.

So she hadn't dated out of fear. And maybe something else. Maybe she hadn't dated because she still loved Flint.

Standing here, waiting for the door to city hall to open, she was forced to acknowledge there could be some truth to that. She still felt something for Flint. Something more than she had wanted to admit even to herself. And that changed everything. Suddenly she didn't want to go into this building. Not with Flint. She couldn't stand the thought that something might happen to him and she might not have the skills to save him.

And just as suddenly, she understood why he hated her doing this so much.

He looked over at her, his dark eyes hard as stones, and she felt a little calmer at the sight of his anger. But then his gaze softened, as if he could see what she was going through.

She looked away. She could do this. She had to. It didn't matter that Flint would be here with her. She would do what she'd always done—try to get everyone out of this alive.

But even as she thought it, she knew it *did* matter. This was Flint, and after all the years of denial about her feelings for him, suddenly she was scared.

Chapter 7

11:01 a.m.

The back door of city hall was opened by one of the SWAT team, who quickly escorted Anna and Flint into the building. A half dozen men had all the doors in city hall secured on the first and third floors and were waiting for orders to storm the second floor again.

"You have your orders for audio and visual?" Flint asked the SWAT team member.

He nodded. "Standing by for audio and visual on your entrance." He glanced at Anna. Flint could see that the man was surprised she was going in, as well.

The attempt to take second floor had ended in a stalemate with the hostage takers holding a gun to Judge Craven's head. Flint had hated like hell to call them off. But had it escalated, Lee Harper might have blown up everyone, including the SWAT team members in the immediate area, not to mention Judge Craven.

Now the two subjects had half a dozen hostages as well as the judge. And in a few minutes, they could add Flint and Anna to their collection.

Flint could feel his heart pounding as they moved deeper into the old building. Their footsteps echoed on the marble floor, the sound eerie in the silent space. Anna looked cool as a cucumber, professional, capable and certainly not scared. But back at the door for a moment, he'd thought he'd seen vulnerability. He even thought he'd glimpsed fear.

He knew now that he must have been mistaken. Just as he'd been mistaken in the ambulance when he thought she wanted to kiss him as much as he'd wanted to kiss her. Yeah, for a moment he'd thought he had seen something of the woman he'd fallen in love with years ago. His mistake.

As they started up the wide central staircase to the second floor, Flint couldn't help himself. "Good luck," he whispered. "Whatever happens—"

"You, too," she said quickly without looking at him, and jogged up the stairs several ahead of him, as if afraid of what else he had been about to say.

11:04 a.m.

Anna could hear someone yelling over the sound of crying as she and Flint reached the second floor. Glancing down the hall, she saw the splintered wood on the floor outside the meeting room where the lock had busted. The door had a hole the size of a fist in it. What looked like a desk had been shoved against the door, blocking a view into the meeting room.

She knew there were SWAT team members positioned close by, but she didn't see a soul.

"You need a doctor in there?" Flint called as they neared the end of the hallway.

The crying halted. So did the yelling. "Get the door open," Anna heard Kenny order, recognizing his voice. "Check to make sure it isn't a trick, then search them."

A moment later she heard scraping sounds as several large items were moved away from the door. Then the desk was slid aside and a face appeared. An older man, his hair gray, face lined, eyes wide, blank behind the wire-rimmed glasses. Lee Harper.

The door groaned open and Anna got her first glimpse of the situation. Her heart began to pound wildly. No matter how many times she witnessed a scene like this, she could never stand the terror she saw in the victims's faces.

Lee Harper, slightly hunched over, stepped in front of her, blocking her view. He wore a police uniform and a large police-issue coat. The coat was open and she could see what appeared to be a homemade bomb duct-taped to his chest. A digital watch was attached to a 9-volt battery and a blasting cap was stuck into a block of green plastic. In an indentation in the explosives was a red toggle switch. Lee held his finger against the switch as he stepped toward them.

Out of the corner of her eye Anna could see Flint studying the bomb with an experienced eye. If there was any chance the bomb was a fake… She waited, knowing that Flint would have made his move by now if that were the case.

"Search them and their bags, but make it quick," Kenny ordered. "I'm friggin' bleeding to death in here."

Anna dropped her bag and stepped back as Lee motioned her to do. He bent down, keeping an eye on them both as he dug through the bag with his free hand, then shoved the bag behind him.

She watched him search Flint's medical bag, noticing the way Lee kept his finger on the switch. It was a real bomb. She saw Flint's grim expression and felt her breath catch in her throat.

Lee did a cursory search of her body, asking her politely to unzip her bulletproof vest, then checking each of the pockets along the legs of her pants before he did the same with Flint.

Anna could sense that Flint wanted to stop this now, before it got any worse. But Lee kept his fingers on the switch. Any movement and the bomb would be detonated. Flint must have seen that in the man's eyes. Anna had. Kenny might be the loud, volatile one, but Lee was the truly dangerous one. Especially after everything she'd learned about him before coming up here.

Past him, Anna studied the hostages. They were all handcuffed to the old radiators along the wall under the large windows. The blinds were drawn, but in the glow of the fluorescent lights overhead, their eyes shone with hope at just the sight of her and Flint. Five men. One woman. Where was Lorna Sinke?

"Help us!" the woman in the corner cried. Councilwoman Gwendolyn Clark.

Anna didn't recognize any of the others, but she could only assume the impeccable man in the dark suit near the councilwoman was her uncle, Judge Lawrence Craven. He appeared to be trying to comfort and quiet her, without much luck.

From where she stood, Anna couldn't see Kenny or Lorna Sinke. She just prayed the woman was still alive and that she could get her to the hospital before it was too late. She and Flint had a lot of people's lives in their hands. She couldn't imagine leaving this room without all of the hostages.

As Lee finished searching them, he seemed to see Flint for the first time. His expression made it clear that he was having second thoughts about letting him into the room. Lee seemed to sense it would be a mistake.

Anna held her breath, afraid what Flint would do if Lee insisted she go in alone.

"Get them in here and barricade the door," Kenny yelled from inside the room.

Anna shifted a little to one side and spotted Kenny. He was on the right side of the room. He hadn't seen Flint yet because he was sprawled on the floor, his back against the wall, his feet splayed. He was yelling obscenities and clutching his upper arm, his fingers dark with blood.

Still, Lee hesitated.

"You have an injured man in there?" Flint demanded.

"Let the doctor in," Kenny called. "What the hell is taking you so long? I'm in here friggin' bleeding."

With obvious reservations, Lee motioned them in, barricading the door behind them. Flint took another look at the bomb as he passed Lee, and they all entered the room.

Kenny balanced the assault rifle on one leg, his fingers on the trigger. Lee still had a finger on the bomb switch. The air almost cracked as if the atoms were charged. Anything could happen in this room.

To make matters worse, Anna saw that several of the hostages knew Flint was a police officer—including Gwendolyn Clark. Her eyes widened in surprise as she recognized him. Did she know he was the head of the SWAT team? Surely she wouldn't be fool enough to say anything. The judge whispered something to his niece that seemed to warn her, as if he, too, feared she would blow Flint's cover.

As Anna stepped deeper into the room, she saw the woman lying on the floor, away from the others, and quickly moved to her.

Lorna Sinke was in her late forties, slim to the point of severity. She wore a pretty blue dress, the front soaked with blood, and held a wadded-up suit jacket to her chest. Anna noted that one of the male hostages wasn't wearing a suit jacket and had blood all over his shirt and hands, but he didn't look injured.

Anna knelt beside Lorna.

"Don't worry about that stupid bitch," Kenny yelled at Anna. "Can't you see I'm bleeding over here?"

As per plan, Flint put down the oxygen tank and, taking his medical jump kit, headed for Kenny, his limp even more pronounced as he moved across the floor.

"We don't need her yet," Anna heard Flint say. "Just try to relax. Let's see how badly you've been hurt."

"It hurts like hell, Doc," Kenny whined. "One of those bastards shot me."

Across the room, Anna leaned close to her patient. "I'm Anna Carson," she said quietly as she opened her bag and pulled on a pair of latex gloves.

"Lorna Sinke," the woman said in a surprisingly strong voice.

"How are you doing?" Anna asked, surveying the situation.

"Not bad considering I've been shot in the chest," Lorna said. It appeared the woman had been shot on the right side. The bleeding had been controlled with direct pressure. She appeared to be experiencing some minor difficulty breathing.

Anna pulled out bandages, blood pressure cuff, stethoscope, trauma dressings.

"I'm going to need something to cover her with," she said, turning to Lee. She could hear Flint behind her, trying to calm Kenny down.

The tension in the room was so thick the air felt too heavy to breathe. Gwendolyn Clark was still sniveling in the corner, but other than that the room had gone silent. Anna wondered if the techs had been able to get the audio and visual in. She didn't dare look up to check.

"Tell me what happened," she said to Lorna. "Do you know what you were shot with?"

"Happened too fast."

"Try to remain still." Anna asked her about her medical history. Was she allergic to any drugs? Was she taking anything?

"We have audio and visual," Max said softly into her earpiece.

She nodded and smiled down at Lorna. "We're doing fine here," she said, taking the woman's free hand. "Don't you worry. Everything's going to be fine."

Lorna gave her a get-real look, as if no one could be that naive.

As Flint opened the medical bag and took out a pair of latex gloves, he could feel Kenny's gaze on him. He worked methodically, taking his time, trying to appear more put out than anything else. A doctor coming in here would be scared spitless, but he knew that emergency-room doctors saw stuff on a daily basis that would curl Flint's hair.

"You a doctor here in town?" Kenny asked.

"Please try to remain still," Flint said impatiently. He could feel the man's eyes on him, sense the growing concern. He kept his face expressionless as he picked up the trauma scissors and, gently removing Kenny's fingers from the upper arm, carefully began to cut away the fabric of the uniform shirt from the area around the gunshot.

"You don't look like a doctor," Kenny said, his voice sounding too high.

"What does a doctor look like?" Flint asked, trying to sound bored.

Kenny had the assault rifle next to him, his hand on it. But he and Flint both knew he would have a hell of a time trying to shoot anyone with it one-handed. And there was no way he could get it up and pointed at Flint. They were too close. Taking the rifle away from Kenny would have been as easy as taking candy from a baby.

But Kenny wasn't the immediate problem. Flint had seen the look in Lee's eyes. He could feel the older man's gaze boring into his back even now. As Lorna had told them, Lee was the smart one. He was also the loose cannon. Flint had seen something in the old man's eyes that had frozen his blood solid. Lee *wanted* to flip that switch. He wanted to end this and was fighting like hell not to.

Flint knew he could take Kenny right now without any trouble. But he needed a better look at that bomb. It had a timer, but that could be set to go off just seconds after the switch was flipped—not minutes. Flint couldn't risk it. Not yet. He would have to wait and see if he could get a few of the hostages out first.

He just had to be careful. If he did anything suspicious, he knew it would push Lee to detonate the bomb and take them all with him.

"What did you do to your leg?" Kenny asked, sounding as if he was in pain, but also nervous.

"Motorcycle crash," Flint said. "I used to like to race bikes."

"No kidding? I didn't know doctors did things like that."

"This is going to sting," Flint warned as he started to swab the area with disinfectant.

"Sting?" Kenny cursed.

Flint gave him a don't-be-such-a-big-baby look.

Kenny calmed down a little, grimacing each time Flint touched his shoulder.

"I have to see how bad the injury is," Flint said as he cleaned around the bullet hole. He didn't want to tell Kenny that the lead had passed right through the fleshy part of his arm. Just a flesh wound. He would live. Unlike Lorna Sinke, unless they could get her to the hospital.

Flint could hear Anna talking softly to Lorna; he could hear the worry in her tone.

"What were you shot with?" he asked Kenny, following Anna's lead.

"A gun."

"What caliber?" Flint asked.

"How the hell would I know? The asshole shot me and then must have thrown the gun out the window." He glared at the hostages.

"Well, you were lucky. The bullet passed right through the fleshy part of your arm and missed the bone."

"I don't feel lucky," Kenny groused. "It hurts like hell."

Imagine what being shot in the chest feels like in comparison, Flint wanted to say. Instead he took his time as he cleaned the wound. He could hear Anna on the other side of the room, working on Lorna, but he didn't dare show an interest. Kenny had made it clear he would just as soon let the council aide die.

Nor did Flint look behind him at Lee. He doubted it would take much of anything to get Lee to detonate that bomb. Flint didn't want to add to the man's suspicions, but he also needed a closer look at the bomb. He'd seen that type of mechanism before and knew he could render it safe if he could get his hands on it before that switch was flipped. Little chance of that.

The timer was the dead giveaway. There were certain things a bomb needed to be triggered. A spark was required to set off the plastic explosives. A blasting cap would do the trick.

And there was only one reason to put a timer on a bomb. To have a delay before the explosion. The delay could be anywhere from seconds to hours.

Flint just hoped the delay would be long enough.

11:54 a.m.

Anna turned to Lee and saw that he was watching Flint like a hawk. She'd seen his suspicion and knew she had to avert it away from Flint.

"I need something to cover her up with," she said. "Lee?"

He turned, surprised she knew his name.

Anna held her breath. She could see him trying to remember if Kenny had said his name in front of her. Otherwise, how would the nurse know his name?

"I need something to cover her, to keep her warm," Anna repeated.

Lee glanced around. This was Southern California. No one wore coats this time of year. No one but Lee Harper. "I don't know—"

"Could she use your police coat?" Anna asked.

Across the room, Anna could almost feel Flint hold his breath. If she could get Lee's coat off, Flint would have a better look at the bomb and its workings.

Lee looked down at Lorna, then nodded slowly. "I didn't mean to shoot her." He shrugged out of the coat, still keeping one hand close to the switch in case this was some sort of trick. Clearly he felt guilty for shooting Lorna and didn't want to see her die.

Across the room, Flint seemed to relax a little as he applied one of the four-by-four trauma dressings to Kenny's arm. "You really need to get a shot of antibiotics so this doesn't get infected. You could lose your arm if that happens. I'd suggest you get to a hospital as soon as possible."

"Yeah, I'll do that as soon as I get out of the country, Doc."

"How is she?" Lee asked Anna quietly.

"She needs to get to a hospital."

"She isn't going anywhere," Kenny snapped, overhearing them. "Are you about done, Doc?"

"Just about."

"I know you don't want her to die," Anna said quietly to Lee.

"Speak for yourself," Kenny snapped. "It's her fault I'm shot."

"She didn't shoot you," Lee said.

"Oh, yeah, then who did? Huh?" Kenny demanded. "One of them did. I wouldn't be surprised if that bitch has a gun hidden under her dress and is just waiting to shoot *you*."

"I'm wearing a bomb," Lee said, his voice deadly calm. "No one is stupid enough to shoot me."

Kenny looked at Lee as if he wouldn't put money on that. "Ouch. Can you be any rougher?" he demanded of Flint.

"Sorry. I just need to make sure I get the wound properly dressed so you don't get gangrene." That shut Kenny up. Temporarily.

Anna feared what Kenny would do once his arm was bandaged. She covered her patient, then attached the blood pressure cuff, pumped it up and listened. Lorna's blood pressure was only slightly elevated, which was surprising, considering what she'd been through.

Anna listened to her lungs. The bullet had missed her heart. Her breathing was a little shallow, making Anna suspect one of her lungs might have been hit. She listened more closely. There were breath sounds on both sides, but none in the lower lobes. A lung had probably been nicked on the lower edge, she suspected.

As she started to put the oxygen mask over Lorna's mouth and nose, Lorna stopped her and drew her close.

Anna bent down, pretending to listen to Lorna's chest.

"There are cookies in my bag," Lorna whispered, her fingers digging into Anna's arm. "They're drugged."

Anna froze, pulling back a little to look into the woman's eyes. Lorna was as tense as a wire strung too tightly, but Anna suspected that had nothing to do with her pain or her fear. In fact, Lorna had been eerily calm through all of this.

Drugged? Anna mouthed the word so only Lorna could see.

Lorna nodded.

Why in the world would the council aide bring "drugged" cookies to work? Anna remembered the special meeting of the council and attorneys, seemingly to discuss getting rid of Lorna Sinke. Had Lorna known about the meeting? Had she been bringing the cookies for the council?

"What drug?" Anna mouthed.

"Xenaline."

Anna raised a brow. Xenaline had the same effect as alcohol on the system. It would give the appearance of being drunk, slurred speech, staggering, an inability to think straight, loss of muscular function, depending on how much was administered. "How much?"

"One, mellow. Three, drunk. Four, a stupor. Six, pushing up daisies," Lorna said matter-of-factly.

Anna thought about the alleged murder of Lorna's elderly parents. Who was this woman? Was this frail little thing capable of murdering her own parents?

Well, this frail little thing had a container full of drugged cookies. Obviously, Lorna Sinke seemed to be quite capable of just about anything. She was the one who'd gotten away from Lee and Kenny. She was the one who had been running the show in this room. And she was still going strong after being shot in the chest.

Anna looked down at the woman with a kind of awe mixed with horror. As sole caregiver to her elderly parents, Lorna had had opportunity, as well as motive. What were the chances that both parents had fallen down the basement stairs and broken their necks? Almost nil.

Anna wished now that she had asked what drug had been found in Lorna's car and ruled inadmissible.

She had a pretty good idea, though. A drug that could make an elderly couple disoriented enough to fall down a flight of basement stairs.

As she looked down at Lorna Sinke, Anna tried to figure out how she could use the cookies without making the hostage takers suspicious. She met Lorna's gaze. "Don't worry, I'll think of something."

Lorna nodded and closed her eyes, a smile on her lips. "Make sure Gwendolyn gets the lion's share."

Chapter 8

Anna looked to the other side of the room. Flint's broad back was bent over Kenny. If she could have reached him, she would have laid her hand on his back. She knew it would have felt strong and warm, as if the memory were from yesterday—not five years ago.

She took a breath, her heart pounding faster. After that first date, Flint had asked her out again. How would she like to have Chinese food at this place he'd heard about?

"I love Chinese food," she'd said in surprise.

"Good. I'd love to have dinner with you tomorrow night."

"Tomorrow night?"

"Too soon, huh?"

The oops sound in his voice had made her laugh. "No, tomorrow would be fine." She'd realized that she wanted to see him again as badly as he did her.

He'd taken her to what turned out to be her favorite Chinese food place near the beach. Then he'd ordered potstickers with the spicy dipping sauce only this particular Chinese restaurant offered—her favorite.

When she commented on it, he confessed. "I called and asked your mother about your favorite restaurant and what to order."

"You *called* my mother?" She didn't mean to sound so surprised that he'd phoned her mother. In fact, she was even more surprised that her mother had known the answer.

"Actually, she put your dad on the phone. He told me you loved this place because of their potstickers."

"How did you find my parents' phone number?"

He grinned. "Do you have any idea how many Carsons there are in the phone book in this area?"

"What if my parents hadn't lived around here?" she asked, amazed that he'd gone to that much trouble—and a little concerned. All this after only one date?

"I might have had to put off dinner for a few weeks or possibly years," he joked.

She shook her head at him. "Or you could have just asked me what I like to eat."

He nodded. "That was an option, but I wanted to surprise you."

He had, in more ways than one.

They'd had a wonderful meal, then walked along the beach, the lights of the city glittering over the bay.

She'd had her reservations about him, but by the end

of the night, she found herself hoping that he would kiss her again. He didn't disappoint her.

Their first kiss had been all fireworks. This one was gentle, just like his arms around her. Flint Mauro was a man of many talents. He just kept amazing her. And he clearly wanted her.

But he wasn't going to push her. He must have sensed the hesitancy in her. He just didn't know why she needed to take it slow, why dating scared her, why getting close to a man terrified her….

Anna listened to Lorna's heart. Strong. She smiled down at the woman. She couldn't help admiring her, the way she'd handled herself through all of this. Lorna looked like anything but a killer. If it wasn't for the drugged cookies, Anna might have convinced herself Lorna had been unjustly accused in her parents' deaths.

No matter, it wasn't Anna's place to judge this woman. But Anna suspected that if anyone could survive this ordeal, it would be Lorna Sinke.

Sitting back, Anna studied the woman. She wondered about the relationship Lorna must have had with *her* mother. Anna couldn't help but think about her own mother and their so-called relationship. Her mother had called the day after Anna had gone out with Flint and invited her to Sunday dinner.

Anna had thought it strange at the time, since she hadn't heard from her mother in months, even though they lived in the same city. Anna saw her dad every week; they had a standing lunch date on Thursdays.

Curious, she'd accepted the invitation.

"Who is this Flint Mauro who called us the other day?" her mother demanded the moment Anna arrived at the house that Sunday. Her sister Emily and husband Lance were there, as well.

Her parents had lived in an upper-middle-class neighborhood in Courage Bay. Her father was an accountant with a large local firm and her mother had always been a stay-at-home mom.

Anna and her mother had never been close. Anna had been the tomboy, all skinned knees and frogs in her pockets. Her mother had related better to Anna's sisters. Candace had been six years older than Anna, and Anna felt as though she'd never known her older sister, who was only interested in dating, makeup and hanging out in her room with her friends when she was a teenager.

Emily, who was three years younger than Anna, played with dolls, loved pretty frilly dresses and took ballet lessons. Anna, who played Little League, hated dresses and had more in common with the boys in the neighborhood, felt like the black sheep of the family.

Only her father seemed to accept her and appreciate her athletic abilities. He'd given her a baseball glove for her sixth birthday. Her mother had had a fit and the two had fought about it.

Anna hadn't wanted to talk to her mother about Flint. She hadn't even mentioned him to her father. It was too soon and she feared talking about him might jinx things.

"He asked all kinds of questions about you," her mother said.

"He just wanted to know what kind of food you liked," her dad amended from his recliner. He smiled at Anna over the magazine he'd been reading. He was a tall, handsome man with brown eyes and hair, and a kind face.

"How well do you know this young man?" her mother demanded. When Anna thought of her mother, she thought of how bony and hard the woman had always felt when she'd hugged her. There was nothing soft there, nothing loving or generous, as if her spare body was an indication of what was inside.

"We've been out twice. He has four brothers, he grew up in Michigan, he's a cop." Anna was gratified to see her mother's horrified expression.

"He sounds quite nice," her father said.

"You think everyone is nice," was her mother's comment. "What do you know about his family? Mauro. I don't think I know that name." She looked toward Emily's husband Lance, the former football star now car salesman at his father's dealership.

"He's only been in town two weeks," Anna said quickly, knowing that Lance would make a point of checking up on Flint. Lance did whatever her sister wanted him to do, and Emily did whatever their mother wanted her to do.

It had been their mother's idea that Lance and Emily wait a minimum of four years after their wedding to have children. "That way, you know the marriage is going to work before you involve children," their mother had said.

As if four years were a magic number. Clearly, all Emily was prepared for in life was being someone's wife and the mother of his children. She had picked out her china when she was thirteen.

Anna had wanted more than that. More than what her mother had wanted. And she'd felt guilty because of it, as if her wanting more diminished what Emily and her mother had. As if they felt the same way.

"You'll have to bring your young man by sometime," her father said when he walked Anna to her car after dinner.

She'd dodged her mother's and Emily's pointed questions about Flint all evening. "I'll give that some thought," she said, telling herself there was no way she would ever subject Flint to her family. "Anyway, I'm not sure he'll call again."

There was a twinkle in her father's eye. "Oh, you'll be seeing him again."

Of course, her father had been right, Anna thought, looking over at Flint. Except neither of them could have predicted how badly it would turn out.

12:58 p.m.

Kenny watched Lee, his irritation with the guy growing. What had he been thinking, hooking up with a guy who was so crazy he'd tape a bomb to his chest? I mean, the guy could flip that switch and blow them all to kingdom come just for the hell of it. If anything, Lee looked more unhinged today than when Kenny first met him.

Kenny had planned to shoot him and put him out of his misery by now, and he would have, if it hadn't been for the damned bomb.

He narrowed his gaze. Had Lee figured that out somehow? Was that why he hadn't just brought a gun like a normal person?

Licking his lips, Kenny told himself he needed to be cooler with Lee. Not a good idea to push the fool over the edge. Better to try to pacify him. What would it hurt?

Once he got his money and was on that plane, Kenny couldn't care less what Lee did. But in the meantime....

"I should put in that call for you," he said. Lee didn't seem to hear him. "Lee?" The old man looked up as if surprised to still find himself here. "I promised you air time on television. I'll tell the cops and get on that. Get you on the evening news. Should be easier than money and a plane, huh. As soon as the doctor gets me patched up, I'll make that call."

He hadn't expected the old guy to dance a jig, but a little enthusiasm would have been nice.

Instead, Lee just looked at him, barely nodding in acknowledgment, making Kenny wish he hadn't bothered.

It was a bad dream. Lee told himself he would wake up any minute, wake up to Francine shaking his shoulder. "You were snoring again," she would say, then smile. "Roll over, honey." And he would, and she would cuddle next to him, slipping her arm around his waist, and he would fall back to sleep.

He closed his eyes for a moment, his finger trembling a little against the bomb switch.

Just do it. End it, he said silently. What are you waiting for? You don't want to be here. You sure don't want to go on television and talk about Francine. Had that been his idea?

He couldn't remember. He couldn't remember anything since Francine had died. No, he thought, it had started before that. He remembered Francine covering for him at a faculty party. The man she'd married, the one who used to be able to recite poetry for hours to his English classes, now couldn't remember the most basic poem.

When he opened his eyes he wished he *had* been dreaming. But he was awake. This was real. His gaze fell on Kenny. Oh, indeed this was happening, and only he could stop it before it was too late.

Too late for what? he wondered. He glanced at the

woman on the floor, trying to remember what exactly it was that had reminded him of Francine.

"Are you all right? Lee?"

He dragged himself up out of wherever it was he spent most of his days now. Limbo.

"Are you all right? You need to sit down?" Kenny was calling to him.

He shook his head. "Fine."

Kenny didn't look convinced. Lee felt beads of sweat break out across his forehead. He felt clammy and cold one minute, burning up the next, as if the fire was in his head.

Kenny was still staring at him, looking concerned and at the same time keeping his distance, as if by staying across the room, he would be safe when the bomb went off. Obviously, Kenny knew nothing about bombs.

The tension in the room seemed to jump several degrees. Anna turned again to look at Flint's broad back. She watched him put a bandage on Kenny's arm. With his large hands, he was having trouble getting the bandage on straight. She stared at his hands. It was impossible not to remember the feel of his fingers on her skin.

The first time they'd made love had been at the beach. Anna felt a familiar ache at the memory. She could imagine the sun on her skin, the soft warm feel of the sand beneath her. They'd spent the afternoon swimming and walking the beach, talking. As the sun slid into the Pacific, they'd stopped at an outcropping of rocks south of town. His kiss had been pure heat. It burned through her to her core. His fingers had felt cool against her skin as he'd brushed glistening sand crystals from her shoulder, his gaze meeting hers.

Yes. Yes. Yes. She'd wanted him as she had never wanted anything before. She'd felt a wild abandon. Giving herself to Flint was impossible—even the thought of surrendering to him frightened her—and making love would have been the ultimate surrender.

The beach had been empty, the day quickly giving way to night. She'd felt the sea breeze coming off the water, warm against her skin as he'd slipped one strap of her swimsuit down over her shoulder, then the other, revealing the pale skin of her breasts beneath.

Flint had let out the smallest of aahs, his gaze skimming over her bare skin like warm fingers. Then he'd met her gaze and kissed her.

She realized he was looking at her now. His gaze seemed to soften at the sight of her, as if he'd known what she'd been thinking about. She felt herself blush and glanced away for a moment, not wanting him to see how much she still ached for his touch.

"Nurse, could you help me with this?" Flint asked softly.

Anna sensed Kenny's gaze on her as she crossed the room. The look in his eyes told her everything she needed to know. If his demands weren't met, he wouldn't hesitate to take it out on everyone within sight.

But it was Lee, the older man, she was still worried most about. He looked exhausted, and yet so nervous he was almost at the point of pacing. He needed the situation resolved, and soon. This was a man who had been pushed into a corner and would do anything to get out. In his emotional state, Anna knew he could detonate the bomb. For any reason.

Or just forget and flip the switch, as if he no longer understood what would happen when he did. Max had gotten all the information he could on Lee Harper. A respected, loved English professor at the local college, he had retired a year ago after he'd been diagnosed with Alzheimer's.

The loss of his wife had only added to his stress, which in turn had sped the disease. Lee couldn't be trusted not to flip the bomb switch at any time.

Anna moved in beside Flint and began to help him with the bandage. Kenny watched her for a moment, then settled his gaze on Flint.

"You have arthritis in your hands," Anna said to Flint.

He looked up at her in surprise, but caught on quickly to what she was doing. "I don't think that is any of your business, nurse."

"Sorry." She turned back to Kenny and felt him relax a little, thinking the doc had a reason for not being good with bandages.

The moment she'd secured the bandage to Kenny's arm, he ordered both Flint and her back. They moved across the room from him, over by Lorna.

Anna checked her patient. Lorna was awake and having a little more trouble breathing, but definitely alert.

Anna looked past Lorna to Flint. "If we can take Kenny out, I think we might be able to reason with Lee," she whispered to him.

Flint gave her a look as if to say he wasn't so sure about that. "Let's get Lorna out of here first."

Lorna mumbled something under the oxygen mask.

Anna moved it a little so she could hear her.

"Get the bastards," Lorna whispered. "Don't worry about me."

Anna smiled down at the woman and put the oxygen mask back. "You just take it easy, okay?"

Lorna's eyes glinted and she nodded.

"If everything goes to hell, you take Kenny," Flint said. "I'll take care of Lee and the bomb."

Anna nodded, not wanting to think about Flint that close to the bomb should it go off. She'd had a little experience with bombs in Washington, D.C. She knew Lee wasn't wearing enough explosives to level city hall. That would take a truckload. But there was enough to take out this room—and possibly the outer wall.

"What are you doing?" Kenny demanded, swinging the rifle toward them. "Stop whispering."

He grimaced and looked at his arm. He was in obvious pain, but that wasn't what had him so strung out.

"You got something in that bag for the pain?" Kenny asked her. "Some Percodan or OxyContin."

"The police wouldn't allow us to bring in any of those kinds of drugs," she said.

Kenny swore and came over to grab her medical bag. He dug through it. "You've got to have something. What's this?"

"It's a drug for congestive heart failure. It would definitely calm you and might relieve your anxiety, but it probably wouldn't help much for the pain."

"What kind of pills do you have?"

She shook her head. "Everything we have, cardiac drugs and drugs for narcotic overdoses, have to be administered through an IV or IM."

"IM?"

"Intramuscular." She'd seen how jittery he'd become and recognized the symptoms. "The doctor could call and get something prescribed for you."

Kenny looked at Flint, hope in his eyes. "You could get me some Percodan? Enough to last me for a while?"

"It's a very addictive prescription drug," Flint said, and frowned.

"No shit, Doc. My sister used to get it for me, but you bastards killed her."

"Your sister was a doctor?" Flint asked.

"Nah," he said with a laugh. "She was a products manager for a company that tested car engines. But she got me some drugs sometimes." Kenny looked as if he wished he hadn't said anything. "She knew I needed them or she wouldn't have got them. My sister was a good kid. She took care of me. Loaned me money and did nice stuff like that."

"What happened to your sister?" Anna asked, not wanting to think how she'd obtained the drugs.

"She was killed in a basement fire after the quake," Kenny said, an edge to his voice. "The fire department didn't get to her in time. She was trapped inside. This city killed her just as sure as it killed Lee's wife. His old lady was crushed when the convenience store where she worked fell on her."

"So that's what this is about," Judge Craven said from across the room. "You blame the city for the aftershock of an earthquake, a natural disaster?"

Kenny shot him a withering look. "Where was the city when my sister was burning to death, or when Lee's wife was lying under that store roof? Anyway, I told all of you to keep your mouths shut. Especially that dumb broad."

"I am not a dumb broad," Gwendolyn snapped. "I happen to be a respected member of this community, and I'm sick of watching you all cater to these…criminals." The last she directed at Flint and Anna.

Anna gave her a pleading look to shut up. Gwendolyn returned it with a dirty look.

"I can understand how you must feel," Anna said quickly, turning back to Kenny, who was glaring at Gwendolyn. Anna pretended to tuck a piece of his bandage in, trying to draw his attention away from the councilwoman. "That must have been a terrible loss for you."

"Yeah. Lee wants an apology from the mayor on the television news," Kenny said. "I want a hell of a lot more than an apology. The city owes me big-time and it's going to pay."

Anna glanced at Flint. That was the connection between the two men. Death. And someone to blame. Kenny blamed the city for his sister's death. She had also been his source of pills. Probably his source of income, as well. Kenny wanted someone to pay. Lee, she thought, just wanted his anguish to be felt, his voice to be heard. And if that bomb went off, it would be heard loud and clear, the repercussions felt for a long time to come.

"The city owes me." Kenny was looking at Anna as if he expected an argument out of her.

Not likely. She'd been trained to deal with hostage takers and knew that you played along, were always compliant, never argued. Everyone in the room seemed to understand how that worked except Gwendolyn Clark.

"I'm sorry to hear about your sister," Anna said. "I'm sure she was a nice woman."

"Yeah." Kenny looked around the room, as if trying to decide who to take his frustration out on.

The phone rang and Anna knew it was Max's doing. He was monitoring the room from the audio and video devices that she knew were peering out of the air vents, although she hadn't dared look up.

Kenny picked up the phone, seemingly irritated that

he was interrupted. "Where the hell is my money and my plane?" he shrieked into the receiver.

Anna could hear Max's side of the conversation in her earpiece. "It takes a little time," Max said to Kenny. "While we're waiting, why don't we talk?"

"If you think you're going to talk me out of my demands—"

"I'm working on your demands. I also don't want you hurting anyone else while we're waiting. So, are you from Courage Bay?"

"I know how this works. I tell you my pathetic life story and you pretend to feel sorry for me, act like you care about me, and I start feeling bad and you talk me out of this." Kenny laughed. "Save it for some sucker."

"I'm sorry to hear about your sister, Kenny," Max said. "Patty Reese. The two of you were close?"

Kenny let out a groan. "Okay, so you know about my sister. You also know that she died because the city didn't get to her soon enough to save her."

"A natural disaster like an earthquake definitely stretches the city's ability to help everyone," Max agreed.

"Don't give me that. The city is to blame," Kenny snapped. "You owe me. You let my sister burn to death."

Anna was surprised to see that Lee had moved over beside Kenny. He'd been so quiet, she hadn't heard him.

Kenny seemed surprised and a little upset to see Lee so close, as well. He stared at Lee for a moment, then said into the phone, "I need a video camera," as if it was an afterthought. No doubt it was. "We're going to make a statement to the press. You're going to make sure it's on the television news." He looked up at Lee, then nodded and said into the phone, "Leave the camera outside the door. No tricks."

"Can you give me something in return as a show of faith here, Kenny?" Max asked. "I got you the doctor and nurse. I need some hostages so I can say to my bosses, he's working with us here."

Kenny was already looking at the hostages. "Sure. You can have a councilman."

Obviously Kenny had changed his mind about releasing Gwendolyn Clark, Anna thought. But she knew Max's priority was to get Lorna out of the room and to the hospital.

"I was hoping for the injured woman, Kenny," Max said. "I just don't want her to die on us. That would definitely slow down your demands."

"Just get the video camera," Kenny insisted. "I'll give you a councilman and then I'll send out the video cassette with the bitch."

"Along with the doctor and nurse," Max said.

"Sure." Kenny hung up.

Anna shot a look at Flint. Kenny was being too agreeable. This didn't feel right. She could see that Flint shared her concern.

Just minutes later Anna heard the tap at the door. Kenny removed the handcuffs from the councilman with the blood on his shirt. Anna saw the man give Lorna a reassuring smile as he let Kenny shove him toward the door, the barrel of the assault rifle pressed to the back of his head.

The councilman opened the door, Kenny staying behind him as he picked up the video camera. Once the councilman had the camera, Kenny backed him up slowly through the door into the room, grabbed the camera, shoved the councilman out and barricaded the door.

"One hostage out," Flint whispered. But he looked worried, Anna thought. Kenny was being too accommodating.

The room filled with a heavy silence as Kenny handed the camera to Lee. The older man set the camera on one of the shelves along the far wall. Still keeping that one finger on the bomb toggle, he turned the camera on with his other hand.

The camera began to roll. Lee stared into the lens, swallowed, then pulled a sheet of paper from his pocket and slowly read, his voice full of emotion, his words obviously carefully chosen.

"Francine Harper was my wife of forty-seven years. Her death devastated my life. She was everything to me. But she is only one of the souls lost during the aftershock that hit this area almost two months ago," he said, reading the sheet. "The city wasn't prepared, and because of that, lives were lost, families were destroyed. The city council talks about money and manpower. How much is a life worth? What if it was one of their loved ones trapped for hours under the roof of a convenience store? Wouldn't they find the money for manpower then?" He looked into the camera. "The city can no longer make excuses. Another earthquake here is inevitable. Steps must be taken to see that there is the manpower to save the lives of the people who depend on this city."

Tears welled in his eyes. He folded the paper awkwardly with one hand and put it back into his pocket and turned off the camera.

Kenny had been watching silently, contempt in his expression, but also a wariness. Like the rest of them, he wasn't sure what Lee would do now.

1:33 p.m.

Kenny looked up to find Lee standing over him, his finger stuck in that damned bomb. For a moment he almost told Lee what he could do with that bomb, but something in Lee's gaze—

"It's time we released more of the hostages," Lee said.

"Okay," Kenny agreed. What did he care? "You can have any of them you want. Except for the judge. He stays. No matter what."

Councilwoman Gwendolyn Clark heard the exchange and stopped sniveling, her eyes following Kenny, her face flushed with the thought of getting out of the room alive.

Lee nodded slowly and reached for the phone. "We will be sending out several hostages with the video camera. The tape is to run on the news."

"The earliest we can get on will be the five o'clock news," Max said.

"Five o'clock news?" Kenny snapped. "I'm not waiting around till five o'clock for some damned—"

"That will be fine," Lee said, and took the phone from Kenny's hand. "That will be fine." He hung up.

Kenny stared at him. Who the hell did this guy think he was? Lee was a total wacko. A wacko with a bomb, he reminded himself.

Anna couldn't imagine Kenny waiting around until five o'clock for his money, let alone the news. Not only that, Lee would have no way of knowing if his tape had made the news, since there was no TV in the meeting room.

Clearly the only way to get these people out of this room safely was through Lee.

"I'm sorry about your wife," Anna said quietly to the elderly man.

"Francine," Lee said on a breath that could have been a sob.

"That's a pretty name," she said. "You must have loved her very much."

He nodded, as if unable to speak, and met her gaze. "She was a good woman."

Anna wondered what his wife would have thought of this.

"I just had to do…something," he said, as if reading her mind. He looked ill. His face was pale and his eyes were fogged over with tears or grief or the disease that was eating away at his brain.

Kenny had picked up the phone once Lee moved back to his position near the door.

"Don't tell me what I agreed to," Kenny was yelling into the receiver. "I said I would give you a hostage. I did. Now I want something more from you. I want my damned money."

Anna could hear Max through her earpiece negotiating with Kenny. "It will make it easier to get the items you requested if Lorna Sinke doesn't die. It would definitely be a show of faith and help me get the people in charge of the city to speed things up."

Kenny actually seemed to consider this. He glared at Lorna with obvious animosity, then looked at Gwendolyn Clark. She had been listening to Kenny's end of the conversation, as well, and now started crying loudly, saying, "Please let me go. Please let me go."

"You can have a woman," Kenny snapped. "The councilwoman broad. I'm sick of listening to her."

Anna felt her heart drop. If only Gwendolyn would just shut up. Like Lorna, she wanted to strangle the woman.

Gwendolyn quit crying. She wiped her tears and looked more eager than ever to get away. She didn't seem to have any problem leaving her uncle, the judge, behind, or any of the rest of them.

"It would be easier to take the injured woman out now," Max said. "The medical personnel can bring her out with them. If she dies, there could be a problem getting you a passport."

"Listen—"

"I'm doing the best I can here, but I'm only the chief of police," Max told him. "I take my orders from the commissioner, and ultimately we're looking at the FBI getting involved. Their policy is not to negotiate at all. But if you prefer to take your chances—"

"Take her—take the shot one," Kenny said. "Just get my money and get me out of here!" He slammed down the phone.

Anna let out the breath she'd been holding and turned to look at Lee. He seemed to sag with relief. She had hoped she could talk some sense into him and stop this, but she now saw that it wouldn't do any good. He didn't want Lorna to die, but he obviously had lost control of what was happening here—if he'd ever had any control.

This situation was so volatile that either Lee or Kenny could set the other off. Anna realized that if Kenny really did let her and Flint take Lorna out, the rest of the SWAT team would move in right after.

"You're sending her out? She's going to die anyway,"

Gwendolyn screamed. "Don't you leave me here. I'm hypoglycemic. I have to eat or I'm going to be sick."

"Shut her up," Max said into Anna's ear.

"Let me see what there is to eat in this bag," Anna said, going to the one Lorna motioned to. She found the container of cookies, hesitated. Gwendolyn was working herself up again, crying and pleading for someone to do something. One cookie, mellow. Three, drunk. Six, too many.

"Would you like a cookie?" Anna asked, cringing at the thought of what she was about to do. But she had to get Gwendolyn calmed down before this escalated or the councilwoman would get them all killed.

"No!" Gwendolyn cried "I want out of here. I can't stand this any longer."

Anna practically shoved a cookie into the woman's mouth.

"I'll take one of those," Kenny said. "Don't feed them all to that sow."

Anna carried the container of cookies over to Kenny. He took one, popped it into his mouth and chewed, then spit it out with an oath. "What the hell is that taste?"

She stared at him.

"Almond," he snapped. "I hate almond flavoring."

"I'll have one," D.A. Lalane said.

Anna had been trained to save lives, not take them. She walked back over to Gwendolyn, afraid of how much of the drug Lorna had put in the cookies. If Lorna was right, one cookie wouldn't hurt them, and it might keep everyone calmer. She fed one to each of the hostages. She could hear Lorna grumbling behind her oxygen mask to give the rest to Gwendolyn.

"Give me another one," Gwendolyn demanded angrily. "You care more about a murderer than a council-woman?"

"My job is to see that the injured victim gets the care she needs," Anna said to the councilwoman. "I'm trying to save her life. And yours. You have to be quiet."

Gwendolyn gave her a look that said she didn't have to do anything. "You tell that cop to get me out of here or else."

Anna didn't need to ask who "that cop" was. Flint. Gwendolyn had recognized him and was now threatening to blow his cover unless she was released. Anna shoved a cookie into Gwendolyn's mouth, tempted to feed her the rest.

As she turned, she could see that Kenny had heard Gwendolyn. He was frowning. She just hoped he thought the councilwoman was referring to him because of the uniform he was wearing. Clearly, Kenny didn't like Gwendolyn. He was looking at her as if he couldn't take much more of her. Anna knew the feeling.

It would seem strange not to offer Lee a cookie. He already seemed dazed and she feared that the drug might have an adverse effect, but she had to make the offer.

"Would you like a cookie?"

To her relief, he shook his head. He seemed despondent. More and more she feared that the Alzheimer's had helped him make this horrible decision and ultimately would lead him to a worse one.

"Nurse?" Flint called. "Help me take apart one of these meeting tables so we can use it as a stretcher to get the patient out."

Anna joined him in the corner, away from the others. "Gwendolyn is threatening to blow your cover," she whispered as she bent down next to him.

"I heard." He removed one of the legs from the conference table and shifted to unbolt another. "I think I can talk Kenny into letting you and Gwendolyn take Lorna out," he said. "Gwendolyn's a big woman. She should be able to help carry—"

Anna shook her head. "Send two hostages. You're going to need me—"

"Hey! No whispering over there," Kenny yelled.

They removed the other table legs and carried the top over and put it down next to Lorna.

"On the count of three," Flint said, slipping his hands under Lorna's shoulders as Anna went to her feet. "One, two, three." They lifted Lorna onto the table top, then put the oxygen tank next to her. She didn't even groan, but Anna could see that she was in terrible pain and seemed to be having more difficulty breathing.

But she was alert and staring daggers at Anna, probably because Anna hadn't given Gwendolyn enough cookies to make her comatose. Anna glanced over her shoulder at Gwendolyn. The cookies didn't seem to have had much effect. Maybe the drug was slow acting. Or maybe because of Gwendolyn's size, it took more than two cookies to mellow the woman.

"You aren't going to leave us here," Gwendolyn cried. The judge tried to hush her, but his niece hadn't paid any attention to him from the start. Anna had seen other hostages who lost control during situations like this, the stress too much for them. But she'd never come across one quite like Gwendolyn Clark.

"You can't leave us," Gwendolyn screamed. "Do something. Stop these men." She was hysterical, crying and screaming and looking right at Flint. "Isn't that what you're paid to do?"

Chapter 9

"Shut up!" Kenny yelled, and pulled a pistol from behind him.

Flint hadn't realized Kenny had another weapon other than the assault rifle. Kenny pointed the pistol at Gwendolyn, who was screaming, her words almost unintelligible. Almost.

"You're supposed to protect us, isn't that what you're paid to do?" Gwendolyn screamed at Flint. "Now you're just going to walk out of here and leave us?"

Anna rushed to the woman, knowing now that Gwendolyn was determined to blow Flint's cover and get him killed—if Kenny didn't shoot her first. She practically stuffed a third cookie into the woman's mouth.

"Get out of the way!" Kenny was yelling at Anna.

Lee was trying to grab Kenny's arm to stop him from pulling the trigger.

Anna could hear Max in her earpiece. "Quiet her down. Whatever it takes. *Anything*. She's going to get everyone in there killed."

"There is no reason to get upset here," Anna said calmly. "Everything is going to be fine." Anna turned, putting herself between Kenny and Gwendolyn. "I think we should let the councilwoman help carry Lorna out. I'll stay behind. That way I can change your bandage when the time comes."

"Get out of my way or I'll shoot you, too," Kenny snarled. "That bitch isn't going anywhere but the grave."

Flint stepped between Kenny and the two women. Kenny was just itching to kill someone. This was going to come to a head and quickly. The problem was, Lee had moved back by the door, seemingly disoriented. Flint feared that if Kenny fired that gun, there was a good chance Lee would detonate the bomb in a knee-jerk reaction.

Flint estimated how long it would take him to get to Lee if that happened. He needed to know how much time Lee had programmed between the flip of the switch and the blast. Probably not long enough for Flint to reach Lee to get him and the bomb out of the room.

Worse, there was a good chance that Flint would be wounded if Kenny started firing. But Flint stood his ground, protecting the woman he loved, his logic as fouled up as his feelings.

Anna must have seen it, too, because the damn woman stepped around him and put herself right into the line of fire.

"You don't want to shoot anyone," she said quietly to Kenny. "You don't want anything to hold up your money or the plane. Doctor, maybe if you called, you could get Kenny some pain pills. That arm must be killing him."

Flint stared at her back, wanting to throttle her. But when he looked at Kenny, he saw that he had lowered the gun, and Flint realized something that Anna obviously had seen right away. Kenny was a junkie and he needed a fix.

"My arm *is* killing me." Kenny glanced at Gwendolyn, daring her to make a sound, but didn't raise the gun.

Flint couldn't believe the way Anna had handled the situation. His heart was pounding, his legs were weak. He watched Anna, awestruck by how calm she appeared, how well she was handling Kenny, handling all of them.

Kenny had the gun resting on his thigh now. He seemed to have backed off. For the moment. Flint had to get Anna and as many of the hostages out of here as he could. But he was aware he couldn't take down Kenny and disarm the bomb on Lee by himself.

He knew Max would take advantage of the situation when the door opened again. Anna seemed to know it, as well. This wasn't what Flint had hoped for, but there was no way to contain this situation other than by force. The next step was to get Lorna out of here and to use that diversion to do a full breach.

Meanwhile he had to start thinking like the SWAT team commander he was, not the lovesick fool he'd been. Anna was right, he had to admit. He needed her if he hoped to stop these two. The thought killed him. If he hoped to do his job, he had to keep Anna here with him. He couldn't do it without her. Once the team went full breach, he needed Anna to take down Kenny while he took care of Lee and the bomb.

He looked over at her. She seemed so fearless now, but by their second date, Flint had known something was wrong. Anna had seemed afraid of intimacy. Not afraid. Terrified. At first he'd thought it was just him. He did come on too strong—especially when he wanted something. Also, he was a lot larger than she was, stronger, and he'd worried that he somehow frightened her.

But he'd been smart enough not to question her about it. Instead he'd done everything possible to make her feel comfortable around him. He'd known he had to move slowly, carefully.

Still, he couldn't help but wonder what it was that had frightened her so much. A love affair gone wrong? Something had happened to make her afraid of men, and Flint had been determined to find out what it was and to help Anna get over it. And Anna had seemed just as determined to keep whatever it was a secret.

2:14 p.m.

"Calm down. Everything is going to be fine." Anna spoke loud enough for everyone in the room to hear as she met Kenny's gaze. She couldn't believe Flint. He'd tried to protect her. What if Lee had flipped the switch on the bomb? There was no way Flint could have gotten to him in time. And what if Kenny had shot him? Where would that have left them all?

She'd feared this might happen. That Flint would be so busy trying to protect her that he would forget his job. She shot him a look. His chastised expression made it clear he'd realized what he'd done. If everything went wild in here, he couldn't protect her even if he tried. She saw that in his eyes, the pain, the realization.

She could feel the rampant beat of her heart as she met his gaze. They both knew it would be hell getting out of here alive unless they could get everyone quieted down and do their jobs, forgetting what had once been between them.

"If you can talk your way out with Lorna, I want you out of there, Anna," Max said into her earpiece. "That's an order."

Anna could feel Flint's gaze, warm on her skin. She looked up into his eyes. Max hadn't said anything about Flint going out with them. Just the thought of leaving him here in this room was too much for her. She understood his need to protect her too well. She had to find a way to get them all out of here. She couldn't leave Flint. He wouldn't be able to neutralize two men, especially these two men, alone. Even if he could disarm the bomb in time, someone needed to make sure that Kenny wasn't going to slow him down. That someone was going to be her. Come hell or high water.

If any more shots were fired, she knew Max would go tactical real quickly, sending in the SWAT team, guns blazing in the hopes of saving as many of them as possible.

She'd seen this sort of thing in Washington, D.C., a few years ago. The team had come in and literally thrown the subject wearing the bomb out the window. The area below had been cleared for just such a maneuver. The man had already activated the device before going out the window. The bomb had exploded between the fourth and third floors on his way down. It had taken out all the windows on that side of the building, but the hostages were unharmed. The man wearing the bomb was lost in the explosion.

Anna knew that was exactly what Flint had been ordered to do.

"I can't take this anymore," Gwendolyn cried, sounding a little drunk. The cookies weren't acting quickly enough. Anna had to shut the woman up.

She stuffed another cookie into Gwendolyn's mouth and, trying to keep her voice calm, said, "Doctor, could you toss me the tape from my bag." She just hoped four cookies didn't kill the woman.

Gwendolyn's eyes were like saucers as she looked up at Anna, obviously suspecting what she had in mind. The councilwoman frantically tried to swallow the cookie. It was clear that once she did, Gwendolyn was going to blow Flint's cover and do even more damage. The stress of this situation aside, this was a woman who was used to getting her way, no matter who got hurt in the process.

"Here," Flint said, but instead of tossing her the tape, he brought it over to her. His fingers brushed hers as he handed her the tape, and she felt heat ripple through her, warming her skin.

Do Whatever It Takes. Wasn't that what his T-shirt had said? Her stomach knotted at the thought that she might have created this man. He had wanted to be chief of police when they'd been together. All her talk of SWAT, was that why he was now the head of the Courage Bay team? He had been risking his life since she'd left him and she suspected it was for all the wrong reasons. And now he was ready to take a bullet for her without even considering his own life.

What surprised her was that she felt the same way. All that telling herself she was over Flint Mauro—well, it had obviously been a lie. The feelings were still there. So were the reasons they couldn't be together. Reasons she had magnified by taking this job.

But they were on the same team now. In this together in a way they hadn't been when they were engaged. And that made her feel closer to Flint than she had before.

The moment Gwendolyn swallowed the last of the cookie, Flint helped Anna tape her mouth with several pieces of tape as the councilwoman struggled, her eyes glaring holes into Flint and Anna. If looks could kill, they'd both be dead. Ditto if Gwendolyn managed to get the tape off.

"You are going to get us all killed if you don't shut up," Anna whispered as she applied more tape.

Two large tears coursed down the woman's cheek. Hatred radiated from her eyes as she struggled against the tape on her mouth, desperate to rat them all out, wanting blood, just not her own.

I will get you fired, the look said as she glanced from Flint to Anna and back.

"Better than getting us *killed*," Anna whispered.

Gwendolyn was struggling to get the tape off her mouth, her eyes mean with anger and open threats. Anna reached for one of the medical bags. As much as she hated to do this, she was going to have to give the councilwoman something to settle her down.

She pulled out a vial of a drug that should put Gwendolyn Clark out like a light. Add the four cookies and whatever drug was in there— Because of the woman's size, Anna had a feeling it would take an elephant dart to put Gwendolyn down. But still, in good conscience Anna decided to cut down the dosage. She didn't want to kill Gwendolyn, just shut her up.

* * *

Flint saw what Anna planned to do and turned a little to shield her actions from Lee and Kenny. The two men couldn't have been more dissimilar. Kenny wanted money and a plane and a passport. Lee just wanted someone to validate his pain. Flint feared the homemade bomb taped to the older man's chest was the way Lee planned to get that validation—not on some video on the nightly news.

At first Flint hadn't understood what would make a quiet, law-abiding, educated man like Lee Harper ducttape a homemade bomb to himself. He could understand taking over city hall—even as desperate and futile as that was.

But the bomb had thrown Flint until he'd met Kenny. Then Flint had understood. The older man had known his partner was a loose cannon. Lee had taken things into his own hands, building the bomb, knowing it would trump anything that Kenny tried to threaten him with. This would end when Lee said it would—and the way he'd planned it. And there was nothing Kenny could do about it.

Flint wondered if he and Anna would be able to do anything about that, either, as he looked at Lee. The man had his finger on the switch and there was something deadly and final in his filmy gaze.

Flint looked at Anna. She was something. What a remarkable woman. That alone added to his fear that someone as unique and wonderful as Anna might not see another sunrise if things went badly in this room.

He would protect her to his death, he thought, and smiled to himself. Thank God he hadn't let her come in here alone. He couldn't bear the thought of watching all of this on the video at the Incident Command Center.

Together they just might be able to pull this off. He had to hang on to that hope. He couldn't contemplate the alternative. They would do their jobs, because as Max said, they were the best at what they did. Anna sure as hell was, he thought grudgingly. She was flat amazing. Max had been right in his appraisal of her. Flint couldn't imagine what would have happened in this room if she hadn't been here.

Now, if only Kenny kept his part of the bargain and let them take Lorna out. He turned so no one could see him signal Max that it was almost time to go full breach. Flint felt his heart pound a little harder. Once SWAT went tactical, he and Anna would really be on their own.

2:33 p.m.

Seeing the needle and realizing what Anna had in mind, Gwendolyn kicked out at her. Anna moved to the side and shoved up the sleeve of the woman's cotton shirt as Gwendolyn fought her.

"What are you doing?" Kenny demanded, suddenly appearing next to her after he shoved Flint aside with the assault rifle. He held the pistol in his other hand at his side.

"Just trying to calm down the councilwoman," Anna said without looking at him as she hurriedly jabbed the needle into Gwendolyn's arm. The woman let out of a muffled howl behind the tape on her mouth.

"I thought you didn't have any real drugs in there?" Kenny said, suspicion in his voice.

"Nothing for *pain*," Anna told him. "This should put

Ms. Clark out for a little while." Gwendolyn was glaring daggers and working furiously to get the tape off her mouth before the drug could take effect.

Anna turned to look at Kenny. "I didn't think you would want that sort of side effect."

Kenny nodded, though he still looked suspicious as he stared down at the councilwoman. Then he turned to look back at Lee and Flint. Lee was standing over by the door, his finger on the toggle switch to the bomb. Flint had moved over by Lorna on the makeshift stretcher.

"Sit down," Kenny ordered Flint, who squatted next to Lorna and pretended to check her vitals. "Tape the rest of the hostages's mouths, then sit down," Kenny said to Anna.

She did as he ordered, then quickly went to join Flint and Lorna, afraid Kenny would try to separate her from Flint.

As she checked Lorna's vitals herself, she glanced at the hostages. They all looked calmer. Gwendolyn looked smashed, eyes unfocused, zoning out. *Finally* silent.

Lorna moved her oxygen mask aside. "Gwendolyn's an idiot," Lorna whispered. "I'm surprised she didn't get us all killed. Someone ought to put that woman to sleep."

Anna wasn't surprised at Lorna's suggestion, given what she knew about the cookies. She had to admit she'd wanted to ring Gwendolyn's neck herself. The councilwoman had almost blown Flint's cover—and had definitely put all their lives at risk, especially Flint's.

"She only got elected because she was related to the judge," Lorna whispered.

Apparently, Gwendolyn had ears like a cat and the constitution of a Mack truck. She raised her head and glared at Lorna even in her drunken state. She mumbled something behind the tape, but the only distinguishable part was "my uncle the judge's help."

The councilwoman had worked a small hole in between the strips of tape with her tongue.

Kenny looked up, his eyes widening as if a light had come on. He walked over to Gwendolyn and ripped off the tape. She let out a yelp and called him a bastard.

"The judge is your uncle?" he asked her.

Judge Craven was trying to shush her from behind his tape, but Gwendolyn was having none of it.

"That's right," the councilwoman said, her words slurring, but still clear enough that they all understood. "I'm Judge Lawrence Craven's niece. You have no idea who you're messing with. My uncle will see that you rot in prison, if not go to the electric chair."

"Shut up, you stupid woman," Lorna rasped.

"If you don't die, I'll get you fired," Gwendolyn said, glaring over at her.

"Have another cookie, Gwendolyn."

Gwendolyn narrowed her gaze suspiciously. "You put something in the cookies."

Yes, Anna thought, but what had Lorna planned? Surely not to kill the woman. Given what Anna knew about Lorna, she suspected the cookies had been more to discredit the councilwoman. Maybe a drunk-driving charge, since Gwendolyn would have appeared intoxicated after eating a few.

Anna wanted to believe that had been all Lorna had planned. Not murder.

Not that it mattered anymore. Both women had worse to worry about than their plots against each other.

The phone rang.

"Look, I'm tired of waiting," Kenny barked into the

receiver. "If you don't meet my demands, I'm going to kill the judge's niece."

"Good choice," Lorna whispered, pulling aside the oxygen mask again.

Anna put it back in place and motioned for Lorna to keep quiet.

Gwendolyn looked up and tried to focus on Kenny as he went to stand over her. The judge was trying to say something from behind the tape over his mouth.

"You hear me?" Kenny screamed into the phone. "No, don't give me any more excuses!" He slammed down the phone and looked around the room as if daring anyone to say a word or he would shoot them.

"You promised to send out the woman and the video camera," Lee said.

Kenny glared at him, but said nothing.

2:42 p.m.

"It's time," Flint whispered to Anna. He looked into her eyes and knew she understood perfectly. This situation had reached the point where they had to make a move now.

"I'll take care of Kenny," she whispered.

Flint nodded, feeling his heart rate pick up. He was worried about what she had in mind.

"Stop whispering over there," Kenny yelled to them.

Flint leaned back against the wall. Anna sat on the other side of Lorna and continued to monitor her patient.

Kenny paced back and forth against the far wall, his gaze moving from Lee to the hostages to Flint and Anna. His expression soured at the sight of Lorna.

Flint let his focus return to Anna. She was so beautiful. He'd thought his memory had been prejudiced by his love for her. But he was wrong. She was even more exquisite than he remembered. There was a softness to her face as she took Lorna's blood pressure, her hands so sure.

He had known by his second date with Anna that he wanted to marry her. He'd been smart enough to keep that knowledge to himself. His friends would have thought he was crazy. He didn't even know this woman, they would have argued.

But he did know her. He could feel a connection between them that was so strong it made his knees weak. Except Anna was keeping him at arm's length emotionally. Sure, she accepted his dates. They would talk and laugh and kiss, but he could feel the wall she had erected between them.

Flint was determined to tear down that wall even if he had to do it brick by brick. He knew he had to gain her trust to get to the reason for her reserve, her terror of men. So he bided his time. He didn't push. He waited.

It wasn't easy. He wanted to call her parents and try to find out what had happened to Anna to make her this way. He did find out that she hadn't dated much. She said she'd been too busy going to college, training to become a paramedic, too busy working after that.

He didn't buy it. Not a woman who looked like Anna.

When Anna's mother called to invite him to Sunday dinner, he was delighted. But when he told Anna, her reaction surprised him. She was angry and upset.

"My mother just wants to interrogate you," Anna said. "You don't know what she's like."

No, he didn't. When one of his brothers had come through town, Flint had made sure Anna got to meet him. He wanted his whole family to meet Anna, but they lived all over the country. Her parents lived right here in town and she hadn't ever suggested taking him home to meet them.

"If you want me to, I'll call your mom and tell her I can't make it," he said.

Anna looked over at him, tears glistening in her eyes. "No," she said, and moved to him, cupping his face in her hands. "No. I've been wanting you to meet my dad."

He felt as though he'd just scaled Mt. Everest. "Great. I'd love to meet him, and don't worry about your mother. She can interrogate me all she wants. Really."

Anna only nodded. "With my luck, my sister Emily and her husband Lance will be there, too."

He lifted her chin to look into her beautiful eyes. "I don't mind meeting your sister Emily and her husband Lance."

"You can say that now," she said.

He laughed. "Wait until you meet my brother Curtis. His idea of dressing up is putting on his cleanest overalls. Did I mention he raises pigs out in Michigan?"

"There is nothing wrong with raising pigs or wearing overalls," she said indignantly.

"I know," he said, laughing. He'd pulled her into his arms. "But when we have dinner, he always has to tell me the name of the pig we're eating at the time."

She laughed then, not sure if he was serious or not. "Thank you."

"I haven't done anything," he said.

"Yes, you have. You just don't know it."

"Anna," Max said in her ear. "I want you and Flint out of there. Try to get Kenny to let you take out the wounded woman now. Once through the door, the team will move in."

She nodded slowly and held up her fingers to answer yes, then took a deep breath, her gaze going to the hostages. Gwendolyn Clark was staring at her. Even as drugged as she was, the councilwoman had seen Anna nod and recognized her action as some type of signal.

Gwendolyn was obviously dying to tell Kenny. Maybe she thought the information could buy her a way out of here.

When Anna looked over at the judge, she saw that he, too, knew what was going on. He nodded and closed his eyes, no doubt assuming Anna's signal would put an end to this one way or another.

The phone rang. Kenny picked it up, grimaced in pain and let out a string of obscenities.

"I just wanted to let you know we are getting what you asked for, but I need a show of faith from you," Anna heard Max say through her earpiece. "Give me the wounded hostage and I'll try to get things moving faster."

Kenny let out an oath and slammed down the phone.

"You want me to look at your arm?" Anna asked quietly as she got up and started toward him. She heard Flint's softly spoken oath behind her. Her heart was pounding so hard she feared he could hear. She licked her lips, her mouth dry. "You might have gotten it bleeding again."

"No, you've done enough damage." He took a couple of deep breaths. "I've got to have something for this pain."

Anna nodded, having been waiting for this. "I can have the doctor call or I can see about getting you something." She motioned to the phone.

He looked at her as if he wondered how she thought she could get him drugs when he had a half dozen hostages and he couldn't get squat.

"May I try?" she asked.

"Whatever." He turned away in disgust. "Just get me something to take the edge off the pain." He turned back to her. "Nothing so strong it knocks me out, or you'll be the person I shoot before I go down, got it?"

She nodded. She understood a lot more than he knew. She saw that it wasn't the pain in his arm that he needed the drugs for. He looked like some of the strung-out addicts she'd dealt with in D.C. Edgy and unpredictable. Only one thing on their minds: their next fix.

Kenny's "fix" was the prescription drugs his sister used to obtain for him.

"I could see if I can get you some OxyContin," she said, pronouncing it "oxycotton" like on the street.

He turned to look at her, his mood picking up. "Like they're going to give you the drugs. They haven't given me anything I've asked for. I guess I'm going to have to start killing people. Maybe then they'll take me seriously."

"I can tell them that we have to have the drugs within the next thirty minutes," she suggested.

He eyed her. "Like they'll listen to you."

She lifted a brow. "I'm a woman and a nurse. Women can be more persuasive than men. Even doctors." She already knew that Kenny was a raving chauvinist. It went without saying that he thought women had it easier than men in his world. "Women have their ways."

"You'll need a doctor's signature to get a prescription," Flint said, sounding very much like a doctor.

She shook her head, still focusing on Kenny. "The police chief will figure it out."

Kenny smiled ruefully at that, then looked her over. "You married?"

She could feel Flint's gaze on her as she shook her head. "I came close once."

"Yeah, me, too." Kenny still didn't trust her his expression said. "You wouldn't be trying to pull something, would you?"

She shook her head slowly. "I just need to convince the police chief that we have a better chance of getting out of here safely if you're comfortable and not in pain."

He still looked doubtful. He was sweating, his face flushed. He needed the drugs and soon.

Anna hoped Max was already getting the prescription filled. "The police might have enough time to get the pills before your helicopter gets here. Otherwise, you might have to make the trip without them. But if you'd rather have the doctor try…" She turned to go back over by Lorna and Flint.

She knew Kenny was imagining flying to another country in a fancy private jet, high on his favorite drug, rich and looking forward to his dream future.

His need for the drugs was strong. But so was his fear that a mistake would land him in prison or a cemetery. She turned to give him a tired, bored look, as if it didn't matter one way or the other to her.

Kenny glanced toward the phone, then motioned her over to it with his gun. "But if you do anything or say anything you aren't supposed to…"

She just nodded and picked up the receiver. She almost dialed the incident command number. Instead she looked at him. "Is there some way to reach them or should I dial 911?"

He seemed to relax a little, relieved she hadn't known the number, as if that renewed his faith that she was no more than a nurse, and nurses were safe. "Here's the number the cop gave me."

"Nice work," Max said into her earpiece as she dialed the number Kenny had scribbled on a scrap of paper. "We're getting the prescription filled. Try to stall him as long as you can."

"This is Anna Carson," she said when Max answered. "I'm the nurse inside city hall. I'm going to need a prescription filled for my patient." She looked up. "Kenny, is there anything you're allergic to? Any medications you've taken before and had side effects?"

"Nah, nothing."

"Is there any drug you're currently taking?" she asked.

"Just get me some damned painkillers," he snapped.

"I have to ask these questions," she said, unruffled. "Sometimes if you've taken something for a long time and you take something else, it can kill you."

That stopped him. He rattled off a long list of prescription painkillers he took, depending on whatever his sister had been able to get for him.

She nodded. "No adverse side effects?"

He gave her a look like she had to be kidding. "Tell them to hurry with the drugs or I'm going to start shooting. I'm sick of them, okay?"

"Okay." Then into the phone, she said, "I need Oxy-Contin. Do you need me to spell the name of the drug for you?" She gave Kenny a look like "dumb cops."

He chuckled and shook his head.

Anna spelled the name out, then gave the dosage required. She looked over at Flint. He was watching Lee. She'd almost forgotten about Lee. Almost. He seemed to be lost in a daze, distancing himself from everything that was happening in this room.

When she looked back at Flint, he winked at her. Her heart did a small roller-coaster loop in her chest as she held his gaze for a moment.

"Tell 'em to leave the drugs outside the door," Kenny said.

"Yes, just leave them outside the door," she told Max.

"Tell him I'm doing everything you've asked," Max instructed. "Can you get Lorna out?"

Anna looked at Kenny. "He said he would get it right away if we release Lorna Sinke." She used "We," wanting him to feel she was in this with him. Her look said, *Why not? Let's humor them.* She glanced at Lorna.

Kenny shook his head. His gaze scanned the hostages, halting on Flint. He didn't like Flint's size and he no longer needed a doctor.

Anna held her breath. Kenny shifted his attention to Gwendolyn Clark. She looked completely out of it, finally.

"Give them Lorna," Lee said, startling them both. Kenny's head jerked around. Clearly he didn't like Lee giving him orders. The two glared at each other across the room.

Anna moved closer to Kenny and whispered, "Let them have Lorna. She isn't going to make it anyway." It was a lie. Lorna was strong and tough. She should make it if Anna could get her to a hospital. But Kenny didn't know that. "That way, when she does die, it won't be here. It will be better for you, you know."

He glanced over at Lorna. Lorna had her eyes closed.

"Fine, trade her. But I want those drugs and I want them now."

"It will take two hostages to carry her out," Anna said, hoping he went for it. She didn't dare look in Flint's direction.

"That wasn't the plan," Max said into her ear. "I want you out of there."

Kenny stood staring at Lee as if waiting for Lee to give him another order. There was a tightness to his mouth that Lee must have noticed, as well. When Lee didn't say anything, Kenny said, "Take the lawyers. No one cares if attorneys die." He indicated the district attorney and city attorney.

Lee reached into his pocket with his free hand and held out the keys to the handcuffs.

"Lorna's coming out with the lawyers," Anna said into the phone and hung up. As she reached for the handcuff keys, her fingers were trembling. If she could just get three of them out of here without another incident...

She moved to the two attorneys and uncuffed them. Both rubbed their wrists and quickly got to their feet, moving toward the makeshift stretcher Lorna lay on. Anna went over to check her patient. Lorna was still hanging in. Anna couldn't believe how tough she was as she checked her pulse one last time.

Lorna reached up to pull aside the oxygen. "Thank you." The mask fell back into place. Anna met the woman's gaze, held it for a moment, then nodded for the men to carry her out.

Lee moved to push aside the desk blocking the door. The D.A. and city attorney lifted the table with the injured woman on it. Anna steadied the oxygen and walked as far as the door with them. She could feel the assault rifle on them, Kenny watching every move. Was he really going to let them leave?

She was afraid something would happen at the last moment to keep the three hostages from getting out.

The D.A. and city attorney waited as Lee unlocked the door and opened it a crack. Anna could see that the hallway was empty. But she knew the SWAT team was there, ready. She prayed nothing happened to keep Lorna and the two attorneys from getting through that door.

She let go of the oxygen tank as the men started through the opening with Lorna on the makeshift stretcher. Just a few more feet and they would be out.

"Just a minute," Kenny said behind Anna.

Chapter 10

3:11 p.m.

Flint knew why Kenny had stopped them. He'd heard the councilwoman. She'd obviously come to and seen what was happening.

Flint had been watching Kenny's eyes. He saw the slight change in the man's manner, recognized it and knew just an instant before Kenny pulled the trigger that he'd heard Councilwoman Gwendolyn Clark say, "They're cops!"

Shoving himself off the wall, Flint dived toward Kenny.

The blast of the assault rifle exploded in the room, thundering off the walls as bullets riddled the plaster just past Anna and Lee.

The sound of the gunshot reverberated through his

head as he struggled on the floor with Kenny, trying to get the rifle away before Kenny could get another shot off. Kenny was stronger than he looked. It wasn't until Flint heard the report, felt the searing ball of fire burn through his flesh that he realized Kenny had pulled the pistol and fired.

"No!" Anna cried as all hell broke loose, just as she'd feared. The D.A. and city attorney lunged out the doorway at a run with the stretcher.

Behind her, Anna heard Flint come off the wall and hit Kenny, heard the rifle hit the floor and the two of them scuffling. Anna saw the expression on Lee's face. Her gaze locked with his and she pleaded silently for him not to flip that switch.

From outside the room came the quickened beat of footfalls as the attorneys ran down the hall with the makeshift litter and Lorna, and the SWAT team burst out from where they had been waiting.

Everything happened so fast, she didn't have time to take a breath. Before the SWAT team could get past the makeshift stretcher held by the two attorneys, Lee had slammed the door and shoved the barricade against it, all the time keeping his finger on the bomb switch.

The first shot had startled her. The second one turned her blood to ice. She spun around, the report still echoing in the room. Kenny was on his knees, holding the pistol to Flint's head. "Call them off!" he screamed. "Or I'll kill the cop."

The SWAT team rammed the door. Anna knew any moment they would be dropping in from the ceiling.

"Hold your position," Anna yelled. "Officer down. Hold your position."

The battering of the door stopped. She thought she heard a creak overhead. She held her breath, staring at Flint. He was sprawled on the floor, his shirt dark with blood, his eyes closed.

In the deafening silence that fell over the room, Kenny slowly straightened, his face twisted in anger.

Anna thought for a moment he would shoot her, as well. Kenny stared at her, the gun raised, his hand shaking with what she could only assume was rage. The man wasn't stupid. He'd known a trap had been set for him when the hostages were released. That would be the last of them to leave this room alive, Anna thought.

She looked past Kenny to Flint, praying he wasn't seriously injured. She'd stopped the breach to save his life, and now realized that decision might have been at the cost of all their lives.

"Is Flint alive?" Max said in her ear as she stepped past Kenny and dropped to her knees beside the only man she'd ever loved.

3:24 p.m.

Flint had a flash of memory as painful as the bullet that had torn through his flesh. The morning he was six and his mother had walked down to the corner market to get milk. Her husband had already gone to work so she'd left Flint's older brother Curtis in charge of everyone. She had gone to the corner store before and knew she wouldn't be gone but a few minutes.

A teenager with a gun was robbing the market when she walked in the door. The kid panicked, turned and shot. She died instantly.

Flint didn't know why he had to think about that

morning now. Maybe because he associated all pain with the loss of his mother that day. It was impossible for a kid of six to understand why things like that happened. It was still hard for a man of thirty-four to accept that kind of loss.

His father had done a great job caring for five kids by himself, but Flint had sworn that his children would have a mother to raise them to adulthood—the one thing he had envied his friends and Anna.

She had the kind of family he'd always wanted; a mother, father, a stable household and only one sibling. He'd had four brothers, way too many when he was the youngest. Anna's life had sounded like heaven to him. He'd imagined the house Anna had been raised in and wasn't surprised that Sunday when he'd gone there for dinner to see that he'd been right.

It was a *Leave It to Beaver* kind of house in a classic neighborhood where men mowed their lawns on Saturday afternoons and kids played ball in the quiet street and mothers made pot roasts for dinner and baked homemade pie for dessert.

But the moment he'd walked in that door so many Sundays ago, he'd understood some of Anna's reservations about his meeting the family.

Mary Louise Carson was nothing like her daughter. She was tall and gangly, cold and distant. There was something brittle about her, an edge. She did interrogate him, but not out of interest, he thought. She seemed to be looking for his flaws.

Anna's father, Bob Carson, was a warm, nice man, quiet but interested, and obviously a huge fan of Anna's.

Emily and her husband Lance were reserved at best, suspicious at worst. It made Flint wonder if Anna had

had another boyfriend before him, one who had caused all this distrust.

"Does your family live around here?" Anna's mother asked after they'd taken a seat in the living room.

Flint shook his head. "My mother was killed when I was six."

"Oh, I'm so sorry," she said, and shot a look at her husband.

"It was tough growing up without a mother," he said. "But my father was in construction and he worked very hard and we never went hungry. There was a bunch of us, so he had to work a lot." He laughed. "I was the youngest of five boys. I always wondered what it would be like to get all new clothes when mine wore out."

Everyone chuckled at that. But he could see that Mary Louise thought him from poor stock in more ways than one.

"Your father raised you five boys," Bob said. "You must be very proud of him."

"I am," Flint replied. "He really did work to be both father and mother to us. The older boys helped. I was the youngest, so I had to learn to be pretty tough to survive." He stopped and looked up from his plate. "Don't get me wrong. It was a lot of fun. You can't believe the pillow fights we used to have." He'd laughed and the mood lightened a little.

"Is your father still alive?" Bob asked.

Shaking his head, Flint said, "He died the year after I became a police officer. I was glad he at least got to see me in uniform."

"Do your brothers live around here?" her mother asked.

"They're all over the country," he told her. "We get

together for weddings and funerals, that's about it. I'd always hoped we would live closer so we could have those big family get-togethers." He glanced at Anna. "I guess I'm going to have to make my own big family."

Mary Louise made a distasteful face and asked about his job and his plans for the future.

Anna changed the subject and, after dinner, she excused herself to give Flint a tour of the house and backyard.

"I told you it would be horrible," she said. "I'm sorry."

"It wasn't horrible," he said, and pulled her behind an apple tree to give her a kiss.

She looked into his eyes, her gaze softening. "My dad likes you."

"That's good, right?"

"That's very good," she said.

"Anna, sometime will you tell me why everyone, you included, is so suspicious of me?"

Her smile faded. "It's not you."

"Whatever it is, will you tell me?"

"Sometime."

That's why he'd blown it with Anna, he thought now. Because he'd had an image in his head all these years of this perfect family he would build, as if he could remake history, have his mother back, change everything. He'd thought he could make his own family with Anna. He hadn't considered how Anna's own past would play into their future.

"Flint—Flint?" she whispered next to him now. Something warm and wet splashed against his cheek and ran down his neck to his shirt. He opened his eyes and saw that she was crying softly.

She backhanded her tears as she worked, dragging

one of the medical bags over to her. "You're going to be fine," she said. "Just fine. You hear me?"

3:29 p.m.

Kenny stormed over to Gwendolyn and jerked her head up by her hair. The councilwoman let out a shriek of pain.

"What did you say?" he demanded.

Lee was mumbling in the background, "I told you not to shoot anyone."

Gwendolyn was still shrieking, sounding more angry than hurt.

"What did you say about *cops?*" Kenny slapped her, startling her into silence for an instant. "What did you say?" he demanded, pointing the gun between her eyes.

Gwendolyn's gaze jerked from Kenny to Flint, then Anna. "They're cops."

Kenny stared at her for a long moment, then turned slowly to look at Anna, his gaze so filled with hate, it took all of her willpower not to flinch.

"You're a cop?" he asked, daring her to deny it.

"I'm a SWAT team paramedic," she said.

"What the hell is that?" he asked.

"I'm sent in to help the victims of situations like this."

He swung his gaze to Flint on the floor. "You're not a doctor. You're a cop, too."

"His name is Flint Mauro," Anna said.

"He's the head of the SWAT team," Gwendolyn blurted, then looked at Anna as if to say, *There, that pays you back for taping my mouth and injecting me with something.*

Kenny was shaking his head as if in disbelief that

Flint and Anna had thought they could get away with this. "You came in here to do what exactly?"

"To help the injured," Anna said.

Kenny shot her a get-real look. "You came in here to stop me."

"We came in to try to keep anyone else from getting hurt," she explained.

"And you've done one hell of a job," Kenny said. He looked at Flint. "You got yourself shot. And *you*—" He turned to Anna. "You got the council aide out of here, didn't you? Too bad you weren't smart enough to get you and your buddy out of here, too. Move out of the way. He's a dead man."

Anna stood slowly, blocking Flint's body with her own as she moved closer to Kenny and lowered her voice. "You kill either of us and you will never see the money or the plane. The only reason the SWAT team isn't swarming this room right now is because I stopped them."

She saw the hesitation in his eyes. He must have remembered her calling out, "Hold your positions."

"If you fire another shot," Anna said, "I won't be able to stop them. I don't think I need to tell you what will happen." She glanced over at Lee, who was visibly shaking, his finger still on that damned switch. "If you want out of here alive, you won't kill anyone."

The phone began to ring.

Anna held her breath, afraid it would stop after the first ring, a signal that Max intended to go to a full breach. When the phone rang again, she felt sick with relief.

Gwendolyn started crying again, a drunken kind of wallowing-in-self-pity sound.

"You shot him," Lee was still saying. "This is not what I wanted. Not this. Not any of this."

"Shut up," Kenny ordered, his voice sounding almost normal as he ignored the phone and walked past them to peer out through the blinds. He was careful to keep his body behind the wall, careful not to let the marksmen across the street get a shot. "Everyone just shut up."

Then he walked to the phone and picked it up. "Get me what I want now or I'm going to kill them all."

3:32 p.m.

"Talk to me," Anna said as blood bloomed through the fabric of Flint's shirt. She knelt beside him and lifted his shirt. He'd been hit in the side, away from any vital organs, but he'd lost a lot of blood already.

Hurriedly she applied pressure to the wound to stop the bleeding, digging with her hand for the trauma dressings and bandages in the medical bag. She tried to lose herself in the motions. *Don't think about this being Flint. Just do your job.*

But then she met his gaze and her eyes burned with tears at the sight of him wounded, hurt, in pain.

Flint was looking up at her, smiling. "You are something, you know that?"

"It's the pain talking," she said as she worked to stop the bleeding, pulling herself together, not wanting him to see how vulnerable she was when it came to him.

Behind her she could hear Kenny on the phone, his anger growing as time passed.

"Unhook the brace," he whispered.

She frowned down at him.

He winked. "I'm going to need all the mobility I can get."

He didn't really believe he could do anything after this injury, did he? What was she thinking? He was Flint Mauro. The Do Whatever It Takes guy.

"I'm going to have to take your brace off," she said, loud enough that Kenny could hear her. She could feel him watching her.

Flint groaned as if in pain and closed his eyes. She took off the brace, wondering if the groan was real or for Kenny's benefit.

When he opened his eyes, she said, "I think the bullet went all the way through."

"That's nice," he said.

She stared into his handsome face, fighting tears. She had to get him out of here. Had to get him to a hospital.

"Don't look so worried," he said, watching her closely. Too closely. "I've been wounded worse than this."

The tears welled and spilled. He'd been wounded more seriously in the years she'd been gone? She hadn't even known. He could have died and she wouldn't have known.

"I don't think you should try to get up," she whispered.

He smiled. "I can walk. Don't worry."

It killed her to see him shot, in pain, bleeding. But if he couldn't walk, it would be hell getting him out of here.

"If you're thinking of trading me for the pills, forget it," Flint said. "He's not going to let a cop leave here and you know it."

That's exactly what she'd been thinking, but she knew he was right. She finished bandaging his side. The bleeding had stopped. As long as he didn't move—

"Don't worry about me," Flint said. "Kenny will let you leave for the pills. Make the exchange."

She shook her head. "I'm not leaving you. Once Kenny gets the pills, we wait for them to work." If Kenny didn't kill them all before that. "It will be my best chance of getting close enough to disarm him."

Flint looked as if he wanted to argue, but the cop in him had to know that that was the only way out of this. There was no talking either Lee or Kenny down.

"I'll do my part, count on it," Flint said, obviously trying to hide the pain from her.

She knew he would at least kill himself trying.

Behind her, Kenny quit yelling into the phone at Max and slammed down the receiver.

A tentative knock sounded on the door. The pills. She closed her eyes for a moment in thanks, then stood and turned, still shielding Flint's body just in case Kenny was thinking of finishing him off.

"That will be your pills," she said.

Kenny looked at her for a long moment. Another knock. Then another.

She could see his need to kill someone weighed against his need for the pills. Clearly he wanted to turn the assault rifle on the door and kill the messenger. Or at least kill Flint. But maybe Kenny had taken her warning to heart. At the very least, the last thing he wanted was for the person at the door to leave. He could always get the pills and then kill someone.

"Go to the door," he said, motioning to her. "I'll be right behind you." He stepped up, poking her in the back with the rifle barrel. She sent a warning glance to Flint as she moved to the door and shoved the desk aside.

Lee, to her surprise, moved out of the way as Kenny

pushed her toward the door. She watched him, suspecting he would be upset about Kenny taking the drugs, maybe even worried.

But his face was expressionless, his gaze on Flint. He seemed to expect trouble would be coming from that direction when it came. Smart man.

"Open the door...slowly," Kenny ordered.

Anna did as she was told. She could see movement on the other side through the hole in the door. She started to reach to open the door, but Kenny stopped her.

"On second thought, tell them to just put the package through the hole," he said.

Anna reached through the hole. It was just large enough for her hand. She felt the container of pills drop into her palm. Slowly she pulled them back. Turning, she met Kenny's gaze and held the drugs out.

He grabbed the container and motioned for her to push the desk back across the door.

"I'd be careful taking these," she warned after she'd barricaded the door under his watchful eye. She'd ordered him a much stronger dosage than he usually took. One would knock someone Kenny's size on his ass.

But she knew Kenny's body had probably built up a resistance to the drug. He would require a higher dosage just to take the edge off the pain. She was also counting on him downing extra pills because he hadn't had them for a while. "I wouldn't take more than two of those at a time."

"I'm sure you wouldn't," he said, sticking the pistol into the waist of his uniform and laying the assault rifle on a chair next to him to free up his hands. He fought to open the container. "Damned child-proof caps."

She held out her hand.

He stared at it, then her, and tried to strong-arm the lid off the container, causing more pain to his shoulder. In frustration, he shoved the container of pills at her.

She opened the lid easily and removed the cotton before handing it back to him. The container was filled with pills.

He stared down at them as if in awe, then motioned her away, waiting until she was at Flint's side, kneeling on the floor next to him, before he looked lovingly at the pills again, then spilled three into his hand and swallowed them dry, closing his eyes.

His entire body stilled. Anna looked at Flint. He shook his head, shifting just slightly. She knew he was as impatient as she was, but he agreed with her plan to wait for the pills to act was the best one.

Kenny's eyes flew open and he glared at Flint. He expected Flint to try something. He would be waiting for it now that he knew Flint was the head of SWAT. Anna had the best chance of disarming Kenny when the time came because he didn't really understand that she, too, had SWAT training. He thought she was just a paramedic.

She could feel Flint warning her to be patient, as if he, too, could feel the clock ticking. As wired as Kenny was, he would react badly to any attempt to disarm him in spite of the drugs he'd ingested. That short-barreled assault rifle could kill everyone in the room before Anna could get Kenny down. With luck, the drugs would slow his reflexes enough for her to get the upper hand.

Meanwhile there was Lee. Anna glanced over at him. He was standing by the door as if he knew not to get too close to the windows, his finger on the bomb switch, his gaze on Kenny. It seemed he was more worried about

Kenny than anyone else in the room. At least for the moment.

More than ever, Anna knew it wouldn't take anything for Lee to go off, literally, and to take them all with him.

Anna waited, afraid what would happen next. She splayed her fingers on the floor in front of her, pretty sure Max had a clear view from the video camera in the vent. No. No. No. Do not breach.

"You plan to make a move when the pills do their job," Max said in her ear.

She smiled, signaled yes. She just prayed the pills would act quickly—but not too quickly. If Kenny thought she'd had something else put in them, he would shoot her.

She had no doubt of that as she met his gaze across the room.

Chapter 11

Flint waited, stealing a glance to where the tiny video and audio wires hung down from the air-conditioning vents, then he closed his eyes.

He wished he could try to get up, wished he was sure he would be able to when the time came. He was going on blind faith. In his heart he believed he could force his body to do whatever was needed to help save the people in this room. To save Anna, he believed he could perform miracles. At least, he hoped so.

He tried not to think about how dangerous it would be when the two of them made their move. He trusted Anna to handle her part.

With a wry smile, he realized that if anyone could pull this off, it would be Anna. Max had been right about that.

She was remarkable. Flint still couldn't believe how she'd handled herself during all this. The woman had nerves of steel. She knew just what to say and do. If Gwendolyn Clark hadn't flipped out—

Anna laid a hand on his arm. Warm, soft, reassuring. He opened his eyes and smiled up at her. Her eyes said, *Not yet*. He'd seen that look five years ago, the night he'd finally gotten up the nerve to ask her to marry him.

They'd been on the Ferris wheel at the county fair after eating cotton candy and corn dogs and going on all the rides. Anna had known no fear. She'd wanted to ride everything, even the huge roller coaster.

That night he could deny her nothing. He won her a giant Panda bear, which they ended up giving to a little girl who'd been crying because she'd dropped her ice-cream cone. The little girl could have been theirs, with her big brown eyes and golden hair. Flint felt an ache like none he'd ever known for a family of his own.

As the night wound down, Anna wanted to go on just one more ride, the only one they'd missed. They climbed on the Ferris wheel, the basket rocking as it neared the top and the city lay before them, glittering like diamonds in the summer night. He looked over at Anna.

Kissing her was as natural as taking his next breath. He bent toward her, brushing his lips across hers. He heard her soft intake of breath and pulled back to look into her beautiful brown eyes. Then he cupped her face in his hands and kissed her with a passion he hadn't known he could feel. Anna surprised him with her own passionate response, giving as good as she got.

He could feel some of that reserve of hers evaporating, yet he still didn't know what she was so afraid of. Not him, he was sure of that. Marriage? He hoped not.

But as he took the ring out of his pocket, he felt her start to tremble. She was shaking her head, tears running down her cheeks. "Flint, no…"

He stuffed the ring box back into his pocket and took her in his arms. "Talk to me, Anna. What is it? I know you're afraid. Is it me?"

She shook her head.

"What, then?"

"My sister."

"Emily?"

She shook her head. "Candace."

Candace? She had a sister named Candace? This was the first he'd heard about her. He thought about the photos he'd seen on the mantel at her house. No photo of a second sister. Frowning, he met her gaze.

"What happened to Candace?" he'd asked, knowing it had to be something so terrible that the family couldn't have her photographs around. Something so horrible that it kept Anna from trusting in his love for her….

Anna was looking down at him now, worry in her expression. She couldn't have been more beautiful. There was a radiance about her. He'd known from day one that she was special. That was one reason he'd wanted to make her his wife, the mother of his children.

Now, though, he realized just how selfish that had been. He'd wanted her all to himself. And when she'd talked about becoming a SWAT paramedic, he had been terrified he might lose her. And because of that, he *had* lost her.

"Flint?" she whispered, and cupped his cheek in her warm palm. "Are you sure you're all right?"

His eyes burned with regret. "I'm sorry, Anna," he whispered. "I was so wrong five years ago."

"Stop whispering over there," Kenny snapped.

"I'm just fixing his bandage," Anna said over her shoulder.

"Just patch him up and then get over here," he ordered.

"We can't wait, Flint," she whispered as she pretended to work on his bandage.

He nodded. "Let's do this."

Anna stared down at him, surprised by the look she'd seen in his eyes earlier. But that look had been replaced by one of determination. "Are you sure you can move?"

He gave her one of his quirky smiles and flexed his legs, trying to hide his grimace of pain from her. "No problem." He gave another signal to Max, using Anna to shield the sign from Lee and Flint.

"What's taking so long?" Kenny demanded suddenly, standing over them.

At first Anna thought he was talking about her checking Flint's bandage, but then Kenny added, "They should have gotten the money by now. They're just stringing me along, aren't they?"

"I'm sure they are doing everything you asked them to," she said.

"Yeah, right." Kenny glared down at Flint. "Like sending in some SWAT commander posing as a doctor. I should kill him right now."

"He was just trying to protect me," she said, shifting a little to put herself between Kenny and Flint. "You would have done the same thing for your sister."

Kenny was silent. The drugs had stilled the restlessness in him some and, she hoped, hopefully slowed his reaction time.

"I should check your bandage," she said, pushing herself to her feet. She felt Flint's fingertips brush her wrist as she rose. "Why don't you come over here where I can get more light?"

4:32 p.m.

Surprisingly, Kenny did as she told him. It was the calm in her voice, Flint thought. No matter what Kenny said or did, Anna just didn't get rattled. At least not on the surface. Flint had seen how she'd been trying to hold it together when he'd been wounded. She'd been scared that Kenny would kill him. Did he dare hope that there was a chance for them once this was over?

Max was right, Flint acknowledged once again as he watched Anna lead Kenny over to the window and realized what she was up to. Anna was damned good at this. Better than him. He let his emotions get in the way. He couldn't make that mistake again. Anna could teach him a thing or two about control and courage.

He watched her talk Kenny into opening the blind so she could inspect his injury and put a new bandage on it.

She was setting him up for a sharpshooter to take him out. Then it would be a matter of talking Lee down—if Lee didn't flip the switch at the first sound of gunfire.

Flint glanced over at the older man. Lee looked as lost as anyone Flint had ever seen.

"Lee," Flint said quietly, "could you hand me that?" He motioned to the second medical bag, the one Anna wasn't using. He had to get Lee closer, if he could. He also wanted another look at the bomb. If there was any chance he could diffuse it rather than have to take out Lee….

The timer on the bomb gave him hope that Lee had programmed in a few minutes at least before the bomb blew up if Lee flipped the switch. *When* Lee flipped the switch.

Flint held no hope that he would be able to talk Lee out of it. He'd watched the older man deteriorate in front of his eyes all day, becoming more vague, seemingly more distant. It was clear that Lee had hoped no one would get hurt, but he seemed beyond that now.

Lee seemed to be in a daze, and it took him a moment to respond. Flint hated to think where the elderly man's thoughts had been as Lee bent awkwardly to pick up the bag from the floor and carry it over in his free hand. He set it beside Flint, his expression confused.

"I'm all right," Flint said, trying to comfort him—and also keep him close. "We're going to get these people out unharmed."

Lee's expression didn't change, but his gaze flickered to Flint's, and in that instant, Flint saw something that froze his blood. Lee Harper had already accepted that none of them would leave this room alive and that their blood would be on his hands for eternity.

Flint looked away, not wanting the man to see just how hard he planned to fight to keep that from happening. He'd gotten another good look at the bomb. The moment the marksman took Kenny out....

4:37 p.m.

"We can't get a clear shot," Anna heard Max say into her earpiece.

She tried not to let her disappointment show and she looked over at Flint. She had gotten Kenny by the window, opened the blind. Even if the shot missed, she was ready to take Kenny down. He'd ingested the drugs, his reflexes had to be slower. Flint had even managed to get Lee close to him.

She fought the tears of frustration and fear. The hours in this room were taking their toll. But it was Flint she was worried about. She needed to get him medical assistance. She needed to get these people out of here.

Kenny put down the blind again, moving away from the window, just as Lee was now moving away from Flint. The look on Flint's face echoed her own disappointment. They were on their own now. They would have to make another opportunity. Meanwhile, the drug she'd given Gwendolyn was wearing off and Lee wasn't looking good.

Max needed to reassure Kenny and soon. He needed to reassure them all.

Anna felt sick as she went over to Flint. He'd lost blood and should be taken to a hospital, yet Anna knew that trying to talk Kenny into letting Flint leave would be a waste of breath and only make matters worse. Not only that, Flint was their only chance of disposing of the bomb.

The phone rang. Kenny picked it up. "I'm tired of waiting." He was no longer yelling, and the quiet tone of his voice was more frightening. He listened. "Well, that's not quick enough. No, you can't have a hostage." He glanced at his watch. "If I don't have some proof that you're doing what I want, I'm going to kill one person every fifteen minutes. You got fifteen minutes." He slammed down the phone.

4:42 p.m.

Flint saw the look on Anna's face and knew, even before she came over to whisper to him, that Max was calling for a full breach in five minutes. She checked his bandage and he saw her fingers tremble.

Five minutes. Flint reached up, his fingers trailing down the side of her neck until he found her pulse.

It was strong, just like Anna. He had seen her disappointment, as acute as his own, when the sharpshooters hadn't taken a shot at Kenny. Flint wanted desperately to get her out of here.

He looked up at her, wanting to memorize the exact color of her eyes. He'd remembered them as being golden brown. But he saw now that there were spikes of gold— like flames—in the honey-brown.

Her pulse quickened under his fingertips, her flesh warm to the touch. He used to go down to the beach to watch her surf, awed by her talent. God, she was beautiful. All California girl. Her skin lightly browned by the sun and smooth, smelling of tanning oil and the Pacific.

She'd come out of the surf, saltwater beading on her tanned limbs, the surfboard under one arm, contentment softening her face.

It was that image that he thought about now; Anna silhouetted against the Pacific as the sun dipped slowly into the horizon.

"Lee will flip the switch," he whispered. "I'm not sure how much time we'll have." Flint was staking their lives on having a few minutes to get Lee to the window and out. He hated that that was his only choice. He would rather have tried to disarm the bomb.

He refused to believe that would be all the time they would have left together. Fate couldn't be so cruel to let Anna come back into his life, only to have him lose her. He prayed he would have a chance to get her back.

The words seemed to stick in his throat. "You'll have to keep Kenny busy."

"I'll do whatever it takes."

He smiled at that. His motto. At least it *had* been his motto. He felt as if everything had changed now. He'd changed. He didn't know who he would be if he ever got out of this room, out of this building. But he knew he wouldn't be the same man who'd come into it.

Kenny leaned against the wall, pretending to drift with the drugs, all the time watching the two opposite him. The cops.

He was not a happy camper. The only thing he'd gotten that he'd asked for was the pills. The video camera had been Lee's dumb idea. How would they even know if his stupid statement aired? It wasn't like they had a TV. If Lee was so smart, why hadn't he thought to bring in a TV set? And some food?

Kenny had let Lee take Gwendolyn to the bathroom just off the meeting room. Lee had made her leave the door partway open and now Kenny had to listen to her whine. He should have just let her pee her pants. Would have served her right.

Kenny's stomach growled. He hadn't eaten since that fast-food breakfast burrito this morning on the way here. What he wouldn't give for a cola. Hell, a beer.

He smiled at the memory of Lee sitting in the passenger seat of Kenny's car at the fast-food place. Lee hadn't wanted anything to eat. He'd wanted to take his own car, but Kenny had insisted they go together. If he'd known the guy had a bomb strapped to him, he would have let Lee have his own way and go alone.

Now Kenny wished he'd thought to at least bring a

candy bar. What had made him think the city would get the money and the plane and passport before lunchtime? Bureaucracy never moved fast, he knew that, but he also knew they were stalling him, thinking they could out-wait him. As if he had someplace to go, something to do besides sit here.

But he didn't like the way the two cops kept whisper-ing to each other. He'd thought about separating them. Even thought about cuffing them instead of the hostages.

It seemed like more trouble than it was worth, though, and he couldn't trust Lee to do it anyway. Lee had screwed up everything he'd touched. Kenny wished the old fart would take his finger off that bomb switch. But even then, Kenny knew he'd be afraid to off the guy for fear the bomb would blow. Wasn't that what his sister would have called irony?

But as he watched the two cops, Kenny had an idea, one that gained appeal the more he thought about it. He liked the woman. He intended to keep her here until the end. But the guy cop he could live without, and it was time to send a message to the city. Forget waiting fif-teen minutes. He needed to let the world outside this room know he was tired of waiting and wasn't taking it anymore.

"You've made me a believer," Flint whispered to Anna, his gaze caressing her face. "You are definitely good at this. Better than me." He'd always been on the outside, giving orders, busting down doors, dropping in from helicopters. The easy part.

He realized he'd been dead wrong about what was right for her. He'd wanted to make this perfect little life with Anna at the center. He'd wanted to limit her possibilities to fit what he saw as her role not only in his life, but in the world around her.

"I was wrong, Anna," he whispered. "You're great at this. Much better than me."

She smiled as if she knew how hard it was for him to admit that.

"I was one selfish bastard," he whispered. "I was so damned wrong." He looked past her. Kenny was standing against the far wall, looking almost as lost as Lee. The pills had obviously taken effect or Flint figured he'd have been dead by now. He owed Anna his life. He just hoped the drugs would slow Kenny when Anna made her move.

The clock was running down. It was going to be time soon. Lee was still standing by the door like a sentry, but he didn't seem to be paying any attention to them. Flint knew he could be wrong on both counts.

He looked at Anna again. "I'm sorry," he whispered.

She met his gaze and nodded. He saw her swallow, and tears glistened in her eyes before she looked away. This wasn't the time, he knew that. But he feared there might never be a time.

"I never stopped loving you."

She didn't look at him. She swallowed again and bit down on her lower lip.

There was a thud overhead. "What the hell?" Flint heard Kenny say.

Flint looked away from Anna, afraid of what he would see.

Kenny was staring up at the ceiling, cold fury in his eyes.

Flint followed his gaze to the wire the SWAT team had installed for audio and visual.

Chapter 12

"What the hell?" Kenny cried again, shoving the pistol into a stunned Lee's free hand. "Anyone moves, shoot 'em."

Lee took the gun and pointed it at Flint, suspicion in his gaze, as well as confusion and fear.

Kenny dragged a chair over, climbed up and grabbed the wire, jerking it hard. It disconnected from the equipment and came snapping down like a whip. He had already spotted the other one and was sliding the chair across the floor toward it.

Anna heard Max swear softly in her ear as Kenny grabbed the second wire and jerked it free. He hurled it in the direction of the hostages, then jumped down, the veins in his neck bulging as he cursed the city and the cops and the sons of bitches who thought they could fool with him.

Gwendolyn was shrieking again, demanding that something be done in a voice that was only slightly slurred now that the drugs were wearing off.

Flint had pulled himself up against the wall. Anna could see that he was in terrible pain but she knew that he was getting ready for what was to come—all hell breaking loose. She was to take out Kenny, but he was raging again and expecting trouble.

The phone rang.

"That is going to cost you!" he screamed into the phone. "You hear me? You want to listen? Well, listen to this." He set down the phone, grabbed up the assault rifle and emptied a clip into the vent covers, sending a shower of debris down on them.

Before anyone could move, Kenny stepped to Flint and slammed the butt of the rifle into his head. Anna saw Flint fall over as Kenny grabbed her and dragged her to her feet. She struggled to free herself, to get to Flint, but Kenny had his arm around her neck and was cutting off her air as he pulled her away.

She couldn't see Flint, couldn't see if he was all right. Lee had moved and was now standing over him.

"You killed a cop," Lee said, his words like a blade to her heart.

"No!" Anna cried, trying to get to Flint, but Kenny only tightened his hold.

Past Lee, she caught a glimpse of Flint sprawled on the floor, unmoving. She began to cry, unable to hold back the tears, all her wonderful cool gone.

"Drag him out into the hall," Kenny ordered Lee. "Hurry. They want a hostage, they can have this one."

Anna fought to free herself of Kenny's hold, but he was strong, and with each struggle he only cut off more of her air. Black dots danced in front of her eyes and she could feel the pistol barrel pressing into her side. Why didn't he just kill her and get it over with?

Lee took his finger off the bomb switch and grabbed Flint's legs as Kenny half carried, half dragged her over to the door. Kenny shoved the desk aside and waited for Lee to pull Flint closer before he opened the door, staying back so he couldn't be seen from the hallway. So the SWAT team outside couldn't get a shot.

Flint couldn't be dead, Anna thought. Not after everything they'd been through. It wasn't over. It couldn't be. Flint was faking it, waiting for an opportunity. Lee had finally taken his finger off the bomb switch. Flint could stop him now.

Lee dragged Flint out into the hall and quickly put his finger back on the switch. Anna caught only a glimpse of Flint's body as Lee closed the door—just enough to see the lack of color in his face, not long enough to see if his chest rose and fell.

But she knew he wasn't faking it. If he had been, he would have overpowered Lee. He would have ended this.

And she was helpless to do anything. Kenny was slowly choking the life out of her. She could feel her will to live slipping away with it.

As Lee shoved the barricade back in front of the door, she quit fighting Kenny, all the fight gone out of her. Her knees buckled and Kenny let her sink to the floor at his feet.

"Anna?" Max said into her earpiece.

The phone rang. Kenny picked it up. "That's one.

I'll kill another one in fifteen minutes," he said, and slammed down the receiver.

5:09 p.m.

Blades of afternoon light sliced in through the blinds and flickered across the floor as a police helicopter thrummed past outside.

Anna looked across the room. Her eyes felt as if they were filled with sand. Grief and exhaustion made her limbs numb. She tried not to think how many hours she'd been in this room or how little time she had left on earth.

Kenny had been watching her from under hooded eyes. She knew who his next victim would be. A heavy silence had filled the room. The hostages were quiet. Even Gwendolyn. Kenny had said he would kill another hostage in fifteen minutes. Anna saw him look at his watch, then at her. It must be getting close to the time.

She closed her eyes and fought the image of Flint's lifeless body being dragged out of the room. She couldn't bear the thought that he was gone. That she would never see him again. It filled her with an emptiness that consumed her.

Lee shifted his position by the door. She glanced over at him, surprised at her own disinterest. Was this what happened to hostages after hours under constant threat of death? They became listless, the fear having drained them until they just wanted it over.

Lee looked as tired and lost as she felt. Why didn't he flip the switch? Or did he even remember why he had his finger on it? Anna wondered why Max hadn't gone full breach. She'd expected it as soon as the SWAT team found Flint's body.

She looked into Lee's dark eyes, idly wondering what he was waiting for. Max had called to say Lee's video was running on all the five o'clock news stations in town. Kenny said he didn't give a damn.

Kenny knew he wasn't going to be getting any money or a plane and passport. He was angry, bitter that the movies and TV shows lied. She watched him glance at his watch, counting down the minutes, daring the SWAT team to come and get him.

Lee shifted again. He must know what Kenny had in mind. Would he try to stop Kenny from killing her? She wondered with the same disinterest that she felt about the bomb going off.

Flint opened his eyes and knew right away that if he was dead, he hadn't made it to heaven. Not if T.C. Waters was here. He stared into the older cop's face for a moment, then tried to sit up.

T.C. pushed him back down. "Take it easy. You're in no shape to be moving. I've called for a stretcher."

Flint looked around, not surprised to see that he was in one of the rooms on the second floor of city hall. "Anna?"

T.C. shook his head.

"Max went full breach?" Flint asked, pushing T.C. back and sitting up. For a moment everything went dark, and he had to put his head down to keep from passing out.

"Max is holding, waiting for an update," T.C. said. "We're just minutes from full breach. You got one hell of a knot on your head and you're bleeding like a stuck pig."

"Give me your radio," Flint demanded. He hit the talk key. "Max, it's Flint. Hold your positions!"

"What's your status?" Max asked.

Flint knew he was asking about his medical condition as well as about Anna. Flint wished he knew. By now Kenny could have killed her. There was no doubt in Flint's mind that Anna would be next.

"I'm going back in," Flint said. "I'm going to need a few minutes inside before you come in."

"Negative. T.C. reported that you're wounded."

"T.C. exaggerates. I'm fine. I'm going back in. I can do this."

"Put T.C. on," Max said.

T.C. was shaking his head.

Then Flint heard Max ask, "T.C., is he up to it?"

Flint shot T.C. a look.

T.C. took the radio Flint handed him. "You know Flint," T.C. said, his gaze locked with Flint's.

"Answer the question," Max snapped.

"I'd put my life in his hands," T.C. said.

Flint managed a smile. "Just patch me up and get me a weapon," he told T.C.

Flint didn't need T.C. to tell him that he wouldn't be on his feet long. He didn't need T.C. to tell him that he'd lost a lot of blood and that he wasn't as strong as he probably thought he was. T.C. was smart enough not to tell him anything as he helped Flint up.

The radio squawked. "Flint?"

"Here," Flint said into the radio. "I'm ready to roll, Max."

"I'll stall Kenny. You've got two minutes once you're inside."

Two minutes. He knew what he had to do. Take out the bomb, one way or another. He couldn't be sure that

Anna would be able to help him. He pushed away the thought. Somehow he'd get her out along with the rest of the hostages. "Two minutes," he said into the radio.

Gritting his teeth to hide his pain, he looked up for a vent. He felt woozy and his side hurt like hell. But his body wouldn't let him down. It couldn't, not now. "Can you connect me with Anna so I can tell her the plan?"

"Yes," Max answered. He didn't have to say, If she still has her earpiece. If she's still alive.

"Then let's rock and roll," Flint said, turning to T.C. "Show me which vent I need to take." There were a half dozen men in position to storm the meeting room. "Full breach two minutes after I drop into the room."

T.C. exchanged a look with the other team members, then said to Flint, "This way, boss."

Flint gave his men a nod. He couldn't have handpicked a better bunch for the job.

As he and T.C. reached the entrance to the air-conditioning vent, Flint turned to him. "No matter what happens," Flint said quietly, "get Anna out if you can."

"She's the one who broke your heart, isn't she? The one you were engaged to."

"Yeah." Flint pulled up a chair, climbed up painfully and lifted the vent cover. The duct work was large enough for a man his size, but just barely. He stopped to catch his breath, hanging on to the opening, suddenly afraid he'd been wrong. Maybe he couldn't do this. Maybe his body would let him down.

"She dumped you," T.C. said below him.

"Yeah."

"So what's changed?"

"I have," Flint said, and wasn't surprised when T.C.

was suddenly beside him on a chair, helping him into the duct. Without looking back, Flint began to crawl quietly into the darkness.

Flint had been dating Anna for almost six months when she'd finally confided in him about Candace.

They'd gone for a walk after dinner at one of the small fishing shack cafés. Anna had been unusually quiet all night. In his pocket was the engagement ring in the small velvet box he'd been carrying around for months.

But that night he had the awful feeling that she was going to break up with him. The warm night air smelled of salt and fish. He'd come to love Southern California. Anna had taught him to bodysurf. He loved the sea and Anna. In his mind they would always be linked.

"Candace was my older sister," Anna told him, as if the words were a stone that had been lodged in her throat. "She was murdered."

He stopped and, taking her arm, turned her to face him. "Anna, I'm so sorry."

She bit her lower lip. "She was killed by her fiancé."

He stared at Anna, suddenly understanding her reluctance to date, let alone trust a man.

"We all loved him." She was crying, the words tumbling out. "He was funny and fun. He was like a big brother. He used to take me and Emily along on some of their dates and he would buy us ice-cream cones. He was so…perfect. He was family."

Flint could only shake his head.

"We didn't know. He fooled us all. Except Candace." Anna's voice broke as she choked back a sob. "She had put off the wedding. We were angry with her and questioning what was wrong with *her*. She knew she shouldn't be marrying him. But she never said anything. Probably because we wouldn't have believed her. Even when we saw the bruises, we didn't suspect anything. Darrel said love had made her uncoordinated and joked that he hoped their kids inherited his genes."

Flint looked away, the sea wallowing restlessly in the horizon. "She tried to break it off," he said, knowing that was the case even before he looked over at her again. Waves lapped at their feet, but neither of them seemed to feel the cool water.

"He said he would rather see her dead than with anyone else," Anna told him.

"What happened to him?" Flint asked.

"He turned the gun on himself after he shot her."

Flint had squeezed her hand, finally understanding why she'd been so scared of falling for a man. With his other hand, he'd cupped the back of her head and gently pulled her to him. He'd cradled her in his arms, the surf foaming around their ankles, the lights coming down on the beach as the warm darkness settled in around them.

5:16 p.m.

The phone rang, startling everyone in the room. Kenny dropped the rifle. It clattered to the floor, and it took him a few moments to pick it up. The drugs *had* slowed his reflexes, Anna thought. He'd taken a couple more of the pills, breaking the container to get them out rather than ask her to open the cap for him again.

He glanced at his watch now as the phone rang again, then blinked and picked up the receiver.

"The video Lee Harper made aired," she heard Max

say to Kenny via her earpiece. "The governor called me. He's authorized me to make a deal."

She saw hope shine in Kenny's glazed eyes for a moment, then quickly die.

"This is another stall, isn't it," Kenny snapped.

"I'm going to have you out of there within the half hour," Max said. "You have my word. But only if you don't hurt anyone else."

In answer, Kenny swung the assault rifle in an arc and pulled the trigger. Anna dove for cover as bullets riddled the wall behind her. Plaster showered down on her and the hostages. Her ears rang from the noise, and then there was an eerie silence.

She waited for Max to say something.

Silence in her earpiece.

Kenny hung up the phone. "I think he's finally realized I mean business."

Anna knew that Max hadn't meant that Kenny would be leaving on a jet plane. Within the hour, Max would have them all out, one way or another. The SWAT team would be coming in soon. All hell was about to break loose. Max had been trying to warn her.

What about Flint? Why hadn't Max said something about Flint? Because he was dead.

She stared at the bullet-riddled wall over the hostages, then at Kenny, anger shaking off her earlier numbing despair. She wanted to be the one who took down Kenny. He'd killed Flint. She felt her blood coursing through her extremities again. With it came a heart-wrenching pain, but also a calculated fury.

"We're coming in. Be ready for the phone call," Max said in her ear.

She was ready.

5:19 p.m.

The afternoon sun dappled the floor of the city hall meeting room. Kenny stared at it, the assault rifle across his lap, the pistol within reach.

The drugs were working. He could feel the mellow along with the melancholy that often came with it. He felt defeated, but then he'd felt that way much of his life.

As he looked across the ransacked room, blood on the floor, a dull constant ache in his arm, he told himself he wasn't going to be getting money or a plane or a passport to some safe foreign country. The bastards had lied.

The kicker was, he didn't want to go to some foreign country anyway. With his luck, people there wouldn't speak English. He'd have to learn some damned foreign language, and what would he do once the money and pills ran out?

He glanced over at Lee. What a crazy bastard. This was all his fault. Him and his stupid ideas. Kenny wished to hell he hadn't gotten involved with the old fool. His life would have been a hell of a lot better if he'd never met Lee, never heard his hard-luck story. Kenny had enough hard-luck stories of his own.

He wished he were in that dinky drab apartment he was about to be kicked out of. At least he still had cable TV, and there were a couple of beers in the fridge. He could be watching "Wheel of Fortune" right now, his feet up in his ragged recliner.

Under the fluorescent light inside the meeting room, he watched the nurse-cop get up and come toward him. He told himself maybe under other circumstances he might have asked her for a date. He doubted she would have said yes, but *maybe* she would have gone out with him. No chance of that now. He was going to kill her in a few minutes.

"How's your arm?" she asked, coming to stand directly in front of him.

He motioned her back with the rifle.

"Your bandage needs changing," she said.

He shook his head. At the back of his mind he was considering who he'd kill after her. He'd save the judge for last, but eventually he'd kill them all, and then Lee would blow them both to hell—if he didn't do it sooner.

The idea of going out in a blaze of glory rather than with his hands up had some appeal. Kenny wasn't wild about jail. He'd been there before. Prison wasn't too bad. They at least had HBO and you got fed.

"It looks like your arm's bleeding again," she said. "You need to stay still."

Maybe he would just bleed to death right here. That's where the cops would find him. Dead against this wall.

No, that would be worse than prison.

"Leave me alone." He pointed the barrel of the gun at her, his words slurred. The drugs had knocked him on his ass. He wanted to blame the nurse, but she'd told him not to take so many.

She knelt beside him and he remembered how she'd opened the child-proof cap on his drugs. His eyes smarted with tears. Hers had been the only kindness he'd had since his sister died. She began to undo his bandage. He was going to hate to have to kill her.

Lee blinked and looked around, surprised to find himself still standing in some room. He didn't know where. He didn't know how long he'd been standing here. He didn't seem to be wearing his watch.

As he looked down at his wrist, he saw the device taped to his chest and frowned, his finger twitching, his body going cold as he remembered getting on the Internet, searching for bombs.

Francine. She was gone. That's why he was here. That's why these people were here, he thought as he looked around the room, saw their fear, felt his own.

Francine. He missed the way they used to make cookies together. He was always in charge of cutting up the nuts for the oatmeal cookies he loved.

They used to joke that they had assisted living. He assisted her and she assisted him.

He remembered her crying and frowned. They'd been to see his doctor and gotten the bad news. Alzheimer's. The doctor said he had Alzheimer's and was losing his mind.

Tears blurred his vision. Francine had told him not to worry. She'd take care of him. But Francine was gone, her death an ache he would no longer endure. He knew she was waiting for him on the other side. So what was he doing standing in this room? He could no longer remember. He could no longer wait. It was time he joined his wife.

Kenny still had the assault rifle resting on his lap, but he'd pulled out the pistol and was holding it in his free hand, the barrel pointed at her chest.

He wasn't as out of it as Anna had hoped. "Leave the damned bandage alone," he snapped, motioning her away with the pistol.

The hostages had been silent as death. But now she heard the rustle of clothing. Like her, they knew something was about to happen. They just didn't know what.

Anna looked into Kenny's eyes, wondering what he was thinking.

"Get back."

Something in his tone made her rise to her feet and step back slowly. She glanced at the hostages. Gwendolyn's eyes were wide as saucers, her face tear-streaked. She was staring at Kenny, no doubt hoping he wouldn't change his mind about who to kill next.

Kenny got to his feet. It must be time. She stopped and estimated the distance between them and the best way to get the assault rifle and pistol away from him.

He glanced at his watch, then quickly back to her as he raised the barrel of the rifle a little higher, taking aim.

The phone rang. Kenny froze. It didn't ring a second time. He looked down at the phone lying on the floor, then back up at her. Did he realize it was a signal?

"Anna," came the soft whisper in her ear, the familiar voice sending goose bumps over her skin. Flint.

Tears sprang to her eyes and she had to close them for fear Kenny would see and know. Relief made her weak. Flint was alive! No matter what happened in this room, Flint was alive.

"Baby," Flint said, his voice breaking.

I'm here, she wanted desperately to answer. *I'm here, Flint.*

"Get ready. I'm coming in the vent near Kenny."

She opened her eyes.

Kenny was smiling ruefully. "It's time. Turn around."

"I love you," Flint said.

She blinked back tears and looked Kenny in the eye. "Yes," she agreed. "It's time."

The vent behind Kenny banged down in a thunder of noise and dust as Flint Mauro dropped into the room.

* * *

Flint hit the floor hard, the jarring drop knocking the wind out of him. Pain shot through him and his side was on fire, his vision blurring for an instant. He didn't need to look to know that he'd started the wound bleeding again.

He shot a glance in Anna's direction. She was already moving, flying at Kenny.

Flint didn't have the time to wait to see if she would succeed. His gaze leaped to Lee.

"You don't want to do that," Flint said quietly, shaking his head as he moved swiftly toward the older man, keeping the trauma scissors in his hand hidden. "Let these people walk away now. You don't want any more blood on your hands."

Lee stumbled back. Flint heard a grunt come out of Kenny, then a loud thud as he hit the floor.

There was that instant when Lee had looked relieved to see Flint alive, relieved that this day would finally be over. But clearly Lee was determined not to leave this room alive.

As Lee flipped the switch, Flint launched himself at the older man—and the bomb.

Chapter 13

As Lee removed his finger from the bomb, he looked at Flint, regret as well as resolve evident in his expression. Lee closed his eyes, waiting for the inevitable. A small hand on the watch began to tick off the seconds.

Flint thought it was funny what came to a person's mind at a moment like this. Bomb squad guys had jokes for such times. "You have the rest of our life to dismantle this bomb" or "Your only mistake will be your last."

Grabbing Lee, Flint shoved him back against the door and looked down at the bomb. He could feel sweat drip off his forehead as he produced the trauma scissors and cut through the duct tape that held the bomb to the elderly man.

The pain in his side was making him nauseous, the pain in his head blurring his vision. He ripped the blades down through the tape on one side and then the other, feeling the seconds ticking by. He was still on his feet. That was about all he could say.

Flint knew his orders. Get Lee out a window. But the windows were on the far wall and he'd have to get the man over there. He had to throw him out and pray that Lee dropped far enough before the bomb went off so the hostages handcuffed to the radiators by the window weren't injured.

There was a second option—one Max wouldn't have approved. He could free Lee and get rid of the bomb.

Timing was everything, Flint thought, and wanted to laugh. He tried not to think about Anna, or what was happening behind him. Or that any moment he might feel a bullet from Kenny's weapon rip through him.

He had two minutes from the time he hit the floor to when the rest of the SWAT team came into this room.

The duct tape cut, he started to peel the bomb off the old man, a little surprised Lee made no effort to stop him. Instead the elderly man seemed to be watching, as if he were a spectator, interested in what Flint would do next.

That's when Flint saw that Lee had put in a fail-safe mechanism. If Flint removed the bomb, it would blow instantly.

Anna grabbed Kenny's wounded arm and twisted. He had already proven how strong he was. And she knew he would be fighting to the death.

He let out a cry. The assault rifle clattered to the floor, but as she started to go for it, he backhanded her with his good arm and sent her sprawling.

She kicked out, striking him in the face, then lunged

toward the rifle. He already had his hands on it and was trying to swing it around to fire at her.

She struggled with him, kicking at his body, connecting with his shoulder, making him howl in pain as he fell backward, hitting hard on the floor.

Behind her, she knew Flint was trying to disarm the bomb. She refused to let herself think that at any moment they could all be blown to smithereens. She wanted to get Kenny. He had hurt Flint, almost killed him. Still might. She couldn't let Kenny get the rifle, no matter what she had to do.

She swung an elbow into his face and felt his nose break, heard him squeal. His fingers on the rifle loosened just enough that she got better purchase. She jerked it away from him, rolled and swung it around, pointing the barrel end at Kenny. "Don't give me an excuse to kill you," she yelled.

He stared at her. "Some Florence friggin' Nightingale you are."

Flint's gaze flew to Lee's. The older man was looking right at him, a smug, satisfied expression on his face.

Swearing, Flint glanced down at the timer. Seven seconds had gone by.

He jerked the man off his feet and felt pain sear up his side. The window. He had to get Lee to the window, but his arms felt like lead and the dark spots were back dancing in front of his eyes. He saw Anna on the floor with the gun. Kenny on his hands and knees.

Flint pulled Lee toward the windows, feeling as if his feet were running in slow motion. He hadn't been expecting Lee to punch him in his wounded side. He felt the air rush from his lungs as he doubled over, losing his grip on Lee.

Before Flint could react, Lee broke loose and ran toward the windows. He was fairly spry for his age. Or maybe like Flint, the old man had willed his body to perform out of necessity one last time.

Flint watched as Lee launched himself, dipped a shoulder to take the brunt of the panes and dove through the shattering window.

Glass and bits of wood sprayed the hostages.

For an instant Flint saw Lee Harper silhouetted against the afternoon light.

Then the man dropped, disappearing from sight.

Flint stared after him for only an instant before he hurled himself at Anna to shield her body from the explosion.

At the impact of falling on her, a blanket of darkness dropped over him. He didn't hear the explosion, feel the debris that fell from the ceiling or smell Anna's scent as she cupped his face, her tears falling on his cheek, and cradled him in her arms.

Like Lee, Flint was in his own world now, far from the pain of this one.

For Anna, everything was a blur. The SWAT team had come into the room, taking Kenny Reese down just before the bomb exploded outside.

It had been her voice saying, "The keys to the handcuffs are in Kenny's pocket." She remembered someone crying. It could have been her. She thought she recalled Councilwoman Gwendolyn Clark threatening to sue the city.

She'd helped get Flint on a stretcher and rode in the

ambulance to the hospital, but the image that stayed in her mind was of him dropping down through that vent. Her hero. Flint, strong, courageous. Flint, vividly alive.

At the hospital, the emergency staff had taken Flint to surgery and had patched up her cuts and scrapes. Max had driven her home to her apartment.

That night she slept on the deck. She couldn't stand being inside. She had wanted to stay at the hospital with Flint, but Max had ordered her to go home.

She waited for his call, afraid when the phone finally rang.

"Flint's out of surgery and in recovery," Max said. "He just needs rest now. There is nothing more you can do. Get some sleep. You've been through a hell of a first day of work."

Out on the deck, she sprawled on her back, staring up at the stars, listening to the ocean. It had never sounded so sad to her before. The stars blurred. She hadn't really let herself cry yet. She'd passed exhaustion hours ago. Now she felt jittery, as if her nervous system had been amped up and she might blow a fuse at any moment. She closed her eyes, but the darkness seemed worse.

She stared up at the stars again, trying to find one to wish on. It had to be the right star. She made her wish. Flint was going to be all right. He had to be. The surgery had gone well, Max had told her. And Flint was strong.

Tears blurred the stars overhead as she thought about him saving her life tonight. He'd come back for her. Alone.

He could have been killed. They all could have been killed, but Flint had saved her. Saved Kenny and the hostages. Lorna was in the hospital. Her surgery had gone well, too. She was expected to make it.

Only Lee had been lost. She felt a deep sense of sorrow for the tormented man. He was with Francine now. That was all he'd really wanted.

Flint had tried so hard to save him, but sometimes saving another human being was impossible. Some people didn't want to be saved.

She must have slept because the phone startled her eyes open. The sun was up, casting her view of the ocean in gold.

She went into the apartment and caught the phone on the fourth ring.

"Anna, it's Dad."

Taking a deep breath, Anna sank down onto the edge of the bed, overwhelmed at just the sound of his voice and surprised to find she was crying.

"Honey, I heard what happened. Are you all right?"

She couldn't speak. The sobs hurt her throat and her eyes ran with tears.

"Anna?"

"I'm all right."

"I'm calling you from the Sacramento airport. I'll be in Courage Bay in two hours. Can you pick me up at the airport there?"

She was so relieved that he was coming. "I'll be there. Dad?"

"Yes?"

"Thank you."

"See you soon, honey."

When she'd hung up, she looked around the apartment, spotting Flint's old faded T-shirt in the wastebasket where she'd thrown it—when was that? It seemed like another lifetime ago.

She pushed herself up and walked over to the wastebasket. She'd been so sure she was over Flint. Slowly she reached down and picked up the T-shirt, bringing the soft, worn cloth to her face, breathing in the remembered scent of him. Crushing the shirt to her chest, she called the hospital. Flint's T-shirt was clutched in one hand when she was told that he'd survived the night. She hung up and sobbed in relief into the cloth.

A while later she went to shower and change clothes. She had to see Flint before she drove to pick up her father at the airport.

The airport was busy as usual. She stood in the visitors area, watching for her father, wondering if he would recognize her, she felt so different.

He spotted her and waved, frowning a little as he came closer. Then he was through the door and she was in his arms.

She didn't break down until they reached her apartment. "Flint almost died," she said, crying again. She couldn't remember ever crying this much. Except when Candace had died. "Flint risked his life for me."

"Anna, Flint is the head of the SWAT team," her father argued. "He would have risked his life no matter what."

She shook her head. "This is all my fault. I'm the reason he joined SWAT. This isn't what he wanted. He did it because of me."

"Honey," her father said, taking both of her hands in his. "You can't take on responsibility for the whole world."

"That isn't what I'm doing."

"It's what you have always done, Anna. I watched you after your sister was killed. You seemed to think you could make everything right. I watched you try so hard to be Candace for your mother."

Tears welled in her eyes at the realization that it was true. Only she'd failed to replace the daughter her mother had lost and she'd seen that failure every day in her mother's eyes.

"What about what you want, Anna? If Candace was still alive, what would you be doing right now?"

She stared at him. "I don't know."

"You wouldn't be a paramedic on the SWAT team, would you?"

She got up and walked across the room.

"What do *you* want?" he asked. "What do you want right now?"

She turned to face him. "I want Flint to live. I want to get the chance to tell him how sorry I am."

Her father lifted a brow. "If you had only two minutes to talk to him, what would you really want to say to him."

She stared at her father. "I'd tell him that I still love him, that I doubt I ever stopped loving him."

Her dad nodded and smiled. "And?"

"And...I want to be with him."

"What about your job?"

She shook her head. "That's what broke us up before." She sat down heavily in one of the overstuffed chairs. "Nothing has changed and yet everything has changed. I've changed," she said, looking up at him. "I don't know what I want to do with my life anymore. I just know that I desperately want Flint in it."

"So you would give up your career for him? That must be horribly frightening to think you love him that much."

She smiled at her father. "It scares me half to death.

Do you think I'm wrong to give up what I love for a man?"

"Do I think you're wrong to love a man that much?" He shook his head. "The question is, how much does he love you? Does he love you enough to let you make the decision about your job?"

"You don't think I should quit my job."

"I can't tell you what to do, Anna. But whatever it is, do it for the right reasons."

"Is that what you flew up here to tell me?"

He smiled. "I had to make sure you really were all right."

She nodded. "I am. But I feel like I've been given another chance. I just don't know to do what."

"Don't you?" her father asked with a smile.

Flint opened his eyes. At first he didn't see her with the sun streaming into the hospital room. She was sitting in a chair by the window, her hair glowing golden in the sun, her head down as if she had been here for some time, waiting.

He didn't move, didn't dare breathe for fear she might be a mirage and, if he blinked, she would be gone. He'd been dreaming about her. In the dream, she lived with him in a house with a view of the ocean from the patio, and palm trees and a pool.

He couldn't remember the wedding in the dream, but he was acutely aware of the gold band on the finger of his left hand and the way he woke up next to her each morning.

And of course they had kids. He could hear the little darlings coming down the hallway toward his and Anna's bedroom. The patter of tiny feet moving on a wave of giggles and bright morning sunshine. He smiled. He had waited in the dream for his and Anna's children to come through the open door of the bedroom with an expectation that was more like an ache.

But then he'd opened his eyes and seen that he was in a hospital room. The disappointment had been acute until he'd seen Anna sitting in the chair by the window. He'd felt a surge of hope so elusive that he'd held his breath, afraid to say anything to her for fear this, too, was only a dream.

"You're awake."

His heart swelled at the sound of her voice. She stepped out of the sunlight, no longer silhouetted against the window, her face coming into view. No mirage.

She reached to ring the nurse and he saw that her hands were shaking.

"Anna," he said, his mouth so dry it came out a whisper. He didn't take his eyes from her, afraid he might blink and she would be gone again. She had a bruise on her forehead and a small cut at the corner of her mouth. When she moved, he saw her favor one side as if it were sore or injured.

But she was all right. He could see that in her eyes. Her brown eyes, which filled with tears as she touched his hand. Just a brush of skin against skin, as if she were afraid to touch him, afraid she might hurt him.

They had survived. His heart swelled at the realization. And they'd done it against all odds. He felt choked up as he recalled how close they had come to not being here.

"The hostages?" he asked, his throat aching.

"They all got out. Lorna came through surgery. She's expected to make it. I heard that the other hostages have been coming by to visit her." Anna made a swipe at her tears. "She really was something under fire, wasn't she?"

"Like someone else I know," Flint said, and tried to sit up.

"Easy." She touched his shoulder. "The doctor said you're lucky to be alive. You lost a lot of blood and you have a concussion. You've been out of it for the last forty-eight hours."

He hadn't realized he'd been gone that long. It surprised him.

"You got hit so hard…"

He saw the tears glistening in her eyes again. He reached up to take her hand, awkwardly thumbing the inside of her palm, trying to find the words he needed to say.

"You were amazing," he said, looking into her eyes.

"You were the one who was amazing."

He shook his head, then stopped because it hurt too badly. He took a breath. He couldn't remember ever being this tired, this filled with emotion. He knew he needed to sleep, to get his strength back, to make sure he said the right words to her.

But his need to tell her how he felt outweighed everything else. "I was wrong about…everything."

She tried to hush him. "The doctor said you had to lie still and get rest."

The nurse came into the room and hurried to his bedside. "So you're awake," she said, and set about checking his vitals.

He kept his gaze on Anna, frustrated that he hadn't been able to say everything that was on his mind. He could feel exhaustion making his body heavy, his eyelids almost impossible to keep open.

The nurse turned to Anna. "He really needs his rest."

"No," Flint managed to say, but he felt her hand slip from his. He'd never been able to hang on to this woman. "I have to tell you—"

"All that matters is that you get better," she said. "Rest. We'll have plenty of time to talk later."

He fought to keep his eyes open. He could feel fatigue dragging him back under. But it wasn't the wounds that were causing him the pain. "I have to tell you, Anna," he whispered. He felt her lips brush his cheek. "I have to…"

As Flint drifted back to sleep, Anna stared down at his pale face and the bandage on his head, both in stark contrast to his black hair. Her heart swelled with relief that he had awakened. He had scared her so badly.

The doctors said that between the loss of blood, chance of infection and the concussion, Flint was very lucky to be alive. She'd stayed by his side most of the last forty-eight hours, fearing that he might not survive after everything he had done to save her and the lives of the hostages. It broke her heart, knowing he had tried to save Lee, as well.

She closed her eyes at the thought of Lee and what had happened to him. Kenny had been taken into custody. He was facing a variety of charges that would put him back in prison for a very long time.

Gwendolyn Clark was suing the city. Her uncle, Judge Craven, had commended both Anna and Flint, saying they had done an outstanding job under the worst kind of conditions.

"You still here?" Max asked, peering in through the hospital room door.

"He woke up," she said, and heard her voice break.

Tears welled in her eyes and she fought them back, not wanting to cry in front of her boss.

"You know how tough he is," Max said, joining her. "How could you doubt he wouldn't make it?"

She could hear the relief in his voice. He'd been afraid, too.

Max was shaking his head as he looked down at Flint. "He's a damned fool. He had no business going back into that room. Always has to be the Lone Ranger." Max smiled as he turned to her. Taking her arm, he led her out of the room. "You look as if you could use a little rest yourself. Did I mention that the two of you did a hell of a job?"

"We were just doing our jobs," she said.

Max made a rude sound. "Save that for the press. This is you and me, Anna. I should never have let the two of you go in there. I'm damned lucky you didn't all get killed. I would never have forgiven myself."

As they left Flint's room and walked through the hospital, suddenly she needed to see the ocean, hear the surf breaking on the sandy beach, smell the salt and feel the sun on her face. The hospital hallway seemed too narrow, too confining, too much like the meeting room at city hall.

"Are you all right?" Max asked.

She nodded. Flint was going to make it. Everything was all right. "I just need...rest," she managed to say.

Max nodded. "An experience like you've been through... Of course you need rest. Why don't you go home? I'll hang around here for when Flint wakes up again. It's over, Anna." He patted her shoulder.

Over. Until the next time.

Max seemed to read her thoughts. "Things will look different after you've had sufficient rest."

She wasn't so sure about that, but she nodded and walked out into the last of the day's sunshine, gulping the air, choking back tears as she headed toward the car, where her father was waiting for her.

"How is Flint?" he asked.

She brushed at her tears. "He woke up. That's a good sign. The doctor thinks he'll pull through as long as the wound doesn't get infected." She began to cry again. "I'm so scared, Dad."

"I know, honey. But you're both alive and both heroes."

She shook her head. She felt like anything but a hero.

"Anna, you should be proud of what you were able to accomplish. Flint couldn't have done it without you."

"Dad, I never understood why he didn't want me to be a part of SWAT until we started in there and I realized I might lose him."

He raised an eyebrow. "Lose him? Anna, you broke off the engagement five years ago."

She shook her head again. "It's all so complicated and confusing. I think I made a terrible mistake."

"Leaving Flint?" he asked.

Looking away, she took a breath and pulled herself together. "Maybe everything I've done was a mistake."

He laughed softly. "Anna, you've been so successful at everything you've attempted. How can you possibly say that?"

"Dad, I've been involved in hundreds of incidents, some more dangerous than others," she said, trying to put the feelings into words, trying desperately to understand it herself. "But when I was in city hall with Flint, trapped in that room, knowing we were probably going to die..." Her voice trailed off. "I'm not sure what happened. It just changed everything."

Her dad nodded. "Let me drive. There's someplace we need to go. Someplace you've put off going for years."

She stared over at him, afraid she knew where he was taking her. The last place on earth she wanted to go.

Chapter 14

Flint drifted in and out of consciousness. He couldn't tell what was real and what was a dream. Had Anna been here in his hospital room at one point? He couldn't be sure. Had he told her how he felt? He'd rehearsed the words in his head so much, maybe he only thought she'd been here and that he'd told her.

This time when he woke, the sun had set and the room was dim—and empty. No Anna. He felt desolate and tried to tell himself it was the drugs and the pain. But he knew it was the fear that Anna was gone from his life.

He closed his eyes and let himself drift. Memories washed through the drug-induced mist behind his eyelids.

He thought about Anna. About having a wife who was a paramedic on the SWAT team. He wouldn't deal with that now. He could think about happier times. He pictured her standing in the doorway, wearing that old T-shirt of his. She was smiling. Her laugh hung on the air, a wonderful, joyous sound.

Flint clung to that sound as he drifted off to sleep.

Anna walked across the perfectly groomed lawn, her father at her side. The sun had sank behind the palms and now cast long shadows through the cemetery. She had cried so much, her throat was raw and her eyes felt scratchy and dry. She feared she had no more tears, as if her grief was a well that had finally run dry.

As she looked over at her dad, she realized how much she missed their weekly lunches. She felt she was losing everyone who mattered in her life and she couldn't bear it.

There had been too much change. Her parents' divorce. Their moves to other cities. Even Emily leaving for Seattle.

"Remember the day I told you that Flint had asked me to marry him?" she asked her dad softly as they walked.

He nodded. "I was surprised, and sorry you'd turned him down."

"You asked me why. You asked me if I loved him," she said.

"I remember." He stopped walking, and she knew without looking that they were almost to her sister's grave.

Tears burned her eyes. It was impossible to explain how she felt. Even to her dad. She'd promised herself she wouldn't cry, and yet her eyes blurred with tears. "I can't…"

He stepped to her, forcing her to look up at him.

"Candace's death affected all of us in different ways. I don't have to tell you what it did to your mother. Emily was so young, it didn't have as much of an impact on her as it did on you."

"Dad—"

"I think you're trying to make up for what happened somehow," he said, sounding sad.

"I can't see how my becoming a paramedic has anything to do with what happened with Candace."

"Can't you? Isn't she the reason you were determined to join the SWAT team?"

Anna shook her head, more in frustration than anything else. "Even if it is—"

"Candace was killed by a man who had sworn to love her," her dad said. "Don't tell me you're not afraid that you might make the same mistake. It's why you turned down Flint's proposal the first time."

She looked away, surprised her father knew her so well. "Do you remember how much we all loved Darrel?" she asked. "He seemed so perfect, not just for Candace but for our family." She turned to look at him again. "I knew something was wrong toward the end. Candace wasn't happy. She tried to talk to me about it but I told her—" She choked back the tears.

"I told her it was just cold feet," she continued, needing to finally tell someone. "I loved Candace but I thought she was going to mess everything up. I didn't care if she was happy or not. I wanted her to marry Darrel. Darrel was family, he loved all of us…" Her voice broke. She'd loved Darrel, and maybe that was what hurt the most. Anna had loved Darrel like a brother, the brother she'd always wanted. "I never told anyone before what I said to Candace, how I encouraged her to marry Darrel when she didn't want to."

"We all loved Darrel." Her father lifted her chin so that their eyes met. "I was no different than you, Anna. I wanted Darrel in our family. Candace tried to talk to me once about the problems they were having." He looked away, swallowed. His eyes were shiny when he met her gaze again. "I told her every couple has problems."

Anna felt as if a weight had been lifted off her shoulder as she stepped into her dad's arms and he hugged her tightly.

"We have to quit blaming ourselves," he said, pulling back to wipe his eyes. "All of us."

Anna stared at him and saw something she had missed before. She'd been so caught up in her own guilt over Candace that she hadn't seen it before this moment. "You think Candace confided in Mother."

Her dad winced. "I think your mother is carrying more guilt than she's been able to handle for many years. Over Candace. Over you."

"Me?"

"I know your mother wishes she could go back and do things differently," he said.

She stepped back from the hug. Her dad had always made excuses for her mother. She looked past him toward the sea. It was her compass, she realized. She felt grounded when she had it as a place to start. The one thing she'd done right was to come back here. "Doesn't Flint seem too perfect to you?"

Her dad laughed. "No man is perfect, honey. There was something terribly wrong with Darrel, Anna, you know that. He was crazy jealous of Candace...."

"What if there is something terribly wrong with Flint?"

Her dad smiled and shook his head. "Anna, you have to trust your judgment. I trust it. You're in love with him. Listen to your heart."

"What if my heart is wrong?" she asked, her voice sounding close to tears. Just like Candace's heart had originally been. Anna could remember only too well when Candace was happy with Darrel, the way her whole face would light up when he walked into a room, or the way she smiled when she picked up the phone and it was him calling.

Anna remembered because she'd hoped that one day she would meet someone like Darrel. And she had met someone who made her feel airborne at just the sight of him, whose voice made her heart beat a little faster. She loved Flint and it scared her to death.

"Anna, you're a smart woman. I have a feeling you've already figured this out for yourself. Whatever happened in that room at city hall…" His gaze met hers and she saw the pain and worry. Her father didn't like her being in this dangerous job any more than Flint. The difference was, he hadn't tried to stop her.

She hugged him again.

"Are you all right?" he asked, pulling back to look at her.

She smiled through her tears. "Maybe I went into this for all the wrong reasons, but I'm good at it, Dad."

Taking a breath, she finally turned to look at her older sister's grave. Her father stepped closer to the headstone. Anna hung back. She hadn't been out here since the day of Candace's funeral. That should have told her something, she thought.

She stood, hearing the ocean on the bluff below, smelling the sea, a breeze whispering in the tops of the tall palms nearby.

Finally she joined her father in front of Candace's headstone. "Beloved daughter and sister," the inscription read above the dates of Candace's life. Such a short life. Anna realized a day hadn't gone by that she hadn't felt guilty.

Her dad took her hand, his gaze on the gravestone. He'd been right. He'd told her she needed to come up here. Her life had somehow been all tied up with Candace's, as if she felt she had to make up for her sister's life being cut so short.

But the last few days she'd realized she couldn't bring her sister back, no matter how good she was at saving other people. This was her life and she had to start living it for herself.

She'd been afraid to marry Flint. Afraid of so many things. The SWAT training had made her feel safe. But after what had happened at city hall, she knew there was no magic bullet. Life was a gamble. All the training in the world couldn't protect her.

Nor would it have protected Candace. Nothing could protect a person from the people she loved. Nor from a broken heart. Or even worse. Nothing could make Anna safe from her fears of intimacy and motherhood and living in her older sister's shadow.

The realization that she was scared to death of being a mother surprised her. But she saw now that it was true. Her own mother had been such a disappointment to her. What if Anna was like her?

Even as the question formed, Anna knew the answer.

She wasn't her mother. Nor was she her sister Emily. Or her sister Candace.

Too bad that revelation hadn't come five years ago, she thought with a wry smile as she looked down at her sister's grave. All these years she'd felt responsible for encouraging Candace to marry Darrel. Her family had failed Candace, but even if they hadn't, Anna wondered if they could have saved her sister. The other times Candace had broken up with Darrel, she'd always gone back to him. As Anna stood looking down at her sister's grave, she knew why. Candace had loved him. She hadn't been able to let go of him even when she knew she should have.

No wonder Anna had been so afraid of love.

The breeze coming up off the Pacific sighed in the palm fronds as she and her dad walked back to the car.

Max called Anna at home that night. "I've got some bad news about Lorna Sinke."

Anna held her breath. She'd just seen the woman at the hospital earlier that day. Lorna had been conscious, her condition still critical, though.

"She's dead, Anna. I'm sorry."

Anna gripped the phone, shaking her head. She'd failed. Tears stung her eyes.

Max sighed. "I don't want you blaming yourself, Anna. You did everything possible."

He knew her too well. She was mentally beating herself up because she hadn't gotten Lorna to a hospital sooner.

"If you hadn't gone in there, a lot more people would have died," he said.

But she hadn't saved the one person she'd gone in for.

"This probably isn't the best time, but I also wanted to ask you when you thought you'd be ready to come back to work," Max said. "I'll understand if you want more time...."

"I need to talk to Flint first."

Chapter 15

One week later

"You can go home this afternoon," the doctor announced as he came into Flint's room.

Flint thought about going home to his boat. It had been his sanctuary before Anna had come back to town. But just the thought of it now...

"Thanks, Doc." He turned to look out at the skyline. He could see a little blue of the Pacific in the distance. He wondered where Anna was.

She'd come by every day, but whenever he tried to talk about what he needed to say to her, she'd stopped him, insisting they would have time to talk once he was out of the hospital.

He turned at the sound of the room door swinging open, hoping it would be her.

"How ya feeling?" Max asked, coming into the room. "You don't have to look so disappointed to see me."

Flint laughed. "Sorry. I just thought it might be… someone else."

"Anna?" Max pulled up a chair as the doctor left. "I heard she's been by every day."

How was it that Max managed to hear so much? Flint wondered. "Doc says I can leave this afternoon."

"You need a ride out to the boat?" Max asked.

Flint shook his head. "I can drive, and I guess the team brought my car over."

Max leaned forward in the chair. "Did the doctor say when you can come back to work?"

Flint hadn't even thought about getting back to work. It surprised him. There'd been a time when all he thought about was work. But that had been to keep himself from thinking about Anna. "Six weeks before I can do much of anything."

"So you're going to be on the desk for a while," Max said thoughtfully.

The chief hadn't just stopped by to check on him, Flint realized.

"You've been through a hell of a lot," Max said. "That kind of experience can change a man."

Flint remembered how he'd felt when he'd been wounded, lying in that hallway, knowing Anna was still in there with a killer and a suicidal man with a bomb. "What is it you're trying to say?"

"Just that your priorities might be different now. Some men wouldn't be able to go into another situation like the one you just lived through."

Not if Anna was in that room, Flint thought. Was that what Max was getting at?

Max tossed an envelope next to Flint on the bed.

"What's this?" he asked as he picked it up, half afraid to open it.

"Just take a look."

Flint carefully pulled the sheets of papers out of the envelope. He frowned as he saw what they were and looked up at Max.

"It's an application for assistant chief of police of Courage Bay," Max said.

"I can see that."

"The position is opening up in the next six weeks. I thought you might be interested."

"You think I can't do my job anymore?" Flint asked.

"No, I'd put my money on you any day. I just think that you might have joined SWAT for the wrong reasons." Max held up a hand. "Don't get me wrong. You're great at your job. But I've seen men who have joined the force who are running from something, a loss of some kind. That kind of gung-ho, do-whatever-it-takes attitude gets the job done, but doesn't lead to a lifetime of happiness."

Flint knew he had been that kind of guy, so he didn't even bother to argue.

"You said a long time ago that one day you wanted to be chief of police," Max was saying.

Back when Flint had been engaged to Anna.

"Well, I have no intentions of giving up the chief of police job for a very long time, but I'd be damned proud to have you as my assistant chief, and I'd put in a good word for you with the hiring board."

Flint stared down at the papers. Wasn't this his dream just five years ago?

"You don't have to make up your mind now," Max

said, getting to his feet. "I don't need your answer for a week or so. You're getting a jump on applying. Take your time." He patted Flint's shoulder. "You and Anna did one hell of a job in there the other day, Flint. I'm sure you won't be surprised when you hear about the medals the two of you will be receiving."

"We didn't do it for medals."

"That's probably why you both have so many of them," Max said, stopping at the door to smile back at Flint. "Give the future some thought."

Flint stared after him. He hadn't been able to think about anything else.

Anna called the hospital that afternoon but Flint had already been released. When she called his home number, there was no answer. She didn't leave a message because what she had to say, she needed to say in person. She'd waited because she didn't want to have the discussion in a hospital room.

She had just hung up when the doorbell rang.

"We need to talk," Flint said when she opened the door.

She stared at him. He looked paler than he had at the hospital.

"Are you all right?" she asked, ushering him into the apartment.

"Fine."

"I thought you weren't supposed to get out of the hospital for another few days?"

He turned to look at her as she closed the door. "I'm an exemplary patient. I also heal fast, and I couldn't stand lying there any longer." His gaze softened as he seemed to search her face.

"Sit down," she said, suddenly afraid. He checked out early to come see her?

He sat down gingerly on the edge of the couch.

"Can I get you something to drink?"

He shook his head. "Anna?" He glanced past her to the rest of the apartment as if he thought he heard something. "Could you sit down?"

She nodded, too nervous to sit, but anxious to hear why he'd come here like this.

"I have to know where we go from here," he said.

She'd dreaded this day. "I have to be honest with you."

Flint felt his heart drop, his mouth suddenly go dry. He watched her get up and walk to the deck. Beyond her he could see the Pacific, a shimmering, undulating silver backdrop.

"I've been lying to myself." She turned to look at him.

He held his breath. Don't let her tell me she doesn't love me. I know that's a lie. But does she love me enough to give me another chance? That was the question, wasn't it?

"I'm trying to understand what happened five years ago," she said quietly.

"Look, I was a fool. I had no right making you feel like you had to choose between a career and marriage to me."

"Flint, I knew how strongly you would feel about my being on the SWAT team before I even brought it up."

He shook his head. He could see where she was headed. But if she tried to tell him that they were all wrong for each other…

"I think I chose that career path because it was an easy way out of the relationship," Anna said.

He'd thought his heart couldn't drop any farther. He pushed himself to his feet, his gaze locking with hers. "Don't you dare try to tell me you didn't love me."

She smiled sadly and shook her head. "I'm through lying to myself. Or you. I loved you so much it scared me, Flint. I felt as if my life was spinning out of my control. It was one of the reasons I decided to join SWAT. I thought it would give me the control I'd lost."

He cocked his head at her. "But that meant leaving me."

She nodded. "You were the reason my life was out of control."

He stared at her. "So now you have your life under control again. That's what you haven't been able to tell me. You don't want me fouling it up again."

She smiled and shook her head. "The incident at city hall proved how little control we have over our lives. Those hostages probably thought they were in control when they got up that morning."

He frowned and reached to take her hand, turning the palm up and staring down at it for a moment before he planted a kiss in the center and released it.

"The day at city hall made me realize something I had been denying for five years," she said.

Finally it was coming. The real reason she'd left him. Hadn't he known all along it wasn't SWAT? It was him. She hadn't wanted to marry him.

"I love you," she said simply. "I never stopped loving you. I tried. I thought that once I had the career I needed, wanted, I would get over you. But when Max called and offered me the job, I couldn't wait to get back here. I told myself it was because this was home and that it had nothing to do with you. But that was a lie, too."

He felt his heart lift like a hot-air balloon. Did he dare hope? "Are you trying to tell me that you still love me?"

Anna nodded, tears making her eyes glisten. "Is there any way we can start over?" As she waited for his answer, she thought of everything they'd been through since the first day they met.

"We can't go back. There is no changing what has passed," he said. "We have to find a place to start again."

"Is that possible?" she asked, her heart in her throat.

"Anything is possible with you in my life," he said, his voice cracking with emotion.

She took a breath. "I was hoping we could take it slow. A lot has happened." She waved a hand through the air, but he had to know she was talking about city hall. Was it possible those hours trapped in that room had changed him, as well? "I feel like we need to sort out some things alone before we talk about a future together."

Flint nodded. Five years ago he would have seen her need for space as her wanting out of the relationship, and would have fought her tooth and nail. He couldn't have given her the space back then and they both knew it.

She waited, wondering if the two of them had changed enough over the last five years, over the last few weeks.

Flint smiled and reached out to take her hand. "Take as much time as you need. I'm not going anywhere."

Two weeks later

The sun glistened low over the Pacific as Anna walked down the dock. She was surprised to find out Flint lived on a boat. She realized how little she knew about him. He'd never mentioned wanting to own a boat while they'd been together.

It rattled her more than she wanted to admit that she might not know Flint as well as she thought she did. Over the past two weeks he hadn't called. He'd sent a bouquet of flowers and a note saying he was there for her if she needed him. Oh, how she needed him.

Her footsteps echoed on the worn boards of the dock.

Flint's boat was a thirty-five-foot motorized trawler, blue and white, sitting in a slip at the end of the marina.

As she neared it, the sun caught on the stern. She stumbled as she read the lettering on the side. *Anna.* He'd named the boat *Anna?*

"Hello?"

She was startled to see Flint appear from belowdecks. He was wearing nothing but a swimsuit, his body glistening with sweat, tanned, beautifully sculpted. He looked healthy in spite of the scars, some newer than others. Several she'd never seen before.

She stood staring at him. He looked wonderful. Her heart leaped at the mere sight of him.

"You all right?" he asked, moving across the deck to jump effortlessly down beside her. The dock swayed a little and she felt as if she didn't have her sea legs. A born surfer and she felt so off balance he had to take her arm to keep her from falling into the water between the dock and boat.

"Anna? Are you sure you're all right?"

She looked up into his face. "You named your boat *Anna.*"

He nodded. "What else would I call her?"

Tears blurred her eyes. Water lapped at the sides of his boat. She shook her head.

"Would you like to see it?" he asked softly. He was

still holding her arm. He gave it a playful tug and she let him help her onto the boat.

It was cool belowdecks. She felt a little better, a little more stable. She'd had a lot to think about the last three weeks, but one thing she knew soul-deep. She loved this man. She would always love this man.

"I didn't know you wanted a boat," she said, turning to look at him.

He had pulled on a shirt and was buttoning it as if he thought his lack of clothing was making her uncomfortable.

She stared at the last glimpse of chest, wanting to put her palms flat against his skin, knowing it would be warm to the touch, smooth.

"Flint." His name came out on a breath. She stepped into his arms. It was so easy that she wondered why it had taken her so long.

He wrapped his arms around her, cradling her head in one large hand as his other arm encircled her waist and pulled her closer.

His body was warm and strong. She let herself lean into him, let him take the weight from her. From deep within her came a feeling so strong, it made her catch her breath: this was where she belonged. This was where she had always belonged.

Flint held her tightly, afraid to let her go. Why had she come here? She felt so right in his arms. Did he dare hope?

She pulled back a little and looked up at him. It had been so long since he'd seen desire in her eyes….

"Anna?" It came out a whisper.

She pulled his head down to hers and kissed him,

taking his breath away. He pulled her closer. Her lips parted. He kissed her, heart pounding.

"Make love to me," she whispered against his lips.

He pulled back to meet her gaze, saw that devil desire in her eyes and something more. Love.

Sweeping her up into his arms, he carried her back to the stateroom.

Her fingers worked his buttons, freeing him of his shirt as he lay beside her on the bed.

He lifted the thin cotton top she wore, pulling it over her head. Her body was as he remembered it, a little fuller, her breasts wonderfully round, filling her bra to overflowing.

He bent to free a rosy-brown nipple from the silk cup and slipped it into his mouth, her flesh warm on his tongue.

Desire rippled through him, waves of memories mixing with the Anna lying next to him now. They fought to strip each other, her need to feel his bare skin seemingly as desperate as his own.

When they were finally naked, Anna let out a long sigh as their bodies melded together. His lips grazed across hers, the sound of her name flowing out on a warm, soft breath.

She reveled in his touch as his fingers brushed across her flesh, sending trails of fire through her blood.

He pressed her to the mattress, his gaze meeting hers. She prayed he wouldn't speak. They had never needed words, communicating instead through touch and gazes and soft, sweet groans of pleasure.

His fingers caressed her, finding the once familiar spots, discovering new ones that spurred her desire until she was panting, her body glistening with sweat, her need for him almost more than she could stand.

She looked up at him, a plea in her eyes.

He entered her, filling her, completing her. She rocked against him, clutching at his shoulders as he drove himself deeper and deeper in her. She matched his movements, the pace picking up to a frenzy. She arched, her head thrown back as he brought her to climax and quickly followed, his cries echoing her own.

Anna lay spent in his arms, her cheek pressed against his chest, his arm around her. She could hear him breathing, hear the beat of his heart begin to slow. She closed her eyes, savoring the quiet after the storm. There were so many things she wanted to say to him.

But as she looked over at Flint lying next to her, his arm draped across her waist, she knew there would be plenty of time to talk about the past. *And* the future. Neither of them was going anywhere.

Epilogue

It was a warm, sunny Southern California day on the beach when Flint proposed to Anna again.

He knew in his heart that the third time really was the charm. He'd held on to the ring, but now he wondered if he should have gotten her another one, a new one for a new beginning.

"Anna," he said as she came up from the water, smiling, her surfboard under her arm, her tanned skin glistening with droplets of water. He'd never seen anything more beautiful in all his life.

She dropped onto the towel next to him, smiling, happy, completely content. He could see that all the ghosts from her past were gone. Anna had become her own woman in ways he doubted she'd dreamed possible.

They'd spent the past few weeks either at his boat or

in her apartment, hardly ever apart. Neither had returned to work. Max had given them both a leave of absence.

"You know that I would never again try to stop you from doing whatever you wanted with your life," Flint had told her over and over.

She'd smiled and nodded. "I just have to decide what's right for me."

Now he turned to her, getting to one knee in the sand as he reached into his pocket for the tiny velvet box holding the engagement ring.

She seemed to be holding her breath, her eyes wide, and for one awful moment he thought she might bolt back toward the Pacific.

"Anna," he said, and cleared his throat. "Will you marry me?"

Anna held his gaze for a long moment, reveling in this man she'd fallen in love with, then she looked down at the ring in the velvet jewelry box. Her heart leaped to her throat and her eyes welled with tears.

"Oh, Flint," she said. "You saved my ring."

He seemed to be holding his breath. He let out a long sigh and smiled as he reached for her hand.

She watched as he slipped the ring back on her finger. It felt so right. "I'm never taking it off again."

"Does that mean you'll marry me?"

She laughed and realized she hadn't said yes yet— and Flint was still on one knee in the sand.

She threw her arms around him. "Oh, Flint, I thought you would never ask." She laughed again and he joined her. It was a wondrous sound that drifted along the beach to a background of waves lapping at the shore. "I can't wait to marry you."

* * *

"Come on in," Max said as Flint opened the door to his office and stuck his head in. Max beamed at the sight of Flint and Anna together. "Congratulations."

"Thank you," Anna said. "I'm so glad you're going to be the best man."

"I wouldn't miss it," Max said.

"I've already asked him to keep the second week of June open," Flint told Anna, then turned back to Max. "Anna wants to get married on the beach. It will be small—mostly family, a few good friends."

The first time, they had planned a large, traditional wedding. This time, they both realized they didn't need that. They'd changed and now wanted a small and intimate wedding with just close friends and family.

"Please sit down." Max took his chair behind his desk again. "I wanted you both to hear the news first. The bullet that killed Lorna Sinke didn't come from either of the hostage takers' weapons."

It took Flint a moment to understand what Max was saying. "But those were the only two weapons the subjects had, other than the bomb."

Max nodded. "Kenny Reese and Lorna Sinke were wounded with the same weapon."

Flint blinked. "Kenny said he thought one of the councilmen shot him and had thrown the gun out the window, but the team searched the area…"

Max nodded. "I suspect whoever shot the two didn't throw it out the window but hid the gun in the room and retrieved it, taking it with them when they were rescued. We had no reason to search the hostages."

Flint was shaking his head. "You think this is the work of the Avenger, don't you."

"The Avenger?" Anna asked.

"Someone has been taking the law into his own hands," Flint explained. "If he doesn't think justice was done correctly, he makes sure the person gets the death penalty."

"You think that's who killed Lorna?" Anna said, clearly upset.

Max nodded. "So no matter what you did that day in city hall, you couldn't have saved Lorna. The Avenger would have gotten her at the hospital or one day after she left. She was a marked woman."

Flint couldn't believe this. "You're saying that one of the people in that room at city hall could be the Avenger."

Max nodded. "Of course we can't say for sure. We've got to run comparisons with the other deaths we've attributed to the Avenger. But there's a good chance this killing fits the pattern. From everything you've both told me and what I've learned from Councilwoman Gwendolyn Clark, Lorna Sinke was about to be fired from a job she had held for years." He glanced at Anna. "Add in what she told you about the cookies she'd brought to work that day and her animosity toward the councilwoman…"

"You think this Avenger, whoever he—or she—is, felt Lorna had escaped justice in the death of her parents," Anna said. "So without even a trial, this Avenger killed her?"

"We can't ignore that possibility." Max studied Anna closely. "I know you liked her."

"I didn't want to see her die," Anna said, thinking about the people in that city hall meeting room. "I'd put my money on Gwendolyn Clark."

"We have no proof, and we have the previous cases to consider, but I can assure you we will be keeping a close eye on all the former hostages," Max said. "By the way, that assistant chief job is yours, Flint, if you're interested." He smiled. "I assume you told your future bride that you'd applied."

"No." Flint looked over at a surprised Anna. "I was waiting until I was sure I had the job. How do you feel about being married to Courage Bay's assistant chief of police?"

Her eyes shone with tears. "I am going to love being married to you, no matter the title."

Flint hugged his future bride, anxious to hear those wedding bells ringing.

"I suppose this would be a good time to tell you, Max," Flint said. "Anna would like to stay on as your SWAT paramedic."

Max's gaze went to Anna in surprise. "You're sure. After that first day of work—"

"She's too good at what she does," Flint said.

Anna smiled. "It's only until I get pregnant, and I have to be honest with you, Max, we've decided to start a family right after the wedding. But until then…"

Max beamed. "I couldn't be happier for the two of you."

Flint recognized that smile of Max's as the chief leaned back in his chair. Was it possible Max had gotten Anna back here, hoping this would happen?

Flint met his boss's gaze and knew he owed Max a debt he would never be able to repay. He smiled. "Thanks." He looked over at Anna. She was smiling at Max, as well. If their first child was a boy, Flint was pretty sure Anna would agree that his name should be Max.

* * * * *

Wedding bells and shotgun fire are ringing out in Lonesome, Montana. Read on for another Colt Brothers Investigation novel from New York Times *bestselling author B.J. Daniels.*

Bella Worthington took a breath and, opening her eyes, finally faced her reflection in the full-length mirror. The wedding dress fit perfectly—just as he'd said it would. While accentuating her curves, the neckline was modest, the drape flattering. As much as she hated to admit it, Fitz had good taste.

The sapphire-and-diamond necklace he'd given her last night gleamed at her throat, bringing out the blue-green of her eyes—also like he'd said it would. He'd thought of everything—right down to the huge pear-shaped diamond engagement ring on her finger. All of it would be sold off before the ink dried on the marriage license—if she let it go that far.

As she studied her reflection, though, she realized this was exactly as he'd planned it. She looked the beautiful bride on her wedding day. No one would be the wiser.

She could hear music and the murmur of voices downstairs. He'd invited the whole town of Lonesome, Montana. She'd watched from the upstairs window as the guests had arrived earlier. He'd wanted an audience for this and now he would have one.

The knock at the door startled her, even though she'd been expecting it. "It's time," said a male voice on the other side. One of Fitz's hired bodyguards, Ronan, was waiting. He would be carrying a weapon under his suit. Security, she'd been told, to keep her safe. A lie.

She listened as Ronan unlocked her door and waited outside, his boss not taking any chances. He had made sure there was no possibility of escape short of shackling her to her bed. Fitz was determined that she find no way out of this. It didn't appear that she had.

In a few moments, she would be escorted downstairs to where her maid of honor and bridesmaids were waiting—all handpicked by her groom. If they'd questioned why they were down there and she was up here, they hadn't asked. He wasn't the kind of man women questioned. At least not more than once.

For another moment, Bella stared at the stranger in the mirror. She didn't have to wonder how she'd gotten to this point in her life. Unfortunately, she knew too well. She'd just never thought Fitz would go this far. Her mistake. He, however, had no idea how far she was willing to go to make sure the wedding never happened.

Taking a breath, she picked up her bouquet from her favorite local flower shop. The bouquet had been a special order delivered earlier. Her hand barely trembled as she lifted the blossoms to her nose for a moment, taking in the sweet scent of the tiny white roses—also his choice. Carefully, she separated the tiny buds, afraid it wouldn't be there.

It took her a few moments to find the long, slim silver blade hidden among the roses and stems. The blade was sharp, and lethal if used correctly. She knew exactly how to use it. She slid it back into the bouquet out of sight. He wouldn't think to check it. She hoped. He'd anticipated her every move and attacked with one of his own. Did she really think he wouldn't be ready for anything?

Making sure the door was still closed, she checked her garter. What she'd tucked under it was still there, safe, at least for the moment.

Another knock at the door. Fitz would be getting impatient and no one wanted that. "Everyone's waiting," Ronan said, tension in his tone. If this didn't go as meticulously planned, there would be hell to pay from his boss. Something else they all knew.

She stepped to the door and opened it, lifting her chin and straightening her spine. Ronan's eyes swept over her with a lusty gaze, but he stepped back as if not all that sure of her. Clearly he'd been warned to be wary of her. Probably just as she'd been warned what would happen if she refused to come down—or worse, made a scene in front of the guests.

At the bottom of the stairs, the room opened and she saw Fitz waiting for her with the person he'd hired to officiate.

He was so confident that he'd backed her into a corner with no way out. He'd always underestimated her. Today would be no different. But he didn't know her as well as he thought. He'd held her prisoner, threatened her, forced her into this dress and this ruse.

But that didn't mean she was going to marry him.

She would kill him first.

Love Harlequin romance?

DISCOVER.

Be the first to find out about promotions,
news and exclusive content!

 Facebook.com/HarlequinBooks

 Twitter.com/HarlequinBooks

Instagram.com/HarlequinBooks

Pinterest.com/HarlequinBooks

ReaderService.com

EXPLORE.

Sign up for the Harlequin e-newsletter and
download a free book from any series at
TryHarlequin.com

CONNECT.

Join our Harlequin community to
share your thoughts and connect
with other romance readers!
Facebook.com/groups/HarlequinConnection

HARLEQUIN

Heartfelt or thrilling, passionate or uplifting—Harlequin is more than just happily-ever-after.

With twelve different series to choose from and new books available every month, you are sure to find stories that will move you, uplift you, inspire and delight you.

SIGN UP FOR THE HARLEQUIN NEWSLETTER

Be the first to hear about great new reads and exciting offers!

Harlequin.com/newsletters